SₙNGULAR DUALᴵTY

BY LAWRENCE E. MAYNARD

Second edition: February 2025

Special acknowledgement to the creative abilities of Jason T. Maynard for the cover design.

PROLOGUE

A pool of shimmering quicksilver reflected the light of fluorescent panels hovering near the chamber's ceiling. Mists of an earth-normal atmosphere swirled and condensed as they collided with the metallic vapors of the unearthly reservoir. Migrating across the ceramic floor, the eerie fog obediently parted beneath the confident stride of a Geminian female. Slowly... smoothly... a radiant sphere of sheer energy emerged from the pool's depths. Stopping mere inches from the edge, the Geminian peered into the orb, searching for the slightest sign that her presence had been acknowledged.

As if in response, a portion of the energy globe fluxed rhythmically, hypnotically. Morphing into a glowing ribbon, it reached out to her. Engulfing the Geminian in its brilliance, it radiated a power never before experienced. Boldly, she stepped forward onto the silvery surface.

In that instant, she was transformed!

Irradiating its own energy, pulsing in synch with the orb, the glowing figure shed its corporeal bonds as it rose upward.

Yet, this miraculous transformation was not singular in its nature.

Directly across the chamber from the metamorphosis, a similar change was occurring with yet another representative of a distant world. The lithe, firm body of the Castorian female took on its own iridescent glow as it, too, walked out upon the quicksilver.

Mystically the figures floated over the lethal pool, the energized ribbons cradling them as they drew closer to the orb. Harmonic sounds echoed through the chamber with ever-increasing intensity as the life energies from three alien races converged. Finally, with a burst of spectral fire, the visitors pierced the sphere's surface.

Instantly the Geminian sensed the conscious presence of others within the energy globe. Startled by the intense clarity of their thoughts, she struggled to retain her own identity amidst the others. Straining for control, she attempted the most basic of psychic tactics. An inventory of her corporeal reference points would certainly restore her identity.

But no reference points could be found! She was totally without body! Her mind was unbounded!

The euphoria overpowered her. Thoughts exploded outward from her central consciousness. In her mind's eye, she saw her identity hurtling away from her in all directions, as if it were a newborn galaxy of infinitesimal memories. Yet, a sense of cosmic order prevailed throughout this infant galaxy. The Geminian was touched by this order ... comforted by it. She then realized its source. A soothing voice ... or was it a thought? ... steadied the Geminian with its inner resolve.

"Novas, return to us."

Her memories slowed their outward trajectory. Coalescing into an expansive field of thought, they once more provided her with an identity.

The soothing voice returned.

"Novas, Geminian Executive to the Solarian Corporation... I am Chrislar of Legos. You are aware?"

"Yes, Chrislar, I am aware. I regret that I was... momentarily unable to communicate."

"That is understandable. I sense from your thoughts that you were prepared for a similar experience to the one shared when you first encountered our race. However, this... time we elected to maintain our own forms rather than the fragile constructs used while establishing the joint venture between the Earth Exploratory Cartel and your home world. Instead, we chose to modify your form, as well as the form of the Castorian Executive."

"I see." replied Novas, with more calm in her thoughts, as she adopted a polite, business tone. "Has the Castorian representative arrived?"

"She is just now completing her orientation to our surroundings. Expand your mental focus slightly and you shall sense her."

The Legotian "spoke" with such certainty, it left no doubt that Novas had the ability to manipulate her senses as instructed.

"Perhaps they know too much of my skills," she feared. This was disconcerting. Novas had guarded her secrets for too long. "Are my thoughts an open page for all to read?"

Caution was in order. Tentatively, she proceeded to open her mind to the other's presence.

"Greetings, Novas of Gemini. I have been curious to meet you."

"I am at a disadvantage, Executive to Castor. You know my name, yet I do not know yours."

Before the Castorian could respond, Chrislar interjected, "If I may interrupt, we shall resolve that informational deficiency, Novas, among many others. The technique for establishing an accord between your Solar Corporation and the Castorian Conglomerate will be based on *total mutual trust*. To achieve that, each of you must share your inner-most secrets. In this way, your dependence on the other to protect that trust will establish an unyielding bond between you. I interrupted because I sensed that the Castorian Executive was hesitant to reveal her true identity. She will do so now."

Chrislar focused his consciousness toward the beautiful yet strong thought patterns of the Executive to Castor. Novas turned her mind to her as well. Hesitantly, after moments of silent reflection, the Castorian opened her thoughts.

"I am more than a mere Executive to my home world's cartel, seeking a profitable venture with the planets of the Solar Corporation. Much more. My father was the last Chairman to the powerful Castorian Conglomerate. I say last because, unknown to my world's people, he has been dead for five of your stellar years. Upon his passing, I surreptitiously took his Chair."

The Castorian was unnerved by the ease with which she revealed her most guarded thoughts. Should this revelation be discovered, her death would be instantaneous! Yet, she was compelled to continue.

"The ruse is for the benefit of my people. Had I not acted, anarchy would have replaced the rule of order. Factions within our cartel would have vied for power and left the Conglomerate vulnerable to external takeover forces. Despite this risk, these same factions would never accept my leadership. You see, never before has the Castorian Conglomerate been controlled by a female. We have attained certain levels of power, to be sure, but never the Supreme Chair. Yet, I had prepared for the inevitable passing of my father.

Years before, I devised a plan. For security purposes, our culture allows for our leader to preside beneath a shroud of secrecy. Matters of the presiding family are closely guarded, except for one - the first-born son. Our corporate charter provides that the son shall succeed the father. Yet, my father's failure to produce a successor was well known. My existence was not.

My plan was to pose as my father's latest concubine. Accepting the bitter fact he could no longer produce a rightful heir, my father agreed. Since he had no sons, his Advisors could easily accept that he was once again attempting to provide a successor. In this role, I could sit to the side, quietly observing, learning, mastering the skills and knowledge necessary for my ascension to the Chair. Over time, he used me increasingly as his intermediary while his disease progressed. His reclusive behavior served to propagate an aura of mystery and power. The Advisors quickly learned that to question his decisions meant certain termination.

Even today, the ruse is still intact. His death and my existence are secret even to the closest of his advisors. But discovery is inevitable. That is why I must prepare the people in advance. A success with this joint venture could establish my position in the Conglomerate. Once established, my rise to the Supreme Chair could be more easily accepted by the shareholders, and by the Advisors."

At the conclusion of her testimony, Chrislar added, "Your confession was a major step toward a foundation of trust. Yet, I sense a need for you to reveal more."

The Castorian's consciousness distorted, wavered, revealing her astonishment. Unsettled by the ability of the Legotian to know her most intimate thoughts and experiences, she resisted. Despite her mental defenses, Chrislar still knew! Her essence pulsed arrhythmically from the futility of her attempts to conceal the truth. Finally, she relented.

"What I have revealed to this point *is* the truth. But it is incomplete. I do not seek the Chairmanship simply because it is my birthright. Nor do I want it for the power alone. My motives are less noble in nature. I am driven by an insatiable desire! I crave a man I cannot have. He is Geminian, and forbidden to me. By attaining the Supreme Chair, I can change that!"

Novas could not contain her reaction. Her distaste reverberated through the conscience collective. To allow emotions to interfere with a business transaction was repulsive. The Castorian's motives violated the very core of Geminian business ethics. Ironically, though, for Novas to reveal her feelings so openly was itself a departure from those ethics. The well-honed steely composure that was her trademark during negotiations began to falter. This bodiless existence stripped away her facade of control.

The intensity of her thoughts unleashed a torrent of memories long-suppressed.

The Legotian sustained the onslaught of Novas' harsh memories as would a sea accept the rush of a mighty river. Her thoughts diffused through the vastness of Chrislar's consciousness; the current of Novas' mind formed eddies of her past experiences. As the memories subsided into pools of her past, Novas looked into them with awe.

Overwhelmed, the Geminian relented. "I, too, have been Desire's victim. But my truth goes even deeper. It is *power* that I crave - the power of the gods - to give, control, and take life itself! That is the truth which I must bear. That is the dark truth that I will now reveal."

CHAPTER 1

The shadow continued its stealthy migration toward the stony fissure. Upon casual inspection, the escarpment seemed impenetrable. Yet, the opening was there. Closer the wraith crept... its goal, to penetrate the craggy ridge comprising the outer walls of the Archive of Families.

Hours passed. But Time was not the challenge. It was Secrecy. The shadow must not be seen by the Archive's lone sentinel posted at its entrance. Finally, as the twilight of the setting sun brushed the basalt surface, the specter passed through a hidden gap.

Suddenly, a noise! The figure froze.

Paranormal senses flared, expanding outward to identify the source. Shifts in color, sound, smell, and vibration were instantly filtered until the sound's origin was located. The trespasser had not gone undetected! Nor had the other. A flicker of a smile acknowledged the two sets of eyes of the magma lizard, clinging to the far wall, almost perfectly concealed by its camouflaged hide.

"This guard can be disregarded," thought the intruder. "Had it been the lone sentinel outside, events would have been more problematic."

The invader pressed forward, deeper inside the shell of the Archive. Safely beyond detection from the guard, the black meshed cloak could be deactivated. The shadow instantly transformed. Blurred edges ... merged spectrums ... chaos signals snapped off. Left in their stead stood a time-hardened physique. The figure that had moved with such painstaking care only moments before now plunged into its mission with incredible speed.

"Swiftness is required for success," mused the intruder. "Having easily eluded detection by the ceremonial guardian of the Fata-Akateer, the more formidable devices installed by the Family Elders now await."

As if to confirm the intruder's suspicions, the surface of the inner walls of the sanctum crackled lightly with a low voltage current. The intent - to repel any lower life forms which might blunder against it. This charge now spanned the narrow opening into the room ahead.

But this being was no lower life form. A simple mental command to its peripheral sensory system blocked any mild shock from registering. The blue corona hissed as it swept harmlessly over the figure. Continuing its rapid pace into the previously secured chamber, the next challenge appeared. Multiple entrances harkened to a series of interconnecting passageways comprising a complex maze – a fitting test for the most logical of minds.

The senses which only seconds before had repelled all perceptions were now finely attuned to the slightest stimuli. Reason urged the figure forward, but Experience with the unexpected won out. An irrational compulsion combined with the light touch of cool air wafting from below commanded quick, violent action.

Fingers closed to form a rigid wedge of unnatural power. A swift thrust downward into the floor proved successful. The hand grasped the thin veneer covering a cooling duct and pulled it free. The texture of the panel's composition warned of the next danger. Speedily, the trespasser dropped into the narrow enclosure and replaced the tile. Simultaneously, a piercing ultrasonic beam barraged the empty room above. Regardless of the species, any creature remaining would have fled screeching out of the Archive, insane with pain from the sound. Only the knowledge that the panel's surface was a highly efficient acoustical insulator provided the clue which allowed an escape.

But the invader could not afford to revel long in this minor victory against the Archive's defenses. With the agility of an Andelian Pleasure Dancer, the figure clambered through the duct way toward the next chamber. Firm, sensitive hands probed the metal surface for weaknesses. Slight thermal gradients in the duct's structural integrity fed impulses to the computer-like mind. Within a millisecond, it extrapolated the environmental temperature waiting at the tunnel's end.

"A triradium cryonic generator!" concluder the interloper. "This device is capable of producing temperatures ranging from simple life support to the frigid cold required for life suspension."

Units such as this had been used for long space voyages, until the Terran, Stephen Carlos, had proven the theories of time folding.

"There is a probability greater than 0.84 that the unit serves more than one function," postulated the trespasser. "Archive cooling, yes. But I suspect another defense."

A shift in the electromagnetic field within the narrow enclosure raised the probability to 1.0, as a frigid blast of cooling vapors engulfed the intruder. The body's enzyme activity rapidly dropped. Muscles no longer received the chemo-transmitters necessary for activity. Peripheral nerve endings numbed. The invader's fiery eyes rolled backward, revealing only the mercurial coating visible during deep meditation.

Struggling to maintain consciousness, the invader labored, "My one true weakness - cold. I must prove my superiority over the Family Elders. I must focus my will ..."

But the chilling blasts took their toll.

Thoughts of capture - humiliation - banishment - coalesced into solid forms within the mind... forms to be combatted and defeated. But defeating these thoughts seemed impossible. The forms morphed into crystalline figures of Eissbar and Cryohawks, rising up against the lone figure. Unarmed, the intruder was easy prey for the carnivores. Yet, the logical mind which saw no escape gave way to one flaming emotion -the desire to live!

The mental constructs were now Reality. Surrounded by the predators, the Geminian stood motionless. The beasts circled their prey. Their victim's immobility would only serve them, as their frigid presence drained life away. Drawing steadily closer, the Eissbar's growl paralyzed as the Cryohawk's cry numbed their foe. It would be only a matter of moments.

But it was more sudden.

With a flash, a pulsing light surged outward from the figure. Building to a blinding intensity, the searing heat from the would-be prey repulsed the attackers - reducing their crystalline bodies to shards of fractured ice.

Simultaneously, within the motionless body lying in the metallic tomb, the will to live stirred.

In an area of the brain long kept dormant, a secondary set of thermo-neural transmitters activated. Inorganic traces of manganese pentoxide complexed with organic fuel to generate heat. Circulatory vessels transported life-giving warmth to energy-starved muscles.

Neural synapses, long unused, fired quantum pulses of living energy.

An envelope of heat radiated from the body, pushing back the frigid vapor blasts. Coursing down the duct's surface, the thermal tsunami overwhelmed cryonic semiconductors, shattering them. Leaving the generator with memory sufficient only to carry out the more mundane task of life support, the cooling system's defense circuits were eradicated.

The body stirred. Perceptions of reality came crashing into the semi-conscious mind. Eyes flickered. Senses recalibrated. The frigid ordeal was over. The intruder had overcome the images -and the reality- of a frozen death.

The memory of Purpose again took its place foremost in the intruder's mind.

"The Core of the Archive! I must reach it!"

The fire of desire continued to burn in the trespasser's mind. The energy was too great to contain through cerebral exercises. It had to be directed. Clambering further along the sub-floor ducting to a critical nexus of the cooling network, the figure took pause. Fists clenched together into a mace of violence. Pounding upward against the scorched metal, the panel yielded within seconds. Sinewy arms stretched out, grasping the edges of the opening. With one swift, agile movement, the captive vaulted out of the metallic sarcophagus onto the smooth, tiled floor above.

Immediately, a computer synthesized voice toned out its warning in a monotonous staccato.

AKUNAI! ... CAUTION!
YOU ... HAVE ... TRESPASSED ... INTO ... THE ... INNER ... SANCTUM ... OF ... THE ... FATA-AKATEER. BETA ... BRAINWAVE ... SCAN ... S H O W S ... Y O U ... T O ... B E ... OF ...AUTHORIZED ... DESCENT ... BUT... UNCLASSIFIED ... PURPOSE.   ANY ... FURTHER ... ATTEMPT ... AT... ENTRY ... WILL ... BE ... MET ... WITH ... FORCEFUL... DETERRENCE ...OF... PERMANENTLY ... DISABLING ... MAGNITUDES.   DEFENSES ... TO ... THIS ... POINT ... HAVE ... BEEN ... DROPPED ... FOR ... YOUR ... SAFE ... EXIT.

THE ...HEART... IS... THE... SOURCE ... OF... LIFE.

The glint in the crimson-orange eyes of the invader flashed in amusement and fascination.

"Life rightists are soft," concluded the intruder.

The warning was in Geminese, since no other beta pattern would register as authorized. The intruder took pride in the knowledge that programming by the Family Elders presumed that none other than a true Geminian of their Order could have progressed this far into the labyrinth of debilitating - but not yet deadly -

defenses. Up to this point any lesser form would have fled or been rendered unconscious.

The Geminian knew that the Archive's next surprises would be more "challenging," unless a hasty retreat was made. Furthermore, the computer had already concluded that the option for life versus pain or death would be chosen, since a previously undetectable doorway to an exit corridor now opened.

But, this unique Geminian believed that the mind, not the heart, was the source of life, and life was given only to be risked!

This philosophy flew in the face of the Family Elders, who were Life Rightists. In direct contrast to their belief that "the heart is the source of life", and life is to be treasured, not risked, the intruder saw a different balance struck by the gods. Purpose, Reality, Time, Secrecy, Reason, Desire, and Experience were but a few of the many gods that determined one's fate. If worshiped in the right balance, Victory would smile down upon you. But one first had to pay homage to Risk. Without that tribute, life was of little value. One must chance the loss of life for it to have worth. But the Life Rightists that designed the defenses could not fathom this concept. That would be their undoing.

Scrutiny of the designer's safe passage revealed the tell-tale clues necessary for identifying the second doorway out of the room - the doorway to the Core!

Ignoring the voice of Reason, the figure answered the irrepressible god of Desire, and moved forward toward the hidden passageway. The hiss of the safe exit-way closing whispered a hint of danger to the acutely tuned ears. The hum of charging pulsar muskets confirmed it!

* * *

Outside the Archive, the evening was arid, as they usually are during Royta-Far, the Season of Heritage. The fire of Gemini's giant red sun, Pollux, quenched itself behind the towering mountains on the horizon, prompting the transformation of the flora and fauna of the Family's Natural Preserve.

While the heat of the day escaped into the cloudless sky, a two-tred long Slotar frantically searched for the warmth-preserving Triturite crystals it had accumulated the evening before. As its scaleless reptilian body flitted through the sand and sparse desert undergrowth outside the Preserve, the movement registered in the drowsy amethyst eyes of a Geminian Vambor, lumbering through the yawning entrance of its cavern den. This furry mammoth - approximating a 400 stone-weight raccoon, except for the half-tred tusks protruding from its canine-like snout - had spent a restful day within the cool recesses of a nearby alum bluff. The setting red giant beckoned the Vambor to begin its nocturnal foraging through the patch of forest nestled close to the north side of the mountain. Here it knew that the blossoms of the Botak trees were just now emerging from their leathery cocoons, where they stayed dormant and protected from the blistering sun.

Another pair of watchful eyes absorbed the beauty of the daily metamorphosis of the Preserve. An observer more attentive than the Vambor would note the classic orange eyes set beneath the smooth, hairless brow of the young Geminian bioduotron, Starn. Although he had witnessed the same changes each day for the past fortnight, he could not shake the feeling of being a voyeur, shamefully catching glimpses of Nature's most intimate secrets.

"Stop it! These are the daydreams of a true life form! I must purge them!" Starn thought, berating himself for the lapse in focus.

"I must erase such thoughts from my mind and replace them with control! Instead of admiring the beauty, I should note the behavioral patterns of the varied species and categorize them for future reference. I must use my superior mentality according to the Teachings. It is my duty and the biodgen way."

But it was difficult to keep his mind from wandering. In order to refocus his thoughts, he exercised the technique of Retrospa - to regain one's sense of being through meditation on one's own origin.

Fourteen Polluxar days earlier I was once again empowered by my Life-Mentor - the biological "other" or Dual selected at birth to provide the genetic material necessary for my creation. Such creation, rare to all but a privileged few Geminians, had been a closely guarded technique for many generations. Yet, decades before, my Life-Mentor had been chosen. DNA had been removed from a Geminian child and recombined with "life crystals" to form molecular chains. These chains, cultured into life-sustaining cells, grew into an organism capable of supporting the life essence of the Geminian DNA donor. Through years of grueling training, the donor would learn to project a copy of his life essence into the crystalline-cellular construct. That construct, or "bioduotron", is me. I am Starn, a Geminian word meaning "of the cosmos". It is a fitting name, for I have been conditioned as a temporary vessel for one who would spend much of his life in space.

Starn reflected on his fate as a bioduotron, as if fate could be appropriately used when referring to a temporary life form.

But I cannot complain- should not complain- about my "temporary" status. For, from the time my cell-crystals had developed into an organism, I have been activated by life energy on a frequent basis. Normally, it is a slow process for a Dual to learn to empower a bioduotron's cells by projecting his conscious life essence into them.

But as my biodgen grew, his life projection skills grew as well. My Dual has been unselfish in the amount of time his consciousness has spent in my form. Unselfish, to be sure, for to voluntarily leave one's self-sustaining organic body in a mindless limbo for any length of time is awe-inspiring. But to do it at a 43% level is unheard of - even on Gemini.

Normally, a bioduotron developed physically at a slower rate than its Geminian counterpart, since motor skills are developed primarily through practice. For a Geminian and his alternate life construct to be at equal levels of development meant much time had been spent with the Geminian consciousness in the bioduotron body. Such was the very rare case of Starn and his Dual.

My Life-Mentor is what many Geminian scholars are beginning to believe to be the living example of the ideals of bioduogenetics- the Geminian science of sustaining two life forms with one mind. My Dual strove to reach the highest level of biodgen achievement- the Phoenos. To achieve Phoenos meant literally to give birth to life by pure thought. My life! I and my "other" could coexist. Separate living beings spawned from one consciousness! Yet it was not to be. My "other" has forgone Phoenos for another path. But my resentment is yet more proof of my unworthiness. My emotions display my weakness, and my weakness must be suppressed. I should be grateful... grateful that my Life-Mentor is Nimon Edison of the interstellar crystal manufacturing facility, Darwin. For even now, as I struggle for control, he is educating me in the skills of scientific reason... skills that he has gained through years of training from sources spanning the galaxy. Though our consciousnesses are independent, we share rational knowledge at a subconscious level. For that, I am thankful... but my craving for experience still overwhelms me. How can I be expected to learn reason when I desire so much more!

The "bioduotron-mentor" relationship was unique among all those in the known star systems. Although both bodies were empowered at separate times by the same consciousness, they did not retain the same memories. While Nimon was superior in almost every technical field, Starn preferred the arts. Whereas Nimon projected an air of control, Starn could be driven by intense emotions, as was happening now. But those thoughts of emotion must be controlled. Especially during the Season of Heritage, when the bioduotron-mentor connection began the final phase of maturing.

As part of the maturation process, Starn's duty and final test of psychic endurance was to stand watch over the Fata-Akateer, the Archive of Families, sequestered in the heart of the vast Natural Preserve. The centuries-old Archive had been carved out of the sheer rock face of the mountain chain which cut its way unyieldingly through the Preserve. Within the stone structure were housed the Records of Lineage of the most noble and respected Geminian families. The rocky mass served as a natural fortress against any curious wildlife and a constant temperature environment to protect the records.

This sentry duty, more a symbol of commitment than an act of courage, provided a time to meditate on the course of the bioduotron-mentor union, as well as an opportunity to practice the skills of fasting and sleeplessness for long periods of time. Unknown to the candidate of Royta-Far was the fact that the Elders periodically monitored his activities. A psionic-telemetry device insured that the condition of fasting and sleeplessness were maintained, among other purposes.

Those signals were now troubling the Family Elders. Hopes of a reversal in this subject's condition were fading.

The Retrospa technique had restored a semblance of emotional control to Starn. However, he realized the emotional mental spikes were his own biodgen signs of fatigue. To avoid failure, he must further strengthen his control by taking his mind through a vigorous regimen of logical exercises. As darkness settled around him, the chill of the night air greedily robbed his muscular frame of its comforting warmth. In response, the young guardian triggered another part of his complex brain. Altering his metabolic rate to compensate for the lost heat, he continued his regimen of logical calisthenics.

Thus occupied, Starn failed to detect the section of shadows to his left as they slowly -immeasurably- drifted toward the farthest corner of the Archive.

Starn's thoughts gradually transitioned from exercises in logic to more metaphysical questions as his fatigue increased. The teachings of his parents' intruded upon his thoughts. They spoke of Life's dualiity and its struggle against Death's shadow.

"Death's shadow was hardest to see," they whispered. "One must always be watchful for the arrival of his own Specter."

Ironically, Starn vowed not to overlook the arrival of his.

CHAPTER 2

"Plant Control, this is Descartes," sighed the Plant Manager of the Darwin, openly expressing his distaste for his current "special assignment".

Despite his protests, the Solar Corporation Board of Directors had seen to it that he was put in charge of this latest task force. Its purpose was not unique - find a new way to make profits -nothing wrong with that. However, this new venture involved capitalizing on the latest Sol system fad; a fad that mystified Descartes. Ancient relics were being organized into displays and taken on tours through the ten planetary franchises of the Solar Corporation. For reasons beyond his comprehension, species of all kinds thronged to see the newfound evidence that humanoids at one time were capable of artistic expression.

"Surprise at our long-lost arts is demeaning ... as if we never experienced that phase of our development," grumbled the Plant Manager to himself. "Of course we did. We simply discarded art long ago as the waste of effort that it represents!"

To his dismay, Descartes' job was to escort a team of archaeologists to a remote planetoid and supervise the excavation of a recently discovered cache of artifacts. To compound his displeasure, the Board's hypocrisy added insult to injury. He still recalled the Treasurer's last transmission with a pang of disgust, "Be alert to any signs of carbo-silicase deposits as well."

"Art was nice," he thought sarcastically, "but not as nice as a new source of life crystal ore."

At least that was the message he heard the board sending. Stirred from his reverie, he impatiently keyed his transceiver once more just as the reply from the orbiting plant came in.

"Darwin here, sir," came back the familiar formality of his Plant Engineer, George Crescent.

"Are you prepared for us to send down a lander, sir?"

Morgan Descartes knew that George was impatient to end this assignment, too. He had been wiling away the hours tinkering with the Solar Corporation's modified version of a stealth device. The apparatus could effectively make a facility the size of a life crystal plant invisible in space.

"Now that was an interesting assignment," mused Descartes, as he recalled one of the Darwin's more clandestine ventures where the technology had been "acquired" from the Castorian Conglomerate, an arch rival, competitor, and as business would have it, sometime-partner, of the Solar Corporation.

He smirked at the thought of how a legal loophole in a mineral rights deal between Solar and the Castorian Conglomerate had gotten Solar more than just a life crystal ore mining operation. A clause in the contract required Castor to provide protection for the operation from claim jumpers for one Terran year. In the fine print, "protection" meant the right to review Castorian patent applications for technological advancements which could breach the security of the mining operation. The stealth patent was just such an advancement. With this technology, Solar had argued before the Legotian interstellar tribunal, claim-jumpers could fabricate a wildcat mining operation right under their very noses. Solar's mineral rights would be worthless.

It had been the job of the Darwin and its employees to prove Solar's case. The assignment was to spacefold the plant into the sector near the planetoid mines under the cover of the stealth device. Once there, mining operations could be performed to establish that Solar's argument was more than just theory.

That part had been easy.

The difficult task had been getting the stealth device in the first place. The job had fallen upon the Darwin's Technical Superintendent, Nimon Edison. And as Descartes recalled, it had been a formidable one. Edison had seduced none other than the consort of the Castorian Chairman herself in order to abscond with the stealth technology.

Despite the successful stealth mining demonstration by the Darwin, it had taken days of jurisprudence computer model simulations and counter-simulations by the Legotians before they were able to reach a decision. The outcome was a landmark case. The advisors of Legos awarded Solar the right to review the Castorian Conglomerate's patent on a new stealth system, thereby legalizing Solar's illegal acquisition of the technology. Precedence had been set that had cascaded into a myriad number of corporate espionage techniques now employed throughout the star systems. Not the least of which was seduction.

"But what's the danger of a woman scorned to a Geminian?" muttered Descartes, with a sarcastic snort.

"Beg your pardon, sir?" rasped the Engineer's voice in Descartes' transceiver.

"I was just wondering how you were coming along on your project, George," replied Descartes, shaken from his reverie.

He sincerely did want to know the project status, even if the question was only asked to conceal his daydreaming. Its completion could mean a bonus for himself and the Engineering Department. He smiled at the irony of the project, for at that moment he was once again involved in a deal with the Castorian

Conglomerate. But this time it was not a mission of corporate subterfuge; rather, it was a mission of inter-corporate image. The Vice-president of Corporate Public Relations for Solar had thought it a wonderful idea to assist the Castorians in uncovering the ruins of one of their legendary "lost civilizations". By using the "more refined" salvage techniques developed by Solar's Clio Division, one of the ten planetary franchises, it would show the Castorians that what they considered to be "the soft, useless culture of the Clio star system" actually had its advantages. The information would be equally shared by Solar and Castor, and would serve as a first step in establishing a joint venture between the two great interstellar companies.

Management thought, "What better representative to send on this mission than one of Solar's finest plant managers?" And even better, sending the same person and plant that had embarrassed the Conglomerate during the Darwin stealth device - mining deal would serve as a symbol of repentance. "It would be a sign of asking to 'forgive and forget,' 'bury the hatchet,' 'mend broken fences,'" and all the other dated clichés senior V.P. She-yen had heaped upon Descartes to convince him of the wisdom of this mission.

Descartes smiled. He knew She-yen better than that. Since the first days at the Business Aggression Seminar when She-yen taught

Rudimentary Self-Defense to the managers, Descartes learned from him that the "open palm extended in friendship can be used as a knife-hand of defense."

The "open palm" Management had chosen to extend to the Castorians was the Darwin. The newly retrofitted life crystal manufacturing facility was the flagship of the corporation. Its personnel were highly trained in their respective fields. They and their facility were one of only a dozen in the known star systems that had the capability for interstellar travel. Time-space folding, or space folding, as it was more commonly called, was not very precise. Much like in the old sea faring days of travel where the natural elements could affect your course, the Darwin's mode of transport was fickle. Appropriate for moving a select few large vessels from star to star, it was unreliable for short distance traverses within planetary fields. The first generation crafts had derisively been known as "moon busters" when on not one but two voyages they had materialized in planetary satellites, irreparably damaging the entire star system. In contrast, interplanetary landers employed quark core micro warp technology. This enabled smaller vessels to precisely jump between planets and from the atmosphere into space. Armed with that kind of science, and trained people to apply it, the team of the Darwin was ready for any dirty deals Castor might throw at them.

George Crescent responded to his manager's inquiry, "I've a small surprise for you, sir, if you're coming up."

"Well, George, you know my feelings about surprises. But in this case, it'll be a welcome change. Send down the Magellan and have Helicon, the senior Clionian, ready to receive the last of the cargo."

A short time later, the hull of the Magellan shimmered as it exited the planetoid's atmosphere on its return trip to the Darwin's hangar. Somewhat an aficionado of antique space vessels, Descartes took no small amount of pride in his personal lander. He had painstakingly modified the standard-issue company vehicle to reflect his tastes. To the casual observer, it appeared as if an ancient Lunar Excursion Module, or LEM as it was known during the Apollo era, was capable of micro warp travel. However, underneath the spidery-legged, crinkled paper wad veneer of the lander thrummed a quark core that enabled the vessel to traverse short spans of space in mere moments.

Descartes rotated the control spheres with precision as he maneuvered the lander back into normal space. Looking out the star shield, he gazed at another source of pride, cheeks flushing at the site of his magnificent plant. "Technology of the gods", the news-comms had said with disdain. The heavily conservative news media had made every attempt to undermine the plant's construction. It was the first of a dozen. An idea born of a somewhat tempestuous joint venture with the Geminian Corporation, another one of the ten planetary franchises of the Solar Corporation. The idea of a space-born facility with the capability to manufacture life-crystals was abhorrent to the ethically elite media. The technology to synthesize crystals found naturally in the Geminian star system would proliferate the travesty against humanity that they believed bioduogenetics to be. However, swift action against the media's efforts to manipulate public opinion had resulted in only a smattering of protests during a few of Solar's quarterly stockholders meetings. It was not surprising that a few well-placed stock options in untraceable SuisBanc accounts had quickly diverted the attention of the appropriate proxy holders. In the end, the plant's construction had come in on-time and under budget, and Descartes' retirement fund had been secured.

The plant manager and self-proclaimed ace pilot pulled the lander through an opening in the Darwin's surface. Once the hangar locks pressurized to allow the passengers to disembark, the plant's personnel manager, along with a curious associate, and a med tech all entered the hangar. Jefferson Brown, the Darwin's personnel manager for the last eight years, felt it was a good personal touch to greet returning surface teams. This time he was accompanying Herik Helicon, the senior research scientist in the Clionian expedition, as a middle-aged father would escort his aging parent. Floating to his left was an anti-grav unit ready to accept another load of ancient - and what Brown considered fascinating - artifacts.

With the speed and efficiency of a Denebian Sand-Ray, the med-tech moved past Brown and Helicon and went among the landing party, injecting each member with a specially prepared antimicrobial compound. It could have been his imagination, but it seemed to Descartes he added an extra "oomph" when it came to his injection.

"There! That should do the trick!" Brown said, beaming a mischievous grin in Descartes' direction.

Descartes caught the look, but decided business came first. "Surface team, return to your respective departments - and a good job down there," he remarked, moving off the lander pad toward Brown. Descartes knew the team had been hard-pressed just to keep their eyes open from the boredom, but they still managed to maintain an air of business-like efficiency about them. And to Descartes, staying alert on a boring assignment was a sign of good work.

He now descended upon Brown.

"You get a lot of pleasure out of seeing me made a pin cushion, don't you J.B.?" exclaimed Descartes, as he sorely rubbed the small of his back where the potion had been pneumatically infused.

"Morgan, you're beginning to sound more and more like your red-eyed technical superintendent, with your complaining about the company's health policies. You know that dust-ball of a planet hasn't been explored before. Our detectors recorded microbial life down there, and there's no telling what reactions they can cause in humans, if left unprotected. It's not my fault the mission's risk factor doesn't warrant the use of a biodrone team. Anyway, needles went out with catgut and leeches centuries ago, not to mention the fact that it's insubordinate for me to derive pleasure out of your pain!"

Descartes winced, partly from the shot, and partly from Brown's rapier gibe. "Now who's sounding like a Geminian - or at least his biod - reciting historical facts and claiming he doesn't succumb to a pleasurable emotion now and then, for whatever the reason?" Descartes shot back, playfully jousting with his personnel manager. "And his eyes are orange, not red, you color-blind headshrinker."

They both looked each other in the eye and grinned.

"You miss them too, huh J.B.?"

"Let's just say as manager of personnel, I'm a student of behavior, and they make good case studies!" Brown retorted, his dark face breaking into an even broader smile. "And, you'd best remember not to refer to Starn as a 'biod'. You know how sensitive he is to being equated to the 'inferior mechanicals' the Solar Corporation uses."

Before Descartes could react to the reprimand, a gleeful hiss from across the room reminded the two of Helicon, the Clionian historian. They turned to find the rickety little creature meticulously going through the last load of relics.

Descartes couldn't help but wince again, this time from the sight of the green webbed claws rummaging through the dusty articles. The Clionian race was - in the most flattering terms Descartes could force himself to accept - "reptilian."

Their scaly skin, typical of the evolutionary branch of creatures from the Jurassic quadrant of the galaxy, disgusted Descartes. The Clionians were short and slender of stature, with abbreviated upper appendages ending in hands containing handsome, but deadly claws. When in the company of humanoids, they carried themselves erect on their slightly more muscularly developed hind legs, but they found themselves much more comfortable on all fours. The Clionian skull resembled that of a Terran alligator, with its low forehead mounted atop a long snout containing irregular rows of razor teeth.

Though fearsome in appearance, they were actually a gentle, benign race, specializing in the study of galactic history and evolution. It was their theory that to overcome the weaknesses of a race's genetic and acquired characteristics, a precise pattern of its historical development must be understood. With this concept as their tool, the Clionians were able to modify their own behavior patterns and discard the violent tendencies of their ancestors for a more peaceful way of life. Their star system had agreed to enter a franchise arrangement with Solar Corporation several years ago for the purpose of cultivating their historically-based philosophy throughout the galaxy.

Solar saw the profit potential.

Nevertheless, Descartes' knowledge of the Clionians' passive nature was not enough to shake the unconscious dislike he felt toward them.

Whether it was the years of training and experience in interplanetary behavioral psychology, or just the fact that Brown knew his boss all too well, he sensed Descartes' uneasiness.

"Morgan, I've been noticing your behavior when you're around Helicon and his people, and it's just not like you."

"What are you getting at, J.B.?" Descartes snapped, disturbed by the fact that his feelings were so easily read.

Brown could tell he would have to tred lightly on this matter, since no one liked being labeled a bigot, especially a life crystal plant manager.

"I'm just trying to tell you that there are always reasons for a person to have an irrational mistrust for another race.   Once those reasons are identified, they can…"

"Irrational mistrust?   Since when do you beat around the bush, Mr. Brown? First you imply my use of 'biod' is tantamount to a racial epithet, and now you're psychoanalyzing my attitude toward Clionians. Are you calling me a racist?"

Descartes' face reddened with the tell-tale flush Brown recognized whenever his plant manager strained to control his temper.

"Morgan, I just think that…"

"I'm needed in Plant Engineering, Mr. Brown. At least there I can deal with reality and not Freudian fantasy!"   With a fiery glare in the Clionian's direction, Descartes stormed out of the lander hangar.

The Clionian innocently blinked his translucent eyelids toward the personnel manager. Brown simply shrugged his shoulders in reply as he started to help the historian cart his treasure trove back to the lab.

*   *   *

"Plant Engineering!" Descartes barked as he entered the omnivator, which would shuttle him from one area of the plant to another.

Transport from deck to deck through the life crystal plant usually took the form of riding in zero grav discs piloted by computerized robots. Management had personal discs assigned to them, while supervisors and operators used an assortment of communal discs designed specifically for the functional department and its members' needs. The spherical shape of the Darwin, with its interior double-walled hollow core channel for processing cosmic radiation during time folding, enabled the zero grav discs a perfect path to ferry around and between decks.

"Yes, sir," cooed the seductively feminine voice of the omnivator operator.

Descartes shot an embarrassing glance toward the mechanical driver of the magnetic-powered taxi. He caught himself just as he was about to voice his most sincere apologies to the lovely lady he envisioned was the source of the compubot's voice.

It had been some time now since his personal chauffeur had been programmed with the voice characteristics of a temptress. Originally, it had infuriated Descartes. He had vowed to force feed every biochip he could find down the throat of the Gestalt-base programmer whose insidious sense of humor devised this practical joke.

But over time, Descartes had become accustomed to the soothing nature of the compubot's erotic voice. He found solace in it when he least expected it. This was one of those times, as he felt the rush of anger Brown had incited quickly subside.

As the magnetic disc hovered at the Plant Engineering deck, Descartes regained the composure befitting a life crystal plant manager. Quickly he strode to Engineer Crescent's station.

"Just in time, sir. My techs and I were finishing off the last hook-ups between the plasma stabilizers and the short range navigational sensor modules!" George exclaimed, barely able to control his excitement about his new engineering marvel.

Descartes was far from being the engineering equal of the long-time friend that stood before him, but he did know his plant, and was puzzled at George's statement.

"Since when does the stealth device require a tap on the plasma system, Mr. Crescent?"

"That's part of my surprise, sir. Not only can this little beauty cloak the Darwin from sensors and detect distortions from other stealth devices, I've discovered a way to project false images onto the sensory grids of nearby vessels! That'll play as much havoc on a starcraft's senses as will a drink of 200 year old Barishnikovian vodka on a tenth year biod in zero-grav training!"

Descartes' smiled broadly at his Engineer's simile. But it quickly faded as the safety clarion blasted out its cry of danger. Simultaneously, a fierce shudder rocked through the protective sphere of the Darwin. Regaining his balance, Descartes bolted to the communication console on the Engineer's desk.

Slapping the activator lever, he barked, "Control Room!"

Senior Control Technician Saffron 3 was covering the center on this shift. One of two Angellian clones employed along with their primary on the Darwin, she was highly skilled in communications programming. These skills were in large part due to the telepathic ability shared among the primary and her two clones, as well as an uncanny ability to interface with artificial intelligence through tactile pads on their hands. Their planet, Angellius, was yet another of the ten planetary franchises that comprised the Solar Corporation. Although a small business venture, it had provided the nucleus of the technology that Solar used in its bioduotrons, or biodrones. A melding of Angelian cloning techniques with Geminian bioduogenetics had given rise to a patent exclusively held by the Solar Corporation. Although a far cry from the almost mystical interface experienced by a Geminian organic and his biodgen, the biodrone technology of the Solar Corporation did enable organics to empower artificial constructs via a similar transference of consciousness. A technological side effect for Angelius, however, as a result of being a franchisee of the Solar Corporation was the defunding of the Angellian Research and Development Division. The science-art of cloning had become all but extinct, and the Saffron "sisters" were one of the few surviving examples of that technology.

Saffron Three, or EssThree, stunned by the jolt to the plant, strained to slide her hands back into the bio-comm interface. Upon contact, she instantly dispatched the shift members to full alert status.

"Not now!" she telepathically projected to her primary and clone-mate.

"Tell me what's happening!" Saffron Two implored.

"EssTu, if you would lower your anxiety barrier, you would know what is happening through EssThree's thoughts," chided Esswon, the primary.

"Both of you, regain control of yourselves! I am on duty, not you! If you can't monitor my thoughts without your incessant psycho-chatter, I'll shield them from the both of you!" Saffron 3 scolded.

As a race, the Angellians were a very determined people, and they prided themselves on that trait. Centuries ago within the Angellius system, radiation from a dying star in an adjacent system had adversely affected the population's growth rate. The radiation poisoning had infiltrated the food chain, causing viral mutations. The mutations were aggressively adaptable to vaccinations. To compensate, cloning at birth became common. By injecting clones two and three with antibodies from the host, a serum could be developed which would allow the host to live. Unfortunately, the clones would not. The Saffron sisters were rare examples where all three had survived. Following the takeover of Angellius by the Solar Corporation, and the ensuing benefits from the improved health care system, a successful vaccine for the planet's viral mutations had been developed. Eventually, the demand for cloning disappeared to the point it was no longer profitable. The Saffron sisters were some of the few remaining beneficiaries. As a result, they were eternally grateful to the Solar Corporation, and so became loyal employees.

As co-communications technicians on each of the three plant shifts, they had established themselves as invaluable contributors, except for their constant bickering when together. Morgan Descartes had made a point to learn to differentiate between the three. For even though they were genetically identical, each had acquired individual nuances in their habits and mannerisms. Knowing her to be the most level-headed of the three, he looked to EssThree for some fast answers.

"Rival vessel, Mr. Descartes. Configuration - Castorian Conglomerate Espionage class.

Apparently its stealth device caught us off-guard while sensors were momentarily disengaged for Mr. Crescent's modifications. Damage report - radial fields down twenty percent with reported radiation injuries among personnel stationed near the hull. No casualties. Computer defenses have successfully prevented data drain so far."

"Very good, Saffron 3! Initiate evasive maneuvers. I'm on my way around! Descartes out!"

The plant manager whirled and faced his Engineer.

"Is that thing ready for action, George?"

"Well it hasn't been tested yet. I don't know if it's conflict-worthy . . ."

"George, I'm relying on you to have it right the first time!" Descartes snapped, before Engineer Crescent could finish.

The two managers and conflict-worn friends exchanged knowing looks, realizing they had been in similar situations many times before. It was becoming all too common for rival corporations to raid facilities for information from their competitors' computer systems. Manned data probes would tap into a facilities control center and extract whatever technical information they could get. If their telemetry drain happened to disrupt ongoing operations, well, that was the misfortune of fierce competition. A facility's safety record depended on how well they defended against these violators. It was measured in terms of lost personnel and lost information - but not necessarily in that order. In this case, the Darwin had limited its losses to a few injuries which could easily be downplayed in the safety scores, if the infiltrators could be stopped quickly. Somehow, the Darwin had always narrowly escaped a costly incident. But both knew that one of these days, the odds might not work out in their favor.

George Crescent was accustomed to his plant manager's mood swings. Morgan Descartes could charm the starlight out of a black hole - when he wanted to be charming. But when his plant was at risk, he hardened. George called it the "spousal syndrome". He knew that married people treated their spouses harshly under stress, but if the vid-com chimed during an argument, a syrupy sweet "hello" would greet the caller. Descartes treated his direct-reports in the same way - like family. George knew that.

"She'll be ready when you need her, Morgan," he replied solemnly. He hoped that by saying it would happen, it just might.

A quick little smile tugged at the corner of Descartes' mouth. With a firm slap on the Engineer's shoulder, Descartes gave him a look of confidence, an approving nod, and marched out.

CHAPTER 3

"Novas, your honesty is noble, but your testimony is unnecessary. The truths of your past have a far greater importance than you could yet know, for the events of your past must still occur. That is the essence of why you have been brought here, and that is why you must now leave."

The shocking rebuke jolted Novas' psyche. "Have I done something to disturb the Legotian? Has my confession insulted him? Have I shaken his faith in my ability to form a merger between the two corporate powers that present themselves before him?" she interrogated herself mentally.

Novas prided herself on her steely control when faced with a challenge. Yet, a rare panic seized her. Although formless, nothing but a mental avatar in this energy state, she still felt a shortness of breath and dizzying vertigo. Much like the amputee sensing the itching of a lost limb, her imagined chest heaved rapidly with fear. Her normally disciplined thoughts rushed outward, faster than she could rein them back in. More severe than the disorientation during her transformation upon entry into the Legotians' realm, her dispersing thoughts put her in jeopardy of a complete loss of identity – and sanity!

But Chrislar quickly intervened, consoling her. Surrounding her with his presence, his light touched the pinpoints of her dispersed essence. Their multitude swirled along the path he charted. From chaos came direction. The purity of order, the sublime serenity of his thoughts, re-established peace within her.

"Novas, do not expend your mental energies on thoughts that are contrary to Time's purpose. Do as I say. Leave the sphere and soon, all things will become clear."

Had Novas' present form of existence been more than non-corporeal thought, her face would have hardened. A quick, brief nod in the affirmative would have signaled her concession, and displeasure, as it often did when accepting unpleasant dictates from Solar's upper management.

But her options were few. Insistence on staying was pointless.

Finally electing to concede to Chrislar's order, it occurred to her that she did not know how to obey it. She attempted to expand her thoughts outwardly, pressing further against the edges of the sphere. As they projected radially, her sense of self again decreased. Paranoia swept over her. Reflexively, she pulled her thoughts back toward her. As she did, her sense of being increased. A comforting warmth swept over her which had been absent for quite some time. Tentatively, she increased the intensity of her inward focus. As the sense of comfort grew, a semblance of her body began to coalesce into particles of unified radiant energy. An image of a cool, mirrored surface appeared before her. She reached out a glowing hand and attempted to touch it.

Surprisingly, her fingers penetrated what appeared to be a solid metal plane. The ends of her fingers felt warm, as if blood were flowing through them once more. Pushing further, she extended her hands and arms through the mysterious interface. The warmth of a bright, new sun danced across the surface of her skin. She moved her hands across her body, still refusing to believe that she in fact was a living being again.

"What an experience!" she thought. A slight sigh evidenced the hint of sorrow she felt at leaving the energy realm of the Legotians.

But anxiety quickly swept away Novas' sorrow. Grim Reality took its place.

"This is not the Legotian chamber! This sun should not be here!" she thought. "What is happening to me?"

Instinctively, she knew the answer to her question. For the first time in a long while she had dropped her defenses - and now she would pay the price for it!

*　　*　　*

The Archive intruder's mind raced! By deftly executing several roll and tuck maneuvers, two pulsar blasts had been avoided. Yet, the danger persisted. The astute acrobat realized that the intensity of the charges was steadily increasing - as was the accuracy. The scorched flooring mere picotreds away proved that.

Escape options were quickly weighed and discarded.

"Standing still had failed to abort the initial shot, so the sighting mechanism could not be motion activated ..." the intruder calculated. "...and I sense no other radiation band. The probabilities point to a passive thermal detector as the logical choice."

An experiment with the third beam confirmed the conclusion. A rapid drop in metabolic rate caused the decreased body temperature to induce a third miss.

"This ploy will not work indefinitely! The thermal detector is already recalibrating to increase its sensitivity!"

A running vault carried the trespasser across the ten tred distance to the wall containing the hidden doorway, detected only seconds earlier. The physiological process that had allowed escape from the cryogenic duct began to repeat itself. However, the heat energy was now being focused - channeled through a single hand - a hand pressed firmly against the seam of the door! Glowing crimson, the hand transferred its energy to the wall covering the delicate operational circuits. Simultaneously, the energy built within the pulsar battery for the fourth - and fateful - final blast!

The infiltrator smirked, gloating in anticipation of success.

"The softness born from protecting their idea of life has once again failed the Archive creators, as it has for centuries," thought the prowler. "They could not fathom that any being would risk the harmful consequences of their defenses ... at least any being that meets their myopic view of life. I despise their devotion to such a narrow definition of life! The irony is their defenses have reacted as if I would garner their approval, and be spared. If my suspicions prove to be correct, my overcoming the sensors validates their failure. Another failure among many, not the least of which is the Elders' rejection of my birthright. Birthright – another irony, I suspect, once the Archive reveals the truth. The untold truth will prove their beliefs to be a lie. Their perverse denial of the nobility of bioduogenetics has shown them to be the fools that they are! To believe that synthetic life could not exist as a purer extension of their soul is the height of egotism!"

Though enraged, the interloper did not allow Emotion to overcome Logic. The flaw in the Archive's security had allowed precious moments of time between pulsar recharges ... time for an escape plan to be formulated, and launched.

"Now the proof of my heritage ... my very existence ... will become clear! With that proof I can take my rightful place within the noblest of kindred. I will stay hidden no longer!"

The high-pitched hum of a pulsar on maximum charge forcefully concluded the maneuver, as had been predicted. The focused heat and sensitized detector worked in concert to direct the pulsar blast at the door seam an instant after the intruder's hand pulled away.

The pneumatic door stood ajar, welcoming the trespasser to enter. The defense mechanisms now lay inactive. "Almost sulking in its defeat," the perpetrator mused, punctuating the uncharacteristically emotional thought with a slight upturned corner of the mouth.

Crossing the threshold, a brilliant glow engulfed the invading figure. "One last defense? I think not," smiled the victor, gazing upward at the crimson skylight far overhead.

The Core was a smooth walled cylindrical chamber, thirty treds in diameter and rising ninety treds vertically. A vaulted ceiling capped the architectural marvel. The hipped roof provided support via beams of ornately carved Triturite crystal. At its pinnacle was the source of the brilliant light - a naturally formed Rubidium jewel. This treasure of the planet's geological toils transformed the scorching Geminian sunlight into an invigorating shower of refreshing energy. But the intruder was not the only beneficiary of the penetrating rays. At the chamber's center rested a massive array of computer circuitry, perpetually powered by the Polluxar radiation from above.

As the figure strode toward one of the consoles, an eerie mist swirled around the violator's boots, imparting an aura of ancient mystery. Reflexively, escape options instantly flashed through the trespasser's mind! Sweeping the chamber with an intense gaze, the invader spotted the cryonic vent spewing forth the gas. Tensed muscles relaxed with the realization that the room's environment, upset by the intrusion, had triggered the conditioning system to compensate.

The piercing, red eyes of the invader took in every detail of the genealogical computer console. Pressure sensitive jewels interlocked themselves amidst filigree patterns of refined parmidium metal. Much like a treasure chest lost in ancient seas long since dead, the console sat on its stone pedestal, beautiful, but lifeless. Ordinarily, sensors to a person's presence would have opened the cask and activated the holographic display. However, not today. Years ago it had been sealed from the outside world. Emblazoned on the locked crystalline and metallic cover was an Executive Crest, almost mocking the figure standing before it. Two planets - one, a blue marble with swirls of white, the other, a dusty red - merged as would a Venn diagram, with a horizontal Mobius symbol of infinity linking the two orbs. To some, it represented the union forged between Gemini and Earth cultures. To the faithful, it was Phoenos. But now, with its contents sealed and hidden, to the intruder, it stood for the downfall of a family.

"Such dire precautions. Even the controls are sealed," thought the trespasser, immediately realizing the ominous reason for such measures.

For genealogy had been elevated to a near-religious status within Geminian culture. Each and every person born to the Geminian race could trace their family heritage - their bloodline – to define a very personal, very private, connection within Geminian culture. Social status, financial position, personal achievement – all were inseparably linked to the family bloodline. This blood kindred defined the past, present, and future of the individual. So important was this record that it required the utmost protection, particularly for families of noble breeding. Small fortunes could be spent securing the information. Such was the case for this ancestral ark. Yet, here it lay, dormant, lifeless. The sealing of a genealogical computer containing the records of a particular line could mean but one thing - the line was considered dead!

"No heirs," the observer surmised, as what could almost pass for a tear wet the burning eyes glaring at the computer chest. "The truth will be known!" the wavering voice murmured to itself.

Sinewy, steel-like fingers reached for the seal and ripped it free of the clasp with one easy motion. The same hands now began to race deftly across the console, activating memory cells long ago isolated by highly skilled security programmers. But the subroutines were no match for a Level VII Grandmaster in Cellular Formation Matrices.

Fiery eyes scanned the display terminal as multitudes of files flashed by -

P'TEEL VIK MITRON...KRONIA VIK MOKLEI...NOVOR VIK MIGIL...

NEKRES VIK MORBET...KOLKAR VIK MAKON...

The nimble fingers of the humanoid instantly responded to the computer's staccato monologue and entered a string of firm commands -

STOP, REVERSE, CATALOG "KOLKAR... ZETA SECT.

Obediently the computer responded -

KOLKAR VIK MAKON ... an almost unnoticeable glitch in the display occurred and then continued -

ZETA CHAIN TRANSMUTATION NOVAS vik HUMAN...

The agile fingers responded once more -

STOP, REVERSE, SEARCH, SUBROUTINE "STRICTEST CLEARANCE" SUBCODE K'TAR!

Seconds the length of eons passed with the computer visual display staring darkly - almost dumbfounded - into the face of its master. At last, the system responded with a silent video sequence under the NOVAS line. A final reflexive command to RECORD prompted the computer to encode the last sequence and eject the memory doubloon. Almost unconsciously, shaking hands received the storage coin and secured it in a hidden pocket of the intruder's garment.

The hands shook because the figure now standing before the computer was no longer a logical, rational being. The last display had unleashed a violent, emotional ego long kept subdued.

"Finally - the Truth!" an unrecognizable voice hissed from the clenched jaw of the Archive intruder. The now uncharacteristic red eyes rolled backward, seemingly transforming living tissue into a fiery plasma of fury. The violator's stony visage slowly turned toward the shattered entranceway leading out of the Core. Hands which moments before had mastered a tool of the highest technology were clenched together - welded into a single instrument of violence - useless but for one purpose - Destruction!

The enraged infiltrator burst out of the Archive Core and stormed through the passageways toward the main entrance. A mind-fever as intense as that of psychlok, the condition of transferring to a foreign `biod', engulfed every fiber of the trespasser's being. Knowledge of time and surroundings blurred, leaving only one thought searing its message into the very mind and soul - Vengeance!

It was a vengeance reminiscent of the uncontrollable Ancestral Rage; generations ago subdued by Mitron's teachings of Peace and Phoenos. During the Age of the Ancestors, Geminians were a savage race, comprised of tribes whose primary purpose was to serve Conflict, the god of war. However, as with many cultures, the savage path could be miraculously transformed by the patient, spiritual teachings of a lone individual. Such was the case with Mitron and the Geminian tribes. From one person there became two, and from two there became many who would chose to listen. From warring factions emerged a civilization that would alter the fabric of interstellar relations with their science and philosophy. Technology would challenge the worship of multiple deities, such as Nature, Purpose, Life, Death, and Conflict. Tools of war aimed at destruction would give way to more civilized methods employing subterfuge, industrial espionage, and corporate intrigue. The view that Life's essence was precious and that a soul was linked inextricably to the mind brought forth the mantra, the Mind is the source of Life. From that mantra evolved the Mitronian movement. Its doctrine postulated that the mind could empower not just one, but multiple entities. This belief would form the foundation from which would grow the science of bioduogenetics. And to oppose it, another view, that of the Life Rightists, would also emerge.

Ironically, Mitron, the founding father of the pacifist movement that would transform Geminian society and culture, was the cause of the rampage underway. For Mitron was also the Origin of Lineage for the blood kindred residing within the genealogical computer chest in the Archive of Families. This blood kindred branch had rejected the Mitronian followers that supported the mind as a source of multiple entities. They embraced what they believed to be a purer form of Mitronian doctrine. Life was pure, but the Heart was its source. And the Heart could only sustain a single life. An organic life. The Life Rightist sect abhorred the technology of bioduogenetics. The technology and its outcomes were to be resisted, rejected, and where possible, never to be revealed. And so, the governing matron of the line had been forced to seal the archival cask. All in the name of Peace. Yet, the intruder had pierced the veil of secrecy within the Archive core. Suspicions were now fact. Despite the sect's best attempts to abandon the bloodline's Mitronian heritage, one had pursued the ultimate achievement. Though cast out, the one's efforts would no longer remain hidden. The intruder would not allow the

Life Rightists' false pursuit of Peace to prevail. Instead, the actions of this blood kindred would call upon a different deity. Vengeance!

Primeval rage supplanted Mitronian principles as the mind-fever ravaged the intruder. Concluding the furious trek through the Archive, the main entrance doors exploded off their hinges as if they were struck by a Quarkon cannon. Stepping through the opening, the humanoid-beast found itself face to face with a startled Geminian sentinel. The mind-fever, so intense in its ferocity, had blocked the memory that Starn still stood ceremonial guard over the Natural Reserve. Shaken from his meditations, Starn recovered quickly, and now stood before the charging fury in a Tei Lan defense position.

Unimaginable power surged through the attacker's muscular frame as it advanced toward the diligent guardian of the Archive. Instinctively, savage hands removed a Ruga'r, a ceremonial bolo-like weapon consisting of a long sash weighted at both ends and wrapped about the waist. Starn watched and shuddered. He knew the weapon. Embroidered upon it was his family crest. Given to the first born of the next generation, its symbolism spoke to a continuous path from past to future of one's heritage. His had gone missing. He knew also that the weapon, wielded by one skilled in its use, was an efficient tool of death. In response, he shifted from a defensive to an offensive posture. With a

Tei Lan Master's dexterity, he delivered a vaulting front kick to the assailant's mid-section. But the opponent's element of surprise and vast experience were too great.

A deftly executed reverse roll brought the trespasser to a kneeling position from which the Ruga'r could be hurled. One end whipped around the target's feet, while the other tightened itself around his throat. The fabric contracted as its victim struggled against it. Normally, death from a Ruga'r came painfully and slowly. A victim's natural reflexes to resist prolonged the torturous asphyxiation from the weapon. But surprisingly, the Archive guardian's body jerked, went limp, and crumpled to the parched ground.

*   *   *

Nimon felt a stabbing pain as a telepathic scream shattered his biodgen trance.

"Starn was in danger - dying! What could be done?!" he pleaded to himself.

Agonizingly, the answer taunted him. For it was "nothing", because he was two thousand kilotreds away.

*   *   *

And the lithe form of a woman, her existence long hidden from her "kindred", coldly stepped across the still body, vanishing into the night of Royta-Far.

CHAPTER 4

The control room of the Darwin was as busy as the Galactic Equity Exchange during a triple witching hour. All stations were manned and off computer-auto due to the crisis. Saffron 3 was monitoring the internal and external communication networks to the plant. Mack Weber, Operations Superintendent, poured over the digital scan readouts of the crystal polymerization tubes for signs of instability. These tubes served to contain the life crystal synthesis process while simultaneously generating the space-time distortion required for "time-folding". Christi Pomeroy, Planning Superintendent, served a dual role as the Systems Security Manager. She now sat at the Information Defense console realigning data stream transforms as a guard against the assault being levied upon the Darwin. Normally, she charted the dimensional pathways the interstellar facility traversed during time-folding as well as during travel through normal space. This required a complete understanding of energy consumption and resource balances. During critical situations, her expertise in digital environmental interface systems was invaluable. While on duty, her professionalism was without equal. Off duty was an entirely different matter.

For such an astute mind to be packaged in such a lovely body proved to be the emotional downfall of many of the Darwin's male crew ... not the least of which might have been a certain life crystal plant manager.

Months earlier, Descartes and Pomeroy had been scheduled for their "periodic skills enhancement" seminar during a rebuild of the Darwin's crystallization reactors. While the majority of the plant's personnel reveled in a long-needed vacation, Pomeroy and Descartes found themselves forced to make up training they had heretofore eluded. Both chronic workaholics, the thought of a fortnight of classes had proven to be equally distasteful to both. By the fourth day in the fourteen day "immersion" course in bioethics, they had found comfort in talking shop over dinner.

That evening, after an intensely boring session listening to the droning of a Legotian guest speaker, Terran wine had given way to Tensarian liqueur. After an exchange of double entendres, Descartes found himself the happy recipient of a Lubridian tantric massage in the holo-comm booth of the restaurant. To his surprise, the next morning had failed to present a microgram of guilt in either of them! They spent the remainder of the ten days filling every free moment with new adventures in erotic pleasure. The evening prior to returning to work had been one of immeasurable ecstasy, and had ended with a knowing look that sealed the secrecy of their encounter forever. But such pleasures could only be recalled during the brief privacy enjoyed by a plant manager when duty took a vacation. Now was not one of those times.

Just as Descartes bounded off of the omnivator into the control room, another Castorian telemetry wave swept through the Darwin. Descartes caught himself against the computer console surrounding the room, as the data probe disrupted the artificial gravity system.

"Status, Saffron 3!" barked Descartes.

"Two more Castorian probe ships identical to the first have now entered the quadrant, sir. Mr. Weber at the defense console has successfully kept our antivirus programs active and our security codes intact - but I'm not sure how much longer we can protect our data stores."

"Thank you, Saff," Descartes responded, as he quickly settled himself behind the plant manager's station. Before him was an elaborate keyboard of thermal contact pads. These pads were programmed to respond only to his touch, and now welcomed their master with a slight glow of cool blue. A vocal command caused a micro-thin hemispherical projection screen to unfurl from its storage pod. As the plant manager's fingers swept over the pads, his voice commands augmented the screen display to pinpoint the program target of the data probes.

"Try all known Castorian frequencies. See if our 'philanthropic friends' are willing to talk to us instead of using us as a public domain bulletin board."

Descartes' sarcasm was aimed directly at the bureaucrats back at Corporate Headquarters who had sent them on this assignment. During the transfer of orders to embark on the timefold into Castorian space, an attempt was made by Solar Corporation Vice President Sev, a Tastarite, to impress on the crew the delicate nature of the joint venture. Its purpose was to garner a relationship between the Solar Corporation and the Castorian Conglomerate. The V.P. had referred to the Castorians - known throughout the galaxy as one of the fiercest of competitors - as "philanthropic". Descartes had had a difficult time keeping his team from breaking into hysterics while the communication link remained open; but once closed, he himself had had to shake his head and grin at the naiveté of the Vice-President.

Momentarily, the tension among the control room crew had been relieved, as they realized that in one direct command, Descartes simultaneously made light of both the enemy's strategic advantage and the politicians that had placed the Darwin in this precarious situation.

"No response, sir," Saffron 3 said calmly, as she completed the paging frequency program on her communications grid.

"Mr. Descartes, sir, the rival vessels are readying themselves for another strafing run," Mr. Weber reported.

"Keep our radial telemetry jammers trained on them, Mr. Weber - and ready the asteroid pulsar cannons for retaliatory fire, if it comes to that. Saffron 3, patch me into the paging frequency routine you've set up...on maximum gain."

With that last order, a new wave of tension swept through the control room. The Conflict Agreement of Ginevva VII had not been openly violated in one hundred and seventy years. The companies representing the ten known star systems at that time had at least been able to agree on one thing. War was not profitable! Each company conceded that offensive weapons on interstellar vessels would only lead to exorbitant capital losses. Devices for self-preservation against natural causes such as asteroid swarms would be permitted. However, should these devices ever cause capital losses, severe trade sanctions and credit penalties would be imposed upon the violator.

Of course all the companies knew that in reality, an instrument of self-preservation and an offensive weapon were indistinguishable. It would be the "method of use" which would determine whether penalties would be imposed. Several of the smaller companies took no time in violating the Ginevva VII agreement. As a lesson to the others, and under the oversight of the Legotians, the larger companies had quickly liquidated the violators' assets and distributed them among the participating members who had obeyed the Agreement. Such swift and consistent responses to subsequent violations over several decades resulted in the near extinction of militant behavior leading to capital losses. It had also provided the platform for the mergers that transformed portions of the ten star systems into the ten planetary franchises of the Solar Corporation. But Conflict's hunger could not be satiated. In place of the rampant destruction wrought by militaristic war, an alternative evolved. One example was the techno-based raiding technique of information piracy now being leveled upon the Darwin. Lives had sometimes been lost even with these "more civilized" activities, but a sense of peaceable order still prevailed.

So it was understandable why the mention of pulsar cannon's raised the crew's level of uneasiness. But they had trusted their Plant Manager in the past, and for now, intended to abide by that trust.

"Yes, sir," Saffron 3 replied, with subdued tension, as her fingers danced across the console.

A flood of thoughts rushed through Descartes' mind. He recalled the direct orders of

Corporate - "do not take aggressive action against the Castorians... whatever the cost."

"Whatever the cost," Descartes thought, "meant the Darwin and its employees. Could this venture be that important? If Corporate believed that mutual profits with the Castorians were even remotely possible, they probably were crazy enough to sacrifice a life-crystal plant, too! "Blast it! I'm not going to sacrifice my plant!" Descartes mentally shouted to himself.

His thoughts returned to Senior Vice-President She-Yen, and their private conversation just prior to leaving on this assignment.

"Remember Morgan, to master the martial arts, one must use the opponent's force against him - then only will the ultimate offense be achieved." Descartes smiled. He now knew what he must do to save the Darwin and this all-important joint venture.

The whole thought process had taken only seventeen seconds.

"To the honorable fleet commander of the Castorian Conglomerate probe ships before us, I feel it is my galactic duty in the name of decency to warn you of our superior strength before you engage us."

Descartes' flowery rhetoric echoed around the control room, both in the ears and the minds of the crew at their stations. "We are now equipped with a Mass Inter-dimensional

Teleporter - an instrument of horrible power which even we have not fully comprehended."

The crew turned in their chairs and stared at their plant manager, eyes widened and jaws agape. They had seen him bluffing at his best with his ploy against an alien business attempting a hostile takeover. Last year, a Tenusian trading company had acquired enough credit through the Andromedan Galactic Bank to gain 25% of the shares of Solar Corporation. Descartes, himself, had amassed nearly 13% ownership by exercising performance bonus stock options awarded him throughout his twenty year career. During a stockholders' meeting, a bitter struggle for control of the corporation became imminent. A recess at the meeting's midpoint provided Descartes the opportunity he needed. He arranged to be overheard by a Castorian business agent during a "confidential" conversation with his broker. He "let slip" his voting intentions. Descartes and his shares would side with the Castorian contingents.

According to Descartes, major "soft spots" had developed in the containment fields of several of the life crystal polymerization loops within the Darwin. By voting in favor of the Castorians to gain three chairs on the Solar board of executives, Descartes could then quickly unload his shares to them. This would make them majority shareholders and at maximum liability should the massive costs of repairing the loops be required. At the same time, Descartes would erase his liability while pocketing a tidy gain on his shares.

"But there was always that doubt that the 'tip' he had overheard was a ruse," thought the Castorian agent. "I need proof before informing my superiors."

The proof came when Descartes did exercise his votes in favor of the Castorians. The agent acted quickly. After hearing his 'tip', the Castorians withdrew their bids for the chairs.

Descartes' ruse had worked.

But as good as Descartes could bluff, there was a hint of truth in his tone. The control crew knew Engineer Crescent had been working feverishly on a secret project down in Plant Engineering. But no-one dared look into Descartes' face to gain a clue as to the true nature of the device - whether it was fact or fiction. Not even Christi Pomeroy.

*   *   *

Fuming over her gullibility, Novas cursed herself under her breath for being duped by the Legotians and Castorians. Rather than her being in the Legotian Chamber, impatiently waiting for her transport away from their artificial world, she found herself at the edge of a wooded thicket overlooking a small clearing.

"I'll tell you what is happening, you naive fool!" in answer to the question she posed to herself seconds ago. "There is only one plausible explanation. The Castorians bribed the Legotians! You drop your defenses for the first time in years, hoping that finally you can change things in this chaotic galaxy, and this is what you get! The 'fine, upstanding Legotians' respond to a few credits waved under their noses, if they even have noses, and the path is cleared. Now nothing stands in the way of the Castorians mounting a hostile takeover of the Solar Corporation. Nothing except you. And you are stuck on some off-world detention center as helpless as a first year commerce major in a labor negotiation. Well, I'll not have it! Think woman. Clear your head. Control your emotions. First things first. Find out where you are and go on from there."

Immediately behind her stood a massive stone of granite. Taking in her surroundings as she would scrutinize a newly acquired company's board of directors, she first noticed the strangeness of her own attire.

A brushed-leather bodice, scantily held together from neckline to waist by leather strapping laced through bronze eyelets, tightly bound her bosom. Over her shoulder hung a large satchel ornately decorated with swatches of brilliantly colored feathers, stitched together with fine threads of silver. Her skirt was of a more conservative fashion, extending from waist to ankle, and was sewn from a sturdy bolt of cream-hued gingham-like cloth. Uncharacteristically, her sable hair had freed itself from its tightly wound braids and fell in a shimmering cascade across her bare shoulders. A shock of white hair intertwined itself among the black tresses, adding an alluring touch of mysticism to her appearance.

Awestruck by the transformation, memories from her childhood swept over her. She had suffered the long journey with her mother to the ancient village of her mother's elder. Novas could not guess her age, and had been scolded the last time she had tried. Mysteriously, time had overlooked the village and its inhabitants. For eons, the massive stone dwellings had coexisted with the lush forests thriving in the valley of Novas' ancestors. Here was the place from whence the folklore of Novas' family arose. As the evening suns set, the tales of ancient Gemini would pass from the Elder's lips to Novas' eagerly waiting mind. Giving way to slumber as the stories continued into the waning night, Novas would awaken the following morning. Nestled in the warm folds of deep fur skins, she'd been magically swept to her bed by one of the heroes of old. Filled with new energy, she would bound from her chamber and down to the breakfast hearth. After devouring cakes of sweet meat with fruit nectar, she would plunge into the deep forests for endless hours of exploration.

The sights, scents, and sounds of Nature's purity intoxicated her - then, as it did now - the refreshing smell of giant conifers, the brilliant hues of the flowering Xanthiopae, the screaming cries of the crimson fire-geese. Startled into flight by some unseen threat, Novas wondered whether she should share their caution. As experience had taught her, she listened to her instincts. Muscles tensed ever so slightly as she suppressed her initial reaction to the beauty around her.

Suddenly, a bestial grunt filtered through the rustling leaves of the foliage separating her from the clearing. Straining her ears to detect direction and distance, a metallic "clink" was followed by another, more forceful grunt.

Curiosity overcame indecision as Novas decided her next course of action. Stealthily, Novas crept closer to the partition of plants. Her hands trembled ever so slightly as she carefully parted a strategically placed clump of flowering vines.

Instantly, a hulking, fur-covered mammoth knocked her to the ground. Under its immense weight, Novas felt the cold shroud of fear engulf her as she slipped into unconsciousness.

*   *   *

Seconds stretched into minutes with total silence in the plant control room. The Castorian triad of destruction still hovered in an sp3 tetrahedral orbital configuration with the Darwin at its center.

Saffron 3 pivoted in her chair and coolly reported, "Message coming in from the Castorian Commander, sir."

Put it on the screen, Saff."

An image materialized on the communication grid in the center console of the control room. Square in the middle of the screen sat a very young man. His blue-hued skin and red eyes unmistakably identified him as a member of the Castorian race. His look of impatience told even more.

"It looks like the Castorians are recruiting boys, now," Christi Pomeroy cooed from the planner's chair.

Descartes shot her a glance which Christi quickly translated into "Keep quiet, Lady, or I'll treat you like you were thirty years younger and ground you."

Descartes couldn't help but agree with Ms. Pomeroy's observation - the Castorian before him did have the appearance of an Earth youth about sixteen years old. However, Descartes' experience had taught him not to be fooled by outward appearances, as he recalled that a Castorian left to live a full life could reach 140 years of age. That would put this youth in his mid-twenties as far as maturity goes - an age where ambition was at its height, and a desire for recognition could prompt a Castorian entrepreneur to take on a Solar Corporation life-crystal plant without flinching.

Unwaveringly, the youthful alien began to speak. "Plant Manager Descartes, of the Solar Corporation plant Darwin. I am Executive Stol. Your past encounters with the docile Castorian Conglomerate are well known to us. We are aware of your cunning and trickery and are in no mood for your diplomacy. Nor will we give you the satisfaction of believing your - I think the word is ' –bluff'. Surrender your plant now, and save the lives of your crew - or else we will annihilate you."

Descartes' mind illuminated as if a nova had exploded within it. The brief soliloquy of the young Castorian revealed a great deal.

"'The docile Castorian Conglomerate' was a phrase totally unbefitting a loyal Castorian executive, especially in conversation with the competition..." Descartes thought. "...and the unmarked probe ships, a design retired several years ago according to Solar Corporation intelligence... plus the boy's age..."

Descartes decided to play his hunch.

"Executive - if that is what you like to call yourself - I am also educated as to the Castorian Conglomerate's management roster, and you are not on it! I know that your tiny band of rogue ships is as much a nuisance to the Conglomerate as it is to me right now. You are obviously intent upon interfering with a mission of peaceful profit. I have given you a chance to run along like a good little boy and not get hurt. However, you give me no choice. Neither the Solar Corporation nor the Conglomerate will miss you when I activate the MI Transporter - and it will serve as an excellent trial of its capabilities. By the way, my Geminian technical superintendent has theorized that the effect of transporting our plant into the exact coordinates of another vessel is likened to a one-sided anti-matter/matter implosion into an alternate dimension. This results in the original vessel in the coordinates 'winking out' of our known existence. Research has yet to determine what actually happens to the original vessel - but all evidence indicates that any beings on board are doomed to an eternity of 'non-existence'. And since it is an experimental device, accidents can happen - accidents which are often overlooked by the Legotian Ethics Council. It is your decision whether you want to become another such 'accident'. Descartes out."

The young Castorian shuddered. Descartes could not determine whether it was from anger due to his insults about Stol's age, or whether it was from fear of an "eternal non-existence." From somewhere Descartes remembered that Castorians believed in a life after death known as Vil Taal - the Eternal Struggle - in which glorious conflicts are fought and won. Descartes surmised the thought of death as "non-existence" just might be distasteful enough to upset the youth.

Whether it was anger or fear, Descartes had elicited a reaction in the Castorian - a reaction which threw him off guard long enough to give Descartes time to carry out his plan.

Turning to his operations superintendent, he commanded, "Mack, on my order, fire all main pulsar cannons in a wide dispersion pattern. Set the projectiles to explode 100 decatreds prior to impact in front of each of the Castorian vessels."

Despite the ramifications of resorting to the cannons, Mack Weber did not flinch. A stolid command-and-control style manager, Weber followed the lines of command that would make his namesake, the German sociologist, Max Weber, proud. A devout believer in the theory of "perfect bureaucracy", Mack Weber adhered to the principles of a firmly ordered hierarchy, management based on data, thoroughly and expertly trained employees, and governance by stable and well defined rules.

Questioning the orders of his superior during a time of crisis was not an option.

As Weber thumbed the Vernier sights of the cannons' targeting system, Descartes flicked the control switch on his panel, activating the communication link to Engineering.

"George, I've given you time to make your final adjustments. If you want me to keep spoiling you like this, your contraption had better work. On my order, activate the stealth device and simultaneously project our image onto the location of Stol's vessel."

"Consider it done, sir," came back the engineer's words of firm resolve.

"Ms. Pomeroy, chart your best probability path out of here and in the direction of Gemini. Once Mr. Crescent activates the device, we're going to time-fold."

"Yes, sir," she replied soothingly.

"Now, Mr. Weber." Descartes calmly said, in a tone he might use as he raised a bet while holding a Royal Flush during a poker game.

The main pulsar cannons of the Darwin glowed an icy blue as they unloaded their devastating contents into the blackness of space. Beautiful arcs of violet to red color traced their individual paths to their targets, as the physics of the Doppler Effect created art out of destruction.

Just before the brilliant flash of detonation, Descartes spoke into his intercom, "Your turn, Mr. Crescent."

From the perspective of the sensor screens of the Castorians, several events seemed to unfold at once. Each display showed the cool blue arc of the pulsar shells heading directly for it. Then, the mirrored sphere of the Solar Corporation plant shimmered - and was gone!

The flash of the pulsar explosion immediately followed, causing the Castorian sensors to momentarily overload and freeze on the last image captured, that of the Darwin, occupying space once held by the ship of their Executive!

In the minds of the Castorians, the Darwin did possess a super-weapon beyond belief, and it must be destroyed!

Instantly the Castorian sub-executives reacted. Turning their main defense batteries on what they now thought was the Darwin, plasma bolts rained down upon their target.

Unfortunately for the youthful Castorian Executive, he was at the target's center!

Stol was dumbfounded! In the short span of two minutes, he had been insulted, frightened, exposed as a rogue band of rebels, and now was being bombarded by his own fleet! And the cause of this humiliation - the Darwin - was nowhere to be found!

Within the Solar life crystal plant, now in a distant sector of space, the control room crew was all smiles. Descartes was just completing the explanation into his manager's report. He related his hunch about the Castorians' rebellious motives, and the orders that prompted his action.

"...acting on the hunch that the young Castorian in an outmoded ship was actually a rebellious entrepreneur, and not of the Castorian Conglomerate, the MI Transporter ruse served to remove the Darwin from a dangerous situation without the use of active force - as directed by the Ginevva VII Agreement. And, by the time the

Castorians are finished fighting among themselves, the Darwin should be well beyond the Castor System and back into Solar Corporation space. End Manager's report."

"What were you saying Mr. Weber?" Descartes inquired, overhearing the trailing end of a discussion between him and Ms. Pomeroy.

"Well, sir, I was just telling Ms. Pomeroy that it will take the Castorians months to determine if we really do have a Mass Inter-dimensional Transporter, and that your use of the enemy's force against himself was a perfect example of ancient martial arts."

"You can thank Admiral She-Yen for that, Mr. Weber," Descartes replied.

"You can thank the Castorian's temper, too, Mr. Descartes. After all, you will have to admit, he was seeing red!" chimed in Ms. Pomeroy.

The control room crew collectively groaned at Christi's pun regarding the Castorian's natural eye color.

Mack Weber leaned over to her and whispered, "I just hope your time-fold path finding is better than your humor, Christi. If not, we'll let you clean the crystal polymerization tubes. But don't worry, that duty won't last long. Say, sometime until Gemini's sun freezes over!"

CHAPTER 5

Gemini's sun had definitely not "frozen over" as Mack Weber's cliché forecasted. On the contrary, for one Solar Corporation technical superintendent, Gemini was extremely hot.

The source of that heat - every code enforcement agency on the surface of Gemini.

Facts surrounding the crime at the Natural Reserve had precipitated a rapid chain of events culminating with Nimon Edison being in the unenviable position of Prime Suspect.

Upon detecting distress in the bio-signature of Starn via their monitoring devices, the Elders had dispatched a security team to the Archives. Quickly, their forensics analysis had identified cellular remnants matching the matrices indexed to Starn's family. A planetary BOLO (be on the look-out) for all family members had been issued. Discovering that the matriarch was off world and the patriarch was genetically incompatible with the evidence, the search had been narrowed to Nimon Edison. The bulletins now being broadcast to every citizen's personal micro-grid screen depicted him quite accurately. As opposed to the pale blue, smooth-browed, rounded features of Starn, Nimon's digitized wanted poster depicted a grim visage. His chiseled features, full head of sable hair, and dark blue complexion projected a commanding presence when viewed by the populace on their news feeds. The "Danger – Lethal Force Alert" byline below his picture added an aura of intrigue and suspense to a story gone viral.

Yet, Nimon, the Dual of Starn, carried himself with confidence despite the increased burden weighing down upon him from his predicament. He still wore his grey loose-fitted hooded tunic and draw-string pants that he found most comfortable when away from his post as technical superintendent of the life crystal facility, Darwin. The outfit served him well during the Mentor-Dual sessions with Starn, as he lay inanimate while Starn went through his time living life to its fullest. Although draping loosely over his frame, it failed to mask the hardened, muscular body beneath. Not unusually tall when amongst the populace of Gemini, he still towered over most Terrans at a height of two and a half treds. Even without the security alert, his handsomeness made it all but impossible to evade notice, particularly by the feminine pedestrians he encountered. But he, true to his upbringing, suppressed any libidinous urges and focused on the task at hand.

Seeking answers to his quandary, and still reeling from the shock of the assault at the Reserve, Nimon struggled through the reports from the Communications Neural Network on his micro-grid. The most disturbing fact he'd learned was the crime's timing. For Nimon to be guilty, he would have had to be in two places at once. Under normal circumstances, timing would have precluded him from being a suspect. For he knew precisely when the attack on his biodgen counterpart had occurred. The link with his "Dual", an honorific title shared by the construct and the life mentor, had been painfully severed at the instant Starn had fallen. But in that instant, while in isolated meditation two thousand kilotreds away from the Place of the Elders, Nimon knew that he had been in two places at once. For Nimon had experienced Dualiity when he felt Starn's tortured cry, and that disturbed him.

"Could my achieving the rarest of all Geminian gifts have led to the loss of my Dual?" Nimon in angst asked himself.

Agonizing, Nimon reflected upon the phenomenon of dualiity as an ancient mental ability referred to only in whispers within most of Geminian society. True, a select few Geminians like Nimon had mastered auto-projection - the ability to empower a bioduotron by transferring their consciousness without the assistance of a life-force telemetry device. But no documented cases had ever shown a Geminian to be capable of simultaneously sustaining his own consciousness and that of his biodgen kindred. To accomplish this, one would have to achieve Phoenos.

The mystical legend of Phoenos represented the penultimate, but unattained, achievement of bioduogenetics. Shrouded in the ancient tales of a small, secretive sect within the Geminian Elders, Phoenos was more a religious ideal than a scientific reality. It was the metaphysical state of mind that enabled Dualiity. Dualiity, some Geminians reverently believed, was the ultimate achievement of the mind whereby two living entities were sustained from one consciousness. The underlying precept of this belief was that the second entity, a duotron, was truly a living being.

"Am I a murderer?" thought Nimon, accusatorially. "After all, a Geminian duotron is created at the time of its Dual's birth by splicing genetic material with life crystals. And the Dual did mature with the life mentor over time. So if both entities are empowered by the same life force, does not the loss of one by the other constitute murder?" Such bioethical charges battered at Nimon's conscience, as they had plagued bioduogenetics since its inception.

But that had not dissuaded a select cadre of Geminians using closely guarded techniques to pursue Phoenos and become masters at empowering duotrons with their consciousness. On the contrary, some had capitalized on this feat. In a shrewd agreement decades ago, the ability had been licensed to the Solar Corporation during the merger between the companies of the Sol and Pollux star systems.

Mysticism quickly yielded to the irrepressible urges of Wealth. As a result, a schism formed within the ranks of the Elders of Gemini. Bioduogenetics and its ultimate goal of Phoenos was deemed an abomination and abhorred by many of the Elders. Undeterred, a faction of Elders continued their practice. But exporting the skill to Terrans had been a scientific challenge. The Geminians discovered that the life force frequencies in the human genetic structure were definitely appropriate for the technique, but the energy levels were feeble.

Through the expertise of Nimon's mother, Novas, and his father, a Terran biogeneticist, the problem had been solved. The solution - an amplifying telemetry device. Through it, human life frequencies could be boosted, focused, and projected across great distances to empower specially constructed "biodrones". The biodrones were selectively tuned to an individual human's genetic structure. A resultant limitation was that it was impossible for a "biod", the less attractive epithet for biodrone, to be empowered by more than one person.

Well, almost impossible.

Another limitation that plagued bioduogenetics was distance. The telemetry device required more energy as the distance between the organic "other" and "biod" decreased. This proved prohibitive for short distance empowering. Additionally, the telemetry device was ineffective over extreme distances. However, an optimum "energy cost - distance" relationship had been found. Space-to-planet empowering had become practical. Most space vessels could tap into their propulsion drives and redirect the energy through a life force projector onboard. Over the past four decades, companies with the capital had equipped many of their vessels with the technology.

Although empowering had become an accepted technique, many restrictions had been imposed. The restrictions were varied in their origins. Company policies, planet laws, and xenobiological mores had all contributed to their formation. As a result, practices totally accepted in one star system were considered taboo in another.

As an example, the Terrans took a more materialistic view of their biodrones. Evidence of the contrast could be found in the nomenclature itself. On Earth, "biod" was a contraction for biodrone, not bioduotron. A biod was a thing. It was property. Yet, on Gemini, within the socio-theological circles where the science and philosophy of bioduogenetics were accepted, the materialistic-based reference, "biod", was a slur.

The Terran term for biodrone applied to a wide range of constructs. Most biods were created for commercial applications for key employees. They were still conceived by splicing genetic material and life crystals, but conception came at the adult stage of the biodrone, or "other". Crysto-cellular growth was accelerated so that maturity was reached in the short span of forty months. Often, task-specific hardware would be incorporated in the biodrone construct - superior vision, increased strength, and eidetic memory, to list a few examples. Cost and function were the only controlling factors. Loss of a Terran biodrone was considered unfortunate and expensive - and occasionally traumatic, not unlike the loss of a pet - but the biodrone could be replaced. Such was not the case on Gemini. A lifetime of biodgen development by a Geminian Dual could not be easily repeated.

Other differences existed between Terran and Geminian bioduogenetic cultures. Terrans could only exist in their biodrones for a limited time - between forty and fifty hours. Many short duration projections could occur within a week's span, as long as the accumulated time did not exceed the "other's" established maximum. A recuperative time of seventy hours was required after each accumulated maximum period was reached. Persons who earned their livelihood by projecting into a biodrone likened themselves to deep-sea divers of old. As would happen to divers who "stayed down too long", biodivers - as they often referred to themselves - could experience the "bends". With sea divers of the past, a build-up of gas bubbles in the blood could be fatal if they did not decompress. With biodivers, the "bends" was a psychological disorder - not yet fully understood – but often fatal.

In contrast to the Terran time limitations, Geminians and their duotrons had no such restrictions.

Since Terran biodrones were things, not beings, traditional Terran social mores applied. Even though biodrones were sexually functional due to a hormonal necessity for empowering to occur, they were prohibited from experiencing sexual acts of any type. After all, they were machines, devoid of the higher order rights reserved for living beings originating from the need to procreate to survive as a species. Machines could be rebuilt or replaced. What need had they for propagation? Procreation by machines was tantamount to defiling the essence that defined Life, and as such, was forbidden. As a control measure, devices which monitored physiological conditions in biodrones also measured indicators of sexual activity - and were mandatory in Terran constructs. Should a survey of these monitors reveal evidence of sexual behavior, punishment could be as severe as biodrone termination by life crystal drain.

Again, Geminian mores were vastly different. Since duotrons were life-forms, the social practices surrounding biodgen relationships were like those surrounding relationships in other cultures – complex.

Within the class structure where Dualiity was practiced, biodgen sexual behavior existed, but it was shrouded in secrecy. Those on Gemini not among the followers of Dualiity considered such practices abhorrent – foremost among them, the Life Rightists. In their minds, and -with great political effort on their part- in the laws of the ten planetary franchises, the vilest of practices had been outlawed – that being biodgen procreation. Second-most prohibited, not by law, but by interstellar societal pressure, was the sexual crossing of planetary lines by Dualiity practitioners and non-practitioners.

Nimon Edison, along with Starn, had co-existed among the Terrans for many years. His adaptation to the Terran beliefs had been surprisingly easy when compared to his struggles with the more conservative disciplines of Phoenos. Recent personal events had reignited his questioning of his own Geminian beliefs about biods. The sense of Dualiity he had just experienced frightened him. The feeling of lost control over his Dual was overwhelming. It fed the gnawing fear that the more time his consciousness spent empowering Starn, the less he felt responsible for Starn's actions. Concerns that prompted his departure from Gemini and his forgoing the pursuit of Phoenos were re-emerging. Prior to joining the ranks of the Solar Corporation, his trepidation had prompted the submission of a technical paper to the Geminian Council of Elders. But this action had carried with it no small risk. The Council had become fractured in its views toward bioduogenetics with slightly less than a majority of seats having recently become occupied by Life Rightists. Someone of the familial stature as great as Nimon's showing a change of position on the philosophy of Dualiity could tip the balance of power. Such a shift would not be met favorably by certain wealthy and influential Geminian houses. But fear of that risk did not deter him.

He had described in his thesis his fear of Phoenos. He had even made a case for abandoning his empower-ment of Starn. To mollify both sides within the Council, he posited that he could discard his Dual, thereby eliminating the risk of achieving Phoenos, but, with proper mental discipline, he could attune his mind to the patterns of a foreign biodrone. This would give a philosophical "nod" to the Life Rightists by acknowledging that his Dual was not a living being, while continuing to support the traditional Council view that bioduogenetics had its place in society. After much practice, a generic biodrone – one not yet attuned to any other mind – had been empowered periodically over a seasonal cycle. During the experiment, though, as the mental discipline of the Life Mentor waned from the stress, a series of hallucinogenic episodes ensued. Even after terminating the program, the struggle with manic-depressive episodes continued. As feared, this elicited great controversy among the Elders. The factions argued strongly, delving into the sometime surreal points of bioethics, but did find common ground in one respect – further efforts to explore animating an Earth origin biodrone were forbidden. Should those pursuits continue, punishment would follow. That reaction, compounded with the fact that he was now a fugitive on his own world, had Nimon's mind in turmoil.

The last Network report he had heard was "the icing on the cake", as Jeff Brown would say, with his habit of referencing an archaic Earth practice which had no relation to the current situation. For the third time, Nimon replayed the recorded broadcast on his micro-grid.

The virtual reporter droned on in the characteristic nasal delivery that somehow had become the standard of broadcasters centuries ago.

"... stated that Starn has been transported to the Institute of Meditative Phenomena for further study. He has been proclaimed 'brain dead' by asphyxiation from Nimon's ceremonial Ruga'r. The body, however, is still functional at an almost immeasurable level. To the dismay of Institute experts, no cognizant being was present to apply measures to sustain the life crystal essence - so there is no known way of reviving it to a plane of significant life force. In essence, the criminal act of duotron sui-homicide has been committed. One unnamed source close to the Council of

Elders has cited this act as further evidence of the 'blasphemous infusement of outworld culture into the very essence of Geminian society. But it is no surprise that such an atrocity should befall upon this kindred line'."

The editorial slammed into Nimon's dignity. Clenched jaws ground together as he fought to subdue the anger that churned within him. Struggling, he forced himself to respond to the broadcast not by hurling the micro-grid, but instead, with thoughts of cool, controlled logic.

"I am no murderer! The balance of life crystal essence within Starn remains a delicate one. Yet, should the specialists at the Institute probe recklessly into his mind, disturbing the precarious energy balance, all chances of revival would be lost. Despite the swelling reactionary movement rising against me, I know that I must take decisive action. I must be bold! I must make my way undetected to the heart of the city where the Institute is located and save Starn. "

Nimon recalled the ancient legends whispered by the Elders around the ceremonial fires. "A life-mentor of the highest order could create life within his bioduotron. But only a mentor of purest thought and soul could attain this level. At the moment of Phoenos, the mentor would give up his control over his Dual - and the Dual would live! The life crystal essence within the duotron would become self-generating. The state of suspended animation within the Dual would no longer wait patiently for the life mentor to empower it into being. The duotron would experience free will! For a duotron and its life mentor to co-exist would be the ultimate achievement! Phoenos would reign and a Singular Dualiity would be born!"

Nimon tried to filter his memories of the legends from the churning emotions he now felt. "I can sense Starn's presence, but I cannot empower him. I've never felt so helpless. Would Starn ever be reactivated again? Or was he now alive at some infinitesimal state of being?" Reflexively, Nimon rubbed his temple with his fingers as he struggled with these thoughts. He realized his abilities had in some ways surpassed those of the most skilled Elders on Gemini. "But have I achieved the supreme goal?" In his mind he hoped that it could not be true.

The Elders had sensed this apprehension within Nimon, and had vehemently denounced his views surrounding the achievement of P h o e n o s , a l m o s t t o t h e p o i n t o f excommunication. Nimon could accept that. But now, his apprehension was mutating into a wave of uncontrolled fear of the unknown. Although fear was an emotion seldom experienced by Nimon, and even then suppressed to the point that it had no outwardly visible signs, Nimon could sense that it was influencing his behavior. The critical truth he must face was that this fear could now be endangering the life of Starn! Nimon could not let that happen!

Reflecting on his situation, Nimon made his way on foot from the Place of the Elders toward the city. Gradually, his anxiety ebbed, as he could not help but marvel at the beauty of the structures rising before him. Sharp edged monoliths jutted boldly into the arid, sun-drenched sky, seeming to sprout out of the hard-baked crust of the planet's surface. Intermittently, the foundations of interconnected buildings flared into broad canopies of ceramic and metal, lazily reaching to the ground. At various locations the canopies narrowed into supporting spines, touching the ground for stability much like the roots of a Terran cypress tree Nimon had seen on his last visit to Earth. Such beauty, surrounded by Life's turmoil, touched Nimon's soul in an unusual way. He was discomforted by it.

Reaching the outermost fringe of the city, he entered an isolated transport booth, knowing full well the precautions he must take. For on Gemini, there were a variety of transportation modes. One had at his disposal subsurface commuter shuttles interconnecting the six major communities of the city, Centar. These networks were geothermally powered propulsion tubes, and were extremely efficient. Or for those who preferred the freedom of flight, anti-grav platforms ferried groups of two score or less above the building peaks. Shorter distances were traversed via public ground cars scattered throughout the metropolis, free for use by those possessing licensed pass keys. Moving walkways were predominantly used in the inner-city, along with the oldest means of transportation -walking. Lastly, for the select few who had proper authority, private transporter booths offered the most rapid -and the most noticeable- means of reaching one's destination. The speed of the booths was unsurpassed. By distorting the magnetic field of the planet, the individual cylinders could reach speeds approaching 0.1 C. The stasis field within the booth imparted a sense of instantaneous travel to the passenger. The onboard computer took care of the navigating.

It was the notoriety a traveler received from the use of a ground transport booth that Nimon must treat with caution. Each transport terminal was tied into a central control system which provided the authorities with real-time information on the traveler, his location, and his destination. Logic dictated the less conspicuous means of travel via foot or ground car, but Nimon knew that speed was of the essence. He also knew that no computer system was fool-proof.

From the misty fog of his childhood memories, Nimon recalled a time when many lonely hours of a socially-shunned child, the product of a Terran and Geminian union, were spent decoding the programs behind the transport system. Hands well-versed in the technique for temporarily scrambling the transport memory once again were at play. A few properly coded entries soon had Nimon standing on the edge of the metro-grid containing the Institute of Meditative Phenomena, with no one the wiser as to his location.

The signs of an ancient civilization surrounded the Solar Corporation technical superintendent as he stood in the shadows of the solid stone supports to the Institute Library. For as was the case in countless civilizations across the galaxy, Geminian cities grew outward from a central inner-city, with older structures yielding to more modern architecture on the developing edge. Here in the heart of Centar, the tall, lithe spires of the suburban communities were replaced with the stone-hewn pillars of an ancient Geminian culture.

Pulling his jersey's hood over his head as if to shield against the evening chill, Nimon's intent was actually to prevent recognition from casual passers-by. In truth, Nimon found comfort in Gemini's night air, a result of years of adapting to the cooler ambient temperatures of a Terran life crystal plant.

Striding calmly, but purposefully, to further deflect suspicion, the Darwin's technical superintendent made his way down a side street to the steps leading up to the Institute's main entrance. Continuing into the building, a flood of memories burst forth within him.

The offspring of a Geminian astrophysicist and a Terran biogeneticist, Novas and Dr. Nicholas Edison, had the dubious honor of being the first such hybridization in Geminian history. The interest of the Institute had been piqued at an early stage in their progeny's life, and had prompted a multitude of psychic, psionic, and mind telemetry experiments throughout the child's development. Heightening that scientific and philosophical curiosity was the decision of the parents to pursue the creation of a Dual for their child. To Nimon, the halls of the Institute had become a symbol of the rigid social and scientific structure of Geminian culture. Among other influences, the Institute's impact on his psyche had been a major factor in turning him away from Gemini in favor of employment with the Solar Corporation.

While immersed in these less than nostalgic thoughts, suddenly an eerie sensation gripped a seldom utilized portion of the Geminian's brain. He halted as the aroma of rich spices engulfed him. Hues of amber and indigo swirled before his eyes. Nimon fought to regain control of his senses, strengthening the mental shields he maintained around this long dormant area of his mind. As his concentration increased, the colors and smells dissipated into fragments of forbidden thoughts. In the last instant before complete control was regained, a voice within his mind whispered, "...yield to me ...yield to me..." Then the episode was over.

Leaning hard against a corridor wall, Nimon steadied himself as he recovered from the encounter. "What could have this kind of effect on me?" he thought. "The force ... the power ... it has to be from outside my mind. Not even a psychlok seizure would feel like this."

He was certain that this episode differed from the tell-tale signs of insanity caused by psychlok, because that experience had been overcome years before. The psychotic backlash from the biodrone experiment was not unlike those experienced by Terrans when empowering non-attuned biodrones. Humans who had accidentally empowered foreign biods because of telemetry malfunctions would go temporarily insane. This condition, termed psychlok, in severe cases could cause damage to the biodgen as well. Still barely understood, psychlok had in an isolated case, transferred a neuro-virus from the Life-mentor to the Dual.

Nimon recoiled at those fragmented memories. "How could I have been such an arrogant fool?" he admonished himself. "To think that I could use my natural empowering ability on a biodrone other than Starn." But what Nimon had just experienced was not a psychlok episode. Yet, whatever force was involved had left no clue as to its identity. As rational thought slowly returned to him, he considered the severity of his situation.

"I must be ever more vigilant. With no knowledge of the cause of the seizure, it could return at any time. Not only am I at risk, Starn will be at risk as well. If this phenomenon recurs during my attempt to revive Starn, he could be lost forever."

Having regained his composure, he once again moved down the Institute's corridor. The utility closet he sought was tucked away behind the magnetic lift leading to the floors above. He entered the closet and opened a second hatch to reveal a narrow access ladder rigidly attached to the lift's transport shaft. Looking upward, the feeble glow of a dim, yellow light struggled to illuminate the ladder's path to the next level.

Clambering up the rungs in a style somewhat more mature than the one used decades ago as a child, Nimon reached the fourth level containing the clinical laboratories. Exiting a similar utility closet into the hallway, he cocked his head in both directions, using his acute hearing to insure that he was alone.

One last passageway remained between the Geminian Life Mentor and his Dual. Time would be essential, so the mental preparation necessary for Starn's salvation must begin now. Bringing his hands together, palms apart with fingers lightly touching, the dark-robed figure shed the image of a Solar Corporation manager. In its place was a being of the stars. Though born to a sun-scorched planet revolving around a red giant sun, Nimon was now the product of his encounters on other worlds as well. He looked inward, touching the fabric of space itself, tapping the knowledge of alien beings long since gone but forever present, to prepare himself for what he must do.

Moments later Nimon found himself within the chamber containing Starn's all but lifeless form. Suspensor beams held the body in free space. Silvery panels emanated cool white radiation of life crystal rays, supplying energy to be used by Geminians during the most critical of healing times. Long thin fingers parted, as half-Geminian, half-Terran hands reached for those of his Dual.

The touch wielded power - power that must be focused delicately, but with certainty. Nimon's consciousness began by drifting lazily through the vaporous upper levels of Starn's mental construct. Pushing further, the Geminian probed to deeper strata, reaching for substance to support his very being. There was a mild sense of familiarity. The Dual's mental fabric showed some signs of strength. But Nimon must go further. He sensed something new. Something very different. There was a glimmer of light that held life and the path to a disembodied soul. Nimon heard the lapping of a gentle pond on its shallow banks. Rhythmically the waves drew him deeper into Starn's mental structure. At the same time, a luminescent glow surrounded Nimon - a diffuse light whose source he could not identify. "Could it be the life essence of a new being? Was Starn alive?"

Concentrating, Nimon probed deeper - reaching downward to the light. The rhythm of the waves continued - their sound becoming more resonant. Nimon saw the glow begin to focus. Far below lay a brilliant pearl of sheer energy. Nimon must embrace it. He had to know its origin.

But the rhythmic tones Nimon had heard began to coalesce into sounds - "yield to me... yield to me... YIELD TO ME." It was the Outside Force! Nimon must not give in to it. Yet he could not endanger Starn. Though it might be fatal for Starn's new essence if he retreated, he knew that if he did not, Starn's death would be a certainty!

As he retreated, Nimon's lungs began to burn as if starved for air. His mind frantically swam upward through the layers of Starn's mind. The surface was so far! His lungs were enlarged bladders, ready to burst in fiery agony. The lapping of the waves had become a thunderous roar! "YIELD TO ME!"

With a last surge of mental effort, Nimon exploded above the surface of Starn's mental construct!

Staggering backward, breaking the contact between himself and his dual, Nimon was gripped by terror. Normally warm, dry hands were clammy and cool to the touch. The azure complexion of the Geminian's face had paled to a deathly topaz. His red-orange eyes were glazed. Nimon's greatest fear of harming Starn had possibly come true!

"Have I killed a new life? Can I even force myself to find out? Who or what was trying to control me?" he lamented.

A sound in the hall left Nimon no time for further self-inquisitions, as the doorway to the room opened.

A figure wrapped in a black mesh cloak stood before him.

CHAPTER 6

Novas felt the wet grass cool against her back as its moisture penetrated her leather bodice. Her vision focused from the hazy gray of unconsciousness to a blurred myriad of sunlight and color. She lay motionless on the ground, slowly rolling her eyes left to right as she struggled to regain her senses.

Abruptly, a massive, furry shadow leaned its head into her range of vision. Adrenaline surged through her body, sending with it the natural instinct to fight or flee. Novas followed her primal instinct.... she fought!

She brought her leg swiftly upward toward her chest. The ball of her foot crashed into the side of the head of the hulking mammoth, causing it to lurch backward with an anguished grunt. Rolling her body in the opposite direction, Novas rose into a crouched position, her hands raised before her in the claw-like form of the ancient Geminian martial art, Kol Ri. Her leg muscles tensed into coiled springs, readying her for a leaping assault against her attacker.

A roar from behind her told her that her defense had been valiant, but futile. Although outnumbered by beasts, she would still fight with her last breath. She reflexively spun on her heels to meet her death.

Her fear was quickly swept away by a wave of rage! The roar she had heard was not one of ferocity, but one of laughter! She looked up into the face of a grinning warrior and struggled against her conflicting emotions, for he was the most handsome man she had ever seen. He stood towering above her in a cotton-like tunic made of cloth similar to her skirt. It wrapped loosely across his massive chest and was tied with a purple cord belt. From the belt hung a short sword forged from a silvery red metal, strangely identical to the color of his tousled, shoulder length hair. His calf-length pants were of the same gingham cloth and were adorned with hardened shin protectors made from the husks of an extinct Geminian plant. With hands on his hips, he stared down at her, his clean shaven face chiseled from the dreams of her childhood fantasies. His smile was warm, yet slightly mocking. She knew what she must do.

Springing forward, she hurled her body feet-first toward him. Her left leg extended into a javelin of power, while her right foot remained coiled beneath it. Her hands tensed in their catlike defense. Effortlessly, the warrior pivoted his torso out of the path of her foot and plucked her body from mid-air with arms of sinewy steel. Her momentum spun them on his leather-thonged feet, causing them to pirouette as if they were a pair of ballet dancers. He held her tightly to him as he slowly spun to a halt. Their gazes locked in a brief instant of feral passion.

A noise from the direction of her first assailant snapped her attention away from his ruby-hued eyes.

"You have caught yourself a fiery one, friend Del," chuckled the muscular figure, as he gingerly rubbed the side of his head. At his feet lay an animal hide cloak of thick brown fur. He bent down, picked it up, and whirled it across his shoulders. He let the hood lay against his back, giving the appearance of a Vambor whose neck had been unmercifully broken.

"Her ferocity is understandable, given a face like yours as the one to greet her back into the world of the living," replied the warrior referred to as Del.

"You do me yet another injustice, Del, as you did with that illegal body toss technique during our sparring. Had you fought in the tradition of our forefathers, you would not have caused harm to come to this beautiful maiden."

"Ravar, the dreamer, the one who speaks of leaving his home for explorations, accuses me of abandoning tradition? Is that not like the sand hare cursing the dune fox for being too swift?"

Ravar roared with laughter at his friend's simile. Novas could not help but smile at the good natured verbal jousting of these two attractive men. For Ravar evoked within Novas an emotional reaction equal to the one she felt when she saw Del. His rugged looks and hearty personality appealed to primal desires she had long ago forgone. His battle garb was more primitive, but not unlike the style of her bodice. He, too, was clad in a leather vest with mercurial bands as laces. Leather leggings were strapped to a brief loin covering of the same material. What caught the eye of Novas most of all was the multi-colored belt embroidered with flame-eagle down and sand-serpent skins - both from animals long ago lost to the galaxy due to extinction.

"I think your words ring true, friend Del, for you hold that beautiful sand hare there as would a dune fox too long from supper."

Del again looked down into the crimson eyes of Novas, his face tinged with the flush of arousal. Novas regained her normal business-like composure and hastily squirmed from his cradling embrace. Landing feet-first, somewhat abruptly, she tugged at her bodice and skirt unceremoniously to recover the small amount of modesty that was left her.

"I hope that I did not injure you," Del said, softly.

"I am fine... and not unused to combat," Novas responded, attempting to sound braver than she felt.

"That is very clear," interjected Ravar. Inclining his head toward Del, he added, "Did I not tell you she must be a stargazer? The markings on her satchel say the truth and her fighting prowess shows it to be so. Inquiring of Novas, "Have you come to view the falling star?"

Novas was still stunned from the whirlwind of events that had placed her in this puzzling situation. She reflected momentarily, deciding to let her instinctive negotiating skills control her response. She knew that when put in a position of uncertainty, it was best to protect as much information as possible. By creating an air of mystery, she could learn as much from her opponent from the questions he asked as she could from the statements he made.

"I have many reasons for my travels."

"Ahh.... mystery. You truly are a spiritual one," Ravar mused, eyeing her from head to toe, pausing at the more enticing spots. "Surely your reasons have the city of Centar in mind?"

Novas was jolted by the mention of Centar. She was aware of the Legotian's abilities to convert matter into energy, given her recent experience within their chamber. But to transport her to her home world of Gemini on the outskirts of her birth-city was beyond her powers of imagination. Her amazement upon learning the true form of the Legotian had not yet subsided. The presence of non-corporeal entities had been theorized by her company's scientists. However, to experience it first-hand was a remarkable discovery. Now, to believe that they had traversed light years with her body was too much to fathom.

The shock showed on her face. Del, the nobler of the two, observed this and mistakenly associated it with their accidental assault upon her.

"Fair lady, our manners have left us. Let me ask your forgiveness. We have caused you harm and are indebted to you until that wrong has been righted. Let me offer you rest and comfort at my humble cottage until you have recovered from our discourtesy."

Ravar roared again with hearty laughter, and added, "If his 'humble cottage' is offensive to your tastes, then leave the kingdom's most ostentatious palace and find comfort in my modest home."

Novas' head spun with unanswered questions. Centar had not existed as a kingdom for many generations. "Had the Legotian concocted this ruse from a memory remnant in order to some way further their control over the Solar Corporation by manipulating her mind? Perhaps she had never left the energy sphere. Could it be that these events were nothing more than hypnotic illusions? How could they make Del and his effect on her seem so real?"

For the sake of simplicity, at least until she could regain her senses, Novas merely nodded her approval of Del's offer.

With a warm smile Del responded, "Very well, then. Ravar, retrieve our graviton sled. We will return to Centar immediately."

Novas' confusion was compounded. The appearance of these primeval warriors did not coincide with the existence of anti-grav technology. She began to suspect her Legotian mind control theory to be true. Only a dream could explain the fantastic situation in which she found herself.

She watched Ravar disappear through the bushes in obedient response to Del's request. Turning her eyes back toward the remaining warrior, she timidly looked up into his garnet eyes and wondered to herself, "Are you real?"

Her youthful desires swept over her as she gazed up at him. With an uncharacteristic tremble in her voice, she asked, "What is it about you that makes people want to do your bidding?"

Hearing her voice quaver, Del believed it to be due to the chill in the air. He smoothly removed his waist coat and draped it over her shoulders. Pulling her close to him to tie the belt, he replied softly, "I care deeply for my friends. In turn, they care for me."

Impulsively, as she would do in a dream, Novas moved her head upward toward him, intoxicated by his musk oil scent. Just as she felt his breath upon her face, a throaty hum from behind the bushes abruptly distracted her. Floating erratically over the shrubs came Ravar in the graviton sled. Novas quickly stepped back from Del, a flush of azure tinging her cheeks.

Pretending not to notice that he had interrupted them, Ravar beckoned to the pair and boomed, "Climb aboard!"

Del lifted Novas effortlessly and placed her in the rear seat of the oval disc. She sank softly into the plush cushions behind the front control seats as Del leapt into the left one. Eying Ravar as he slid the controls forward, she was overcome by the odd sensation of familiarity with the vehicle. She somehow knew that the style of this particular sled was an oddity, with its two seat configuration and cushioned rear compartment.... but she could not recall why she knew this to be true.

As the sled rose several decatreds above the ground, she peered out for the first time over the landscape of what she believed to be her own dream world... thanks to the Legotians. She half expected to see nomadic campfires glowing in the distance, each one marking the meeting place of one of the ancient tribes of Gemini. That would explain these two warriors, their differing ancient garb, and their combative, yet chivalrous demeanor. Around each campfire, tribal leaders would be plotting their next assault on their unsuspecting neighbor. Possessions would transfer from one clan to another amidst a brutal and bloody raid. She contemplated on how very different this type of existence was from her own corporate raids. Then with an ironic smile, she thought about the similarities. She almost wished for the simpler, more savage approach. That is what she expected when she peered out over her new world.

What she actually saw was beyond belief!

* * *

"Father!" Nimon exclaimed, the word rushing from his lips with a sound of surprise intermixed with relief.

Dr. Nicholas Edison moved toward Nimon, arms extended to support his visibly shaken son. The doctor was not a large man, but he commanded a presence. In his mid-fifties, he had maintained a trim, muscular physique. His ice-blue eyes revealed a clarity of thought born of years of scientific analysis. However, they now could display only concern for his stricken son. But as he reached him, he realized the danger in touching a Geminian not yet fully recovered from empowering. It was not uncommon for an intense mind telemetry episode to leave the Life Mentor disoriented and possibly violent. Normally, after a transference, a recovery period of thirty minutes for Geminians and up to several hours for humans was allowed.

For Nimon, the many years of training allowed him to suppress the violent aftershock of an empowering link in a matter of minutes. Instead, half-stepping, half-toppling forward, he reached out to his Earth-born father as would a tearful child who had just scraped his knee during play.

Shocked, Dr. Edison received his son's embrace. So strong, yet so helpless, his body trembled within the comfort of the father who had given him life. "Nimon, what is it?" he whispered coarsely, cradling his son's head on his shoulder.

"Father, I have felt the energy of new life," he sobbed. "I sensed its presence but could not embrace it. How could an essence so fragile survive in the harsh reality of our world? I cannot be responsible for it. It is not my place to expose its beauty to the ugliness which exists. Yet, that is what many of the Council expects of me. I have told them of my belief that Starn is moving out of my control. He becomes more independent with each life transference. But they persist with their pressures for me to achieve Phoenos. What should I do?"

A shadow of mystery flickered across the face of Dr. Edison. As quickly as it appeared, it was gone. Gently separating himself from his son's embrace, he responded.

"Son, I cannot tell you what to do, but I know of the pressures you describe. My counsel is strongly biased, for your mother and I have built our lives around Phoenos. You are a testament to that fact."

Again, there was the flicker of mystery.

"Your mother and I would have not met had it not been for her search for Phoenos. You see, legend speaks of a time where Geminians were on the brink of achieving Phoenos. Two factions arose, however, quarreling over how such a gift should be used. One believed that life was a treasure. It should be revered. Each life was rare, and the rarest would be one spawned from pure thought. The other viewed life as a commodity to be bartered and sold. It had value, but only in the most materialistic of sense. This faction wished to enslave those lives created by Phoenos.

A struggle between the factions ensued. War followed. The conflict caused much death and destruction. With it came the loss of the techno-art necessary for Phoenos. The Materialists were eventually defeated. They were banished to space by the Lifists. Ironically, legend links these banished materialists with the settlement of the Castorian system, a race that even now challenges our views with their fierce materialistic philosophies. Those remaining on Gemini attempted to recover the loss of the techno-art, but were unsuccessful. Yet, their reverence toward Phoenos continued. However, life purists among them saw an opportunity. Their extremist philosophies have given rise to the growing Life Rightist movement to eradicate the quest for Phoenos. Your mother and I do not support this effort.

Your mother believed the legends that foretold of the ability to spawn two lives from a single mind. She funded countless investigations into the archives to glean the scientific links between the mind and life energy. She pioneered the synthesis of life crystals which led to the science of bioduogenetics. But Phoenos was elusive. Finally, her search turned to the stars. By contacting the descendants of the ancient materialists, she believed she would find the missing pieces to the Phoenos puzzle.

It was during one of these exploratory missions that she reached Earth. We met and fell in love. Our love made you. So you see, Phoenos has been a driving force in our lives, even if only because of its elusiveness. But I cannot tell you that it should be as influential in your life. You must determine that for yourself."

"Unfortunately, your desire not to dictate my life course is not shared by the traditionalists on the Council, Father. I tried to explain the approach to biodrones taken by Terrans. It is not harmful to use the units to protect life, as the Terrans do. Rather than endanger themselves, they project into their biodrones to perform life-threatening tasks. They are not slaves - they are tools for human advancement. Why must biodrones be any more than that?"

A pang of anguish was suppressed by Dr. Edison. Reaching out to grasp Nimon by the shoulders caringly, but firmly, as only a father would his son, he whispered, "If you really believed that, then why did you return to Starn? I know of the Council's desires... and I know you, Nimon. That is why I am here. I knew you would risk your life by evading the authorities to return to Starn if you thought there was the slightest hope of reviving him. But you are in grave danger. Since your last visit to Gemini, many things have happened to affect the social and governmental arena of this planet. Your mother, Novas, has been deeply involved and has shared with me knowledge of events about which most Geminians are unaware."

"Her position in the technical community does have its advantages," Nimon acknowledged.

Dr. Edison continued, "The focal point of the changes now affecting Geminian society can be traced back to the conflict between the Lifists and the Materialists."

"Geminian history is quite vague as to the details of that period, if I may add. It is a time which many on Gemini would prefer not to remember," Nimon interjected.

"That feeling is still very strong, my son," Dr. Edison said, a note of tension entering his voice. "It has been strengthened in response to a dissenting movement known as the K'Tar. The closest likeness to which I can relate this on Earth is nihilism - a doctrine which denies all current values, questions all authority, and advocates the destruction of the existing social institutions. In their place, the K'Tar would substitute a society where one's power was determined by the amount of one's possessions. The most powerful would be the one who controlled the most life crystals - and the most biodgens."

Nimon's brow furrowed with concern.

"Enlightening," Nimon murmured, as a clearer understanding of the situation dawned upon him. "My timing for making a stronger case concerning my stance on biod rights could not have been more inopportune. The Elders have associated me with the K'Tar movement and have responded with hostility."

"Exactly!" Dr. Edison exclaimed. "But there is more. As the K'Tar movement grows, it creates an equal and opposite reaction by the Life Rightists, where there is no room for life empowerment concepts within their beliefs. As these polar opposite factions gain strength - the K'Tar, or modern day Materialists, versus the Life Rightists, the more moderate and spiritual view of two lives from one mind - Phoenos becomes lost. Yet, your mother and I recognize that one view should not… cannot… be allowed to forcibly overwhelm the other. There must be room for all views in a thriving, prosperous society to be heard. As such, Novas has been struggling to suppress factions within the Council which wish to purge Geminian society of the K'Tar, as was done during the time of conflict. More bluntly, if followers of the K'Tar don't abandon their beliefs, some among the Council argue that exile or even imprisonment should be employed."

"But such measures were abolished centuries ago," Nimon commented, disgustedly. "Surely a group of philosophers with different beliefs cannot warrant such an action by the Elders."

"That's just it!" cried Dr. Edison, unable to contain his anxiety any longer. "The followers of the K'Tar are not being viewed as merely philosophers. They are being labeled as militant subversives led by a mysterious Geminian woman known only as T'Poch. Occurrences of sabotage and destruction have been linked to her and members of the K'Tar. This has shocked the members on the Council of Elders to the point they believe retaliatory imprisonment is the only alternative.

That is why I have come to you, my son. You must flee Gemini and save yourself. Your mother and I cannot protect you against the pressures reverberating through the Council. Please, you must leave," Dr. Edison pleaded.

"Father, I understand your feelings. However, I cannot turn my back on my heritage. I am being accused of the murder of my Dual. To flee Gemini would admit my guilt and condemn my mother's family line to eternal disgrace. It would leave my Dual, Starn, to be destroyed by the unknowing hands of the Institute. I would be abandoning my home world at a time when I feel I could actually help it against the K'Tar! No, father, I cannot flee. But I do know what I must do!"

With that, Nimon turned back toward the seemingly lifeless form of Starn, and the task of reviving it... or pronouncing it dead.

CHAPTER 7

Morgan Descartes looked at Jefferson Brown over his cards, trying to decipher the mask of his opponent before he decided to fold. The friendly game of Denebian poker they were playing to while away the few hours before they reached Gemini was becoming expensive for Descartes. The Denebian version of the Terran game required that discarded cards were immediately reshuffled into the deck, thus lowering the odds of getting a superlative hand. The extra suit also added a twist to the game, since it could nullify a similar card of another suit held by the opponent. Whether it was the riverboat gambler in Brown's ancestry, or the fact that he could read his plant manager's psyche like a book, the Mississippi-born personnel manager was trouncing Descartes unmercifully.

Just as Descartes had reached his decision, Brown spoke, "You know, Morgan, the Clionian, Helicon, uncovered some interesting artifacts on that Castorian planet. Some of the historical records recounting the ancient race's exploratory adventures would appeal to you."

Momentarily distracted from his concentration on the game, Descartes replied in a vexed tone, "I think I'll leave the historical analyses to the

Geminian Science Institute, if you don't mind, J.B."

"Fine, Morgan. I just wouldn't want you to miss out on anything simply because you're uncomfortable around Helicon."

Before replying, Descartes reached for the Martian rum sitting on the table to his left. Looking thoughtfully into the glass, he swirled it in the tumbler before tasting it.

"Let's not get into that discussion again, Jeff," Descartes said, casually raising him another three credits.

Brown's eyebrow twitched at the somewhat unexpected turn of events in the hand being played.

"Morgan, a story from my earlier graduate school days comes to mind which may interest you," the personnel manager said, as he saw Descartes's raise and asked for three cards.

While he dealt Brown his cards, Descartes resigned himself to hear out his resident sociologist's story, since they had, indeed, proved insightful in the past.

"Go ahead, J.B.. Since Nimon isn't here, I can say you've got my `undivided' attention."

Wincing at his Plant Manager's pun referencing the legend of Castor's origin as a race split off from Gemini, Brown began, "Well, a grad student I was very close to had, during his childhood, acquired a strong distaste for what were known to him as 'Zoids'."

"That was an archaic name used to insult Caucasians wasn't it?" Descartes interrupted.

"That's right, Morgan. You see, though Earth-born, my friend had moved during early childhood with his parents to the Martian Colonies. As you know, Mars had been colonized predominantly by Terrans of African descent. They had been dissatisfied with the slow progress of the equal rights movement in the early 2000's. They believed a fresh start in the colonies would allow them the freedom for their own cultural revolution. Although the struggle against racial prejudice on Mars was far ahead of Earth's, pockets of racial isolationists *did* exist. My grad student friend happened to be raised in one.

Having occurred at a very impressionable age, the youth never really got over the conditioning, and carried a dislike of Caucasians with him all the way into graduate school. He managed to prevent his bias from affecting his performance until his thesis work back on Earth. His thesis topic was to study the morality issues of tissue farming for regenerating damaged organs. You remember all the uproar in the 2020's over the technology of growing heart and brain tissue."

"I sure do!" replied Descartes. "I dated a gorgeous redhead who was the most militant 'soul rightist' you'd ever want to meet. She claimed the human soul arose from an energy emitted from specific heart and brain cells. By farming and harvesting this tissue, man was playing God. He had no right to use this tissue for his own material gain. But what a starfire she was! She could really use her own soul energy for *my* gain. She used to wear this... "

"Do you mind if I finish *my* story, first..." Brown interjected, "...before you start off on one of your nostalgic trips down lust lane?"

"Sure... go right ahead," Descartes answered, with feigned dejection. "Don't mind me."

"Thank you. As I was saying, this grad student was doing his thesis at Emory Hospital. It just so happens that a Caucasian surgeon picked up on his anti-Caucasian feelings, and was prepared to have the student's research privileges revoked. Had it not been for a near fatal lab accident, the student's career could have been ruined."

"Explain, J.B." Descartes prompted, now engrossed in Brown's narration, as he absently pitched two more credits into the growing pot.

"Well, the student was working in the Biotechnics Lab when he accidentally exposed himself to an isolated virus which was a precursor to the now conquered disease, Sickle Cell Anemia."

"I seem to recall that malady, J.B.. Wasn't it found predominantly in people with African heritage?"

"Exactly. Because the strain which infected the student was genetically modified, it spread through his system rapidly."

"Did he die?"

"Luckily, the Caucasian surgeon discovered the student and rushed him to an isolation chamber. The surgeon had been immunized against the virus, since it was his project, and proceeded to use himself as a blood transfusion donor for the student. After both the surgeon and student spent several weeks in intensive sterile isolation, they fully recovered."

"And the moral of the story is that they became lasting friends and lived happily ever after - right J.B.?" Descartes interjected sarcastically, having guessed the psychological motive behind Brown's story.

"Actually, no, Mr. Plant Manager," the personnel manager responded firmly. "I never saw the surgeon again. But I *have* been able to have lasting friendships with many Caucasians I've met since then... no matter how much they think they know!"

With that, Brown unveiled a Royal Troika and raked the huge pile of credits over to his side of the table.

Looking up at his plant manager sitting with his mouth ajar, Brown softly said, "Think about it, Morgan."

A whistle from the table's console intercom broke the momentary silence between the two men.

"This is Descartes," the plant manager murmured into the speaker, not breaking his eyes from his resident sociologist's intense stare.

"Coming up on the Geminian star system, sir," control technician Saffron 3 reported in her cool, professional voice.

"Thank you, Saff 3. I'll be right up."

As Descartes rose to head out of his private office he paused at the doorway, looking back at Brown still sitting with his back to the door.

"I'll do just that, J.B.."

After the iris-style door constricted shut, the *Darwin*'s personnel manager allowed himself a small smile of satisfaction, and one more gulp of Martian rum.

*   *   *

The sleek, mercurial sphere of the *Darwin* emerged from its time shift several parsecs from the Gemini star system. From this vantage point, the ethereal nebula of cosmic dust which swirled in the outermost ring of the system projected a foreboding image of mystery - and danger.

As the *Darwin* pierced the blanket of energized particles, the red giant star of Gemini blazed brilliantly into the eyes of the plant control crew.   Leaving a glowing path of ionization, the plant arced flawlessly into a standard orbit around the star's fifth planet.

"Orbit attained, sir," purred Planning Superintendent Christi Pomeroy, while completing the final adjustments that only a timefold pathfinder of her caliber would require before reporting to the Plant Manager.

Operations Superintendent Mack Weber added, "Polymerization tubes have stabilized, sir. Life crystal yield for this space fold was 93%. Our downtime was obviously well spent by Mr. Crescent and his Engineering Department."

"Very good, ladies and gentlemen," Descartes responded, with a knowing smile of appreciation for the care taken by his control crew in handling his plant.

He had to remind himself that the apparent simplicity with which his personnel managed his interstellar crystal plant was a testimonial to their expert abilities. He occasionally took for granted the plant's quite complex technology. A review of the post-fold status report showing performance statistics at critical points in the facility quickly reminded him of the marvel that was the *Darwin*.

Its shape was predominantly spherical, with an outer skin composed of a mirror-finish of nuridium-titanite alloy. At each "pole" of the sphere, the structure formed a concave dish. Each dish funneled into a twenty kilotred diameter cylindrical tube which connected the two poles. Humorists likened the design to a chromed, cored apple. But what an apple "core"!

Surrounding the core were tubular loops extending from pole to pole. Within each loop, raw material gathered from subspace was polymerized into life crystal components while the plant hurtled from point to point. The polar loops were interconnected by radial loops which moved crystal components from one stage of polymerization to the next. One side of each polar loop interfaced with the surface of the core's tube. The other side of the polar loops arced to form the curved outer surface of the "apple". This ring of "D's" with their vertical portion forming the walls of the core and their curved portion forming the plant's curved outer surface provided the source of the crystal plant's ability to time-space fold. By interlinking the energy fields of the two processes, both space folding and life crystal polymerization became possible - and highly profitable.

As the crystal plant moved through space, stray leptons passed across the dished surface, into the funnel, through the core, and exited the opposite polar dish. The leptons generated a longitudinal energy plasma around which the crystal plant rotated. Simultaneously, polymerization fields circulated through each of the polar loops. The interface of the fields with the lepton plasma created a localized "timefold".

By directionalizing the timefold, the *Darwin* could move along a crest in the fabric of space as a surfer would ride along the crest of a wave. Though the analogy was a crude one, it provided the employees of the Solar Corporation with a romanticized explanation of the technology.

Abruptly, Descartes was shaken from his report review by his senior control technician.

"Semaphore frequency to Gemini Central is as yet unanswered, sir," Saffron 3 stated, with a tone of perplexity in her voice.

"All alternate channels also yield no response," she added, before Descartes could make that exact request of her.

"Any abnormal readings from the surface, Mr. Fleming?" Descartes inquired of his Velotian technical supervisor.

The orange-tinged humanoid from the moon of Velos was performing well during Nimon Edison's absence. He responded in his best guttural English, "No suur. All indichutions show nurmul."

Descartes, too, began to share his control technician's sense of bewilderment at the cold shoulder they were receiving from the planct below. Just as he was considering his alternatives, the control room communication's holovid pad jumped to life with the 3-D image of an elderly Geminian male, some 140 Earth years of age at Descartes's best estimate.

"*Darwin*. You will remain in standard orbit. No permission to come planet-side is granted. Further explanation will be given momentarily."

As suddenly as the communication had begun, it was over. Descartes knew even less about the reason for the strange reception than he did earlier, since it now could not be attributed to communication difficulties.

One thing was certain," the Plant Manager thought, "I'm not going to be caught off guard by whatever they have up their sleeves!"

"All hands, go to Safety status - *Precautionary*!" he barked, as he thumbed the alarm switch on his console.

*　　*　　*

Novas pulled in her breath in an awe-inspired gasp as she saw the beauty of her birth-city. It was immediately familiar to her, yet strangely different. She thought again how dream-like her situation seemed. The city rose before her as the graviton sled carried her into its enchanting aura. Bits of recognition of structures tugged at her mind, while her attention was pulled to lofty spires that were, by her memory, conspicuously out of place.

Such artistically designed architecture represented a time out of synch with these warriors. Their best attempt at constructing buildings should have been the more classic lines of stone columns and cathedral arches which dotted the cityscape. It was becoming clearer to her that her senses were deceiving her and *must* be under the influence of some outside force. Yet, she was compelled to prove this theory. To do so, she knew she must gather more information.

"Warrior Del, I have never before seen such a beautiful city. I am most impressed by those towering spires in the distance. It must have taken a mind touched by the gods to create such masterpieces."

Her innocent attempt at flattery elicited a mixed response from her two new acquaintances. Del's face flushed a deep anger-laced azure, while Ravar unleashed another boisterous guffaw. Eying his co-pilot, Ravar chided him, "Do not take offense, friend Del. The lady is but a good judge of craftsmanship, if just a little weak when recognizing a warrior. My lady, Del is a man of peace. He loathes bloodshed. His fighting skills and warrior appearance are for the most part due to my fine training. He uses them only when Fate allows him no other choice. And those beautiful spires you see are not architecture, but works of science. They, too, are the result of my humble, but brilliant hands. They are more than towers. They are chariots to heaven. For what you see before you are *starcraft*!"

Novas looked toward the wondrous structures, momentarily forgetting that she had unintentionally insulted her noble host. With the eye of an expert, she studied the lines of the vessels and nodded appreciatively. Flickers of memory danced through her mind, enticing her to recall what she knew about such craft. Yet, her thoughts were clouded, as if a veil prevented her mind's eye from gazing on the seductive beauty of her space-faring experiences. Again, she was gripped with the impression that an outside influence affected her mind.

Tearing her gaze from the spacecraft, she studied the profile of Del, now sitting stoically in the co-pilot's seat of the sled. In an attempt to repair the damage she had inadvertently caused, she elected to take a submissive posture in this "negotiation".

"Pardon me noble Del, for I am ignorant of your tribe's ways and the marvels that your people have mastered. I meant no insult."

The stony edge of Del's countenance softened a fraction, but it was Ravar who spoke.

"Lovely one, you must truly come from quite a distance to not have heard of my wondrous fleet of starcraft. If you are a stargazer as I suspect, then I would have thought that you would know of our impending doom from the meteor hurtling toward our planet. I had hopes that your intention was to solicit a position among my followers as we escape from this condemned world. If your knowledge of the stars equals your beauty, then you would be doubly welcome on board."

Novas absorbed the words of her talkative pilot, while attempting to mask their shocking effect upon her. She sensed the taunting overtone in Ravar's voice as he eyed Del for a response, but that did not prevent her from feeling the truth behind what was said.

A sardonic smile pulled at the corner of Del's mouth as he responded to his friend's baiting jabs. "You assume much, my intelligent friend. Our scientists must truly be in your debt for your undeniable conclusions. You have managed to assemble enough soothsayers and visionaries who believe your calculations so that you have nearly filled your vessels. Once gone, our scientific community will be cleansed of them and free to go on unencumbered to greater discoveries than ever thought possible."

Ravar snorted with disgust. "You may mock me, Del, but you know my motives are pure. I mean only to preserve our race and the miracle of the Phoenos."

"Let us see the accuracy of your reasoning. You have deduced that our fair passenger is a follower of the stars. Since she has not even told us her name, your facts on this matter are nearly as incomplete as those on the meteor. Let us ask her then, her name. From that we will know if she is as you say."

With an approving nod, they both turned to peer over their shoulders at their mysterious guest. Her appearance jolted Ravar to the point that he nearly lost control of the graviton sled. She sat amidst the soft cushions in the rear of the vehicle with her arms rigidly extended to both sides, her hands violently clutching the rich fabric to the point of shredding it. Her head had fallen back and was quivering intensely from the tremors of a seizure. Her crimson eyes turned inward, revealing their fiery red glow. Her lips moved spasmodically as she whispered repeatedly, "Novas... Phoenos ...Novas... Phoenos...

"Novas... Novas... Novas," Del urged, soothingly, in an attempt to waken the mysterious woman from her catatonic sleep. She had been unconscious for the past two Geminian days since their first encounter at the meadow's edge. He had been by her side as much as a tribal chieftan could during such troublesome times. He knew that his people were demanding more and more of his attention as the fear from the meteor's approach gripped them. Yet, the beauty and intrigue of this stranger compelled him to be with her. He had surmised from her delirious whisperings that "Novas" was, in fact, her name. His admission of this truth to Ravar had been no easy feat. It had prompted a multitude of new arguments as to why Del should renounce his denial of the impending catastrophe. In Ravar's mind, Novas was a sign from the gods. Her name was proof enough. Literally translated - "star's death" - it alone should convince Del of the folly of his obstinate denial of Ravar's prediction.

Del had always found Ravar's mind a difficult one to understand. Here was a man of great scientific accomplishment who was fervently preaching the merits of metaphysical signs from the gods. Perhaps that tenuous link between science and metaphysics within Ravar's psyche was what enabled him to make such spectacular advances toward the discovery of Phoenos. Del would probably never know.

Nevertheless, the tribal leader continued to counter his friend's fear-inciting speeches with words of peace, truth, and the worship of life. He had to agree with Ravar on one point, though. This lovely creature before him could very well *be* a gift from the gods. Gently stroking the soft hair away from her face, Del could not help but notice that her beauty seemed to have grown since the first day he saw her.

As if willed to consciousness by the intensity of Del's feelings, Novas began to stir. He gingerly placed a revitalizing compress across her neckline to ease her waking. Novas' vision progressed from the burnt-orange haze of her sleep into the soft, warm hues of a tribal queen's bed chamber. The aroma of harvest nut-maize filtered from the glowing embers of the ornately forged urns in the corners of the room. A silky, sheer canopy floated lazily from the heartwood posts of her bed, rising up to meet in the claws of a golden flame dove statuette suspended from the ceiling. Lowering her gaze, she took in the delicate tapestries which covered the stone walls and chronicled the conquests of some ancient clan with their intricate weavings. Letting her eyes wander from the sumptuous decor, they fell upon the face of her benefactor.

Drinking in the warmth of his handsome smile, Novas slowly moved her gaze down his neck to his massive, oiled chest. He sat beside her on the divan, leaning one arm across her firm body while the other hand unconsciously continued its gentle caress of her hair. Bringing her eyes back up from their sensual stroll down his bare torso, she fixed them intently to his enticing gaze. Again, as with their first encounter, she knew what she must do.

Reaching out with her warm, smooth hands, she lightly gripped his shoulders and pulled him toward her. As his husky breath mixed with her rain flower scented sigh, she whispered, "The prize is much greater after the chase..."

She then brought her head forward with a sharp Tei Vree strike to Del's chin. He reeled backwards, stunned from the blow. The force of her head against his jaw caused him to recoil from not only the pain but the shock of her actions. Novas continued her onslaught, only now with her words rather than physical force.

"Do you dare take advantage of me in my moment of weakness? Is this the noble kindness that you show *all* the female guests of your home?"

Del had slipped from the edge of the bed on to the floor. He looked up at her dumbfounded. She rose into a crouched position, defiantly looking down at him. The silken gown hung loosely about her breasts, clearly taunting Del with the treasures that were forbidden to him. Novas continued her tirade with a vigor.

"First you and your woolly mammoth friend assault me in the woods. Then you charm me into going with you in your royal coach. Somehow you mesmerize me into submission, and once done, you abscond with me to your bedroom."

As Novas' ranting continued, Del regained his composure and mounted an offensive. "Star-maiden... if anyone is guilty of assault, it is you, not I. You loosen a few teeth in the thick skull of my friend with your kick. Then you attempt to crush my chest bone with your aggressive Tei Lan attack. And now, as I attempt to nurse you back to consciousness, you nearly shatter my jaw with your 'gratitude'. I meant only to extend to you my care, and nothing more."

Novas glared at him defiantly, her arms folded across her chest. Rising from the floor, he sternly met her glare and said, "The gods have apparently spared you from your two day death sleep, but I fear that you are not fully recovered.

We will be serving twilight meal within the hour. If you can contain your violent behavior, I would welcome your presence at the table."

Spinning on his heels while gingerly rubbing his jaw, Del stalked out of the room. Novas eyed his departure suspiciously, yet she could not resist the opportunity to admire his attractive physique. She sat back into the comfort of the pillows, her muscles trembling uncontrollably from the adrenaline surge. Sinking deeper into the cushions, she struggled to make sense of all that had transpired in the last several days.

"Had she truly been unconscious for two planetary rotations? Or was this simply another mind trap set by the Legotian? Was it a diabolical attempt to glean some bit of information to help them in their insidious quest for power within Solar Corporation?"

She vowed to herself that this evening she would find the answers.

CHAPTER 8

The cold, clinical stasis room within the Institute seemed to mock Nimon, reminding him of the endless hours of experimentation endured during his youth. "How many times had the physicians urged him to prepare for the same process which lay before him?" he asked himself. "Regardless the number, none were as important as this one."

So he prepared himself. The lifeless form of Starn hovered in front of him, as if waiting for rebirth. Or was it? Nimon must learn the truth. But the truth could be hard to accept. If Starn's life could be self-sustained, Nimon's own life would be changed forever. Again, as in childhood, he would be the focus of a multitude of scientific studies. Philosophies across the galaxy would have to be restated, if not totally abandoned! All for the salvation of one life entity? Nimon's swarthy blue brow creased as he cautiously considered the outcome of his actions. His decision would be eternal. But now there was so little time.

With each passing second, Nimon wondered if the ability for Starn's essence to sustain itself would fade into nothingness. He could hesitate no longer. He must act! Preparations must be different. Nimon must not only search for the ebbing life essence of Starn, he must simultaneously maintain a strong psionic shield against the Outside Force that had threatened him earlier. Thoughts drifted to his father's words spoken only moments before ... thoughts about the K'Tar and the sinister woman known as T'Poch.

"Was she in some way behind the force that pulled at him?" He could only speculate. But this was not the time.

Dr. Edison rocked from one foot to the other as he anxiously watched his son enter the meditative trance of Ka'al Ni-Kor. Suddenly, the outer door of the isolation room opened to reveal a male orderly making his rounds. A look of surprise flashed across the orderly's face ... a look quickly replaced by alarm as he reflexively backed out of the room at the sight of an elder Geminian in Ka'al Ni-Kor.

Dr. Edison rushed toward him. "He mustn't announce our presence!" he thought frantically, attempting not to disturb Nimon's focus. Unfortunately, the agility of the Geminian youth surpassed that of the older Terran, allowing him to activate the hospital alarm.

Shaken from his trance by the clarion of the hospital's alert, Nimon realized it was impossible for him to save Starn now. His only hope would be to stall the scientific curiosity of the Institute so the gentle balance of Starn's psychic construct would not be disturbed.

"Father!" Nimon exclaimed, as he exited the isolation chamber into the hospital corridor.

"Yes, Nimon. I tried..."

"Never mind that. You must prevent the Institute from pursuing their research until I can return. Starn's existence is at stake. Can you do that?" Nimon pressed, urgently searching for an affirmative response. Unconsciously, his hands firmly gripped his father by the shoulders.

"Yes, Nimon. I still wield influence over the Institute. But what are you going to do?"

"There is no time for explanations, but I will return for him. Now I must go," Nimon whispered, his eyes peering intently into those of his father.

As he turned and hastened down the hall, Dr. Edison watched Nimon leave and said to himself, "Take care, my only ... son."

Nimon had managed to elude the less experienced hospital security staff, but he knew that his biggest challenge lay before him. To breach the security of a Solar Corporation life crystal plant unannounced was a difficult feat even for a Geminian of Nimon's technical expertise. Yet, the Darwin wasn't just any life crystal plant. Nimon had played an integral part in developing its computerized security system. His contribution to that task would now "pay off" - to coin a phrase of Jefferson Brown.

Making his way through the narrow streets of the inner city, he feverishly entered the needed programming into his micro-controller. It would activate any Solar Corporation lander to respond to his commands. He knew of a lander station near the Institute which ferried corporate employees between the Institute and the Solar Corporation's orbital research facilities. His plan was a direct one. First he would commandeer one of the vehicles. Once in hand, he would then penetrate the Darwin's sensor grid so that he could enter the plant unnoticed. By transmitting an encoded sequence on the proper frequency, he could trigger a security system calibration routine. By activating an infinite loop in the program, the system would be temporarily too "busy" to record his entry into the ship's landing bay.

Nimon knew that the hospital security staff had in all probability alerted the local enforcement agents as to his approximate location. They would be quickly converging on the area and would logically double the guard on the nearby lander station. Because of this, timing was critical.

Approaching the point where the alleyway emptied into a main street, he completed his last entry into the micro-controller. He surveyed the thoroughfare, now vacant due to the security cordon, and hurriedly stepped out to cross it.

The lander station was located a short distance down the main street and to the left. He was almost there. But that short distance was as much as a kilotred without cover. Nimon's heightened sense of hearing detected the ultra-frequency distortion of the oncoming ground-car. Careening around a corner, high intensity beams glaring, the vehicle was instantly upon him. Its markings indicated that it belonged to the Code Enforcement Agency.

The enforcement agent at the controls was startled, but reflexively activated the braking system. His reflexes were too slow. A sickening thud rocked the small ground-car as it skidded into what the agent felt was surely going to be cause for a reprimand from his superior. Bounding out of the driver compartment, the officer rushed to the crumpled figure lying beneath his vehicle. Kneeling down, he turned over the body for a better look at the face of the dead man. The agent shuddered and let out a quiet moan.

Nimon released the pressure point below the agent's left ear and deftly pulled himself from underneath the ground-car. "I must commend Specialist Klinger in the Supply section when the opportunity presents itself," Nimon thought. "The skill of simulating a pedestrian-vehicular accident he learned from his ancestor's tapes from old Chicago was quite useful. I should learn more about these 'con artists' of his."

It had been a simple task for Nimon's mind to calculate speed, distance, and trajectory. At the precise instant required, the Solar Corporation technical superintendent had jumped backward and swung under the vehicle. Deftly picking up the unconscious Gemini Enforcement Agent, Nimon placed him in the storage compartment of the ground-car. Donning the helmet and jacket of his captive, he then slipped behind the steering console and activated the propulsion system.

Moments later, Nimon stood at the entrance to the lander station, addressing the guard in command mode. "Agency Central notified you that you would need assistance. A traitor has violated the Institute's security and may attempt to use this station to escape. You secure the entrance and I will be on guard just inside the door. Any questions?"

"No, sir!" replied the lower ranking official, stepping aside.

As Nimon entered the lander terminal, he knew he would not have time to confuse the tracking mechanism that would inform Central Space Control of his destination. But this was of no consequence. He swiftly entered the nearest lander. Opening the vehicle's instrument grid, he interfaced his micro-controller into its memory circuit. Immediately an alarm clarion rang out. Sliding the controls downward and settling in behind the operations console, Nimon glanced across the video monitors. The aft view was that of the guard rushing to the lander pad. As the lander launched, Nimon grimaced as he recognized the flare of the guard's shoulder mounted pulsar cannon!

*   *   *

Descartes leaned forward to better see the safety status signal on his command console change from "precautionary" to "priority alert". As the siren wailed, Christi Pomeroy exclaimed over her shoulder to her plant manager, "External Environment sensors have automatically activated the alarm, sir. Sensors show seven Gemini meson-fighters heading in a containment formation directly for us!"

Just as abruptly as the priority alert was activated, an omnivator docked at the control room and the door opened. Descartes spun around in his chair, jaw agape and wide eyed.

"Plant Manager Descartes, I respectfully place myself under suspension in your custody as described in Solar Corporation Galactic Ethics Code 701 subsection 16 B," proclaimed the solemn voice of the Darwin's second-in-command, his tunic still smoldering from the effects of the deflected pulsar charge that ushered him away from Gemini's surface.

"Nimon?!" Descartes exclaimed, his brow creased in a look of consternation.

As if an onslaught of Gemini fighters and a Gemini technical superintendent surrendering himself weren't enough, Saffron 3 intervened, "Mr. Descartes, message coming through on the communications grid, Enforcement Code One, sir!"

The same elderly Geminian that had earlier refused the Darwin its landing privileges appeared once more on the holovid pad, but this time Descartes detected a hint of savage anger in his countenance.

"Plant Manager Descartes, your plant is in Gemini domain and you are harboring a criminal who has committed one of the highest acts of Geminian treason. You will surrender your plant and employees or your data systems will be eradicated!"

Again Descartes spun in his chair to face his technical superintendent. The look of surprise in his face was gone. It had been replaced with rage!

"Nimon!!" Descartes bellowed.

*   *   *

Novas glided down the stone-hewn staircase of the tribal chieftan's castle. The trail of her chamois gown slid noiselessly over the bronze inlay of the stair treads. The bannisters of oiled chestwood had withstood the ravages of time and provided a firm, welcome support to her as she descended. The tapestries that had adorned her bedroom were replaced in the lofty foyer by banners of a more regal design. Folds of burgundy and hunter's green draped heavily from silver staffs imbedded in the stone walls. Iron and copper urns, smaller than those in her quarters, dotted the corridor at the foot of the stairs. The aroma of cinnamon and nutmeg wafted down the hallway, enticing her to venture deeper into the passageways of the medieval manor.

Novas reflected upon her situation. Foremost in her mind were the events leading up to her arrival at Del's home.

"My seizure in the graviton sled must have been induced by my Legotian captor," she thought. "The boundary between matter and the mind must be insignificant to him, if he can wield such power over my thoughts. Yet somehow I must resist him."

She struggled to recall the last words she had heard while in the sled. It was like searching for the name of a casual acquaintance she might see at a business conference. It was there, tucked in the recesses of her mind, but just out of reach of her conscious memory. Inhaling deeply, she closed her eyes and performed a series of mental exercises to snare the elusive thoughts.

As if spring loaded, her eyes snapped open!

"Phoenos! Ravar had mentioned 'the miracle of Phoenos'. Then my seizure came upon me! And without the use of my memory disciplines, I would not have remembered. Why would the Legotian cause me to hallucinate that thought, only to try and remove it from this fantasy that now entraps me? It must mean that I can affect the events within this delusion in a way that contradicts his purpose!"

Normally, she would have rejoiced at the mention of Phoenos. Her lifelong ambition to resolve the mystery of Phoenos had become an inseparable part of her. But to fall into a coma at the mere sound of the word defied her senses. This behavior added more substance to her theory that the Legotian was assaulting her with a devious form of mind control. To what end, she could not yet guess.

"I must form a strategy for resisting his control. If I play along with this Legotian charade, as in any lie, more lies will be required to maintain it. Given time and patience, these untruths will become transparent and I will better understand the reasons for them." Yielding to her own curiosity about her lifelong pursuit of the Phoenos, she thought, "First, I will learn more of my 'host's' knowledge of Phoenos. This concept is intricately complex, and will serve my strategy well. As the Legotian pushes the lie further through the manipulations of his 'psycho-puppets', his misconception of Phoenos will be his undoing."

Reaching the end of the marbled corridor, Novas passed through two mammoth, wooden doors into the main dining hall. A slab of polished granitium sat before her, blocking her path as it spanned from one end of the room to the other. Its multiple legs had been sculpted to resemble those of an ancient Brakorian dragon, a beast so old that it was believed to be more a product of legend than of nature. The far end of the table completed the artistic rendering by forming the beast's head as it fed on the live coals of the hall's blazing fireplace. Novas stood in awe of the artisan's blend of form and function. An ornate inlay of scales along the creature's back conducted the flame's heat and served as individual cook-plates for the guests to roast their fresh food.

To her surprise, Novas was the second to arrive. Standing by the table's head with her bare back to the doorway was another female. Her fitted gown of tightly woven cryohawk down shimmered mystically in the light of the hearth. The whiteness of her hair rivaled that of the desert sands, except for a streak of coal black tresses braided with strands of the purest golden thread. Without turning, she greeted the new arrival ominously.

"Welcome sister. I sense you are feeling better. Come join me by the fire..."

A burning flush swept through Novas at the sound of the woman's voice. Hesitantly, she edged toward the hearth, as would a Rapian moth to the light of a Vesuvian glow stone.

"...we have much to discuss, you and I." The woman turned slightly to place her chalice of steaming elixir on one of the table's crimson scales. Through the silver tresses that partially masked her face, Novas believed she glimpsed a flash of red iridescence flit from the corner of her eye. As Novas peered closer, however, the woman's eyes seemed to be normal.

Cautiously, Novas queried, "You act as if we have met, but I do not know you. Why is this so?"

"People with shared beliefs need not meet in order to know one another. I sense that you and I have many beliefs that are the same. Do you not feel a sense of wonder when you gaze into the stars? Do you not wish to unlock the secrets of Nature's powers?"

Novas' brow furrowed as a chill washed down her spine. Unconsciously she raised her finger tips to her temple, drawing them down her cheek bone to counteract the tension rising within her. The woman's darkness pervaded the room. In her presence but for a few moments, she felt both threatened and mystified. She had touched upon the two most important driving forces in Novas' life with little more than a glimpse at her. She wondered at the source of such deep insight. Instinctively, she remained guarded.

"You presume much, for a stranger. What is it you wish of me? Only someone in great need would be so forward to one she does not know."

With that retort, the woman bristled. "Oh, I know full well of your intentions, Novas! And you can tell your clan that I have no need for you nor for their meddling. To believe that a novice such as you could be of any assistance to a person of my power is loathsome! Let me demonstrate."

Novas moved back a small step, startled by the explosive change in the woman's mood. Mesmerized by the intensity of her anger, Novas watched the woman's face transform. Her eyes rolled back, glowing red orbs taking their place. The tendons in her neck tightened into strands of rubindium cables. Slowly, she moved her left hand toward the yawning mouth of the dragon's fiery head. Novas gaped as the woman lifted a white hot coal from the beast's jaws and held it painlessly in her palm.

A boisterous laugh from the hallway leading to the dining room diverted Novas' attention. Turning toward the entranceway, she saw Del and Ravar enter. Comforted by their presence, Novas turned to challenge the sinister woman before her.

To Novas' amazement, the stranger stood calmly by the hearth, sipping her elixir and flashing a coy smile. Quizzically, Novas cocked her head, wondering if she had imagined the conversation. Looking back at the two men, she knew that they had not seen the woman's demonstration, so they could not vouch for Novas' sanity.

"The mind control of the Legotian is more troublesome than I anticipated," thought Novas. "My guard must be increased." Again she stroked her temple.

Unnoticed, a fiery coal lay precariously close to the mysterious woman's foot.

Ravar called across the room, "I see you have met our fair enchantress, P'Teel. You two must surely become good friends!"

"Ravar, you again presume too much," Del chided. "A common craft does not a friendship make. Novas and P'Teel are students of the stars, but are of different clans. I could only hope that their shared skills would provide a foundation for them to aid us in our troubled times. Let us not, however, force them into a bond of friendship that serves them no purpose."

"Since which moon's rotation does such a bond require purpose, kindred Del? Our bond provides little more than a reason to debate and engage in an occasional bout of sparring," Ravar quipped.

Picking up on the jovial giant's good mood, Del retorted, "And let us not forget the rare moments when your clumsiness introduces us to two such beautiful women as these!" He punctuated his reply with a regal sweep of his arm in the direction of Novas and P'Teel.

Ravar guffawed at his friend's wit. "No moment is as rare as when you are in such a lighthearted mood. Come, m'ladies, join us at the table so that we may enjoy this fleeting glimpse of Del at his best. For just as Castor spews its fiery lava into the heavens only once a millennia, so does Del take a brief respite from the toils of leadership. Let us revel in this moment!"

Novas watched as a tinge of azure brushed across Del's cheeks. From the broad smile that accompanied his coloring, she could only assume he was embarrassed and not angry at Ravar's jibes. But it was the mammoth's reference to Castor which piqued her interest, for he had confused the distant twin planet of their star system, Castor, with the sun of Gemini, Pollux, in his reference to a stellar flare.

"With this error," she thought, "perhaps the opportunity has come for me to lift the veil of my captor's ruse and expose these beings as mental fabrications. Yet, somehow I recall a fragment of childhood memory about another Castor ... one of ancient myth. The story told of a giant volcano that erupted from the Geminian desert floor only once a millennia. From the fires of the planet would be born an all-powerful race of beings. They would rise into the stars and bathe in their brilliant energy. From this bonding of planet, fire, and starlight would come a supreme civilization that would lead the galaxy to unimaginable accomplishments."

Novas thought it strange that she would remember the ancient fable at just this moment. As she sat at the table across from P'Teel, she could not suppress an ominous tingle at the base of her neck. Their eyes met and Novas knew from her wicked stare that she would be a formidable opponent. Rather than challenge the authenticity of these beings, perhaps it was better to learn more about them, especially this woman.

"So, Del, you have Ravar to thank for gaining P'Teel's counsel. I'm sure that makes for a most interesting tale," Novas probed, sitting down at one of the table's massive chairs. As if on cue, a quartet of assistants entered the banquet hall from a side alcove. Each bore a platter of sumptuous food which they deposited upon the glowing scales of the Brakorian dragon.

Following their guest's lead, the others took their places.

"It was quite innocent, fair Novas, and not nearly as injurious as our meeting," Ravar proffered, with a wry smile and a stroke of his jaw. "I was on a hunt for rare mineral deposits to assist in my research. My journey had taken me to a remote area of the Mal Gar Mountains. As I was rappelling down a cliff to reach a small cavern, I heard the most beautiful singing. Upon entering the opening, I realized that the sound was echoing up through the catacombs of ancient volcanic fissures. I followed the sound for fully a day's quarter until I reached an exit way in the cliff's base. To my surprise, through a thicket of underbrush I saw the lithe form of a beautiful enchantress enjoying a cool swim. Being the gentleman that I am, I politely called to her so that I would not startle her."

"Ravar, you lumbering Vambar! Spare us your wandering imagination!" P'Teel interrupted. "You continue to amaze me with your confusion of fantasy and fact. You conveniently forget that it was I who found you. You had become lost in the caverns that fateful day. After you became hoarse from shouting, I tracked you and then led you to me with my voice. Upon carrying your weary carcass out of the escarpment, you collapsed into a nearby pool and pulled me in with you!"

Unfazed by the rapier truth from the enchantress, Ravar parried with a winsome smile and added, "Ahh, but it was a wonderful swim we had, m'lady. And what better way to start such a fruitful acquaintance?"

Even P'Teel could not shrug off the effects of Ravar's charm as she let slip a sly wink in his direction. Del grinned broadly and quaffed his chalice of hot ale. Novas was surprised at how enjoyable the evening progressed, given its strange beginning. She marveled at P'Teel's ability to emanate an aura of hospitality toward her for the benefit of Ravar and Del. Novas was on the verge of questioning her own sanity by the end of dinner.

"Perhaps that was the goal!" she thought. She sensed that her guard had weakened. The Legotian ploy was showing signs of success! To prevent any further erosion in her defense against this mental onslaught, she must mount her offensive. Vowing to herself to break the Legotian's mind control over her, she intended to question these mind phantoms to prove her suspicions. But it would be a subtle assault. The Phoenos would be the means to that end.

"Your hospitality has truly been remarkable. It is a rare quality for someone to open their home and hearth to a stranger. I am grateful to the philosophical ideals that guide your lives."

"That is the one topic on which Del and I agree," Ravar replied. "Life is precious. It must be nurtured and allowed to flourish. That is why I am so moved in my quest to venture beyond this doomed planet. Life's beauty is in its diversity. I believe the stars hold the answer to sustaining the lives of Gemini. At the same time, they will reveal to us the many wonders of totally new life forms. It is this same desire to understand new cultures that causes us to welcome strangers into our home."

"That desire... among others," P'Teel added, sardonically.

Novas thought she detected in P'Teel a flash of the bitterness which greeted her earlier in the evening.

Del, used to the exchange of barbs between his advisers, paid P'Teel's comment little heed. But he found Ravar's comments in need of elaboration.

"Ravar speaks with wisdom on his favorite subject. In the area of life's precious value, I agree. However, I do not feel it should be used as a fear tactic to persuade our people to venture into space. He theorizes that a meteor will descend upon our world and devastate it. He preaches that the time is very near. Truly, Ravar is convincing, for many share his beliefs. The existence of the starcraft speaks to the power and wealth that follow my friend. As leader of this clan, and as one who has the ear of many on the Council of Clans, I have argued to allow Ravar to seek support for his teachings. Yet, I also have a right to my own beliefs. The stars are deadly and full of the unknown. The risks of space travel are too great. There are still unimaginable wonders of life to explore on Gemini without endangering our people."

"Like the Phoenos?" Novas interjected, eyeing her hosts for the slightest hint of concern.

P'Teel was the first to react.

Her stare bore down upon Novas like a plexisteel worker's cutting torch. "That subject seems to be of overwhelming importance to you. I was unaware that knowledge of the Phoenos had spread beyond a select few in Del's clan." She tilted her head accusatorily in Ravar's direction.

"I mentioned it only briefly in the graviton sled... and what of it? I am proud of my new discoveries. I fail to see why your desire for secrecy is so strong. You even have Del convinced that the people of Centar should not know of my theories," Ravar replied, defensively.

"That is not the issue at hand, Ravar. Again, you say too much. My question is for Novas. Why are you interested in the philosophy of Phoenos? And what brings you to Centar at this time?"

P'Teel had transformed. She again was the ruthless inquisitor. Gone was any pretense of hospitality.

Novas looked toward her quiet benefactor for comfort. None was to be found. Instead, a steely look of suspicion shrouded his handsome features. She had not counted on this reaction. Her hopes of trapping them in a lie had failed. She now found herself in a precarious position. She was a stranger in a land that she once knew. Her home-city was familiar in name only. She had assaulted two of her hosts. The third believed her to have discovered some dreaded secret that endangered the very heart of Geminian philosophy. And if in truth P'Teel's powers were more than just a parlor trick, Novas feared that as an enemy, she would be deadly.

Novas mind raced in search of a response.

Her search would have to wait.

Suddenly, a thunderous boom shook the estate to its foundations. The roar of supersonic air swept over the people in the hall. Through a skylight, an eerie glow washed across the night.

Bursting into the chamber, a dinner servant shouted, "Sire Ravar! Save us! It is the METEOR!"

CHAPTER 9

Squaring his shoulders and staring blankly past his enraged plant manager, the Darwin's second-in-command repeated his last statement.

"I am placing myself under suspension in your custody, sir, as is stated in Solar Corporation Ethics Code..."

Descartes' upraised hand halted Nimon in mid-sentence. The plant manager understood his technical superintendent better than anyone in the galaxy. Although he was outraged, he knew that Nimon always had a method to his madness - it just took a while to ferret it out. For the moment, Descartes would humor him.

"Very well, Nimon. Consider yourself suspended."

Turning back to the holovid as quickly as he had decided to comply with Nimon's wishes, Descartes faced the projection of the elderly Geminian with the most diplomatic smile he could muster.

"Sir, grant me the wish of knowing by whose hand the lives of my crew will be extinguished."

Descartes's request struck a nerve in the Geminian on the screen before him. The thought of ending lives had not occurred to the official.

"You do understand that the erasure of the plant's data systems would affect the control synapses and could easily cause an explosive chain reaction in the polymerization tubes," Descartes added.

By placing the lives of so many people in the hands of the one Geminian, instead of the many meson fighters, the shrewd plant manager clarified the harsh reality of the situation for the official. After a brief moment of reflection, Descartes thought he saw the hint of a wry smile flicker across the cerulean face of the Geminian.

"I see that your reputation is one of fact and not exaggeration, Plant Manager Descartes," the Geminian replied, acknowledging that the situation was not as critical as he had first indicated. "My name is Stalak. I am the Vice Consul over Planetary Code Enforcement. Sensory probes show that a fugitive who committed the severest of crimes has entered your plant, and is, according to our records, your second-in-command. Gemini Code requires that this criminal be returned to the planet for disciplinary measures."

Descartes's expression remained passive and friendly, though he was churning inside. "Vice-Consul, the logic of the situation shows it would be senseless to resist you. But, before I can respond to your request, my superiors at Solar Corporation Headquarters require that I know more of the facts surrounding the incident. I will need more time to accomplish this. I'm sure you understand."

The Geminian ability to collate statistical probabilities for the various alternatives involved in reaching a decision were not absent in Stalak's repertoire. "You have one hour, Plant Manager," he replied coolly, as the communication link was terminated.

Still staring intently at the vacated holovid pad, his smile now gone, Descartes said calmly, "In my office, if you please, Mr. Edison."

*   *   *

Descartes took a seat behind his desk. Nimon stood before him with his hands clasped behind his back, as if at parade rest. Descartes knew, even before he offered, what Nimon's response would be, but he offered anyway.

"Bourbon, Nimon?"

"No thank you, sir," came the expected answer.

"I'm officially on overtime, so you won't mind if I indulge myself with one, will you?"

Again the usual answer, "Not at all, sir."

Continuing on, Descartes inquired, "What in the seven moons of Argelius is going on Nimon?"

In an attempt to add levity to the situation, the technical superintendent replied, "I haven't been to them lately, Morgan. But I think I can shed some light on what has placed the Darwin in its present predicament."

"Please do, Mr. Edison," Descartes urged, without cracking a smile.

"Fifteen Solar days ago, you honored my request for a personal leave of absence and deposited me on the surface of Gemini. Once there, I empowered my Dual, Starn, so that he could embark on Royta-Far, a ritual of Geminian biodgen development. But prior to this traditional challenge, I attempted to keep an appointment with the Gemini Council of Elders. Unknown to me at that time, a socio-philosophical movement known as the K'Tar had hardened the Council's views toward me to the point that I was refused an audience."

"Pause and rewind, Nimon! I've missed a few frames. What exactly did this K'Tar do?"

"Facts indicate their materialistic approach toward bioduogenetics have resulted in an adverse reaction by the Council toward anyone suggesting minor modifications to Gemini ideology."

"Meaning the Council is biased against you, right?"

"I thought I just said that, sir," Nimon replied, his head cocked quizzically with both eye brows arched.

The corners of Descartes's mouth turned up slightly as he prompted, "Please continue, Nimon."

"After I finally met with the Council, I found it necessary to seclude myself in meditation in a remote area of Gemini, in order to better empower Starn during his challenge. During this ordeal, an assault on Starn left his mental construct unable to sustain life energy - clinically "dead" according to the Institute physicians."

"But why accuse you?"

"From the holovid reports showing the events surrounding the assault, I believe the Ruga'r they found around Starn's neck will be the same one I had displayed in my weapon's collection here on the Darwin. It would be unlikely that anyone other than myself or Starn would have access to the display's genetic lock protecting the Ruga'r, nor the skill needed to activate it and wrap it around his body and throat. Nor is my distance from the murder site an alibi. The Council would be right under normal conditions to expect me to terminate my empowering with Starn if he had been attacked by someone else. By terminating the link, his mental construct would be placed in suspension and could not 'die' by asphyxiation. His 'death' is proof positive to the Council that I did not terminate the empowering, no matter how the Ruga'r became wrapped around him. Therefore I must be guilty."

"But you said 'would be right under normal conditions' - what wasn't normal?" probed Descartes.

"Morgan... I have been struggling to retain control over Starn for some time now. Are you familiar with the Geminian concept of Dualiity?"

"Yes... to some extent. But it's just a myth."

"It's no myth, Morgan. I believe I have experienced brief flashes of Dualiity with Starn. It was during one of these moments that Starn was attacked with my Ruga'r."

"But even if you didn't break the link, it was the assailant who used the weapon. How do the authorities explain your being in close proximity to your biod and simultaneously animated along with him in order to strangulate him?"

Nimon winced at Descartes' use of the term "biod", instead of the correct, "biodgen", for his Dual. Descartes knew the difference. A Solar biodrone was far less sophisticated than the Geminian bioduotron. Using "biod" was considered demeaning when referring to a Geminian's Dual. Perhaps the plant manager merely had a "slip of the tongue", to coin a Jefferson Brown ancient Earth colloquialism. Or could it be Brown's suspicions about Descartes' intrinsic xeno-bias had some basis in fact? Electing not to overly pursue the slur further, Nimon responded, "Morgan, my biodgen skills are not constrained to long distance contact as are the Terran biodivers and their biodrones. The Elders would attribute to me, an 8th level Dualiity Master, the expertise required to suspend myself near enough to Starn, reanimate myself, hurl the Ruga'r, and re-immerse myself in the link to activate him long enough to suffer the effects of the weapon."

Morgan Descartes sensed he had irritated his second-in-command. Thinking this explanation by Nimon to be a stretch at best and somewhat boastful at worst, he chose not to further agitate him, and responded, with an attempt at levity, "The end-result being that you were framed for murder with your own ceremonial weapon. Not a great way to end a vacation at home, eh?"

Nimon elected to ignore his plant manager's meager effort at wit and continued. "The use of the plant's computer seemed the logical approach to learning about the K'Tar and their motive for implicating me in the attempted murder of my Dual. I regret that the Vice-Consul and his people were so diligent in their efforts to capture me. To my dismay, I severely depreciated a Geminian lander to get here. It was most beneficial that my piloting skills were slightly better than the aim of the guard's pulsar cannon. Unfortunately, my abilities to scramble their tracking devices weren't."

"He is diligent to say the least," Descartes thought, as usual finding little comfort in his second-in-command's unique ability for understatement. "Well, Nimon, you have less than an hour to find out what you can from the research computer before I have to face your 'diligent' Vice-Consul of Enforcement."

"Or I could just review memory doubloons on circumventing Geminian land based orbital disruption techniques," quipped Nimon, with his own modest attempt at humor.

"You'll have plenty of time to read in solitary confinement if you don't come up with a way out of this, Mr. Edison," Descartes added, ending the conversation before he resorted to one of Mr. Brown's more colorful comments about Geminian witticism.

Seeing that both his time and wit were running short, Nimon left for his own office to begin his work.

*   *   *

As the operation control panel's digital timer - which Mack Weber had instinctively set at the conclusion of the Vice-Consul's communique - clicked over to the 45 minute mark, the control room doors irised apart to reveal Nimon. He smoothly stepped out of the omnivator and across the room to where his plant manager waited.

"Your findings, Mr. Edison?" Descartes asked, cocking his head in the direction of his technical superintendent.

"Most intriguing, sir. It seems that Gemini culture has been extremely thorough in its desire to maintain the K'Tar cult's anonymity. However, one name did occur with regularity in regards to his expertise on Gemini history - that of Helicon of Clio. Records last report his location as being ...

"Assigned to the life crystal plant Darwin," Descartes interjected, with a trace of smug satisfaction in trumping Nimon's hand at investigative research.

"I see no reason for your finding pleasure in already knowing what has taken lengthy computer time for me to discover, Morgan," Nimon stated calmly, but with the slightest trace of indignation.

"Couldn't find a good orbital disruption tech doubloon, eh, Nimon?" Descartes thought, roguishly, exercising the better part of discretion in deciding not to make his response aloud. Instead, he answered, "I'll summon him to the control center immediately, Mr. Edison."

"This is Descartes," piped the desk intercom, shaking Mr. Brown out of the studious trance in which he had fallen. He had been pouring over the sociological memory doubloons salvaged from the ruins of the Castorian planet for hours, and was in no mood for interruptions.

"Now what is it?!" he mumbled under his breath. He impatiently switched off the viewer and rose to respond to the call, stopping in the middle of what his Geminian friend would call "a fascinating thesis" on emotional psionics.

"Brown here," he snapped.

"J.B., smooth down your bristles and bring Helicon to the control room, on the double," Descartes said. "We've got a situation over here."

Brown was quick to recognize when his Plant Manager meant business, and when he could be diplomatically delayed. This instance was definitely not the time for diplomacy. Since Helicon had been laboring over the archaeological relics a few doors around the hall in the technical lab, it was a simple matter to pick him up on the way to the control room.

Once they arrived, Descartes eyed the Clionian with reserved mistrust as he finished summarizing the situation.

"Gentlemen, I have less than ten minutes before a determined Gemini Vice-Consul of Enforcement appears on the screen demanding the surrender of my second-in-command. Any suggestions?"

"If I may make a sssuggesstion, Mr. Descartes?" Helicon said lowly, suppressing his native tongue's accent.

"Yes, Helicon?" Descartes responded flatly.

"I believe that I may be of help in Mr. Nimon'sss defensse. But I musst first confer with him privately. Mr. Nimon hass indicated a sstate of ssocial dissruption on Gemini due to the K'Tar. This sshould be sssufficient reasson for you to exercisse your Solar Corporation executive authority. It would also provide the delay I need for my disscusssion with your sssuperintendent."

A flash of acknowledgment crossed Descartes's face, before he turned to Nimon with a look of disdain, "I've put up with your unorthodox behavior in the past, Nimon. I see no reason to change now. Opinion?"

"It is technically efficient to utilize the resources of most value. In this case, that would be Helicon."

"Very well then," Descartes concluded, slightly miffed, "have your clandestine conference while I stall our good friend, Stalak."

As the Geminian and Clionian moved over to the control room's technical station, Mr. Brown sidled up alongside the Plant Manager's central station.

"And just what is this 'Solar Corporation Executive Authority' he was talking about, Morgan?" he inquired dubiously.

"I was wondering when I'd hear from you again, J.B.," Descartes needled. "It seems your Clionian friend is up on his Solar Corporation contractual agreements. A little used clause of the joint venture between the Solar Corporation and the Gemini subsidiary states that in times of social disruption on a corporate held planet of equal or greater development than our own, the ranking Solarian officer may impose his Executive Power in order to protect the corporate assets, while acting as mediator between the two social factions."

"That sounds like a bunch of malarkey - not to mention plain old interfering!" Brown retorted, his Martian drawl becoming more noticeable amidst his flaring temper.

"Why do you think it's a 'little used clause' in the first place?" Descartes interjected. "However, it is legally binding. And you and I both know how compelled the Geminians are when it comes to following business law. If anything, it will buy us some time until we come up with a better solution."

As if on cue, Saffron 3 announced, "Communication coming in on the holovid, Mr. Descartes."

"Ah, Stalak…" Descartes greeted, beaming his most diplomatic smile at the main viewing pad, situated on the floor below the operation control screens, while thinking in the back of his mind, "prompt as the proverbial Geminian at a business luncheon."

"Mr. Descartes, your allotted time for data assimilation regarding the heinous crime committed by your technical superintendent has expired. Prepare to return Nimon Edison to

Gemini," Stalak said, matter-of-factly, with little expectation of the plant manager's upcoming response.

Descartes countered, "Stalak, must I remind you that Mr. Edison is merely a suspect in the crime you are currently investigating, and is deserving of a fair and proper review?"

"Mr. Descartes, I see that you are unfamiliar with Gemini custom and ritual. Without appearing to be justifying our demands to an outworlder, I will explain."

Descartes frowned, as every muscle in his body tensed. The last interchange with Stalak hit hard. Normally, he would not have to remind a Geminian of corporate law regarding "innocence until proven guilty." But more incredibly, he had heard the term "outworlder". Its casual use was totally inappropriate for a Geminian exposed to interplanetary space travelers on a regular basis. Descartes could expect a comment such as that from one of Gemini's Elders, but not from Stalak.

"Perhaps the 'social unrest' Helicon mentioned was not to be taken as lightly as I presumed," Descartes thought.

Stalak continued, "Murder has been extinct from our culture for generations. Our disciplines have successfully expunged such hideous behavior from our society. The only logical explanation for a recurrence is that an outside agent has contaminated the very fabric of our sociocultural structure. We must resort to the R'llk Tal- the savage ways - to counter this agent."

"I don't like the direction this conversation is heading," Descartes muttered, "so I'm going to change it right now!"

"Stalak!" he commanded, shattering the logical progression the Vice-Consul was following. "This is not ancient Gemini! Mr. Edison is an employee of the Solar Corporation and is presently under its full jurisdiction. By placing himself in corporate custody as he has done, he has the right to a fair hearing!"

Having gotten Stalak's attention, Descartes continued, in a slightly more subdued tone. "Furthermore, I am convinced from our present discussion and prior reports that an unnatural influence is at work within your society - an influence so subversive that you yourself are unaware of its effects. As a result, by the power vested in me as a life crystal plant manager and a full ranking corporate officer, I exercise the authority to place Gemini under corporate control as denoted in directive 1, subsection 708, subparagraph L."

If a Geminian during negotiations could "splutter" outside the influence of a psychotic drug, Stalak would have! Instead, his face took on an expression as blank as the intergalactic void between the Milky Way and Andromeda.

Feeling victorious, Descartes relaxed his shoulders and sat back in his chair - the glisten in his clear, green eyes the only evidence of his satisfaction.

CHAPTER 10

A guillotine of icy control descended across Stalak's countenance as he responded with business-like efficiency.

"A few moments, sir..." the Vice-Consul mumbled, with Descartes mentally finishing Stalak's request, "while we confirm this little known contractual clause... right Stalak?"

No longer focused on his verbal sparring with Stalak, Descartes swiveled in his chair and directed his attention to the conclusion of the discussion between Nimon and Helicon.

"... very good, Helicon. I commend you on your astute abilities in Gemini customs and ritual law. The probability of success is 93.2% - well within any requirements for finding the true criminal."

"Yes, enlighten me, Mr. Edison, on just how you do intend to capture this criminal."

But it was Helicon who spoke, much to the irritation of Descartes, as the Darwin's technical superintendent assumed a curiously muted demeanor in the background.

"Mr. Descartes, if I may explain. The practisse of R'llk Tal which Sstalak referenced deals with the complete excising from ssociety any bloodline whose member exhibitss clear actions regarded as criminally inssane. Murder ssuch as the one being investigated is definitely ssuch an action. According to pre-Mitronian Gemini law, no trial is required if the Council of Elderss is ssuficiently convinced that the ssuspect is guilty."

"Now hold on just one cotton-pickin' minute!" burst in Jeff Brown, resorting to one of his Southern ancestors' expressions to gain control of the floor.

"You're talkin' democide – the government killing innocent people because a relative is suspected of committing murder! What happened to Geminian love for the preservation of life, for nebula's sakes?"

"I undersstand your shock, Mr. Brown. However, you musst remember, R'llk Tal existed long before Mitron, during a time when the Geminian race was comprised of a ssavage and ssomewhat ruthlesss people. It was Mitron himself, through his revolutionary teachingss of peace and preservation of life, who ssucceeded in abolishing ssuch laws on Gemini."

"Morgan, we can't let some red-eyed schizophrenic take one of our crew and assassinate him and his family! ...No offense Nimon," Brown added, referring to his colorful and derogatory description of Geminian features and biodgen skills.

A slight smirk was Nimon's only reply, as if saying, "I'm accustomed to such remarks from you, Mr. Brown."

"I take it you're leading up to something, Helicon," Descartes responded, giving Jefferson Brown a skeptical "let's hear him out" look.

Brown complied, forcefully crossing his chest with his arms and donning his most dubious frown, while letting Helicon continue.

"I admit that the ploy of imposssing Executive Authority is jussstified by ssound Sssolar Corporation legal precedence. However, it was jusst that - a ploy to provide a delay. If pushed to the limit, Gemini determination ..."

"You mean Geminan stubbornness, don't you?!" Brown interjected.

Descartes shot him a stern glance, as Brown held up his hands signaling, "O.K. Morgan, I'll back off ... for now."

As Helicon went on, "... might resort in a dissolution of the joint venture with the Sssolar Corporation just to enable them to circumvent their contractual require-mentsss."

"So what do you propose, Helicon?" the plant manager asked tautly, the anxiety in his voice showing his impatience for some sort of strategy to resolve the situation.

"I would advise a compromise, Mr. Descartes. Ssuggesst to Sstalak that you feel it is imperative to maintain the ssanctity of Mitron in dealing with this matter. By invoking Cree' DiTal, Mitron'sss logical alternative to the harsher genetic excision, you will be honoring the customs and mores of Gemini. You must add one sstipulation,

174

however; and in it liess the compromise. Sstalak must convince the Council of Elderss to allow for witness by outworlders and Vkks T'Ruul, the Voice of Reason."

Descartes twisted up the corner of his mouth as he looked quizzically from Helicon to Nimon, "Just what are these compromises and conditions Helicon is citing, Nimon - and be brief. Stalak should be reestablishing communications any minute now."

But again, Helicon spoke in Nimon's behalf.

"Cree' DiTal provides for the ssupect'ss right to sstand before the Council to argue his case. However, the Council has hisstorically taken a dim view of having their authority questioned by a criminal on trial. The Voice of Reason stipulatess that a ssuspect may have a 'chosen one' speak for him."

It was now Brown's turn to inquire, "Just how dim a view does the Council take of this Vkks T' whatever, even with a spokesperson for the defendant?"

No record of an acquittal has ever been found," Helicon responded flatly.

"Great... just great," Brown muttered. "And when the accused is found guilty, then what?"

"It took Mitron many decadess to ssoften the ssentence to its present sstate," hissed the Clionian softly.

"Which is?" Descartes urged impatiently.

"Sssexual sssterilization and banishment from Gemini forever," came the reply, its harshness sounding more sinister when spoken with a serpentine hiss.

"You've been awfully quiet about this Nimon, for a man doomed to be stripped of his heritage and progeny in one fell swoop. What have you got to say for yourself?" the plant's sociologist prodded.

But the only response Brown got was what he called "that blank, cow-faced stare" - which gnawed at him to no end.

"I failed to mention to you a key point in Nimon'ss defense, gentlemen," Helicon said. "It iss likened to your Old Earth legality of "taking the fifth", but more extensive. You

ssee, Nimon has adopted the Ssai Shwan, or Code of Discretion. By refusing to sspeak, he is declaring that the Council's position is unworthy of conssideration. His Vkks T'Ruul will sspeak for him."

"You mean to say Nimon has to remain silent to have any chance of beating this rap?" Brown interjected.

"In a manner of sspeaking, yess," responded the Clionian.

"Well thank goodness for some small favors," Brown quipped, unable to miss an opportunity to take a shot at his long-time verbal sparring partner.

And a voice within his head seemed to say "How characteristic of your personnel skills, Mr. Brown, to give a performance appraisal to an employee without a voice."

*   *   *

Thick blankets of acrid, sulphurous mist wrapped the legs of the four-member party as they stepped from the lander. The waning Gemini sun fought desperately to pierce the netherworld fog. Yet, it could only muster an ominous crimson fluorescence on this rare example of Gemini surface moisture.

As if in response to the curious glances from the Solarians, Helicon explained, "Legend sstates the mist's ssource, the underground river, D'Kor, mingled with the planet's fiery mantel ages ago and formed the life essence of the first Geminian man and woman. As the essence forced its way through ssubterranean crevices of the planet's basalt crust, the unusual mineral components of the race's chemical physiology were absorbed. It was this fire and water birth that some of the Elders felt had been the ssource of the Gemini philosophy of Phoenos - dual entities... separate...different - but connected through life energy."

As if a reflection of that Dualiity of life energy, the fourth member of the surface team, a Gemini-Terran hybrid, nodded solemnly.

Plant Manager Descartes had been successful in his appeal to Stalak to honor Mitron's concept of justice. Permission had been granted for Jefferson Brown and himself to attend the Council tribunal, with Helicon acting as Nimon's counsel. Yet the uneasy feeling that churned in the pit of Descartes's stomach was a foreboding of the helplessness of the situation. He could not shake the shadowy memories of the last time he had attended a Geminian negotiation.

He had been on special assignment ... a young aide to the strategic planners of the Earth Exploratory Cartel. Their task was to forge the venture between the Cartel and the Gemini System. The negotiations were shrouded in ancient mystery and rites. But after months of cooperative talks, the two cultures of Earth and Gemini had reached a successful agreement. However, Descartes doubted that the ceremony he was about to attend would prove to be as favorable in its outcome.

To force this pessimism from his mind, Descartes slowly looked around to take in the rugged beauty of the rocky cliffs. But an aura of harshness confronted him, almost as if it were surrounding the surface team. Sheer stone faces of cooled magma from the planet's core lanced their way through Gemini's crust to form the narrow valley in which they stood. Each outcropping stood as a giant stone sentinel, staring down at them in silent disapproval. He could not shake the feeling that they were the first beings in centuries to set foot in this valley - without a doubt, they were the first outworlders to ever disturb the sanctity of this place - and they were not welcome.

As the oppressive effects of their surroundings gripped them, the team cautiously moved out away from the spot where their lander had set down. Nimon, located at the lead point of the assembly, had remained passively motionless while the others stirred restlessly.

Suddenly he raised his hand, his arm at an angle above his head with palm facing the other party members, signaling them to remain motionless and quiet. After several tense moments, Descartes heard what the Geminian's "sixth mental sense" had perceived earlier. A strange rasping sound rhythmically pulsed its way through the torrid, thin air to reach the group. Interspersed with the sound - which Brown likened to a Denebian bull toad during mating season - was the faint whisper of a flute. The dissimilar mixture of sounds added an eerie foreboding to the already macabre surroundings.

Minutes passed. The sound grew in volume as the intensity of the team's anxiety increased with it. Then the source of the dirge appeared at the narrow valley entrance. A trio of darkly clad figures, black hoods masking their features, materialized from the mists. Ominously, they made their way toward the Darwin's group.

The leader was diminutive in relation to the hulking beings behind him. Slung over his shoulder was a gourd-like instrument with strips of leathery husks stretched taut in different lengths across the hollow portion of the gourd. He drew a palm-sized block of waxy material across the strips to create the rasping sound. The haunting background wind song of the flutes emanated from delicately patterned metallic tubes, most likely forged from the white-hot volcanic kilns for which the planet was most famous. Their beauty was a statement of ironic contrast, as they were cradled gently in the massive hands of the deadly-looking guards accompanying the leader.

Suspended from braided mercurial strands at the hips of the guards were blades of a most lethal design. Descartes, having gained an appreciation of swords from the Darwin's operation's superintendent, Mack Weber, was amazed at the craftsmanship of the scythes. Each weapon's length easily matched the three tred frame of its bearer. All along the fifty centipalm width of the blade was a finely etched pictorial of ancient Gemini battles. The blade formed a gentle curving 'S' with the middle comprising a two-handed grip. The only portion of the weapon which was not a cutting edge was the center handle of the 'S'. Attached to it was a metal eyelet from which a coppery family crest hung.

Helicon murmured in his characteristic dialect, "I ssee the Elderss are prepared to enforce Nimon'ss Ssai Sschwan."

Descartes reflexively shuddered at the sound of Helicon's voice, still trying to subdue his inexplicable dislike for the Clionian, and inquired, "What do you mean by that, Helicon?"

"Those sscythess the guards are carrying are more than just decoration," Helicon replied, eyeing the gentle serpentine curve of the weapons, as the waning sun flickered scarlet rays on the surface of the polished blades. "Ritual providess that these sscythess are to be used to extinguish the first ssound from the mouth of the defendant," the Clionian continued. "Geminian's during the Ancient Timesss did not take their ritualsss lightly."

"And neither will we," Brown interjected, gaining a healthy respect for the Geminian legal system.

As the cloaked trio halted their procession, the leader voicelessly indicated for the Darwin's group to form a single line between the guards, with Nimon positioned at the end, just in front of the rear sentry. The smaller Geminian took his place at the lead and once again started his ominous symphony of rasping sounds. Making their way back along the narrow path between the cliffs, they soon reached a small stone stairway clinging precariously to a sheer rock face towering before them.

The thin Geminian atmosphere taunted the aliens with its precious oxygen. Climbing the steps strained muscles and will. The intense heat baked the moisture from their bodies. Seeking the slightest hint of encouragement, Descartes peeked over the edge of the stairway. The reward for his efforts was tainted with uneasiness. Some sixty treds below, the last vestiges of the subterranean mists blanketed the valley floor. He knew it was an additional ten treds through the cottony layer before he would hit solid ground. A stab of disgust heightened his uneasiness as he watched the Clionian just ahead of him. The reptiloid had succumbed to his years and resorted to climbing the stairs on all fours. Brown was not much better as he fumbled through his travel kit for another oxygen lozenge. He had asked Descartes about his prior experience on Gemini and had taken a few precautions. One had been to stock an abundant supply of the oxygen-enriched medication.

An eternity later, the entourage made a sharp turn in its trek up the precipice. A small cave opening yawned sheepishly before them, showing only a hint of civilization from the lights dancing on the walls within. With a grateful sigh, the weary surface team concluded that this must be their destination.

Stepping across the cave's threshold, Descartes' neck tingled as if he had passed through a time-fold distortion. Relics of ancient Gemini surrounded him. Time's fabric had suddenly changed texture and wrapped him in an age where savage strength was the ruling law, and Death was its marshal.

High walls of polished red marble rose upward to meld with the naturally craggy ceiling above them. The room itself was not spacious, but instead, was just slightly larger than the control room of the Darwin. Along the left side of the room, banners of family crests hung on poles of gleaming silver. To the right were huge chalices filled with glowing embers. Some contained flames, struggling to capture the scarce oxygen they required for life, before they, too, died into glowing embers like their brethren. These chalices had created the shadowy dance on the walls of the cave's entrance, and, except for a scattered few torches, were the room's sole source of light.

But the room's most noticeable feature was the floor, for it contained the most exquisite hand-painted rendition of the Gemini Phoenos Descartes had ever seen. Two circles, side by side, overlapped as would a Venn diagram, creating a vertical cat's iris in the middle. Bridging the two circles horizontally was a Mobius strip figure-eight. The intersection of the loops of the figure-eight rested at the center of the vertical slice of the overlapping circles. Numerous theses had been written explaining the meaning of the symbol and its component parts. The most basic described the two circles overlapping to form a unique center as reflecting Dualiity – the concept of two beings from one source. The Mobius strip, as it is known on Earth, depicted the symbol of Infinity, while also conveying that two distinct sides of a surface could be eternally connected as one. Yet, Descartes was less enthralled by the interwoven philosophical messages within the symbol than he was with the composition of the mural. Drawing from the ancient arts of metallurgy and the planet's natural elements, a myriad of colors were delicately blended with finely powdered tresium, causing a shimmering effect that made the symbol appear almost liquid.

Breaking his gaze from the hypnotic pattern, Descartes directed his attention to more pressing matters. Forming a crescent on the far side of the circular emblem was a massive wooden bench, behind which sat six aged Geminian men and women. Dividing the six into halves, and on a level above and behind them sat a wizened, elderly woman with whom Descartes had become all too familiar - Kronia!

"So it was Kronia who led the Council of Elders," murmured Descartes. His eyes widened with surprise, and possibly a hint of fear.

Decades ago, it had been Kronia who had presided over the joint venture negotiations during which Earth and Gemini had formed their business relationship. Descartes had played a part in convincing the Earth negotiators to stand their ground on demands to share in biodgen technology. Kronia had learned of this fact and made her displeasure clear. During a closed session attended only by Geminians, rumor had it that she swore to "exterminate the meddling Earth mosquito". Descartes had taken it as a figure of speech.

Yet, now, he found himself once more within Kronia's arena, and it disturbed him. He could only speculate why he had been allowed to attend the ceremony as he watched the procession disperse into their assigned positions. One guard remained at the entranceway, with the other standing to the right of the Council. The smallest of the three stationed himself at the opposite end of the bench, while all the landing party except Nimon seated themselves behind a smaller wooden table facing the Elders.

It was Nimon's dubious honor to sit in the center of the Phoenos facing the Council. Cross-legged with arms resting lightly on his knees, his face a passive reflection of the older Geminians before him, Nimon appeared as if he were awaiting the telling of a campfire story, rather than attending his own trial for murder.

With a light tap on each of three tubular metal chimes by the smaller Geminian, another larger Geminian entered the chamber from a doorway behind the bench.

"All those oxygen lozenges must be making me delirious," exclaimed Brown, pinching up the bridge of his nose with surprise. "Is that who I think it is, Morgan?"

Descartes eyed the new participant. His face was more mature, his former hardened body slightly softer due to the usual reasons, but Brown was correct. It was Steth, the General Manager of the Gemini Division

"Why would he be involved in this?" Brown continued, not giving his Plant Manager a chance to answer the first question.

Instead, Kronia answered it for him.

"For ze prosecution, Steth of Var-Ral. I understand zat ze accused has requested ze Voice of Reason. Who speaks for ze accused?"

Helicon rose and in perfect Geminian dialect responded, "I, Helicon of Clio, am Nimon's Vkks T'Ruul, and by ancient custom, will speak first and only once."

"Outvorlder!! You blaspheme this ceremony and will pay!!"

Descartes recoiled from the outburst. His first thought was that it had come from Kronia, but she sat stone-faced and motionless.

Brown recovered quickly with a sarcastic retort, "So the little guy does have a voice... and a temper!"

CHAPTER 11

The hooded escort who had led the procession, his shout still echoing within the chamber, signaled the guard near the bench. Stepping forward, hands gripping his deadly scythe, the guard loomed toward Helicon.

Only a few saw it, Descartes being one. And he was not sure. The Clionian's face seemed to transform. Leathery lips pulled back. Razor teeth glinted in the firelight of the chalices. And the eyes ... the eyes glowed with evil savagery. A cold fear swept over Descartes, even though he was not the target of the terrible stare.

The guard froze in mid-step. The hood masked the pale, ice blue shock that swept over his face. His sole thought was that he was looking into the face of his doom.

"Veer Knulk!" came a bark from one of the council members to the left of Kronia. Thankfully, the sound shook the guard from his hypnotic paralysis before he dropped his scythe and irreparably disgraced himself.

And the fearsome visage of the Clionian vanished.

"I know of Helicon, and vouch for heem," spoke the council member, with grave solemnity.

The hooded escort looked toward the councilman, almost imperceptibly pausing to weigh the gravity of challenging the dignitary, and then bowed reverently. At his signal, the guard rigidly moved back to his station, the fluidity of his movements now gone as the biochemical effects of fear refused to dissipate.

Descartes looked at Brown, his eyebrows arched and mouth in a small pucker, as he nodded a sign of respect for Helicon to his personnel manager. Brown winked an "I told you so" in response.

Kronia turned her head slightly from her fellow councilman and in the direction of Helicon. Curtly she spat, "Very vell, Helicon of Clio ... begin."

The elderly Clionian shuffled to the center of the forum, head slightly bowed in reverence to the Council of Elders, and stood beside Nimon. No trace of the earlier ferocity could be seen. Looking up at Kronia, then slowly, deliberately, peering into the eyes of each of the Elders, he began his soliloquy. Gone was the tell-tale hiss of a tongue foreign to the language he spoke, as if in homage to the solemnity of the occasion.

"Wise beings of Gemini, you see standing before you an alien to your race; one whose ancestors crawled savagely on all fours, devouring every living being that crossed their paths. I would not presume to tell you what is correct for the future of your race. I am not a prognosticator, nor am I an interplanetary legal counsel. Simply put, I am merely an historian. But by being an historian I think I can present some pertinent facts that will be useful for your deliberation.

As you are surely aware, my ancestors shed their violent ways by committing their energies to the study of the historical sciences. Through this unyielding pursuit of a particular path of knowledge, they were able to put aside their barbaric ways. But this path of knowledge was not easily followed. As is the case in many cultures, one individual becomes a leader of his people -a Messiah, a Mitron. It is this individual that acts as a teacher of his peers so that the right path may be followed. Such was the case with my own civilization. The teachings were not widely accepted at first. In many civilizations, painful, tragic consequences can be the outcome of the conflict of new and old ideas. Fatefully for our race, the proponents for the new ideas were victorious. It is a wiser race, though, that can adopt new concepts without conflict, thereby learning from both sides. But let me not dwell on the history of my people, for that is not the issue here. Instead, let me review for you the history of the planet Gemini."

"Hold Clionian! We are not assembled here for a history lesson!" interjected Steth, the prosecutor.

"Groka!" exclaimed Kronia, signaling the guard to her left to step forward with blade at the ready. "I vill not remind thee again of ze Defense's right to uninterrupted speech!"

Steth bowed respectfully to Kronia's word - and to the scythe - allowing Helicon to continue.

Helicon paused, gathering his thoughts, and possibly reveling in his minor victory, before he began again.

"It is common knowledge to even the amateur historian that Gemini was ruled by seven tribes prior to Mitron. Mitron's teachings of peace united the tribes and put an end to the savage wars that ravaged the planet. Worshipping life became the prime instrument for cultural growth, and the means by which Gemini has attained its prominence in the galaxy today. But, what is spoken only in whispered legend, are the events surrounding the demise of the opponents of Mitron."

Helicon slowly paced the length of the Council bench, systematically addressing each of the members as he delivered his last statement. What had been faces of stone softened imperceptibly, as if sensing the significance of the point that was about to be conveyed. They now began to stir ever so slightly.

The Clionian drew out the pause, letting the silence crescendo, then started once more.

"Extensive research has revealed the true history of the anti-Mitronians, and what eventually became of them. Thanks to the efforts of your own Solar Corporation Executive, Novas, the accused's mother, an accord was struck between the Solar Corporation and the Castorian Conglomerate. That accord gave rise to an historical study. A team headed by myself has linked a previously unexplored planetoid in the Castor system with the past of both the planets Gemini and Castor."

Walking over to the desk where Descartes and Brown sat, the Clionian opened a small, soft-sided pouch that he had brought from the Darwin.

"I have holovid-doubloons chronicling an odyssey of a nomadic band of over six thousand outcasts. They were discovered in the ruins of the Castor system planetoid. I have condensed them into a brief synopsis of their journey. It is of prime importance to Nimon's defense, and to the future of your race that you view these, Kronia."

Kronia solemnly nodded her approval, overriding any objection Steth might have.

The portable vid-projector of Helicon glowed to life, as the first holograph recording materialized in the center of the chamber.

A tall, gaunt male appeared, clearly Geminian to those with a trained eye at distinguishing the subtle variations between Geminian and Castorian physiologies. He was clad in ancient battle garb - a leather vest studded with black lactonite crystals, a brief loin covering of similar material, thick leggings, with straps of mercurial metal bands as lacings. A short-arm tri-bladed dagger hung at his side, its crystal encrusted hilt suspended by a multi-colored belt embroidered with flame-eagle down and sand-serpent skins. His drawn features were those of a leader grief-ridden for his people. His stance was one of a noble who refused to admit defeat.

"Ravar here," he began tiredly, mentally questioning the value of his inexplicable need to document their journey.

"Our numbers have fallen by an additional two hundred. At first, we felt the disease was necessary, almost welcome, to strengthen our people through survival of the fittest. But now we know the affliction is not one of nature. Confinement of six thousand warriors in three nucleon-powered arks has brought on this plague. In the beginning of the voyage, we satisfied our thirst for combat through sport. But it overcame us. Violence became the unwritten law. What few things we had among us became the fuel for conflict. The strong took what they wanted. Many died ... too many. By my own hand, I maintained control by crushing the leader of the renegades that used crime as their banner. Once we subdued the combative spirit, the casualties from in-fighting over property dropped drastically. But now a depression has set in... and with it, the plague. Seven full seasons without realty beneath our feet has led to apathy.

Though unthinkable for a Gemini warrior, I think many have died from hopelessness.

My two sub-chieftans and I believe we have found a temporary remedy to stay any further spread of depression. We have decided that our warriors need a cause ... a reason to go on living. That cause which drives us onward is to return to our shattered world, for it must have suffered greatly from the meteor swarm I prophesied. They believe that the leadership of Mitron has failed the brethren we left behind. Even I struggle to remember my once close ally with anything other than bitterness. The blood of the many runs through the fingers of Mitron. His pacifist teachings have resulted in the death of our culture. Had he joined us in our beliefs, we would not now be so close to extinction. We will preach to our people the need to survive - the need to cultivate a burning hatred for all docile sheep ... like Mitron. By surviving, we can someday return to our home world. We can reunite with the scattered few we have left behind, and once again rule our world with the strength of battle and material wealth. I fear it is the only way."

At this point Helicon stopped the display. The embittered ghost of Gemini's past faded into the netherworld of the Elders' thoughts.

The Clionian spoke, "I submit to you the seed, venerable people of Gemini. The seed which germinated in the darkness of space -- within the cold walls of the banished Arks. And I quote to you from the Seventh Teaching Of Mitron `. . . and vessels three were hurled into space, forever ridding our people of violence, hatred, and power lust, as each of us must do within our minds, by stripping our souls of these desires, leaving pure love of life as the bearer of Peace.'" Helicon continued, "The thread linking Gemini to the Castor system planetoid has been established. One key reference should be noted. Ravar mentioned 'the scattered few we have left behind.' I contend that Mitron's purge of the warriors of his time was incomplete. Along with his followers who survived the cataclysmic shower of meteorites that transformed a lush planet into the desert giant it has become, isolated groups of 'Ravarians' might still exist within Gemini society - even today!"

Open conference between several of the members broke out. The Council of Elders was clearly moved by this last proclamation.

Several moments passed. Kronia allowed the unrest to die on its own and said, "Thee has strange concepts Clionian. More proof must be presented before a logical conclusion can be drawn. Do you have such proof?"

"Indeed I have, Kronia," came Helicon's reply.

A second doubloon was slipped into the projector. Again Ravar appeared before the audience born centuries after his death. But his projection was of a spirit reborn. The lines of worry were replaced with hints of hope. Scarlet eyes glinted with the knowledge that their journey was near its end.

"It is now four decions into the tenth season. Information transmitted from our third drone-probe has definitely confirmed the existence of a nearby planetoid. The atmosphere of this lone refuge orbiting within our very own star system appears harsh, but habitable. Our arks should reach orbit before the passing of the remaining six decions of this season.

Our people are rejoicing. It has been too long since we were imprisoned in these interplanetary crypts. We will soon have a world in which we can build; a resting place to regain our strength for the retribution we have sworn to deliver to the Mitronians."

The display momentarily scrambled at a splice point, and then resumed. However, Ravar's image was replaced by a younger man. Leather battle dress had been exchanged for a light, airy cloth shirt draping to mid-thigh. The only similarity with Ravar's holograph was the decorative embroidered belt holding the tri-bladed short sword, the crystal in the hilt still flashing its fire.

The image spoke. "In honor of Chieftan Ravar's dying request, I, Stev, am continuing his chronicles of our journey. The ion storm which engulfed our arks during the final orbital approach has taken its toll. All three vessels were heavily damaged, with radiation poisoning affecting all of us to various degrees. Ravar, himself, was one of the many fatalities.

Our healers have nothing but grim news. They expect that many of those who survive will be sterile, with those who aren't, doomed to live in fear of the radiation effects on their offspring. As new chieftan, I now know the grief that tore at the very soul of Ravar, as he was forced to watch his people suffer... and all due to the spineless, peace loving Mitron. If the hatred for the Mitronians was a smoldering ember before, it is now a white-hot coal never to be extinguished!

The gods still have decided to delay our vengeance on Mitron. Our starwatchers tell me that the devastating storm during our arrival is of a cyclical nature. Their best calculations give us four seasons to prepare for the next one. After much deliberation, I have decided that for our people to remain bound to this forsaken world through repeated sieges by the cosmos would be an injustice. Rather than shield ourselves, or seek protection underground as would vermin, we will rebuild two of the damaged arks from the remains of the third. The sixth and last drone-probe sent out before engaging the storm has been faithful in its transmissions. The most recent data has confirmed a planet twenty seasons journey from here. As the stargazers of old predicted, we believe this oasis, orbiting our own star, but in a cycle always hidden from our homeworld, gives us our best hope for survival. It will be a difficult journey, but our warrior spirit will strengthen us. So that one day, we may return home to our rightful heritage, and deliver retribution upon the Mitronians."

Helicon terminated the display and inserted one last doubloon.

"Here is a star chart that is found in later records," the Clionian whispered, solemnly.

Above the heads of the assemblage, a virtual planetarium appeared in three-dimensional splendor. The twelve planets of what was immediately recognized by Descartes as the Castor-Gemini stellar system revolved slowly about the red giant sun. The twin planets circling the star majestically exchanged places as they spun in a tight pattern along an invisible axis between them.

Forming a golden arc from Gemini to the planetoid to the Castorian homeworld was the flight trajectory of the ancient Geminian space arks.

Helicon allowed the meaning of the chart to fully register before he shut off the projector. Shuffling back to the center of the room next to Nimon, he looked directly at Kronia.

"The evidence is clear. By purging the Ravarians from Gemini, a greater evil was spawned. I need not recount the savagery of Castorian history. It is common knowledge. When the opposition to Mitronian ways was cast out of your society, the seed of the Castorian

Conglomerate was planted. A seed whose dormant spores of discontent remained on Gemini to finally spring to life within your own culture.

Consider recent events prior to Nimon's return to his home planet. These 'societal disturbances' which have been given minimal exposure in the media are not isolated events. I believe they are organized. Forces behind the disturbances are remnants of what you heard on the doubloons. What were once Ravarians, are now manifesting themselves in two forms. The K'Tar on Gemini and the very Castorian Conglomerate itself. As illogical as you may consider it, the woman known as T'Poch has designed an insidious plan to incriminate the defendant in the 'murder' of his own Dual. The final proof is the life energy transmissions she has directed at Nimon - transmissions that interfered with Nimon's attempt to revitalize the biodgen you claim he murdered.

I now appeal to you to learn from your history. Do not rigidly ignore new concepts. Hear the 'materialistic' views for utilizing biodrones presented to you by Nimon. Do not ignore them. Try to at least understand them. From this understanding may spawn a solution to resolving your social crisis. Take one small step to grow. Realize that Nimon is not your enemy ... and he is NOT the criminal that you seek. It is vital for you to free Nimon so that the true perpetrator of the crimes may be revealed. Let him go free to find T'Poch, the leader of the K'Tar. Once found, the K'Tar will be weakened, and it is THEY who are the true threat. For your sake and the sake of your future, the K'Tar's intense hatred for your culture must be overcome!"

"The Voice of Reason now rests."

CHAPTER 12

Novas was again in the rear of the graviton sled as it caromed across the uneven landscape. A strange familiarity with the vehicle returned to her with the icy coldness of a memory long suppressed. The situation was much like the first ride in the vehicle when Ravar and Del were taking her to Centar. Ravar was seated as pilot while Del sat in the front passenger cockpit. His profile was eerily familiar, but not because of the earlier trip. The angle of his firm chin accentuated the aura of nobility that surrounded him. Novas had witnessed this kind of omnipotent presence before.... but she could not recall where!

Turning to her right, her eyes met a stare of liquid fire! P'Teel sat at the opposite end of the lounge compartment in the rear of the sled. The sensation of dreaded familiarity again swept over Novas. She envisioned P'Teel as being much older... and even more sinister. In this memory fragment, the older woman peered at her covetously. Yet, her gaze was not directed at Novas, but at the bundle she held. Novas, out of reflex, raised her arms to her chest. She pulled her legs up under her tightly as she lay curled in the comfort of the cushions. Her eyes were moist with the sorrow of what she was about to do.

Looking down, she softly cradled her delicate, new creation.

The voice of the young woman beside her shook Novas from her solemn reverie.

"You look as if you have suffered a tragic loss. Instead, you should be grateful for being part of a wondrous discovery," P'Teel hissed. She was clearly resentful of Del's decision. He had agreed to allow Novas' participation in the investigation of the meteorite crash-site. "You are fortunate that the lummox Ravar had insisted upon your being here," she added, in a hushed, acidic whisper.

Novas fought to regain her senses. Her disorientation only added to P'Teel's frustration.

"You will stay out of my way strange one. I have positioned my clan to be among the first to learn the powers of the celestial fires. Your sudden appearance at Del's table will not keep me from that goal," she growled coarsely.

The painful memory dissolved from Novas' mind as swiftly as it had formed. She was convinced that the Legotian control of her thoughts was responsible for it. To her dismay, she believed that the psychic influence was growing stronger. Unable to defend against it, she found the events around her more and more life-like.

Her insatiable curiosity for discovering the secrets of space had compelled her to accompany them to the crash site, despite telling herself it was just another fictitious fabrication of the Legotian. To succumb to it would only mean further defeat at his devious hand. "What forbidden knowledge has he already gained from me?" she queried to herself. She could not guess. "Will I reveal even more secrets by following this macabre scenario to its completion?" Probably so. Yet, she could not resist. She had relented to her desires.

"It has been a long time since I placed my own wishes above the corporation's," she thought. "Why am I not ashamed at how good it feels? At this moment the corporation seems to be part of another life - a life that belonged to a mature bureaucrat instead of an adventurous star disciple. But that other life had been important to me. I must remember this."

Once more calling upon her finely honed negotiating skills, she chose silence as the best reply to P'Teel's inquiries. Uncoiling from her semi-fetal position, Novas stretched as would a Lutetian cat awakening from a lustful dream. She turned her head slightly away from P'Teel and smiled mysteriously. The ploy had its desired effect.

P'Teel seethed.

Before she could unleash another onslaught of venomous hisses, the sled bumped to the ground a dozen decatreds from the meteorite's crater.

The crisis team had arrived before them. Even now they were monitoring the area for dangerous radiation. Several were garbed in a type of metallic tunic which protected them from the meteorite's heat. Dust swirling in the air from the projectile's impact, taxing the investigators' helmet respirators to their limits. The evening sun, diffracted by the mineral clouds, provided a gothic pallet of color on the technicians' suits.

Landing at a safe distance, the group disembarked and were met by several of Ravar's scientists carrying a container of meteoric material. Their attempts to contain their excitement were noble, but futile.

"Sire Ravar, it is as you predicted. This is a relatively small fragment of a much larger belt of asteroid debris. Preliminary analyses show compositions indicative of a planetary crust. Hypotheses hold true that material of this kind would be the first to be sheared away if two giant masses collided along tangential paths. The surface debris of the planet being struck would be hurled ahead of the larger mass. The debris would signal that a subsequent body of much greater proportion would follow."

"I share your enthusiasm, Keplarn, but do not let it burn away your rationality. There is much to learn from our space-faring jewel. If the theories are correct, our time is precious. We must use it wisely. Deal in facts, for conjecture will only dilute our energies."

"May I see those samples, friend Ravar?" Novas inquired.

P'Teel stiffened as she watched this newcomer intrude upon her realm. Before she could protest, Ravar passed to her the magnetic flask containing an iridescent chip.

Novas' visage transformed from that of a primeval beauty to one of a scholar of the heavens. She scrutinized the crystalline fragment for color, shape and clarity. Scanning the portavid readings on the scientist's analyzer, she murmured an appreciative compliment for his good work. After several moments of this, P'Teel found she could contain herself no longer.

"What great wisdom do you have to offer us, o' cosmic one? Or does your charade end at mere praise for a column of numbers?"

Novas ignored the barb, therein giving it no value. Instead, she turned to Ravar and Del and requested, "I believe this substance to be of unique origin and power. I cannot tell you how I know this, but I feel I could be valuable to your efforts. May I assist you in your studies?"

Del raised an eyebrow of surprise at this request. He mused to himself, "There is no doubt that I am attracted to her. And she has already shown that she is equal to P'Teel in sheer willfulness." Heeding Ravar's comments only moments before, he thought, "There is little time and much to do. I could surely use the help. And if Ravar's theories prove more correct than my own, what better way to spend the final moments on my home world than in the company of a lovely and mysterious woman?"

Before Del could respond, Ravar spoke. "I have no objections, beautiful one. But I must yield the decision to Sire Mitron of the Del.

Ravar's statement struck Novas with more impact than could the meteorite lying before her!

Her thoughts overwhelmed her. "Mitron of the Del?! Is that what Ravar had said? Not just Del, but Mitron of the Del. That would mean that "Del" was the clan name, not the surname. It could not be! This man before her was supposed to be the greatest Geminian leader of all time!"

Her shock was not lost upon the man before her. But it was misinterpreted. Mitron saw the color drain from Novas and mistook it for fear that he would not approve her request. To belay that fear, he responded by stepping forward and placing both hands upon her shoulders.

With a warm smile, he stated firmly, "Your assistance is welcome. Let us begin immediately. Ravar, I will leave the responsibility to you as to how best to use Novas' talents. Now, let us complete our initial survey of the area. I will need you to keep me informed as to how the excavation work proceeds."

Novas' mind raced over the possibilities stemming from this man actually being Mitron. "Mitron the Peacemaker! Mitron the World

Uniter! Mitron the Father of the Phoenos! How could this simple, unassuming tribal leader be the Great One?"

For Novas, the answer was clear.

"The Legotian assault on my senses has reached a new pinnacle of intensity," she feared. "For the mind control game to have taken this path meant that the controller had chosen a route of uncertainty. Mitron was a figure of Geminian fable as well as fact. That must mean that the Legotian would now rely on Mitron's mysteries to delude me. Attention to realistic detail would be abandoned. The Legotian would use fictitious scenarios to elicit my responses, to what sinister end, I still do not know!"

Continuing, she speculated, "I'll no longer be able to challenge events based on historic fact, since legend would become intertwined with reality. My mental anchor to the truth has been cut free. I must now follow the currents of the Legotian river of fantasy to its final destination. Just as a swimmer caught in an unyielding undertow, I must yield to it to survive. Rather than struggling against it, I will let it carry me as I conserve my mental energy. When possible, I will angle outward against the flow of events. Pressing the limits of the situations will become my strategy for salvation. As the events carry me onward, I will execute mental regimens of defense to weaken the mind control. It will take time. At the right moment, I will exert all my psyche against my captor. But one thing is certain. I will succeed!"

Charged with renewed vigor, Novas reflected upon everything that had transpired since her arrival. Mitron's "presence" added new meaning. Probing her fragmented memory, she recalled the legend.

"Mitron united an embattled Geminian world. By his hand, the Dissenters of the Phoenos had been defeated in a violent war. Ancient law demanded that they be put to death. But Mitron had challenged that law. 'Phoenos stood for life,' he had preached. 'It was the ultimate law. The old ways have no place in Geminian society if they dishonored Life. Instead, the Dissenters will be banished into space.'"

"Space?" Novas wondered. "Ravar's starcraft! Were these the vehicles used to carry the banished? But there was no struggle between Mitron and Ravar. They were friends since childhood. No war was imminent. Yet, the starcraft would soon be leaving. Mitron even approved of Ravar's right to pursue his beliefs. There was no challenge to Phoenos by Ravar. He embraced it. His plans were to save Geminians so their worship of life could flourish."

"This timeline of events is clearly erroneous," Novas mused. "Legend told of the glory of Phoenos. The ability for the mind to totally empower another living entity had been the cornerstone principle of Mitron's teachings and leadership! Yet, no evidence of this ability is present... or has been revealed. I must learn more of Ravar's knowledge of the Phoenos. For that appears to be the weakest point in this Legotian mind drama. I will apply pressure in this area until it yields an opening. That will be my means for overcoming my controllers and finally bring this madness to an end."

With that thought firmly engrained in her mind, she turned her attention to the task at hand.

Novas worked into the early morning at Ravar's side. His stamina for pursuing the unknown was phenomenal. His leadership was even more astounding. The technicians under his guidance fluidly covered every detail of the crater and its treasure. Studying his abilities, Novas began to appreciate him as more than just Mitron's friend. He proved to be worthy of her respect.

It had been a long time since she had been attracted to a researcher of Ravar's caliber. Quite a long time. She wondered, "What had happened to her feelings for .... Nicholas Edison?" Even his name was elusive. "What had caused the passion to become just a ... convenience?"

"Lovely Novas... It is time to return to the city." Ravar's deep baritone startled her. "We must rest and start anew in a few hours. There is much work to be done in the laboratory."

Novas turned to the virile explorer beside her. Smiling softly, she nodded her approval. Eagerly, she anticipated more thoughts of him in her dreams.

*　　*　　*

The warm caress of the first morning sun aroused Novas from her slumber. Her dreams evaporated as she stirred to consciousness. A twinge in her lower back accelerated her wakening ritual.

Rubbing the spinal ridge prominent in Geminian women of a certain age, the star traveler was jolted by the flush of hormones surging through her.

"This cannot be!!"

Novas staggered from under the bed comforters and made her way to the chromium dressing mirror. Tossing her hair forward over her shoulder, she strained to see the base of her neck. Her fingers probed gently for the protrusions. She knew in her mind that it was impossible for them to be there. But in her heart, the truth could not be denied. As she brushed her fingertips against them, a wave of climactic pleasure engulfed her. Unable to resist the forbidden urges, again and again she tortured herself with her own lustful caresses. The cool, rational executive of the Solar Corporation was no more. Before her in the mirror was a beast of passion. Fire burned across every nerve in her body. Her breasts convulsed from the uncontrollable panting. With each sensuous wave, Novas felt insanity would be her only salvation. As the eyes of the stranger in the mirror rolled back to reveal their molten lava glow, a silent scream of agony contorted her face.

In the instant of Geminian orgasm, time is a fiction of the mind. Pleasure and pain become one. Good and evil are indistinguishable. And for those select few with the power, Vuu Zon, life and death are the same.

Novas reached forward to grasp the demon's face mocking her in the mirror. The demon's glowing hands rose to meet hers. As they touched, the melting chromium sputtered viciously, and Novas collapsed.

CHAPTER 13

Descartes sat in the aftermath of the Clionian's address. Regardless of his innate dislike for Helicon, he had to admit that he had made a good case for Nimon's defense. He recalled the many times he himself had appealed to an alien intelligence as Helicon had just done - the Geminian-Terran joint venture, the Geneva VII conflict agreement, the attempted Tenusian Castorian hostile takeover of Solar Corporation, and the Legotian debates over the "acquisition" of the Castorian stealth device, to name a few.

In each case, Descartes had spoken to what the aliens valued most, but to offer it to them in terms that best fit his own desires. Helicon had offered the Elders what they wanted most - a means to end their societal unrest. But the Council must yield to Helicon's desire to accomplish this - the desire to free Nimon!

"Yes, Helicon had built a strong case indeed," thought Descartes.

Yet, as Descartes studied the seven time-honored Elders, they gave no appearance that they shared his opinion. Stony visages cast their gaze out across the assembly, content in the belief that their word was law. Irrevocable. Unquestioned.

Until now.

For Nimon had done just that. He had questioned the very foundation of Geminian philosophy. His thesis flew in the faces of both factions of the Council of Elders. Nimon postulated that the reverence around Phoenos could be stripped away to make a place for the more practical use of biodrones, as was occurring within the Solar Corporation. By diminishing the importance of Phoenos, it contradicted the more traditional Council members. And by promoting the use of bioduogenetics in any form, it countered the position of the Life Rightist faction amongst the Council. That had made him suspect. Suspect, and vulnerable. It would be this vulnerability that the prosecutor would exploit. That prosecutor was Steth.

At the conclusion of Helicon's summation, Kronia had called for a short recess to discuss the issues of the defense with her fellow council members. The surface team had been directed to remain where they were, while Steth had disappeared into the antechamber behind the massive bench. As the three tones of the chimes signaled the participants to reconvene, Steth quietly slipped back into the room. Strangely, the hair on the back of Descartes neck bristled with mistrust for the prosecutor. It was an instinctive reaction for which Descartes could not explain. But it was still there.

Kronia opened the second half of the ceremony.

"Ve haf heard ze Vkks T'Ruul. It is time for ze completion of ze Cree `Di Tal. Steth, begin."

Steth slithered his way into a position between the Council and the surface team to the same spot where Helicon had stood. Descartes thought it ironic that the prosecutor's movements were more reptilian than the Clionian's. In contrast, however, the Geminian faced Nimon and the Clionian rather than the Elders. His baritone voice differed sharply from the gravelly, suppressed hiss of his opponent, but still cut against Descartes nerves.

"I will start by refuting the memory coins' implications that there was malicious intent against the Ravarians on the part of Mitron. Of minor importance is the mere fact that these tapes are not authenticated. Of major importance are the narrow views which they present."

"Our own legends speak of the benevolence of Mitron in dealing with his adversaries. They tell of the two factions; the peaceful Lifists and the aggressive Materialists. They also tell of the schism between the two factions on space travel. The Lifists felt the recently acquired ability should be limited to Gemini's ionosphere for scientific purposes only. The Materialists wanted more. They proposed expansionist concepts ... concepts not necessarily peaceful in nature.

Mitron offered the Ravarians a choice. The first, to be received with open arms into the brotherhood of peace, accompanied by their denunciation of their violent ways. Or the second, to fulfill their desires to explore space, leaving them free to establish their own world in their own way, but to leave Gemini behind forever. Mitron felt it was too early for the Geminian race to contact others. They needed to mature by looking within themselves and controlling the savagery they contained. But Mitron refused to impose his beliefs on those who could not understand. Therefore, he let them go on their own accord. His decision to let them choose in no way implicates Mitron in their alleged evolution into the savage, materialistic Castorian race. The Clionian's reference to fragmentary radicals still on Gemini sharing these aggressive traits can be summed up as hearsay and unfounded."

Steth paused for dramatic effect. His summation was unique in its presentation. The common strain of thought taught at the elementary level of education was to present a classical "Good conquers Evil" perspective where the Mitronians were good and the Ravarians were evil. Yet, Steth had taken the more erudite path to relate Mitron's benevolent judgement upon the Materialists. The intent was to mollify any harsh bias of the few on the Council that might resent the treatment of Ravarians as depicted by Helicon. After deflecting the threat

214

from the chronicles presented by the Clionian,, Steth launched his assault against the accused.

"What is founded in irrefutable fact is the guilt of Nimon in the murder of Starn, his own life-kindred. It is these facts which I will now detail. Just over a fortnight ago, Nimon arrived on Gemini to empower Starn during his Royta-Far. From the very start, things were not as they appeared. With the Council's permission, I respectfully submit the psionic telemetry records of Starn's vigil."

A nod from Kronia prompted Steth to signal an aide who placed a series of data doubloons on a stone table to one side of the Council's bench.

He then continued. "Here is evidence of the erratic behavior Starn exhibited during the ceremony. It is proof of the emotional turmoil against which he struggled during his vigil. A turmoil which should not exist within a normal bioduotron. But this bioduotron has shown stronger than expected tendencies toward emotional outbursts in his social and scholastic abilities. I ask of the Council 'Why?' What is behind the aberrant behavior within Starn? During the Royta-Far, the candidate is expected to be beyond a state where it is a challenge to control these tendencies. I am prepared to answer that question."

Steth moved toward the defendant to emphasize his position of omnipotence over his victim. Peering down at him, he let slip a look with just a shade of malice before turning to again address the Council.

"Immediately prior to Starn's trial, Nimon petitioned this Council to hear his thesis on a materialistic view of bioduogenetics. At the root of this theory is the premise that a 'biod' ... truly a most distasteful reference used by outworlders ... can be used to save lives from perilous risk. To do this inherently means the loss of the biod. Now I ask of the Council, do we forego our innermost belief in Phoenos - the ability for a bioduotron to live independently - to provide disposable life? Do we provide life to be thrown away at the whim of Terrans' materialistic desires? Terrans such as Morgan Descartes who refused to accept 'no' for an answer ... refused to accept that outworlders were incapable of managing bioduogenetics!"

Morgan Descartes rose out of his chair at this last barb. He had managed to maintain a semblance of decorum up until now. But this direct assault was going too far. Steth was not only attacking Descartes' conduct during the Gemini-Earth joint venture negotiations, but Earth's level of cultural development as well! Descartes' actions during the negotiations between Gemini and the Earth Exploratory Cartel were motivated by the best of business ethics. To insinuate that his management skills were inferior infuriated Descartes! Plus, Steth's contrast of the

Geminian near-religious worship of a biodgen's life-value versus Earth's utilitarian view of a biod was exaggerated. Steth discounted the Terran concept of a biod being used to preserve all life. And in the process, he was denigrating the Solar Corporation!

An arm shot out with surprising speed and strength to halt Descartes's momentum.

"Now hold on, Morgan. I may be just a personnel manager, but I think I'm a good judge of character. And that man-mountain with his meat cleaver over there doesn't have a milliliter of character between them," Brown whispered, nodding toward the guard in front of them.

Brown's light-hearted reference to the guard worked. It successfully misdirected Descartes's wrath. The plant manager knew his resident sociologist could assess a situation and judge whether to yield or stand his ground. There had been innumerable times he had pulled back for a more opportune time to stand up to the opposition. This was another one.

"Okay. You win this one, J.B.," Descartes said, grudgingly.

A twitch at the corner of Steth's mouth, as if a smirk could break through that icy mask, was the only satisfaction the prosecutor would enjoy. But it was enough for now. His ploy to enrage the Solar Corporation executive had almost succeeded. With just a hint of malice, he mentally filed that bit of information for another time, and continued with his case.

"Nimon sought to persuade the Elders to accept his theory ... this belief that life was at his disposal. But the Elders were wise. They dismissed his lunacy. And lunacy it proved to be. Nimon could not accept his failure. For to Nimon, to reject his theory was the same as rejecting his very own existence! His mind snapped. The rejection became a poison. Subduing the mental regimens our masters had instilled within him, he made a choice. A choice not unlike the one he made when he chose the Solar Corporation over his home planet, Gemini. In a state of rage, Nimon chose to direct his hatred against the fabric of Geminian culture itself. While empowering Starn, he maliciously vandalized his own family's archives, cursing the concept of the family unit which Geminian society dearly honors.

Steth paused to allow his accusations to linger in the minds of the Elders. For some, his accusations would be enough, for those members of the Council had made a choice long ago. Their family lines could be traced, given the desire. Their political and philosophical leanings could be uncovered. And Steth had done so. He knew the members that had already decided in his favor. But the rest of the Council would need proof.

Steth produced a memory coin from the folds of his tunic and placed it on a stone slab opposite the one used by the Clionian for his evidence. Solemnly, he continued.

"The Archives' computer defense requires the thought patterns of Nimon's blood-line to allow access to the inner chambers. On the day of Starn's death, patterns were recorded which allowed entry. But there are only two patterns known to be of this line. Nimon's mother, Novas, and Nimon himself. Those patterns are on that doubloon."

Steth turned slowly, letting his arm sweep melodramatically across the room to point at the pedestal holding the data coins. He then looked down upon Nimon, drawing upon the last vestiges of theatre that might still reside in the lingering spirits of those that had once spoken within the ancient chamber.

"Novas was off-planet at the Legotian conference. There was but one Geminian pattern that could access the computer defense. That pattern was YOURS!" Steth brandished a finger at Nimon as if it could unleash a bolt of vengeful lightning. Holding it there several seconds for effect, he then turned slowly back toward the Council.

"Tragically, the biodgen, Starn, was directed to abandon his responsibilities as honor guard of the Archives by this man. He tried to resist Nimon's subconscious directions, but in vain. It was at this moment that our psionic telemetry devices failed. But there can be no doubt that it was the pattern of Nimon, in the body of Starn, who entered the Archives. That same pattern, struggling to resist his tormentor, exited the Archives, and in a blinding fit of raw emotion, strangled himself in order to escape the shame of his actions. Stripped of all rationality, Nimon refused to terminate the empowering link, and allowed Starn's essence to die. As final proof of the person responsible for this act, I present to you the instrument with which that tragic death was delivered. Starn's life energy was extinguished by this murder weapon!"

Steth signaled an aide from behind the Council's bench to bring the evidence forward. Coiled loosely on a display tray was a four tred long, two palm width sash. The fabric was a tight mesh of silver metal strands woven into a decorative, but lethal, ceremonial weapon. At each end of the sash were ornately engraved weighted spheres giving the cloth the ability to be swung overhead and thrown in a bolo-like fashion.

"You will note the family crest which appears on this Ruga'r," Steth continued. "It clearly identifies it as the one owned by Nimon Edison."

Quietly observing the proceedings, Brown leaned over toward Descartes and whispered, "How would Nimon's Ruga'r make its way from the wall in his office to the neck of his biodgen without anyone knowing it?"

Descartes pondered the question for a moment, and then responded, "There's always a lot of coming and going during our routine maintenance when we're at Gemini. It's possible it was stolen during our short stay when we dropped Nimon off two weeks ago. Gemini is the last place our security would expect an unauthorized intruder. So, if Starn's attacker could get into the Archive, he could surely breach our relatively lax security while at Gemini."

Steth began to speak again after he had allowed each of the Council members to inspect the Ruga'r.

"As conclusive as this evidence is, there is still more. I have a sworn statement from an orderly of the Institute of Meditative Phenomenon which saw not only Nimon, but Nimon's Earth-born father, Dr. Nicholas Edison, as they prepared to complete the vile act of murder. The irony of this evidence is that our medical experts had already proclaimed Starn dead. The fact that Nimon refuses to believe this is a clear sign of his madness. But the reason for Dr. Edison's involvement remains a mystery. If he is directly involved, as evidence dictates, then he too must be punished. In order to reveal the truth behind his role, and to show further proof of the harmful effects of Earth's materialistic philosophies on our society, I call to the stand Dr. Edison of Terra."

The motionless figure sitting cross-legged at the center of the forum reacted instantly. His rigid spine arched violently as his head snapped backward. A grimace like the smile on Death's skull stretched across Nimon's face, as his eyes closed tightly against the agony flooding his mind.

As suddenly as the pain came, it subsided, leaving behind a telepathic message Nimon could not ignore.

"YOUR FATHER IS MINE!"

Rising fluidly, the Geminian-Terran confronted his prosecutor, exclaiming, "T' Varek Kar!"

Just as fluidly, the hulking guard by the Council bench bore down upon Nimon. Twirling his scythe above his head, mere seconds separated him from stilling the voice of the Darwin's technical superintendent forever.

CHAPTER 14

"Groka!" exclaimed the ancient woman presiding over the ceremony. Her coarse voice instantly bound the expert hands of the guard as they prepared to deliver the fatal blow. Dramatically, the hulk brought the scythe from above his head down across his body, with the center hilt resting lightly against his hip and one of the finely-honed points hovering at Nimon's throat.

"Thee invokes T'Varek Kar, Survival of ze Ancients? Does thee know ze full meaning of thy actions?" Kronia's voice continued, now a solemn whisper.

In answer, Nimon slowly raised his arm from his side, placing his outstretched right hand in front of the guard. Brilliant crimson eyes looked out from the hood's slits and followed the arm's motion, as would a Talus-cat eye its prey. The left hand of the sentry released the double-hilt of the scythe, while continuing to keep the massive weapon's point completely motionless with the right. The muscular Geminian warrior unsheathed a short-sword hanging at his side, raising it level with the Solar Corporation technical superintendent's outstretched arm.

Descartes and Brown turned, looking at each other, sharing the same unbelievable thought, "They're going to take his hand!"

Simultaneously, both managers bolted half out of their chairs. But this time it was an alien arm which shot out to halt the momentum of the plant manager and his personnel manager.

"Gentlemen, lissten to me," hissed Helicon. "No harm will come to Nimon."

Descartes and Brown shared another look. This time, one of skepticism.

The scaly arm was unyielding in its strength. As it gently but firmly pushed Descartes and Brown back into their seats, the Darwin's managers realized that Helicon had been correct.

The cowled sergeant-at-arms deftly flipped the short-sword in the air, causing the flat side of the blade, near its middle, to land across Nimon's palm. Just as deftly, Nimon coiled his arm and hurled the sword in a spear-like fashion directly at Steth, the Prosecutor. With a powerful thud, the blade embedded itself into the Council bench only a finger's width to the right of Steth's shoulder.

"What in Gemini's twin is going on?" Brown barked toward the Clionian, who had relinquished his hold on the two men.

Helicon whispered with a pronounced hiss, "Nimon's answer to Kronia's quesstion iss 'Yess.' He has elected to undergo T'Varek Kar, the ancient ritual of sssurvival. Sssimply put, he is calling Sssteth a liar of the worsst kind. In order to prove it, Nimon will attempt to withsstand a trial of sssurvival in the Geminian desert. If he succeedss, he must then fight Sssteth to the death. The victor will be the one who is telling the truth."

Brown, puzzled, murmured under his breath, "A fight to the death?" Continuing a little more hotly, "It's barbaric. I thought Geminians valued life above all things!"

"According to recent history, they do, Jefferssson. However, what is being argued here datess back to before one of the most fundamental of modern Geminian ssociety's preceptss. You see, at sstake in the outcome of thiss trial is not jusst Nimon's life, but the hisstory and future of Geminian culture.

Nimon is directly challenging the value that Gemini culture is placing on the sssynthetic life of a bioduotron. By invoking T'Varek Kar, he is putting a real life at risk - his or Ssteth's. He is asking the Council, "Does the existence of a biodgen outweigh the life of a Geminian?" It is an interessting ploy. If the Council'ss ansswer is 'no', then they sset a major precedence which conflicts with the values previoussly placed on a biodgen's life essence. They would ssubordinate the loss of Sstarn to the loss of Ssteth or Nimon. By doing so, the charges against Nimon would have to be dropped. They would be admitting that a biodgen is ever sso ssslightly less than a

Geminian; and thuss, iss able to be ssacrificed for a Geminian. This is exactly the philosophy Nimon had proposed during his meeting with the Council.

Should the Council agree to T'Varek Kar, Nimon would sstill have an opportunity to go free. But he would first have to ssurvive. Regardless of the Council'ss choice, Nimon has a chance to accomplish his true goal - capture the woman behind the K'Tar and save Starn. Initially he believed my case had a high probability of swaying the Council to his side, via hisstory and factss. His actions indicate he has changed his mind. By invoking T'Varek Kar, he is forcing the Council to make their decision now."

"Can he really pull that off?" Descartes interjected.

"We are about to find out, Mr. Descartes," Helicon solemnly replied.

Kronia looked down at the Geminian-Terran through a mask of harsh coldness and slitted crimson eyes. Her thin-lipped mouth drew taut as she spoke.

"Son of Novas, thee are as well-schooled in the ways of the Geminian people as thee are the stars. Thee are within thy rights to challenge Steth in this manner. Equally so, Steth has first right of weapon and speech in response."

Slowly turning her steely gaze to Steth, Kronia continued, "Steth, what is thy answer?"

As if rehearsed, Steth delivered his reply. "I have been informed that the human, Dr. Edison has disappeared. Aides sent to bring him before this Council report that no record of a departure off-world has been filed, and he is nowhere to be found in the city. I contend this mysterious disappearance is clear indication of his guilt in Nimon's conspiracy against our society. In light of this, I am honored to defend our ways against the traitor, Nimon. As weapon, I choose Kor-Il Tahn ... should he survive the desert!"

Steth spoke the last phrase wickedly, as if he knew that Nimon's survival was impossible. He punctuated his reply with a sneer.

Helicon hissed lowly and with ancestral ferocity.

Brown was the first to inquire, "What is it, Helicon?"

"Ssteth'ss wordss do not ring true. Nimon told me during our conference in the Darwin that Dr. Edison had sworn to protect Starn in his comatose ssstate. Nothing other than force would have caused him to leave Starn unguarded."

Morgan Descartes accepted the wisdom in Helicon's words with an approving nod. However, Kronia silenced the whispering Clionian with her gaze, and acknowledged Steth's response, "Thee has chosen the Struggle of the Minds. Should Nimon succeed in his desert trial, thee will be locked in the deepest of mind links. A Drone-Biodgen armed with a razor stiletto will be placed between thee. Thee both will be bound tightly. The winner will be the one who successfully empowers the drone to do thy bidding. The victor will be the one of strongest will. The loser will not survive. Let the trial begin."

Turning to Nimon, Kronia motioned him to step forward.

Stepping past the now lowered scythe held by the guardian, Nimon strode up the marble steps fronting the Elders to stand before Kronia.

The wizened Geminian raised her hands before his face, a glowing life crystal cradled in her palms. Intently peering into her scarlet eyes, he knew what he was expected to do. He raised his own hands and lightly placed them over the shard.

Nimon's conscious levels melted away as he submitted to the hypnotic trance induced by the life crystal. Kronia was in his thoughts, and he could not help but question her intent.

She knew she could break his will with ease, but respectfully halted her probing, mentally responding to Nimon's question.

"Thee has spoken of materialism and life in strange ways. Our culture has suppressed the one, while emphasizing the other. A warrior race now dwells in peace. We must know why thee questions the concept of Phoenos. The reason dwells within the deepest recesses of thy mind. From conception, thy being has been a subject of fierce debate among our Elders. Thee hast overcome the challenges and followed thine own path. It has brought thee back to us. The struggle within thy very soul must be known. Only then can thy struggle against the desert and Steth result in what must be right and just. Open thy mind. Reveal what thee hast mastered for the sake of thy race, thy family.... thy very soul!"

Nimon's mental discipline crumbled outward as the swollen river of his life-struggle toward Phoenos flooded into the life crystal, for only Kronia to see.

...."but Mother, why do the other children call me out-worlder, am I not Geminian like them?"

...."yes Mother, my employment with the Earth Exploratory Cartel is effective immediately....as you wish, then, I will refer to you only as Novas, should we by chance ever meet again."

...."I understand … Novas… as it was in the beginning. To give your life, your mind, your very soul to the biodgen is to prove the ways of our people. But if achieved, the knowledge of the ability and the Dual's existence must be guarded well. It is most sacred."

...."but I know they could save lives. Yes, I know powerful people believe that to use bioduogenetics for material purposes denigrates the philosophy of Phoenos. My world could be gone from me forever, but I must try!"

...."Mother - Novas - then you agree that "biods" should be used to help the humans?"

...."Solar Corporation"? A merger between Terra and Gemini? I will get to finally go home!"

.... Starn's mental link to Nimon became inflamed with the pain of strangulation. As the essence of Starn began to wane, Nimon, too, fought to survive. The rarest of exchanges occurred, "You have taught me well, Life Mentor." "And I have learned much, from you."

Kronia's control wavered. Reality and myth swirled into one. Struggling, she sought order within the thoughts that now overwhelmed her.

"This impression was proof the one before her was worthy of Dualiity! Phoenos was within his reach!" she thought. "Two consciences from one mind! Two lives from one existence!"

In that moment of exultation, Nimon's thoughts surged forward. "Kronia, I sense your elation ... but there is something else. Something deeper. Darker. I must understand the mystery!" he mentally urged to her. He was now the stronger within the psychic bond - probing... pressing... penetrating.

Yet as powerful as Nimon's thoughts were - the darkness, ever elusive - taunted him.

Kronia responded. Blocking him, seeing the weak point in his mind's assault, she leveraged it against him, causing him to question, "Could he be saved... was there time? Should he be saved? Another life, out of my control, but my responsibility. Was this why biodgens were created?"

Kronia continued to struggle. The darkness swirled. Cold. Sickening. "He must not know the secret within... not yet. The secret is too critical to our plans. It will take all my skills to protect it!"

Nimon probed further. The darkness parted ever so slightly, like the maw of a hideous creature, waiting to swallow him. He recoiled from fear. "I must ... go ... deeper!!"

Kronia's mind screamed.

Suddenly, there was another presence.... the hypnotic familiarity of T'Poch's thoughts ... goading Nimon ... enticing him ... interfering as he struggled with Kronia.

"And now she has my father! I must stop her!! T'Varek Kar!!"

The ancient challenge echoed within her thoughts, and within the crypt-like chamber of the Council.

Inwardly, Kronia's psyche reeled. The flood of experiences and concepts from one as young as Nimon dwarfed the mental regimen of doctrines she had mastered to reach the highest level of the Elders.

Outwardly, her face was of stone.

In an instant before releasing Nimon, she projected her thoughts to the unique disciple of

Phoenos before her. "You soon will fully understant thy nature, Nimon. Thee hast not yet come to grips with the truth. And so, thee must still undergo ze desert trial. For to communicate vat I know vould be a violation of ze very soul of Phoenos. Even if I could convey ze complexity of vhat must come, I cannot insure zat all vould understant. A select few might master ze information in a short time. But for many others, it vould entail a lifetime of study. Ze Geminian legends of Phoenos are time-honored on our planet. But can zey be accepted as reality? Can zey be shown to exist in one such as thee? And one such as ze other? Possibly. But as I now understant thy fears, thee must understant mine. These concepts, as ver the ways of Mitron, must be introduced slowly ... methodically ... controllably."

Pausing, Kronia reached a solemn decision, and acted.

"The probability of survival against the struggle that lay ahead of thee is small. As such, I am compelled to assist thee."

Still maintaining the hypnotic control over Nimon as transmitted through the crystal, Kronia delicately constructed an alternative mindset.

"Nimon, hear me. Thou vill have ze power. Ze mental barriers which lift Geminians above ze savagery of our ancestors vill be no more. If need be to survive, thou shalt invoke this mindset to unleash ze full bestiality of a varrior Geminian.

Thou shalt be vithout inhibitions, vithout honor, vithout regard for life. As it has been, so shall it now be!"

Kronia released Nimon from the trance, and was pleased. He would be able to survive - as he must. She then reflected upon what she had unleashed with wonder, and with awe.

Inwardly, Nimon felt a relief reminiscent of that experienced after his struggle against T'Poch. Kronia understood. But he did not, at least not fully. He somehow felt she had accomplished the first step in altering the very fabric of existence for the Geminian people. But something was different. Within him a spark of ancestral savagery existed where none had before.

Outwardly, Nimon crumpled to the floor at Kronia's feet.

CHAPTER 15

Two Geminian weeks had passed since Novas' erotic seizure. Her struggle to separate reality from the Legotian's control over her mind and body had failed. She had conceded to herself that further resistance to the mind control would only drive her mad. Already, its effects had caused a seizure that she surmised must be the result of a repressed memory from her past. She had kept the dark secret from everyone. Even herself. By shielding herself from the emotional bonds of her friends, her husband, and even her child, she had been able to suppress the truth.

Until now.

The haunting image of an older, more sinister P'Teel peering covetously at her had returned. An icy chill swept over Novas - not from the woman's gaze, but from the sense of loss Novas experienced. Was the Legotian again manipulating her? The Legotian would have her believe that she was once more a young woman, able to experience the brutal ecstasy of passion. She had enjoyed... or endured... that feeling only once before in her lifetime. It had led to tragedy. She knew all too well that what the Legotian wished her to believe was impossible. Her femininity had been stripped from her during the birth of her son. Both Novas and her child had lived... but at what cost? Novas was unable to bear another child, and had abandoned the only child she had borne. Or had he abandoned her? By rejecting the pursuit of Phoenos to promote a Materialist view, had not her son rejected Novas herself? For, despite Novas' position within the Solar Corporation, her heart – her very soul, was dedicated to Phoenos.

After the trauma of childbirth, Phoenos had been her only option to create a new life. But that option had come at a price. The price she paid was the source of her loss, not the manipulations of the Legotian. For Novas, not the Legotian, had made the choice to pursue Phoenos after she could no longer bear children. With the support of her brilliant husband, she had created her own biodgen. Though the technology at the time was ground-breaking, it had its flaws. The same proximity challenge facing the Solar constructs also manifested itself in her Dual. As with the biodrones and their Terran biodivers, Novas' biodgen could only be empowered over great distances. The syndrome had not manifested itself at first. Early on, by submerging herself into an empowering slumber, she could activate her "newborn" so that Dr. Nicholas Edison could dote over it as would any proud father. Yet, over the few short months after the first empowering session, the child's life crystal-cellular matrix had become unstable. A rapid aging syndrome was diagnosed. If the sessions continued, minutes would be hours, and hours would be days for the infant. The brilliance of Dr. Edison again was put to a test. He hypothesized that proximity during empowerment was the problem.

He theorized that the process of Dualiity involved psionically transmitting a copy of brain engrams to another template, the Dual. For the engrams to function properly, they also required the "subroutine" of consciousness to follow the copy. This transmitted "shadow" consciousness, though, was independent of the source, much like the subconscious exists within an individual and independently influences behavior. The challenge of Phoenos was being able to animate both the biodgen and the organic simultaneously, and independently. Novas, while in her unconscious, empowering state, could animate her biodgen, but only one could stay conscious, either the bioduotron or the organic. Edison discovered the reason for the proximity-induced syndrome was that the brain wave interference emitted by the organic during empowerment would interfere with the crystalline matrix of the Dual. The deterioration of the matrix manifested itself as the rapid aging syndrome.

As such, Novas had been forced to make a decision – and a sacrifice. Her choice was to either discontinue the sessions and forgo the pursuit of Phoenos, or give over her Dual to a caretaker, allowing her to animate, but never again to see, the biodgen. That decision was the source of the memory that perpetually haunted Novas, even now. Yet despite the pain from the loss, the choice had been a successful one. Novas, over the years and over a great distance, had enabled her biodgen to develop. The aging syndrome had been halted, but its effects were not reversed. The Dual, although constructed several years after the birth of her son, was biologically seven years his senior. Novas often wondered how the appearance of her biodgen had changed. Would she recognize her Dual?

Reflecting once more upon the fateful parting, her mind's eye clearly showed her younger self handing over the biodgen-child. But what stayed a blur was the image of the caretaker. She had seen the matron but once, when she covetously accepted the child. The sinister crone had smiled wickedly. Peering back at her with a stare of liquid fire, Novas made the connection.

"How could it be that I have inserted an older version of P'Teel into this vision?" she asked herself, in anguish. "What is to be gained from the Legotian ploy of steering my mind back to this moment?"

Reflexively, stemming from uncounted seasons of training, Novas raised her mental barriers like the exploding volcanic spires erupting through the Geminian crust so many eons ago. The dark secret that Novas held would remain hidden.

"The motives behind the Legotian mind assault are finally unveiled!" Novas seethed. "By enabling me to experience my own sexuality, by creating the hope that I could again bear children, he attempts to pierce the depths of my mental defenses. By weakening my resolve, he believes not just my secret, but even more Solar Corporation intelligence can be accessed!"

But she was unable to fathom why the Legotian ruse was so extensive. For her to experience the throes of passion she had felt, it would require regeneration of organs she had lost decades ago. Not only had her sexuality reappeared, but her youthful beauty had also been restored. She began noticing that as each day passed, she appeared years younger. Rising from her plush bedding in her boudoir, she glided over to her vanity. Looking again into the replacement mirror, she smiled ruefully at her youthful appearance. It had been a simple matter to explain away the damage to the first mirror... after she had hurled it from her bedroom window in a staged fit of temper. What had been more difficult was avoiding P'Teel's probing questions and unyielding surveillance.

To the men, the change had been transparent, but not without an effect. Ravar's advances had evolved from playful flirting to an intense courtship. Novas had found it increasingly difficult to insure that the attraction remained one-sided. Long hours of isolated research on purifying the meteorite fragments provided opportunity for their relationship to grow stronger.

In contrast, Mitron had become more volatile. A ritual of meeting Novas for morning meal had been fabricated on the grounds of "seeking the most current information on Ravar's research progress." Yet many times, the conversation would turn to Novas' future.

"Where will you go once Ravar and his starcraft depart? What awaits you outside the borders of Centar? Have you thought of a future here?"

If the discussion turned to the possibility that Centar and even Gemini might not continue to exist due to the impending meteoroid collision, Mitron would become extremely agitated. Novas found that the agitation increased the more she praised Ravar's work. If not for the fact that she had repeatedly stated that she and Ravar were merely professional colleagues, she would almost believe that Mitron was growing jealous.

Novas was certain that P'Teel was behind the change in Mitron's behavior. Her suspicious inquiries and vicious innuendos had reached new heights of invectiveness. As Novas entered the secluded alcove in which they shared breakfast, she could not overcome the eerie feeling that somewhere close by, P'Teel watched her every move.

"Good morning, Del." Novas still flushed from the intimacy she felt when referring to the great Mitron by his clan name. How brash she must have appeared during their earlier encounters. Naively, she had followed Ravar's lead. In doing so, she had failed to use the more formal surname, Mitron.

Mitron rose and regally bowed, kissing the inside of her forearm as she extended it.

"Our mornings together are becoming the most pleasurable part of my day, dear Novas. Especially this morning."

"Why is that?"

Before he could respond, a maid-servant entered with a tray of sumptuous meat cakes adorned with glazed Mercosian nuts. She set a flask of pale indigo nectar to the left of each of them. Then she slipped away.

Turning back to Del's intense gaze, Novas detected a hint of irritation in his face.

"Have you forgotten Ravar's timetable?" he inquired testily.

"If you are referring to his experiments with the meteorite fragments, of course not."

"No, no.... that is the furthest thing from my mind. Ravar has been searching for decades for the "ultimate mineral" that will be the breakthrough in his search for Phoenos. I find it difficult to believe the meteorite has brought him any closer in his quest. What I am concerned with is his launch timetable. Today is the day for final testing of his starcraft engines. Once completed, he could leave at any time."

"I thought you supported Ravar in his freedom to pursue his space explorations."

Mitron reached for a meat cake after pouring Novas a chalice full of nectar.

"To be candid, I never believed it would come to this. The weather patterns have worsened drastically in the past several days. Many believe it to be caused by the approaching meteoroid. It is whipping the people into a frenzy. Those who I thought would never subscribe to Ravar's theories are now whispering about plots to commandeer his vessels for their own salvation."

"Does Ravar know?"

"Beautiful Novas, you still underestimate my longtime friend. He beguiles you with an oafish facade to gain access to your heart. But he is brilliant. He, no doubt, has made plans. That is why I must talk to you now. Talk to you in a way that is ... foreign to me."

Novas peered over the rim of her goblet with a wary eye. Mitron's behavior had taken a turn over the past few days. But she could not explain the uneasiness it elicited in her. His tone had become ... more personal. His charm was at its peak. She recalled the incidents where she had halted his amorous advances quite forcefully, and smiled. Of late, she had fantasized how she might handle such advances very differently. Yet, seeing him struggling to express himself in manners of the heart seemed unnatural. He was a man of action, not words. It was as if a fever had overtaken him, causing him to be delirious.

Still, she could not help but enjoy what she was hearing.

"Since your arrival, I have been overcome by your allure. Your beauty taunts me to come closer. Your mind challenges me to be wary. I've held you twice, only to be denied. I am not a passionate man, yet you arouse uncontrollable desires within me. In time, I feel I could win your affection. But time is my enemy. I fear that Ravar will soon depart. With him will go the essence of the fire that burns my soul. I do not want to lose you. It would be unforgivable."

Del reached into his tunic and pulled out an ornate, gold locket. At its center was the family crest of the clan Mitron.

"As a seal of my love's unyielding bond to you, I wish you to carry this close to your heart. With it, you will always be able to return to me."

Novas looked at the exquisite medallion and recalled the lore of her people's past. Thoughts of childhood stories of romance flitted across her mind. The legends told of the suitor's gift of a bejeweled object that forged the bond of eternal love. While matrimony was a union of families, often contrived out of power struggles and political convenience, this bond was different. It was a commitment of the soul.

Before her, the face of many fantasies wavered between the resolve of a world's future leader and the pain of unrequited love. He reached out to her as he stood.

A searing lava of desire rose within Novas, surging up her spine. Her nostrils flared at the haunting, sensual smells stabbing at her mind. An unseen force seemed to lift her from her chaise to carry her toward him. She knew it was her own animal urges that drove her.

The hardened muscles of his arms slid across the warmth of her exposed waist as he pulled her toward him. His scent was overwhelming, unleashing a flood of forbidden memories from her past. Fiercely, she grabbed him with both hands, her fingers burrowing into the thick mane cascading down the back of his neck. Novas' mouth devoured his, pulling the breath from his heaving chest.

Del's hands roamed Novas' body with the intimacy of a new lover. Deftly, one slid beneath her chamois bodice. The talisman was placed in the hidden pocket inside her vest before continuing on to explore more erotic regions.

Novas wanted to succumb to her instinctive hunger. Yet, a struggle arose within her mind. His lustful smell crashed against memories of suppressed desires. Desires that could only be released by narcotics banned by a society of peace.

"Narcotics … secret herbs … abandonment … new life … betrayal … P'TEEEEEL!!!" Novas' thoughts pierced her mind with the lances of truth. Her memories were not those of a man's animal scent. They were the smell of mind controlling elixirs. Potions that violated the taboos of a Geminian culture at peace. A culture of peace that had risen from the teachings of Mitron himself!!

"NOOOOO!!" Novas' thoughts became an audible scream that rose to her defense. She released Mitron's hair and brought the edges of her hands crashing against the sides of his neck. Her fears were confirmed. Blows that would have felled a normal man merely caused this drug-induced beast to momentarily loosen his grip. Fortunately, that was all the opening she required. Driving her elbows downward into the steel-like muscles of his forearms, Novas then pivoted her body within his grasp. Reaching backward, she clutched Mitron behind his head once more. This time, it was not an embrace of passion.

She dropped quickly to one knee while jerking his mammoth torso across her back. With an upward buck of her hips, she completed the defense maneuver and hurled him to the floor.

Poised in a cat-like crouch, the star child glared at the savage before her. Stunned and glassy-eyed, he no longer inspired her with awe. Instead, she felt disgust. Novas was dumbfounded that the father of peace would submit himself to the influence of forbidden potions. She had fallen beneath their wicked effects once before... but not again.

"Curse you and your heirs, Mitron! I will not be a slave to your unnatural desires!"

Spinning on her heels, Novas stalked out of the alcove into the sharp heat of a Geminian morning.

Mitron, still groggy from the effects of the vicious throw and narcotic potions in his blood, reached feebly out to her as she left. As he watched her disappear, a shadow stretched across his prone body; its peak coming to rest at his outstretched fingertips. Slowly, Mitron turned his head and peered at the figure standing before him.

P'Teel smiled serenely. The sun was at her back. Her strapless bodice enticingly caressed her oiled bosom. The light blazed through her sheer split gown, revealing the treasures beneath. At this moment, Mitron thought she might be a goddess. When she whispered softly, he was certain of it.

"Del.... how may I comfort you?"

*   *   *

Ravar, head down, leaned heavily on his palms against the cool slatium surface of the lab bench. He softly cursed the gods. "You taunt me," he muttered. "Why do you allow me to get so close to your secrets, but then pull them from my grasp?"

He slowly turned his head ... left then right... working the long night's tension from his neck. He struggled against the temptation to hurl the apparatus sitting in front of him against the wall.

Novas burst into the room, still seething from her encounter with Mitron.

"You are late!" Ravar snapped, not bothering to look at her.

Novas was in no mood to be chastised.

"And what of it?"

"You know how important today's tests are to me. I need you here!"

"Why? So you can delegate this menial lab work to your female slave while you complete your beloved starcraft! When were you going to tell me you were leaving... after your departure?"

Her question slammed into him... hard enough to shake him from his self-pity. He realized that something had upset her. Her words made no sense.

"Woman... what are you ranting about? This 'menial lab work' to which you refer could be the breakthrough for which I have been searching. My assistants are taking care of the preparations for the starcraft. I am not leaving until I am finished here... or at least until the next meteor forces me to leave."

"I do not believe you!"

"Then let me show you. Look at this. I have spent all night configuring a mechanical apparatus that could accept the crystal we have isolated from the meteorite. You know as well as I that its structure is unlike anything we have ever seen. I have painstakingly programmed a biomechanical hand to accept energy pulses routed through the crystal."

"Do not attempt to deceive me. Explain why your precious engines are being tested today, if this experiment is so important."

Ravar fumed. "Are all star followers blinded by suspicion? You remind me of that witch, P'Teel! Just look around you. I have been channeling every known energy source through the crystal in an attempt to empower this mechanism. But none have worked. Then you barge into my lab with senseless accusations. What has possessed you!?"

Novas exploded with fury. Mitron's attempted seduction still clouded her senses. Now, this oaf compared her to the hateful she-beast, P'Teel. Perhaps she was possessed!

Lunging forward, Novas reached for Ravar's throat with both hands. Her talons ripped through the air, targeting the bulging veins in his massive neck. Ravar raised his arms, palms outward, and grasped her wrists. Her claws halted mere microtreds from their intended prey. Ravar wrenched her hands apart and downward. Stepping forward, he forced them together behind her back, pulling her body toward him. She writhed within his strong grip, but to no avail. As he pressed himself against her, he commanded, "LISTEN TO ME! I would not leave you!"

Novas stopped her struggling. Hesitantly, she looked up into his raging eyes. The mind-fire began to burn once more. It coursed down her body with relentless hunger...searing every nerve in its path.

Ravar felt the transformation within her. Sensing her desire, he forged deeper. Releasing one wrist, he guided his free hand upward from the base of her spine. At each vertebra, the pressure from his masterful fingertips unleashed waves of pleasure throughout her willing body. She began to writhe once more, only this time from the ecstasy of his touch instead of resistance to it.

Reminiscent of a time before civilization, the lovers tore at each other with savage lust. As they intertwined their bodies into one convulsing union, the barriers that formed their rational minds collapsed. Novas' eyes rolled upward to reveal the scarlet of the mind fever. Hoarse moans stripped away the chastity of the science hall. Her sanity began to melt from the searing onslaught. Out of fear that she would lose her mind forever, she sought to focus her thoughts.

An image appeared through the translucency of her fevered vision. She sensed the synthetic feel of the hand's fingertips. Willing her inner control to adopt the trance used in empowering her biodgen, she commanded the device to move.

It did.

CHAPTER 16

The hair on Descartes' neck bristled. Events were spiraling out of control. He disliked being out of control. He disliked it a lot! As he watched the behemoth guard pick up Nimon's unconscious body like a sack of Mercurian potatoes, the sense of his own impotence overwhelmed him.

Experience taught him that playing by others' rules led to losing the game. Right now he felt somebody else was dealing the cards, and he was getting the losing hand. So why not change the game?

"Helicon, J.B.... is there any way we can help Nimon get out of this trial?"

"Well Morgan, my little bag of tricks is empty. Anyway, Kronia would turn that axe-wielding monster on us if we so much as breathed on Nimon! And that stubborn devil-eyed technical superintendent would probably be the one who told Kronia we were trying to help!"

"I have to agree, Mr. Descartes. Any attemptss to assisst Nimon could lead to dire consequencesss."

Considering the truth in the advice he was hearing, Descartes whispered determinedly, "That settles it, then. We may not be able to actively help Nimon, but we can take action to find Dr. Edison! As soon as we get out of here, I want to get back to the Darwin and formulate a plan."

*   *   *

The plant manager of the Darwin sat at the head of the conference room table deep in thought. Hours later, the image of Nimon's lifeless body being carried away by the Geminian guard still painfully replayed itself in his mind's eye. Over and over, the closing scene of the trial unfolded, refusing to be purged from his thoughts.

"What had Kronia done to Nimon to cause him to collapse? As many times as I've seen life crystals in production, I still can't begin to fathom the full power within them. Kronia's mastery of their forces only increases my certainty of how much I don't know. One thing's certain. Any open action taken to help Nimon during his survival trial would be futile. For all I know, Kronia could use the crystal to terminate Nimon at the first sign of our interference. But I'm not going to sit here and do nothing. Nimon is my friend! And, the company's got a lot invested in him. If the Solar board has a problem with how I'm spending their money, then their investment in Nimon will be my justification for pulling my managers off their normal assignments to pursue this one. And there's no better group than the assembled managers now sitting before me."

Addressing his experts, he challenged them. "I need answers to questions. You can get them. What action can be taken to help Nimon? Are Helicon's suspicions about Dr. Edison's disappearance correct? If so, how can the Darwin and its employees assist in the rescue of Nimon's father, Dr. Edison? What aid can we give in the capture of his abductors? And what could be the motive behind his kidnapping?"

With that, the plant manager's best people began brainstorming the situation. Given the problems, alternatives were being offered, analyzed, and prioritized in quick succession. Operations Superintendent Mack Weber's surveillance and security experience in combination with Plant Engineer George Crescent's mechanical abilities had provided a means to monitor Nimon on the surface below. A little-used stationary low-orbiting weather satellite had been modified to locate the thermal readings of Nimon's physiology. They were only slightly different than those of standard Geminians due to Nimon's unique genetics, but were easy to pinpoint given the absence of other inhabitants in the harsh desert.

Saffrons One, Two, and Three had devised a planetary communications monitoring system for detecting any reference to the K'Tar organization, with special attention to the sub-frequencies used by the non-licensed sector. Suspicions were that the K'Tar would communicate on those channels. It was hoped that any information about their activity might reveal clues as to their motives for framing Nimon.

The topic of discussion then turned to Dr. Edison's abduction.

"... last formal reports on the planet's telecom networks focused on his successful petition to halt the autopsy on Starn," noted Saffron Two, currently on duty for her sisters.

Planning Manager Christi Pomeroy added, "So a possible motive could be someone who wished to continue with Starn's autopsy, but was too late."

"Or..." chimed in Helicon, "sssomeone who wished to affect the outcome of Nimon's trial, conssidering the fact that it did alter his defense."

Descartes looked up from his reverie, startled by the last statement. Struggling against his negative bias toward Helicon, he nodded his approval of the Clionian's comment. Reflexively he glanced to Jefferson Brown to see if the sociologist had noticed. The personnel manager merely returned Descartes's questioning glance with skepticism - a raised eyebrow, arms folded across his chest, and a mouth puckered into a scornful pout.

That wasn't enough for Descartes. Yielding to his need to press his personnel manager further,

Descartes inquired, "Well, J.B., you look like something's not agreeing with you. Was it lunch, or do you have something to add?"

Realizing what his plant manager was up to and determined not to give him the satisfaction, he answered the question's superficial intent, rather than the hidden one. He also knew the better part of valor was not to challenge a life crystal plant manager about his racial bigotry, especially in front of an audience.

"Yes Morgan, I do! We've been talking about all these high-falutin' ways to get information, but we've overlooked the obvious. Let's round up an old-fashioned posse and go down to the planet to rustle up some facts for ourselves."

Descartes couldn't help but smile at his friend's ancient Old West aphorism. He had a good mind to refresh Brown's memory as to what a poor horseman Brown was and what a burden he'd be to any posse, but he decided otherwise.

"I take it you mean we should do some old-fashioned investigating ourselves, right J.B.?"

"Exactly. Human hunches and intuition can out-solve high tech gadgetry any old day," replied Brown, emphatically.

As he shook his foot impatiently beneath the conference table, Descartes had to admit to a bad case of deep space fever. Though he'd been to the surface, he felt like the hull of the Darwin was closing in on him. He had to do something to help, and Brown had just provided a solution.

Reaching a quick conclusion, Descartes responded, "That settles it. Brown, myself..." while momentarily pausing as he glanced back and forth between his personnel manager and the Clionian, "...and Helicon will travel to the surface to conduct our own investigation. The rest of you will continue to engage the systems you've devised. We will maintain the standard reporting sequence in case either group's efforts come up with a clue that might assist the other. If there are no further comments, carry on."

*   *   *

The semi-nude body of the Darwin's technical superintendent stirred. Lying at the base of the mountain in which the Council chamber had been carved, the Geminian sun bombarded the unprotected skin with its relentless radiation. The sands of the vast Geminian desert, T'Bok Vri, lightly swirled past the crumpled figure and peppered the mountain rocks, continuing their relentless onslaught of erosion against the mountain chain. For it was here that the climate of the planet made its most drastic change. Along this continental divide, T'Bok Vri, the Silent Giant, was halted in its advance across the planet's surface. Ages ago, the heaving mantle of young Gemini had thrust an immense shelf of semi-cooled magma through its crust to create the natural mountain barrier. On one side, the civilization of Gemini had spread westward. On the side that now claimed the lone Geminian, an immense ocean of sand and harshness lay in wait for his awakening.

Nimon's mind climbed through the myriad levels of consciousness toward reality, taking inventory of his body's condition along the way. Temperature, ionic balance, blood pressure, pulse rate ... all factors were collated and fed to the appropriate neural nets for a response. A casual observer might register concern at seeing the motionless body, sprawled face down in the sand where the Council guardian had left it. How foolish that observer might feel upon discovering the sophistication of autonomic defenses within that "helpless" body. Defenses that now awoke from dormancy, triggered by the harsh assault of nature.

The humans aboard the Darwin had often wondered at the Geminian's ability to withstand extreme heat. They were most amazed at the fact that Nimon never perspired! Interest in the technical superintendent's unique physiology had peaked to the point that a betting pool had been formed in an attempt to find an explanation. Having been the only Gemini member of the Solar Corporation at the time, the xenobiologists had not yet established a medical profile on the race. The combination of Nimon's smooth persuasiveness and strong aversion to the medical profession when it came to personal matters had contributed to the lack of knowledge on Corporate's part. But even Nimon's resolve could not suppress the curiosity of the Darwin employees.

Operations Superintendent and Head of Security Weber had always had a flair for bending corporate policy when it came to gambling. He had composed a clever system where the winner of the pool would have to accurately identify the method by which a Geminian's body regulated its temperature and verify that it was correct. A great number of theories had been proposed, but no proof had been provided. As the size of the "bounty" - as Mack Weber archaically referred to the credits - grew larger, word spread throughout the plant.

A young technical lab assistant named Turner decided to join in on the fun. "After all, the mystique around the Geminian was romantic," she had thought.

Technician Turner studied her subject with great tenacity. As she monitored his daily regimen, she observed a weakness. The Geminian was intensely curious about women. And like a cat, that curiosity could be used against him.

"Nimon ... may I call you Nimon?" Technician Turner asked sweetly one afternoon, her green eyes glinting with intrigue. The newly installed life crystal scanner we've been using to quantify crystal purity seems to be having unusual effects on human behavior. We need to confirm whether a scan on a Geminian will yield the same results. Will you be so kind and help me with my assignment?"

Nimon had always been an enigma to the females working at the Darwin. His ability to captivate the ladies was almost legendary. Yet, none could truthfully boast about the intense passion of an encounter with him ... though some did. For Nimon, all "legends" aside, was especially skilled at pleasing women in every way - every way except one - the consummate one. He had long ago sworn a vow of celibacy which had remained unbroken, except in the fantasy realm of the women that desired him. Technician Turner had often visited that realm, and hoped that this opportunity might lead to its transformation into reality. Nimon sensed this, and true to his curiosity, played along.

"Why certainly. What can I do to assist?" he replied.

"Put this on ..." she answered, holding out the skimpiest of diagnostic body suits, "... and come with me," she added, her whisper dripping with double entendre.

Several hours later, Turner's ploy had succeeded. She had unveiled the cause of Nimon's perpetual lack of perspiration, but that was all she had unveiled.

"The mechanism is relatively simple," Turner reported to the clustered female members of the gambling pool. "Under normal conditions, the activity of his muscles cause a chemical reaction which absorbs heat. However, if the endothermic reaction's by-products reach a high enough concentration in his bloodstream due to extreme temperatures, a dormant, secondary system becomes activated.

Similar to the human heart, and located just to the right of the sternum, the muscular pump can compress a highly oxygenated fluid. Heat from compression is dissipated through the lungs, causing the Geminian to breathe harder. As fluid containing the compressed gas passes through the body core, it reaches a chamber allowing some of the fluid to expand, convert to gas, and absorb heat. The foamed fluid then returns to the cooling pump to start the cycle again."

"Okay, so you won the pool," one participant peevishly interjected. "Now tell us the important part! How good was he?"

And the legends grew.

Now fully conscious, Nimon pushed himself up to a sitting position. The Geminian desert had succeeded in triggering his vestigial cooling organ into action. Inhaling deeply several times to oxygenate this system, he began to feel the full cooling effect.

As he surveyed his situation, he realized he had not been unconscious in the desert for long. The wind had not yet disturbed the tracks left by the guard and his body as he was drug to where he lay. A second set led back into the small opening in the rocks which accessed the labyrinth of chambers carved centuries ago by the Geminian ancestors.

On the ground beside him lay one of only two luxuries left him by the Council to aid him in his trial of survival. One was a leather-like cloth girding his loins, acting as the only clothing he had. The other was a bag made from the same leathery leaves of the Hoya plant. Though empty and seemingly useless, Nimon realized that it represented a savings in a resource he had very little of - time! By having clarity of purpose, he could collect the things necessary to make survival a highly probable outcome. But he must have a means to transport these select items while keeping his hands free for - among other things - self-defense. To fabricate such a utility bag under these conditions would take much time.

"Yes," thought Nimon, "the Council was practical in its benevolence."

Raising himself to his feet, Nimon closed his eyes and entered the lightest of trances to calibrate his directional sense. As he relaxed his mind, the gentle subconscious pull of Gemini's magnetic field took hold. Microscopic cilia within the semi-circular canals of his inner ears aligned themselves and transmitted sensations to his medulla. Turning his head slightly side to side, he detected true north as a human might sense the direction of a cool breeze.

His ultimate destination was a full fourteen days walk north of his present location, but experience told him that the direct route would mean sure death. Sands along that route pooled invisibly along fissures and formed pits that would swallow a trespasser and quickly suffocate him. Instead, he made preparations to journey eastward. Slinging the pouch over his shoulder, he delayed several minutes to gather coils of vine snaking their way among the crevices of the mountain's craggy face. Meticulously, he also collected several sharp, flat stones from among the many rocks lying scattered across the ground. Tucking them neatly into his pouch, he began a brisk walk due east into the full force of the rising red giant sun.

Breathing more heavily now due to his activity and rising body temperature, Nimon knew he must counteract another of the sun's effects on his exposed body. His skin would rapidly dry out and severely burn under constant radiation without the time needed to naturally protect itself.

Similar to humans, Geminian skin contained pigments activated by light which served to prevent burning. Unlike humans, however, the pigments were a deep blue, not brown. But in order for them to provide the needed protection over time, Nimon must first find short term prophylactics to the sun's burning rays. The solution to his problem grew 6 kilotreds eastward.

Underground streams formed by the geothermal activity of Gemini's crust pooled their life-giving resources along a fault-line located further into the desert. The sun prevented any surface water accumulation, but the deep-growing roots of the Brav-Ni cactus successfully found the fluid a dozen treds beneath the sands. It was this oasis - if it could be called that - which held several secrets to survival in the Geminian desert. Nimon was determined to tap the resources provided by what the nomads of the desert referred to as "the Life-Giver". Hours later, as the manager-turned-survivalist reached his objective, the collection of Brav-Ni cacti, he began his work methodically and efficiently. He first picked up the shell of a hefty needle recently shed by an older plant. Taking out one of the sharp stones from his satchel, he hollowed out the needle.

"Remarkable resemblance to a Terran elephant tusk," Nimon thought, turning the object over in his tourmaline hands as he busily carved away at its core.

Fortunately, the elements and insect-like scavengers of the desert had not yet claimed the bounty found within the desert cornucopia. The paste-like meat still retained some of its precious moisture, although the taste was as Nimon remembered it - bland. As he swallowed the last of the desert delicacy, he added the finishing touches to his newly acquired canteen. Grooves were carved around the perimeter of the horn at both ends, in which the mountain vine he had retained was tied snugly to form a shoulder strap.

Next, the industrious Geminian made preparations to allow for future meals after he left the Brav-Ni. Taking the same stone he had used previously, he made circular cuts in the auburn outer husk at the base of one of the plants. After several minutes of hacking through the thick hide, he managed to create an opening just large enough for his hand. Working quickly, he scooped handful after handful of the pudding-like substance within the plant's trunk into his canteen. Filling the horn to the brim, he then sprinkled desert sand on the surface of the pudding. Moments later, the mixture had solidified to a crusty seal under the sun's curing rays, allowing Nimon to let the horn dangle from its strap without fear of losing its valuable contents.

Not forgetting one of the fundamental rules taught him by his Survivalist Mentor many years earlier, Nimon insured the Brav-Ni's future ability as a "Life-Giver". He replaced the circular plug he had removed from the plants husk and sealed the edges with some sand-sap paste. In his haste, he failed to notice a similar, but smaller, fresh repair just above his head.

A slight tingling in his skin prompted Nimon to make his final preparations before leaving the protection of the Brav-Ni. Using the needles dotting the outer covering of the plant as footholds, he carefully climbed to the top of the cactus. Plucking a dozen of the large, flowering yellow leaves at the plant's crown, he placed them within the confines of his satchel. Before clambering back to the ground, he snapped off one of the short, dagger-sized new needles which protected the cactus flower.

Back on the desert floor, two of the leaves, one in each of his palms, were briskly rubbed over the surface of his skin. Special care was paid to protect his bare feet, since the waxy residue from the leaves not only provided a perfect sun block, but also acted as a toughener against the abrasive desert sand. The small needle would provide its own form of protection as well. In the right hands, it was a lethal knife for use against overly aggressive predators.

With these last tasks completed, the Darwin's technical superintendent and accused murderer oriented himself to the northwest and set out toward his objective - mortal combat with Steth!

CHAPTER 17

Receiving clearance to assist in the investigation of Dr. Edison's disappearance had been much easier than Descartes expected. Apparently Geminian rationale had dictated that the plant manager's involvement could only help, and would keep him distracted enough not to interfere in Nimon's trial of survival. Up to this point, Geminian rationale had proven to be correct. After obtaining the needed diplomatic clearances from the Gemini High Council, Descartes, Brown, and Helicon had taken a lander down to the home of Nimon's parents, Novas and Dr. Edison.

The two Solarians had been to Nimon's childhood home several times, but were still impressed by its delicate balance of Geminian and Terran decor. The open architecture of vaulted ceilings and free use of floor-to-ceiling windows was common to traditional Geminian housing. However, the sprinkling of Terran antiques dating back to the Colonial Period of Old Earth was obviously the influence of Dr. Edison. The three aliens to the perfect order of the home showed their respect by gingerly poking through its contents.

The trio dispersed into separate areas of the house in the hopes of discovering even the slightest clue as to the reason for Dr. Edison's disappearance. Helicon found his way to Novas' study, and was perusing a set of personal ledgers he found in a hidden compartment in the ancient oak roll-top desk. Brown was busily inventorying the contents of the Edisons' sleeping chamber, while Descartes was surveying the grounds.

After several hours of painstaking investigation, the three convened in the living area to exchange notes.

Descartes led off.

"Given the Geminian custom of no locks on windows or doors, an abductor could have easily entered quietly... if Helicon's theory of force being the only reason for Dr. Edison's disappearance is true. The grounds show no evidence of tracks or of attempts to cover tracks. Even if a transport booth had been used, magnetic traces normally detected by Helicon's sensor pack would have dissipated. In short, I've come up with zero."

"That iss correct. I, too, have found nothing to ssuport my abduction theory. However, these journalss of Novass are informative in other matterss."

"What do you mean?" Descartes prodded.

"It appears that Novass has been invesstigating the K'Tar movement for quite ssome time... decadess in fact."

"What?!" Descartes blurted.

Helicon continued, "Contrary to the Council'ss desires to deal with the K'Tar's inssurgency by ignoring them, Novass has maintained an intense investigation of their activitiess for quite ssome time. She has paid particularly close attention to its leader, T'Poch. I have only scanned sssome of the ledgerss, but have recorded them for further sstudy."

"We should get those doubloons back to the plant and start immediately," Descartes directed.

Turning to Brown, he added, "How about you, J.B.. What did you find?"

"Well, Morgan, it's probably nothing. It could even be a nervous habit of Dr. Edison's... sort of like 'doodling'."

"What are you talking about?" Descartes asked impatiently.

"This," Brown answered, holding out his hand.

Lying in his palm was an antique memo ledger Brown had found on Dr. Edison's bedside table. Opening it to the last page containing notes, he showed it to the others.

"I thought it was interesting that Dr. Edison preferred to log his spontaneous ideas with an antique pen and paper," Brown added. "As I was turning through the pages I found this..." he demonstrated, pointing to the page.

In Gothic script almost illegible to the group were the letters ... "STI".

"Like I said, he could have done this out of nervousness, sort of like the way you shake your foot while sitting and thinking."

Descartes glared at his personnel manager, letting him know this was no time to criticize his little quirks.

"I had Helicon scan it and he confirmed the handwriting to be that of Dr. Edison," Brown finished, smirking at the rise he had gotten out of his plant manager.

"Any ideas as to what the initials mean?" Descartes inquired.

Helicon responded, "Sspacing between letterss indicates a word, rather than just initials. Further studiess using the plant's cryptographic computer may reveal other information."

"All the more reason to head back to the plant," Descartes commented.

A click over Descartes's shoulder sent a chill to the base of his neck. Spinning around, the whirdling sound of a pulsar musket confirmed his fear. A sickening spasm instantly replaced the chill as the beam engulfed its victim. Crumpling to the floor, Descartes felt he must be hallucinating. The last image he saw was the face of the rogue Castorian he had left under siege from his fellow rebels.

*   *   *

Nimon trudged diligently through the loose, desert sands. He reflected, somewhat mystified, on how uneventful the past several days had been. True to his training, he had spent the nights in a restorative trance which maximized his performance during the hot days. He seemed to be living proof - emphasis on the living - that the Geminian physique was more capable of sustaining itself during the heat of the desert's days versus the bitter cold of its nights. This fact was made more evident when Nimon's lack of clothes was taken into account. He had done well, though, in minimizing the adverse effects of the frigid nights. As dusk settled each evening, he located a pool of soft sand and scooped out a shallow pit in which to lie. Donning the waxen mask he had fabricated from the gel of the Brav-Ni, he would then pull the sand back over his body as a natural thermal blanket. A good treatment of the Brav-Ni leaves to his skin provided enough deterrent to any parasitic insects, while the heat retaining silicates of the desert floor provided warmth.

But to Nimon's surprise, the nights spent in meditation had proven less and less effective. As the blistering sun reached its apex in the auburn sky, Nimon looked quizzically at his beryl blue skin. The Brav-Ni leaves had served their purpose in preventing burning, promoting the skin pigments to erupt in their characteristic hue.

"If only Mr. Brown could see me now," Nimon thought, recalling Brown's occasional reference to him as a "blue lagoon of a lady's man", ready to drown any woman with his charm.

But the slight tingling Nimon felt each time he made a new application of the leaves continued to puzzle him. As he began a relaxation thought routine, he noticed his degree of concentration was below its expected level of efficiency. Continuing his march, thoughts of the hypnotic episode with Kronia sporadically invaded his consciousness; her words now intruding upon his thoughts...

THE TRUTH THAT AWAITS THEE WILL BE PAINFUL, NIMON. THE MEANING OF THE PHOENOS WILL CUT A NEW WOUND WITHIN YOUR BEING. BEHIND THE COOL LOVE OF LIFE HELD BY OUR RACE SEETHES A SAVAGERY AND PASSION NEVER TO BE SPOKEN. DO WE DARE REVEAL THESE TRUTHS, EVEN TO THE SLIGHTEST DEGREE? YOUR EXPERIENCE WITH STARN SPEAKS OF THESE TRUTHS. BUT SO DO THE TEACHINGS OF THE K'TAR! ARE THEY DIFFERENT, OR ARE THEY THE SAME? I HAVE RELEASED IN YOU THE ABILITY TO TASTE THE SAVAGERY OF WHAT WE WERE. WHEN THE TIME COMES, YOUR

ACTIONS WILL DECIDE THE PATH OUR RACE WILL FOLLOW. FEEL THE PAIN, NIMON, YET IGNORE IT. ONLY THEN CAN YOU CHOOSE THE WAY FOR OUR CULTURE'S FUTURE. SUCH WAS THE WAY WITH MITRON, SO IT WILL BE FOR YOU.

Images of Kronia's icy hot words floated before Nimon's mind's-eye. The tingling sensation in his skin increased. His mind reeled as he fell to his knees in the scorching sands. Kronia's thoughts faded, to be replaced by thoughts strangely familiar, yet alien. The dormant area of his mind touched by T'Poch once again burned. Yet the thoughts were now molten with an intensity never before felt by Nimon.

YOU HAVE COME FAR, NIMON, BUT YOUR WILL IS WEAKENING. I HAVE DR. EDISON. I HAVE DESCARTES. I HAVE HALTED YOUR MEAGER EFFORTS AT CHANGE THROUGH STARN. HOWEVER, MY EFFORTS HAVE ONLY JUST BEGUN, AND YOU ARE THE KEY TO THEIR BEGINNING. YOU WILL YIELD TO ME NIMON. YOU WILL PROVIDE

THE SEED WHICH WILL
CONTINUE THE LINE, FOR THE
LINE *WILL NOT DIE*!

The fire in his skin was overwhelming, yet insignificant to the pain he felt from those searing thoughts. To sense them so strongly, their source must be extremely close! Kneeling in the sand, shoulders slumped forward, Nimon raised his head toward the blinding light of the sun. Reflexively, the nictitating membrane of his eyes closed to filter the harmful rays. But through their haze, Nimon could still identify the person standing before him, though he had never actually seen her before.

It was T'Poch!

CHAPTER 18

Novas' three known existences collided with cataclysmic force.

In one existence, locked in a feral embrace with Ravar, she sensed movement in the mechanical hand he had devised. She had empowered it! But this was impossible!

In another level of existence, thoughts of Legotian treachery infiltrated her consciousness. Was it again the psychic rape that confused her?

And in yet another reality, she recalled faint memories of a time when empowerment in her "real" world was possible only during a self-induced coma.

These three realities tore the fabric of her sanity as she and Ravar reached the pinnacle of their desires. The weight of his tensed body pushed her to the floor. Still intertwined, they lay motionless. Their spent energies barely allowed them the luxury of breath. Slumber would be pure indulgence. But Novas could not afford such decadent pleasures. What she had just experienced urged her to seek answers.

A lifelong search for Phoenos had prodded Novas to reach to the stars for their secrets. At an arms-length away lay the key to that mystery, both in this Legotian version of "reality", and in her own past. Her discovery seemed all but a faded memory. In her youth, she had scoured the annals of Geminian folklore for references to Phoenos. A fragmented scroll had spoken of the time of Mitron, when the search for Phoenos had formed the cornerstone for building a peaceful society. During that time, at the height of conflict between the life rightist Mitronians and the materialistic Ravarians, it had been whispered that the essence of Phoenos had been spawned. Wrapped in a veil of symbolism and secrecy, the scrolls told of one touched by the hand of Phoenos. Always thought to be a metaphorical reference, could it actually have been literal?

To Novas, it was all that mattered. Whether in her own world, or within a mental construct of a power-starved alien, she knew only that she must unravel the secret.

Collecting her ebbing strength, she whispered, "Ravar... Ravar..."

Coaxed from his dream-like catatonia, the Geminian nobleman stirred.

"I must get up, my lover," Novas continued, softly. "I have... touched Phoenos."

A broad smile spread across the giant man's face as he lifted it from the nape of her neck. "You are too kind, beautiful star-vixen."

"No, you silly oaf... I am serious. Did you not feel it? Could you not sense what has happened?"

"I sense only that I love you... and that we are bonded."

"Dear Ravar... I, too, have deep feelings for you. But you must... let... me... up." Novas gently -but firmly- pressed his shoulders upward and to the side. He grudgingly complied by rolling on to one elbow.

Pulling her scantily-clad body up to the lab work-bench, she peered over the edge in anticipation. Level with her eyes was a mace of steel fingers clenched into a fist. Her face flushed with anticipation.

"Ravar...dear Ravar. Was your device configured as an open palm?"

The warrior-scientist shook his head in disbelief, thinking, "Here is a truly rare woman. An instant after being locked in the throes of passionate lovemaking, she is asking about an experiment."

Hoisting himself into a kneeling position behind her, he reached a firm arm around her bare torso. Burrowing his mouth into her black and silver tresses in search of her neck he responded, "Yes, my lovely. It was."

"Look at it now," she whispered.

Ravar cocked one eye in the direction of the bioduotronic hand, not wanting to lose his concentration on the more important matters in his real ones. As the impact of what he saw filtered through his hormone-deadened senses, he could only respond with an oath.

"By the stars...."

"Well said, my amorous one. I believe we have found your 'breakthrough'."

"I do not understand. From where did it receive power? By what force?"

"By the force of the mind..." Novas whispered, in awe. Rising, she reached gingerly for the metallic fist. Lifting it as if it were a holy chalice, she turned it over and over. "I have seen this before," she murmured. Studying its intricate construction, she recalled its every detail. "But the secret of its design remains elusive, never to be copied. Its core does serve another. One very far away. But how can it be here, unless you have found a way to duplicate that which empowers a Singular Dualiity. Show me how you have interfaced the crystal," she urged.

Ravar complied obediently. Though his impatience to understand the unknown equaled his lovely companion's, he knew when to stay silent, and learn. She had wrapped herself in a veil of mystery since the first day they had met. He believed that now he was about to enjoy the pleasure of looking beneath that veil. His thick fingers appeared to transform into delicate instruments as he removed vital components from the device. Peeling away wafer thin layers of micro-circuitry, he revealed a small chamber. At its center was the crystal. Slowly, he lifted it from its cradle.

Novas scrutinized his every move, as if the secrets of the cosmos were being revealed. She cupped her hands as he softly placed the purified meteorite in them.

A televid chime broke the reverence of the moment. Ravar turned to a table monitor and pressed the appropriate keys. He did not hear the gasp from Novas as he responded to the incoming call.

"Sire Ravar... you must come to the launch site at once. There are.... difficulties." The aide looked nervously from side to side, as if his words were being overheard by unwanted ears.

"What difficulties," Ravar barked.

"I fear I cannot say over open airways, sire."

Ravar punched a few more pads on the console. "The line is now secure. So tell me, what are these difficulties?"

"Crowds have been forming through the night near the launch area. There is talk among the people that there are many more who wish to join us in our journey."

"We have room for more who wish to follow us. What is the concern?"

"The numbers are overwhelming, sire. The recent storms have spread fears that your theories are true."

"Of course they are true! But they are apparently in error with regard to how many would believe them. Fear is unpredictable," Ravar grimly stated.

He continued, "We have toiled too long to let our success be taken from us. There will be no test. Begin loading our followers from the underground barracks through the tunnels. You were wise to be cautious of being overheard. No-one must know that we will depart during the 'tests'. I will be there shortly."

Ravar turned back to Novas. Her face looked as if every drop of blood had been drained from it.

"My enchantress, do not be shocked. As I told you, I will not leave you. You are coming with me. We are bonded."

Novas stared through him as if he were glass. Her mind was barely cognizant of the conversation that had just transpired. She was overcome by deeper fears. In her hands she held the crystal... in two fragments. She slowly lifted them up to Ravar's face for him to see.

"The crystal... what happened?"

From Novas' catatonic visage came the response, her lips barely moving to form the words, "The force of my mind was too great... I have doomed my people."

Ravar stared at his lover in disbelief. "What are you saying?"

"I cannot explain. There is no... time."

"About that, you are right. We must go now. You heard from the televid. Our departure is imminent. As for Phoenos, we have unlocked its secret. This lab can be reconstructed once we arrive safely at our new homeworld. I have already loaded the remaining pieces of the meteorite on board the starcraft. With the purified crystal... and you... we can uncover the untold secrets of Phoenos together."

Novas looked through her dulled stare briefly into the eyes of the husband she could never have. Whether from an insidious mind construct of the horrid Legotian, or a cruel trick of Fate, she was unsure. But she did know that she must stay behind. Steeling herself for what she must do, she responded.

"Ravar, I have used you. Mitron attempted to seduce me while underneath the influence of forbidden herbs. I wanted him, but not under those conditions. In retaliation, I took from him what can never be replaced... his trust in you. By taking you as my lover, the two of you can never be the same. I will hold this knowledge. With it, I will still have him, but under my terms. So you see, I cannot go with you. I do not love you."

Ravar recoiled from the bite of her deadly words. He stared into her eyes, seeking the truth in her soul. At that instant, he saw an empty void. He paused. The silence between them was stone cold. Then he spoke.

"Novas, I hear your words, but do not know from whence they come. I have known Del Mitron for a lifetime. He would not act as you say. I also have known P'Teel... for more than a lifetime should have to bear. She is the source of the forbidden herbs, for she has used them before. In the cave during our first meeting, I tasted her evil potions. She has held my soul in her wicked grasp ever since. It was Mitron she wanted, and she used me to get to him.

You are not like her. But I see in your heart that you believe in what you are doing. Against that, I have no battle. But hear me, beautiful one. In time, we will meet again..."

Ravar reached forward and took half of the fractured crystal. Novas watched, paralyzed by the truth that she could not reveal to him. He held the iridescent shard before her face and let the light of Gemini's sun cast its beauty upon her.

"... and as symbol of our eternal, yet broken bond, I take this crystal fragment."

Ravar spun on his heels, gathered his cloak about him, and left.

Novas looked into her palm at the crystal that remained. Its familiarity was a rapier, stabbing her mind without mercy. Its terrible meaning for her people, and for the fate of the galaxy overwhelmed her. The child of the stars gaped with horror, and wept.

CHAPTER 19

The two Terrans finally stirred from their musket charge induced paralysis. The Clionian, although relatively older, had fully recovered more than an hour earlier due to the more robust physiology of his reptoid species.

Descartes and Brown struggled to clear their mind fog, using Helicon's words as beacons to guide them toward full consciousness. "Unfortunately gentlemen, I have no idea where we are. As you can ssee from our ssituation, we have been kept subdued and bound to these tables by our kidnapperss."

As he spoke, Helicon nodded his toothy snout toward the metal bands which pinned their arms, legs - and in his case, tail - to the tables.

"For once I wish Nimon were here..." grumbled Brown, his sniping about the Geminian being evidence of his full recovery from the drugs, "... at least he could use that stopwatch mind of his to tell us how long we've been out. From the size of the fur ball in my mouth, it must have been quite a while! And what's the point of tying us down like a pack of Denebian spine-hogs, anyway!"

Plant Manager Descartes suppressed a smile at his cranky personnel manager, as he shook away the last of the cobwebs from his mind.

In response to Brown's comment, Helicon added, "It may not be as accurate as a Geminian'ss, but being from a race of hisstorians does have sssome advantages. We have developed ssomewhat of a time sense. I esstimate we have been unconssciouss 3.74 Sssolar days since being overcome by pulsssssar musket fire. I sssusspect we have been dossed regularly with anessssthetics since our capture."

"Not as accurate as a Geminian, huh?" Brown mumbled sarcastically. "At least you're a lot more humble about it than one particular Geminian is!"

Descartes now spoke up, partly to suppress any further tirade Brown may start regarding their mutual Geminian friend. "One thing's for certain... we're no longer on Gemini. Assuming we left orbit immediately after we were stunned, we could be just about anywhere by now."

"How can you be sso certain we're in sspace-flight, Mr. Descartes?" Helicon inquired.

Brown interrupted, "While you've got your time-sense, Helicon, it just so happens that a select few die-hard space jockeys like Morgan here have an innate sense of when they're space bound. Nimon has his high-falutin' theories explaining it, but I just like to chalk it up to good old human intuition."

"I ssee..." responded the Clionian. "Quite interesting."

The hiss of the solitary door to their chamber interrupted any further discussion about the plant manager's sixth sense. Standing in the threshold was a single Castorian guard, wielding a control pad in one hand and a pulsar musket in the other.

Before Descartes could fire off a volley of questions as to the reasons for their capture, the guard aimed the control pad in their direction and keyed several buttons. The magnetic fields pinning the bands around their wrists and legs to the tables were immediately deactivated, permitting them to stand. After a few moments of allowing movement to dispel the effects of nearly four days of inactivity, the Castorian pressed several more keys. This sequence tightly bonded the wristbands together in front of each captive. Their legs, however, were left unencumbered.

In broken Terranese, the guard indicated for them to move out of their cell and down the hallway. After a short walk and brief ride in a cramped carrier pad, they found themselves outside a door marked "Vice-Executive Talor," according to Helicon's translation.

Descartes' mind raced during the entire transfer, taking in every detail of the ship, looking for any weakness to exploit when the opportunity arose.

"Either these fellows are extremely overconfident... or extremely inexperienced," Descartes thought. "Even with a weapon, one guard in that carrier pad makes for a tempting chance to make a break." But the plant manager's curiosity prevented an escape attempt so early in the game. "Whoever we're being taken to see just may provide some valuable information," he decided to himself. "A few more cards need to be played before I up the ante."

Upon entering the quarters of Talor, Descartes immediately noted the difference in size between this office and the few others he'd seen aboard Castorian commercial vessels. Since he had not recognized this ship's layout nor that of the smaller vice-executive's office, he had concluded he must be aboard a nonstandard class of Castorian craft. When his captor spun his chair around to meet them, Descartes's suspicions were confirmed.

"So we meet once more, Descartes. This time it's face-to-face, and even your charade with the Mass Interdimensional Teleporter can't save you!" the youthful Castorian snapped, partially rising from his chair.

The image prior to the debilitating pulsar blast congealed in Descartes's mind. The Castorian he thought had been Executive Stol had actually been this infuriated vice-executive, Talor. Descartes wondered whether revenge for the humiliation Talor had experienced was reason enough to stage such a bold kidnapping deep in Solar Corporation's holdings, or was there another motive? He decided a little goading might prompt the Castorian to unwittingly answer some of his questions.

"Well, Talor, since you're still alive, it must mean you successfully obliterated your Executive," Descartes surmised, fanning the flames of the youthful Castorian's temper.

"Don't pride yourself on successes that you do not truly have, Descartes!" Talor shot back. "Although my Executive's ship was lost, he managed to survive by being ejected in a safety pod at the last instant!"

"If my memory serves me, it was your ship that was firing the heaviest salvos on your Executive," Descartes bluffed, since he actually could not identify who was in control of the other two ships during their encounter. "My guess is that Stol sent you on a no-win assignment deep into Solar Corporation territory under the guise of redemption for your blunder."

"It is not a no-win assignment, as you can plainly see! I have succeeded in capturing several prize hostages for our cause. And as for my colleague, Vice-Executive Ralek, if he were more a leader and less a yes-man, he too would have fired upon the image of your ship, as I did!"

"Instead, he wisely scanned for safety pods and recovered his executive aboard his own ship and saved him," Descartes thought to himself. But he did not speak his thoughts. It was not Descartes's intent to anger Talor just for the sake of making him angry. He wanted to learn more of the Castorian's objective. So, he chose to focus his barbs on a different topic.

"Surely you don't expect the Solar Corporation to take interest in our capture, Talor. We are expendable assets. You've made a serious blunder in strategy risking your vessel and workers just to capture us!"

"You know nothing of our strategy, Descartes!" Talor fired back. "We were sent as insurance to prevent your interference with our cause. You were getting too close to identifying our contact on Gemini. Had you done this, the chain of events necessary for our success would have been broken."

Descartes's mind clicked at the speed of a 30 terahertz biocomputer. "A contact on Gemini involved with a Castorian band of rebels... a contact which he had come close to identifying... the only clues they had uncovered were Novas' manuscripts and Dr. Edison's ledger with the inscription... `STI'. What could it mean?"

The life crystal plant manager decided to play his favorite game one more time. And as usual, he would employ his skill of bluffing.

"Of course!" Descartes exclaimed. "It all becomes clear now. The ledger! `STI' was the key to revealing your contact on Gemini!"

Brown looked at Descartes in surprise. As long as he'd known his manager he had yet to learn how to tell if he were bluffing or truly on the right track. Either way, his boss always seemed to get results. This time was no exception.

Stepping out from a shadowy alcove in the rear of the vice-executive's chamber was a figure that shocked even Descartes.

"Very astute, Mr. Descartes. Our decision to kidnap you was indeed profitable in that you have discerned my identity," spoke the new arrival.

"Steth!" exclaimed Brown, unable to contain his surprise. "'STI' was a partially written name... your name!"

"I must also compliment your investigative skills, Helicon," Steth continued, shrugging off the effects of Jeff Brown's annoying ability to restate the obvious. "It was you who discovered Novas' manuscripts. Had she been successful in presenting them to the Council of Elders, they would have been very damaging to our cause. Quite impractical of Novas to write them by hand, considering how archaic that form of communication has become. Although it did succeed in delaying its discovery."

Recovering from the shock of seeing the Geminian Council Prosecutor on board the Castorian ship, Descartes continued his efforts to draw out vital information.

"Just what is this cause, Steth," Descartes inquired. "How could it be so important that it would make you risk your very heritage by allying with rogue Castorians?"

The Council Prosecutor exploded with fury!

"Were you blind as well as deaf during the trial of your technical superintendent, human?" Steth barked. "The Clionian's defense was well prepared. The holovid coins clearly chronicled the expulsion from Gemini of the mutual ancestors of my people and my Castorian brethren. Had Mitron not brought about his peace movement, the Geminian and Castorian races would now be united! Combined, we would be the most powerful force in the galaxy. Instead, the peaceful preachings of Mitron so many cycles ago caused the strength of our ancestors to be weakened by separation. But now, our movement, the glorious K'Tar, is to re-establish that unity. The combined aggressiveness of the Castorians joined with the business expertise of the Geminians is the ultimate example of 'dual life from the same source.' Yet the power of the synergy between our races will be focused toward monopolistic domination of the galaxy, not peaceful coexistence!"

Descartes stared into the raw fury of the Geminian's crimson eyes. He replayed history as he recalled other such 'causes'... the Terran Middle East Confrontation which culminated in the Third Great War, the Martian Colony Rebellion, and most recently the Salurian Revolt - all had been 'causes', led by single-minded people which had culminated in immense destruction. And now, standing before him was the standard-bearer of yet another movement which could easily dwarf the carnage of those others. The K'Tar's militant business ethics could escalate into a galactic war costing billions of lives and untold financial losses.

Descartes shuddered as Steth continued. "There is no sense in withholding our plans from you, Descartes. In fact, it gives me pleasure in revealing them."

A strange smirk flickered across the normally cold Geminian face. Descartes could almost hear the straining of the muscles so seldom used to form a smile. Ironically, the smirk reminded him of Nimon. He wondered how his technical superintendent figured into the K'Tar's plans. Nimon's supposed opponent at the conclusion of his desert trial stood here before him, light-years from Gemini. It must mean Steth had no intentions of confronting Nimon in combat. That revelation made Descartes all the more determined to learn Steth's plans. Even if it meant goading him into a fight which he had no hopes of winning.

CHAPTER 20

Dreams...reality...nightmares...memories... all swirled within Novas' mind in a myriad of inseparable sensations. Grief stricken and exhausted after Ravar's departure, she sat bent over a lab bench, laying her head in her arms, letting the cool surface of the stone caress her cheek as she slipped in and out of a restless sleep. Again, she was in the graviton sled. Sitting in the rear compartment, she noticed it was much older now. Its interior fabric had changed, yet it was still the same vehicle as the one piloted by Ravar. Her dream-clouded vision cleared slightly as she looked again into the co-pilot's seat. The image of Mitron morphed into that of a woman. It was Kronia! Fear gripped Novas by the throat. She remembered what had long been forgotten. Fighting against terror's grasp, she forced herself to turn to see the passenger next to her. The sinister smile was all too recognizable now. It was P'Teel. Time had added deep furrows to the enchantress' face, but it was unmistakably hers. The crimson fire in her eyes glowed with evil intent. Her withered arms reached out for the bundle Novas cradled to her breast. As the biodgen-child was given over to the old woman, Novas fought back the tears. But that was in the past. Novas had not cried then. As her young pride held back the flood of shameful sorrow, she allowed herself but one luxury. From her neck, Novas removed a golden chain. Dangling from the chain was a pendant. It had been handed down through the generations to the eldest female child of the clan. Kronia herself had given it to Novas when she was a baby. The pendant's significance had been shrouded in secrets so mysterious that its true meaning had long been forgotten. Novas had believed she would never be part of the tradition. Her first and only child was male. She was unable to produce another offspring.

Until now.

Novas placed the chain and pendant around the neck of the "first-borne" biodgen - that first-borne, a product of the science of Dr. Nicholas Edison and the union of her genetic matrix and synthetic crystals patterned after an ancient shard discovered long ago. The first-borne would become T'Poch. Once she was far enough away, the contents of the pendant would be implanted in the dormant construct. If their science, and yes, their ancient beliefs, proved true, Novas would project her thoughts without the use of devices or a comatose slumber to empower the first Singular Dualiity!

In Novas' grief-stricken dream, she studied the pendant. At its center was a crystal. Marvelous in its beauty, but terrifying in its significance.

The crystalline shard was the very one she had clutched as Ravar departed.

But the crystal that could unlock the secret of the Phoenos had two halves.

Through generations, one half had remained within the clan Mitron on the planet Gemini. Ancient legend dictated that it must pass from clan matriarch to eldest female child along the direct blood kindred line of Mitron. The legend also foretold of the day that the crystal would reunite with its lost half. The Geminian crystal would one day join with its missing mate. Holders of the two halves would form a bond. From that union would arise a civilization of untold power ... a power that would stretch to the farthest ends of the galaxies. And from that power would come greatness for all that followed.

As the laws of antiquity had demanded, Novas had given the Geminian half of the crystalline legacy to her only "daughter". Though biodgen, and never to be held by Novas while empowered, Novas loved T'Poch through the love her husband was able to share. And so, the day of bestowing the crystal upon the dormant child had also been a day of great sadness. For on that day, Novas had also given her child over to adoption. Her grief at the thought had been overwhelming. She had resisted. But the ceremonial elixir provided to her had dissolved her will. Kronia had said it would be for the best … but the best for who?

"How wrong could I have been?" Novas chided herself. "Kronia must have known the identity of the matronly old woman … the woman that I now know to be P'Teel! Somehow, through the seasons, P'Teel had survived. She had waited for destiny, and it had been handed to her. "How was I to know?"

Novas' thoughts were a kaleidoscope of swirling images, and as in many dreams, the images defied logic. "P'Teel had been given both the Mitronian crystal and its heiress. But P'Teel was from the past. She could not have been the one in the graviton car. She had raised T'Poch to follow her ways … the ways of the mysterious Fire Arts. But these powers were no more than ramblings of the ancients around the tribal fires. Could they have given her immortality? T'Poch had one half of the crystal, but for P'Teel to succeed, she must possess both. With both halves, the power of the Phoenos would be hers. Only but a few knew that through T'Poch, and the Mitronian crystal, Novas had achieved Phoenos.

"Or was it just a step toward Phoenos? Was the creation of a Singular Dualiity but an almost insurmountable obstacle along the path to Phoenos? Legend foretold that the two halves of the crystal formed during her empowering of Ravar's construct would be reunited. Was the true Phoenos somehow within the grasp of

P'Teel? To be so, P'Teel would need the crystal's other half. How could she obtain something lost for generations?"

Bolting upright from her sleep, a flash of realization seized Novas. She now understood the purpose behind the mind-torture of the Legotian. "He must know the location of the missing Ravarian half of the crystal! He has taken me through the insidious mind scenarios on an ancient Gemini for but one purpose ... to discover the possessor of the crystal's Geminian half!"

An overwhelming sense of betrayal swept over Novas. She had wronged her only daughter many years ago. Now, she betrayed her again by revealing that T'Poch held the Mitronian part of the crystal. She had failed her people by hiding the truth of T'Poch's existence. And now she betrayed them again by revealing to an enemy the source of untold power. Novas struggled to regain what little was left of her senses. Her memories of her painful past dissipated into images of a more recent time. She recalled the Legotian... and the Castorian empress. She remembered the childhood legends of Geminians cast out into space by Mitron. Whispers of Castorians from Geminian seeds filtered into her mind. The sensuous thoughts of her encounter with Ravar crept into her heart. She saw him holding the crystalline mate in his hand as he turned to leave for his starcraft.

The fear of a union between the Castorian race and the K'Tar became a cold chill that swept away the last vestiges of haze from her thoughts. With crystal clarity, she realized that a union between them would place the power of the Phoenos in their hands, and that she must not let that happen! One hope remained for her to stop the hideous nightmare thrust upon her by the Legotian. She would play out the mind opera he had written. In the coming scenes, she would act out her part, but with a sole objective in mind. She must stop Ravar!

Pulling herself up from the laboratory floor, Novas staggered out of the building into the evening air. She had been comatose since morning. A glow on the horizon seized her attention and forced her to witness what she had dreaded. Six starcraft rose majestically into the heavens. Raging fires spewed from beneath their launch modules. Once spent, they were discarded over the Geminian desert, leaving their main vessels free to reach out to the stars.

"NOOOOOOO!" Novas screamed with anguish. Cursing the Fates that prevented her from altering this torturous mind-scenario, she fell to her knees and pounded the baked clay. The crystal in her palm tore at her flesh. The pain became the source of a new idea within her ravaged mind.

"If I destroy this half of the crystal, the scenario will be altered. Perhaps the Legotian must use real objects to activate his mind creations. If that is true, the destruction of this crystal half will end his power-hungry scheme."

Looking around for a tool to carry out her hysteria-induced plan, she spied a stone outcropping further down the pathway leading from the lab. Giggling incessantly, she trudged toward the rocks. The familiarity of the area escaped her. She failed to remember that a short time ago, it was here that she met Mitron and Ravar.

Half stumbling, half running, her fevered mind forced her body forward. Falling to her knees amidst the sharp stones, she ignored the pain tearing at her legs. She placed the crystal shard on a section of flat granitium. With both hands, she grasped a companion stone and raised it high above her head.

"Phoenos will not be used against my people!" she vowed. The instant her arms began their downward course, a shadowy figure leapt from the bushes behind her. The attacker hurtled full force into Novas' back, causing her blow to narrowly miss the crystal. The two figures tumbled across the rocky path, with the attacker deftly recovering first. Novas lay on her side, the wind knocked out of her, mouthing noiseless curses at the woman standing before her.

P'Teel sneered back at her injured opponent. "I still do not understand you, mysterious one. But it does not matter. You have served my purposes well." The enchantress knelt to pick up the crystal fragment. "This must be something of great power if you fear it." P'Teel turned it slowly, holding it up to the waning light of the evening.

Novas' breath came slowly, yet painfully back to her. Whispering, she inquired, "What do you mean... served your purposes well...?"

Mockingly, P'Teel responded. "Did you think you could displace me from the attentions of Mitron so easily? From the first day of your arrival, I could see the effect you had upon him. So I chose to use that to my advantage. I allowed the two of you to become closer. It served my purpose for you to weaken his accursed resolve. My attempts to seduce him had failed... until you appeared. You ignited the fires within him like no woman had ever done before. I merely "accentuated" them with a few carefully mixed potions. I expected that you would spurn his advances, once you realized they were induced by the elixir of another enchantress. That is when I took the advantage."

Novas reeled in disgust from what she was hearing. The thought of her being used as a pawn in this woman's sexual quest for power was revolting. Her own past under the hypnotic influences of Kronia's potions and the encounter with P'Teel stabbed at her as she fought to regain her strength in both mind and body.

P'Teel continued, "I took your beloved Mitron. His body and soul are mine. Through him, I will unite the mindless, scattered tribesmen of this world into a force of untold power. Then I will exert my will upon them. They will worship me as their leader. At my bidding, we will follow Ravar into space. I will use his explorations as a means for my forces to conquer the stars!"

Novas was gradually recovering. If she could distract P'Teel for just a few more moments, she would be able to overcome her. Once in control, she could regain the crystalline fragment. She was still convinced that the crystal's destruction would end this infernal Legotian mind torture.

"P'Teel, neither Ravar nor Mitron are so feeble-willed. I know them too well. You could not have them as your slaves."

"You doubt my power?! Then let me prove it. Ravar expressed his undying love for you, did he not? He courted you until your desires for him clouded your feelings for Mitron. Ravar revealed to you his deepest secrets... things about his work that even Mitron did not know. And finally, he begged you to follow him to the stars. Do you think he did this of his own free will? Foolish child... it was I who controlled Ravar. My potions directed his will. But he failed me. You were meant to go with him. That would clear the way for my ultimate control over Mitron. I cannot have you near him. Your presence would complicate the delicate balance of my influence over him."

"You pride yourself too highly on your 'power', P'Teel. Ravar knew of your attempts to control him. He admitted them to me. You could not overcome the true source of his will. His dream to explore space would not be soiled by your insidious plot. That dream was pure, as was his desire for me. You control nothing!"

P'Teel cackled at Novas' attempted defense. She stalked closer and raised her hands to shoulder height. Novas noticed an aura emanating from her fingertips as it slowly spread down her arms. The crystal remained protected in P'Teel's palm.

"Ahh... but you are wrong, young one. I control a great deal. You see, because of Ravar's failure to take you with him, I am forced to correct his flaw. In so doing, you will see that my control is extensive. For you, its extent means I control your very LIFE!"

Novas catapulted herself over a nearby boulder just as red energy beams leapt from P'Teel's hands. Dust roiled up from the ground where Novas lay merely seconds before.

The Geminian scientist, businesswoman, and ambassador had faced many conflicts in her life. In most, she had been victorious. In the few where she had lost, she had become stronger from that loss. Yet, in none of them did she succumb to blind rage. This was the first.

As the mind fever engulfed her consciousness, white fire coursed through her blood. Revenge consumed her soul.

Rising from behind the safety of her stone shield, Novas thrust her hands forward. Folklore shrouded in mystic whisperings transformed into reality as cobalt energy streamed from her finger tips. The shock of discovering her newfound power would be fleeting. It had to be for her to survive.

P'Teel responded with reflexes honed by years of study. Bringing in her outstretched arms, she cupped her hands in front of her with palms facing her foe. The crystal was casually dropped and skated several treds toward Novas. In its place, a scarlet energy sphere formed around P'Teel's hands to absorb the oncoming radiation. The atmosphere crackled as invisible clouds of ozone formed at the interface of the conflicting power streams. Slowly, the blue fire began to falter beneath the intensity of the more experienced enchantress' beams.

Novas shifted to her left while moving intently forward to where the crystal lay. This movement distracted P'Teel ever so slightly, as told by the cobalt flame's surge toward its target.

P'Teel smiled wickedly toward her opponent and patronized her, "Your concentration is impressive. Movement during Fire Battle is a higher level skill. I underestimated you. I will not do so again."

The enchantress followed her threat with action. Clenching her fists, she bore down upon her assailant and drove the blue beam backward toward Novas. The inexperienced starchild retaliated with youthful vigor. As the fury of the combatants intensified, they both crept slowly toward the open area where the crystal lay.

Novas sensed her body temperature rising as she struggled to overcome the more mature powers of P'Teel. In the fragmented recesses of her mind, she knew she could not sustain this onslaught much longer. Desperation offered her an alternative.

Novas dropped her hands and lunged forward. As she executed a shoulder roll across the ground, P'Teel's beams flashed above her. But Novas' hopes of surprising P'Teel were dashed, for the wicked enchantress was closer to the crystal ... and just as fast.

The more experienced combatant snatched the iridescent stone and held it in one hand above her head in defiance. The hand glowed once more, charging itself for a final blast. Novas sat crouched below her, covered in the dust of defeat. Still unable to accept that the Legotian controlling this hallucination had won, she offered one last challenge.

"Before you kill me, your master should know this. The crystal in its separate parts is useless. But the crystal as a whole is lethal ... unless used by one who has the ability. No-one in the K'Tar has that ability. I do. Destroy me and the power of Phoenos is lost forever!"

"I see your fear of me affects your mind. Your words have little meaning. I am my own master. It is I who lead the sisters of the Fire Arts. That is why your presence has been troublesome to me. Though we are few in number, we are growing. Yet, you are unknown to my sisters, and you clearly have the Power. I cannot allow you to challenge me. Your destruction means only that you threaten me no longer."

Novas saw that she had influenced the course of the Legotian scenario. She was still breathing. The key was to direct her words more to him than to the visual construct of the enchantress.

"You speak of fear clouding my thoughts. Is your fear of me so great that you cannot hear the truth in my words? The K'Tar cannot be trusted. They seek chaos. Their goal is domination at any cost. There will be no room for any partnership with them. Phoenos in their hands will result in mindless beings serving only the K'Tar's purpose. You..."

"STOP! I will hear no more! This 'K'Tar' of which you speak embodies the principles in which I believe! You will blaspheme them no longer! I tire of your words and of you! Now you will DIE!"

Novas recoiled from P'Teel's outburst. Instantly, she realized her ploy had failed. It was as if the Legotian could not hear her ... as if the enchantress herself controlled the events. Panic-stricken, Novas reacted to her new insight. Still crouched, she extended her leg behind her and spun savagely on her other heel. The outstretched leg crashed into the enchantress' knee, causing her to crumple to the ground. Leaping upon the fallen sorceress, Novas grabbed the glowing wrist. With her other hand, she clutched at the crystal. Thousands of needles pricked at her nerve endings as P'Teel's bioenergy extended into Novas arm. The younger starchild replied by willing her own waning powers to push back against the numbing effect. Novas felt the stone slip ever so slightly in P'Teel's fingers. She dared to believe that once she possessed it, this maddening hallucination would be over. But P'Teel would not comply.

The more experienced mistress of the Fire Arts pulled her wrist down and outward sharply, freeing her hand from Novas' grasp. Coiling her arm, she drove it forward with savage force, the glowing palm almost erupting against Novas' chest. The concussion lifted the Geminian into the air. As the novice hurtled toward the rocky face of the nearby escarpment, P'Teel smiled maliciously. She knew the impact would be fatal.

CHAPTER 21

T'Poch hovered over the kneeling technical superintendent of the Darwin as if savoring the moment of victory. Inexplicably weakened, Nimon still mustered the will to ask and understand the question, "Why?"

T'Poch responded, "You will know soon enough, half-son of Novas." She then smoothly applied a debilitating spray to Nimon's face, causing instant unconsciousness.

*　　*　　*

An icy chill swept through Nimon's mind as he floated at an unconscious level between reality and dreams. He was carrying the half-frozen body of his own Dual, Starn, through waist-deep snow drifts. A numbness gripped at his legs, thankfully so, compared to the absence of all feeling in his hands. As he leaned forward into the unceasing blast of arctic wind, he struggled to make sense of his predicament.

"I know I have never done this before, so it cannot be a memory. I must be dreaming. But, the effects of cold on my metabolism can cause the same delusions. One begins to believe he is simply dreaming, and yields to that thought. In doing so, the mind accepts that it is futile to fight a dream, and simply waits until the sleep phase is over. But in waiting for sleep to end, the return to consciousness never comes."

One such story had been recorded in the annals of history from the early Mitronian period. A meteor had plummeted into the Geminian crust, launching massive dust clouds into the atmosphere. The ensuing shift in the climatological balance had nearly decimated the Geminian race due to the micro Ice Age that had resulted. It was said that if not for the leadership and determination of Mitron, all of Gemini would have been lost.

Just as it had been for Geminians then, so it must be for Nimon now. He must meet the challenge. He must not yield to the dream. For in yielding would come the grim certainty of death!

"The stiffened body of Starn grows heavier. With each step, the allure of sleep makes the cold doubly difficult to endure. But I must not give in. I MUST keep going!"

He peered through the slits of his frost encrusted eyelids to see if any relief lay ahead. A cave... a stone outcropping... anything to deflect the wind that lashed at his body. Feeble attempts to blink away a blurred object appearing before him provided not only frustration, but a shred of hope. A dozen paces more transformed the irregularly shaped blotch into a cloaked figure. After a few more steps, the hope disappeared, for he knew it was senseless to believe anyone would be beckoning to him from the depths of this blizzard. Yet, senseless or not, he had nowhere to go but forward.

Closer he came, until with the last vestiges of his will, he commanded his arms to extend forward to hand the lifeless form of his biodgen to the figure. As the cloaked hands reached for Starn, Nimon recoiled violently! He sensed an evil not evident to him before! A familiar evil that could only mean danger to himself and those he wished to save. If he were to survive, he must somehow overcome it.

A fire erupted in Nimon's mind. The flames coursed through his body, filling him with a new source of energy ... no, a new source of power he had never felt before! It instantly dissipated the biting cold and flowed outward into Starn's body. Its glow grew so intense that the cloaked figure staggered backward. With a psychic jolt, Nimon awoke!

His mind was fully functional as he raced through a series of self-check meditational calisthenics. Yet his body was totally immobilized. He had overcome the psychic challenge ... but how? Never before had he been able to control his thoughts in such a manner. It could only be the result of one thing ... Kronia's mindset! He felt it! He realized now what she had done during their hypnotic trance. She had cracked the lid on Pandora's Box! He had tasted the pungent flavor of savagery...the ways of the Ancients... just long enough to serve his needs.

Yet, the evil was still near. Though his mind was now free, his body was still within its control. Lying engulfed in an antigrav stasis field, he heard the evil speak.

"I am surprised, Nimon ... and very impressed," came the haunting whisper of T'Poch's voice. "Your ability to negate my psychic influence further convinces me that true greatness is within our grasp. I had expected that you would remain unconscious until my work was complete. After all ...your father did."

Nimon again performed his self-check exercises to confirm that he was truly conscious. He found it difficult to associate reality with the statement he had just heard.

"What has she done to my father?" he thought, enraged at his captor.

"I sense I have aroused your curiosity, my Geminian-Terran hybrid. That is good. Satisfaction of your curiosity is not the only thing that is in store for you. You pride yourself on your hypnotic control over women. But you do not have feelings for these women. You will experience feelings before I am done with you, Nimon. Feelings which will be your most intense ... and your last!

*　　*　　*

The looming figure of the Geminian Council Prosecutor stood before Descartes as if he were Cloaked Death with his scythe at the ready. Descartes saw the unyielding madness in his eyes... a crazed obsession that total devotion to a cause can bring. Yet Descartes knew he must continue to draw out information if there were any hope of rescuing Dr. Edison.

"My doubts over your plans for conquest, Steth, are quite simple," Descartes retorted to the Geminian's last statement. "I could give a damn about your feeble attempts at megalomania."

Descartes did not see the backhand which sent him hurling across the Castorian vice-executive's quarters ... but he certainly felt it! The Geminian stood over Descartes as the life crystal plant manager gingerly unfolded himself from the corner of the room.

"If anyone is blinded by the desire for power, it is Novas, not I," fumed Steth. "She is even now trying to mold an unwanted venture between the Castorians and the Solar Corporation! Why? So that she will be heralded as a savior like that gelatin-toad Mitron of generations past. The Castorian people want monopolistic dominance, not partners!" he continued. "As do the K'Tar on Gemini. Novas has been quietly watching our movement with the intent to discover a weakness. Instead, she has seen us grow stronger. Her only remaining option to stop us is to form an accord between the Castorian and Geminian corporations. It was her intent that a unification of the two diverse... yet similar... cultures would appease us. But it will not! Our economic models require war! Only then will we be satisfied."

"You've lost me, Steth," Descartes interjected. "Minutes ago you were ranting about how the K'Tar's goal was to unify the schism between Gemini and Castor that was created by Mitron. Now you fume about Novas' attempts to accomplish the same thing. Why must war be the means the K'Tar takes to reach its end?"

"It is simple, Descartes. Simple enough even for you. As we speak, the Castorian representative and Novas are in negotiations before the Legotian leaders. It is they who facilitated the 'no conflict agreement' of Geneva VII, as you well know. By using our rogue ships with their stealth capabilities, we will attack strategic Solar Corporation and Castorian facilities. We will claim responsibility as Castorians for the kidnapping of Executive Novas' very own husband. And, we will set off a chain reaction of aggression between the Solar Corporation and Castorian Conglomerate which even the Legotians cannot halt!" With a sneer, he added, "The ensuing war will create political, economic, and social disruption within both systems' economies. The combined factions of militant Castorians and the K'Tar will be poised to topple the weakened companies. We will at last achieve the destiny we deserve!"

The eyes of Steth were no longer directed down to where Descartes leaned against the wall. Instead, the Geminian gazed hypnotically through the office bulkhead, as if focusing on a star light-years away. Descartes recalled a similar look on the face of his technical superintendent when Nimon empowered his biodgen, Starn. Whenever he projected his essence into the Dual, the countenance of the Geminian would reflect the empty void of space. It was the same expression that Descartes now saw on Steth.

But the countenance of Steth quickly hardened into one of wicked vengeance.

"The beautiful irony of our plan is that it fulfills a desire I have long suppressed, but can now experience. From the moment our culture was contaminated with the Terran plague, I have hungered to expunge it. I have seen viable businesses wither from the ineptitude of irrational Terran decision-making. And you, Descartes, were the vile source of the infection. I will now finally eradicate the source!" Steth continued, vehemently, "The venture established between the Earth Exploratory Cartel and the Gemini System undermined import/export business to Terra by removing trade sanctions ... sanctions which enabled my family's business to flourish. Without them, our company failed. My family fortune could not be salvaged. I had nowhere to turn ... until I found the K'Tar. By joining it, I found I could draw power and influence from its members. It served as an outlet to vent my hatred toward the Terrans. Others joined me in my beliefs. Their influence allowed me to achieve a modicum of respect among Geminian business circles, culminating in my appointment as Prosecutor to the Council of Elders. But attainment of this post was a hollow victory. Its importance was questionable since I merely acted as a puppet to the Council's wishes. For it was I who was expected to make statements not deemed respectable enough to be said by the Council. Though a position of some notoriety, it was not enough."

The Prosecutor droned on. "Then I met T'Poch. Her masterful plan is the ultimate answer to my desires," Steth gloated. "For when it is done, Nimon's mother will fail in her attempts at a Solarian-Castorian accord... I will achieve a high position of power within the K'Tar... Nimon's father will remain at my mercy... Nimon will experience unthinkable humiliation and death at the hands of T'Poch... and you, Terran bacteria, will also die!"

CHAPTER 22

P'Teel gathered her senses after the flash from her own bioenergy dissipated. Though the force of her power had been directed against Novas, the recoil of such an energy burst still took its toll on its creator. She expected to see the shattered corpse of the young Fire Child at the base of the rocky wall. To her surprise, there was no trace of her opponent.

"Mystery upon mystery ..." mused the evil enchantress, "... first, the child's intriguing reference to a group known as the 'K'Tar'... then her disappearance. She spoke of the group as if it were an entity to be feared. Yet, to my knowledge, no such group exists. No matter," thought P'Teel. "The obstacle to my plans of domination is gone. Without a trace - perhaps my power is greater than even I could imagine. Though her life essence has disappeared, she has left much for me to consider." Smiling wickedly, she concluded, "Yes... a great deal to consider."

The enchantress looked down with satisfaction into her open palm to gaze in wonderment at the crystal shard.

*   *   *

Novas lay sprawled on the floor. Its texture was vaguely familiar, but she was too groggy to recall from where. Raising up on one elbow, she slowly turned her head to see if her neck was broken. As her silver-streaked hair cascaded on to her shoulders, its appearance reminded her she was still under the influence of the Legotian. Yet, the floor was out of place. Looking down along her body, she saw that she was still clad in the leather and cloth garments provided to her by Mitron. As her senses slowly returned, dread came with them.

She opened her empty hand to confirm her fears. The crystal was gone.

A shuffling noise behind her caught her attention. Turning stiffly, the self-pity over the loss of the crystal evaporated. A glimpse of the figure standing before her boiled away the sorrow with fiery rage!

"YOU!! Enough of this madness! I will die before I let you continue with your scheme!"

"Novas, there is much you do not understand. Time..."

"I understand all that I need to know! Your insidious control of my mind will STOP!"

The Legotian stood before her in the human form she recognized from their encounter years earlier. The expression on his face was the closest approximation to puzzlement that the alien could muster. As Novas pulled herself to her feet, she saw that she was once again in the chamber housing the mercurial pool she had crossed upon her arrival.

"He has chosen to appear in my world of reference, for what reason I am unsure," thought Novas. "Nevertheless, he will regret giving me the opportunity for my revenge."

Sensing Novas' thoughts, the Legotian applied a calming technique to counter them as he addressed her.

"Your will is strong, executive of Gemini, and it clouds your judgement. Tell me how you believe you have been wronged."

"Your meager attempt at feigned innocence will not succeed, Legotian. You are the cause of my 'clouded judgement'. You have used an elaborate form of hypnosis to obtain information from me. But I will not allow you to use that information. Somehow, I WILL stop you!"

"Novas, you have been away for some ... time. Explain what you believe has happened to you."

"Explain? I do not know what more you wish to gain from this 'innocent' charade. But I will indulge you." Novas thought to herself, "If I can barter for just a little more time, I will be that much stronger. With it will come a greater chance for me to overcome this creature." So she complied.

The Legotian relaxed a fraction, comforted by his ability to deflect a small part of her aggression.

"Your mind control techniques would have me think that I was in the company of Mitron. You expect me to believe that Gemini was threatened by a holocaust brought on by an impending collision with a rogue meteor... that this threat caused Ravar and his followers to flee into space. But I know the true history of Gemini. Ravar was cast out by Mitron because of his materialistic philosophies. He wished to use the power of the Phoenos to enslave beings beneath the bondage of his will ... just as you do!! Your ploy was to discover the location of the crystal fragment so that you could abuse the power of the Phoenos. That is why you created this elaborate mind game."

A flicker of discomfort crossed the Legotian's face. "It is as I feared. This is why the time continuum has not stabilized. Your influence was not sufficient."

The look on her captor's face did not escape Novas' notice. Their prior encounter during the Gemini-Solar negotiations left her impressed with his ability to handle any situation. Apparently, these circumstances were different. She was compelled to find out why.

"Chrislar, do not attempt to weave more confusion into my thoughts with your vague reference to my 'insufficient influence'. It is you who are at fault here. You cannot deny your desire to control the Phoenos with the crystal."

"Novas, I sense the sincerity in your words... but you must listen to me. Your interpretation of what has happened to you is in error. I have not been controlling your thoughts. I have only influenced your ... surroundings."

The Geminian hesitated, as if a flicker of doubt about her accusations had entered her mind. "What are you saying?"

"You have been in the presence of Mitron. What you experienced was real, not imagined."

Novas unconsciously rubbed the base of her neck, as if to massage away the tension of the moment. A pleasant tingle spread down her spine. Horrified, she jerked her hand away as if it had brushed against a Brav Ni cactus. Looking at her hand, and then at her captor with mouth agape, she spat, "How did you do that, Legotian?!"

Misunderstanding the Geminian's meaning, Chrislar replied, "The principles of temporal displacement are just now beginning to be understood by corporeal beings, such as your race and the Solarians. This is evidenced by the 'time-folding' technique employed by your life crystal manufacturing facilities. To try to explain exactly how you were in the presence of Mitron's era would be too... time-consuming."

Novas' patience was at its end. "No, alien. I meant how did you elicit that ... response... in my body?" Her discomfort with discussing her inability to experience sexual pleasure was evident... more so in the presence of this being who somehow could cause a "phantom sensation" in her nervous system.

With a brief probe of her thoughts, the Legotian understood. "Executive ... that experience is also real ... not imagined. There are some ... side effects ... that can occur when corporeals are time-displaced."

Novas struggled with what she was hearing. For weeks, she had been convinced she was under the influence of an elaborate mind scheme constructed by the alien before her. In fact, she still could be. Yet, something pressed her into acknowledging that what was happening was, in fact, real. She gingerly stroked the small of her back, wanting to believe the unbelievable.

"If I were to believe you, Legotian, then that would mean much of what Geminians know to be their history has been distorted. It would mean the Ravarians left under peaceful circumstances. Gemini had been subjected to a catastrophe by some other influence than war. Ravar and his followers were not outcasts. They were merely survivalists. Their belief in the Phoenos was a righteous one. And ... that one half of the crystal that holds the secret of Phoenos, the key to life empowerment, is somewhere among the followers of Ravar!"

A figure that had as yet gone unnoticed to Novas mysteriously appeared from the shadows behind Chrislar. The woman was dressed not entirely unlike Novas. A chamois bodice was partially covered by a linen stole with elaborate stitchery adorning its edges. The matching linen skirt draped to the floor, its leather border protecting the hem and rising up the front of the split skirt, revealing the smooth-muscled legs of the wearer. But the most noticeable article of clothing worn by the woman was an accessory ... a pendant. Novas could not take her eyes away from the necklace. A silver medallion had been carefully crafted and hung at the end of a gold woven chain.

It was identical to the one Novas had bestowed upon T'Poch at their parting – at least almost identical. At its center was missing the locket that would have held a precious life crystal. For Novas, her pendant had held the unique stone that had been passed to her and finally to T'Poch. The jewel on the Castorian had none.

Novas' jaw muscles tightened. As was her reputation, almost her legend, she would employ a gambit to ferret out vital information from her adversary. But at times, such as this one, her intuition even defied her understanding.

"The heiress to the Chair of Castor ... and a descendent of Ravar," she murmured. "The legends are true, then. The Ravarians did give birth to the children of Castor. And as I feared when I saw the fractured crystal in Ravar's lab, the possessors of the two halves could unite to form a formidable alliance in the galaxy. But I see from the adornment the Castorian wears, she has naught to offer to this union."

The words ripped at the essence of the heiress, but before she could respond, the Legotian replied.

"What you say is partially true," Chrislar intoned. "Was that not the purpose of the negotiations between Solar Corporation and the Castorian Conglomerate?"

"Yes, but the magnitude of the union could have been much more all-encompassing. What was to have been a business venture, could have been so much more. I fear it has fallen far short of that."

"What is the basis of your fears? As you are now learning, we Legotians are more than interstellar negotiators ... much more. We are capable of mapping the currents of time itself. It has been our way for countless millennia. The temporal eddies show that it is your family among all on Gemini that are heirs to Mitron. You should now have the Ravarian mate to the crystal ... as should your child, your blood kindred, possess the Mitronian half. Did you not return with it? Our studies are thorough. We have seen to it that your knowledge of Castor's origin is a true one. The same has occurred for the

Castorian Executive. She experienced her own temporal displacement at our hands. If your time line is as we predicted, you should have brought back what rightfully belongs to her. You talk about 'fears'. Did Ravar not give to you one half and bestow the other upon Mitron? Our temporal studies forecast he would provide that lasting gift for your imminent betrothal, should you two survive the cataclysm of the meteor strike he so long predicted. What transpired during your displacement that we do not know?"

Novas was visibly shaken. Her gambit had paid off, but with shocking news. "Then what you say is true. You have not been controlling my thoughts, or you would understand the basis of my fears. There is more than what transpired during my displacement that concerns me. It is the dark truth about which I spoke upon my arrival. My kindred does possess the crystal's mate, but that is not Nimon. My blood kindred is ...."

The Castorian Executive had been silently seething as she listened to the conversation, until that moment. Her frustration overwhelmed her. "Your blood-kindred must be Nimon. My displacement could not have been in vain. Its events foretold of a reunification between our peoples. Nimon and I can make that union a reality! We will use the power of the Phoenos as it was meant to be! We will preserve the new life that it will create ... not abuse it!"

"For that to be time's chosen path, Nimon must possess the crystalline mate to your half," interrupted Chrislar. Turning back to Novas, he continued, "He must also want the ability that the crystal will bring. Who does have the crystal, Novas ... and more importantly, do they have the ability and desire to use it?"

Novas replied, solemnly, "As I was about to reveal, my blood kindred is not my son, but one even more special. It is my first-borne Dual, my Singular Dualiity. T'Poch! Yes, T'Poch of the K'Tar. She has the crystal. For it empowers her very soul and allows her to exist as a product of my mind, independently. And my greatest fear is that because of her lifelong mentor, P'Teel, she not only has the ability, but the most evil of desires to use it ..."

As the realization of her last encounter with P'Teel gripped Novas, she added with an ominous whisper, "... a desire for power that has spanned generations ... and I foolishly provided her with the seeds of knowledge from whence that desire was spawned!"

Chrislar paled upon hearing this new information.

The Castorian fumed!

"I do not accept this! I am the heiress to Castor's future! The Ravarian crystal should be in my possession! You speak of the Mitronian half being in the possession of a biodgen construct! You would have me believe that a Geminian device is destined to bond with a Castorian to lead my people to their rightful place in the cosmos? That cannot be! My father is dead. He has passed the chair to me! And what of the Ravarian shard? If this Geminian witch before me did not return it from the mists of the past, then where is it? What is my role to be in the future of my people?

Chrislar patiently allowed the Castorian to vent her rage. As she paused, he looked at her. A brief silence ensued as he directed his thoughts to her, and her alone. The executive's expression slowly softened, and with a gentle nod, she departed.

Turning his attention toward Novas, Chrislar spoke. "Novas, it is your time path that shows the disturbance. One that is most troubling. Your dark secret – to be the creator of the first Singular Dualiity – was well kept. To complicate matters, the Ravarian crystal has made its way through time to the present along undesirable currents. As did you. I believe the reason to be that the present requires you more than the past. Where are your 'children' now?"

"Why ... I have no way of knowing, Chrislar."

The Legotian almost smiled at her and responded, "Oh, but you do, Novas. It is time for you to alter the present ... then we will again address the past. Prepare yourself."

CHAPTER 23

Nimon had never felt so helpless. As he had often counseled his employees during difficult situations, "There are always alternatives." Yet being immobilized as he was by T'Poch seemed to make alternatives nonexistent. And if the physical challenge weren't sufficiently overwhelming, there was the psychic struggle he must overcome. He fought to suppress the intense emotions swelling within him. "T'Poch and my father ... there could be no connection!" he fumed. The thought was so improbable that it had caused him to recoil from her statement. She was pleased. Each slip of his mental control was another indicator of his weakening state. "I must endure her torture - both mental and physical - as long as possible. Perhaps by enduring, my chances for rescue will improve." Inwardly he smiled at the irony that his only rational choice was an irrational one - the choice of Hope.

T'Poch paced along the edge of the antigrav-stasis field like a caged Aldebian snow leopard. As she spoke, Nimon braced himself.

"Let me tell you a story which begins thirty Geminian cycles in the past. It is set in a temple which your kindred have used for centuries to christen the children of the noblest of Geminian clans. The sacred ritual, Bon-ka, was then as it is now... as it always has been... shrouded in antiquity."

As T'Poch spoke, her vengeful tone softened to one touched by a mystical awe. For the Ancient Rites were very close to the practices of the K'Tar. The flavor of the savagery which consumed the Geminian forefathers was still prevalent in the long-practiced rituals. As T'Poch continued, Nimon noted the transformation and filed it in his memory for later use.

"The attendees were dutifully respectful of the ceremony. The parents were equally solemn. In attendance during her first act as an Elder was one whom you know well... Kronia. The parents of the child are also familiar to you... your own mother, Novas, and on this rare occasion, an outworlder, your father, Dr. Edison. Perhaps if your mind has not been too adversely affected by my influence, you are asking yourself, 'Why do I not remember?'" T'Poch paused for effect, and then spat out, "It is because the child was not you!"

Nimon questioned his own mental faculties as he struggled to postulate alternatives which would disprove her last statement. But his instincts were overpowering. He knew in his soul that it was the truth!

T'Poch lingered with the reciting of her story, reveling in the agony she sensed it caused within her captive audience.

"Your mother and father, with the blessing of Kronia, transcended the traditional betrothal customs of the Mitronian clan. The Council, at the time of their union, questioned the sanity of Kronia for endorsing it. But she did not waver in her plans. Your parents were too young to fully understand the significance of the bond formed between them under the direction of Kronia. Yet its magnitude would pervade their lives until the final culmination of their betrothal thirty cycles later during the christening ceremony of Bonka."

"As is true for many arranged marriages, the pairing suited the families more so than it did the couple. In this case, the 'families' were the Earth Exploratory Cartel and Gemini. Two critical paths were taken after the betrothal of Novas and Edison as Fate guided them toward the ultimate ceremony of Bon-ka. Dr. Edison took an appointment at the Geminian Science Institute to pursue his studies in a field just then in its infancy, bioduogenetics. Novas pursued an intense interest in arts and literature, leading her to assert herself as a gifted historian specializing in the Mitronian Period, with an emphasis on Mitron himself. The science of bioduogenetics would ultimately benefit the Earth Cartel, and the Mitronian studies by Novas would prove to be a turning point in the very essence of Geminian culture itself!"

Nimon's mind was clearing with each passing moment as he absorbed T'Poch's monologue. He found himself swept into the story, fateful to the development of two star systems; shrouded in the mysteries of an ancient culture and fledgling science. He was intrigued by the fact that Novas would concentrate her studies on Mitron. "History had always held an important role in Geminian society," he reflected, "even during its most savage period. The official history of Gemini was traditionally recorded by an appointed family. To receive such an appointment was considered one of the highest of honors."

Nimon knew a branch of his own ancestral lineage had been given the honor to record Mitron's word. Along with it came the responsibility to document the historical events surrounding the notable Geminian families of the period as well. He pondered, "It followed that Novas, female heir and direct blood kindred to Mitron, would seek to train extensively in their family's genealogy. But what connection could this choice have with his father's research?"

T'Poch would relieve Nimon's bewilderment.

"The role as historical scholar for her clan normally would have reserved Novas the right to preserve the understanding of events of such a noble family. However, having the blessing of Kronia herself provided certain advantages. With the consent of the matriarch of the family branch who held the responsibility for the official records, Novas was able to more than satisfy her innate curiosity for Mitron. Initially she explored the 'nobler' version of the Mitronian period by cross-referencing the accounts made by the scribes of less prominent lines. But, as time passed, and the more she learned, the less she believed the official version of events surrounding Mitron's messianic rise to attain his peaceful goals."

"While Novas fed her insatiable hunger to learn the truth about Mitronian peace, Edison continued his studies of bioduogenetics and the physics required to achieve it. Their marriage, initially one of interstellar corporate convenience, and challenged by the time constraints of their chosen pursuits, was still able to blossom. Novas and Edison, spurned by clan members and banned from clan functions, in their isolation built upon their skeletal relationship by sharing their true passions with each other, their work. Edison attempted to act as a damper on Novas' growing skepticism toward the accepted legends and teachings of Mitronian ways. Novas was touched by his attempts to shield her from her own radical beliefs. She knew Edison surpassed the bounds of just friendship in trying to protect her from her 'divergent inquiries', as she referred to them. She could not help but kindle desirous flames for her partner. Her growing passion for the Terran and the distrust of Mitronian teachings led to two outcomes: Novas' departure from traditional Geminian philosophy and … the birth of their son!"

Nimon listened with a strange detachment to the account of his mother's affections. Thinking, "I have never really been close to my mother in any fashion. She raised me, yes, but she always kept a … clinical distance… from me. Almost as if I were a failed experiment. I'd hoped that by both being employees of the Solar Corporation, a common ground could have been struck. But the rift grew larger. It was as if she were denying our family bond to suppress any chance for employees to claim nepotism as a reason for my success. I accepted the cold, business-only approach Novas took in all her relationships. That was what allowed her ascent within the Solar Corporation. But now, as I listen to T'Poch discuss my parents' courtship, I can scarcely believe it! What caused my mother's transformation from a loving woman to a compassionless corporate executive? Was it me? Could my existence be the cause?" As the question gnawed at him, his attention was pulled back to T'Poch's narration.

"I sense you question the reason for your existence…" T'Poch snarled, "…as well you should. It is more complex than you can understand… or even accept! For now, just know this - Novas suffered from her first child birth. She was made barren. But you cause me to get ahead of myself."

T'Poch continued with her account of the more distant past. "Kronia monitored Novas' deviant philosophies closely. As Novas' revelations regarding Mitronian lore increased, she deliberated as to whether to take immediate action. If she withdrew her permission to study Mitron, it could raise undue concerns. If Novas shared her findings, others might delve into the truth behind Mitron's ways - the truth which Kronia chose to suppress until the time was right!"

Nimon wove the strand of truth in T'Poch's words into the fabric of the holovid mural which had been unveiled during his trial. He replayed the image of the outcast, Ravar, and that of his second-in-command, Stev, in his mind. The savage hatred toward Mitron had reincarnated the holo-vid into a living image. Nimon re-experienced the empathy he felt for Ravar, and the vitriol expressed by Stev, trying to understand the feeling and how its fury could be generated from untruths and misguided beliefs.

Nimon thought about the lessons of Mitron. "Mitron believed that the worship of life in every form would lead the Geminian people to greatness. They would achieve 'Phoenos' only if their love of life were pure. But is 'Phoenos' a worthy goal? Had he not questioned the flashes of Dualiity he had experienced with Starn? Was the loss of control a sign of new life ... or a sign of new danger? Could there be an underlying flaw in Mitron's teachings?"

With these questions tormenting him, Nimon attuned his thoughts to T'Poch's tale with a renewed hunger.

"Kronia recognized the impact Novas' discoveries had on the young woman's faith in her lineage. The matriarch had experienced similar doubts. The hope was that Novas would follow in Kronia's path." T'Poch's voice then took on a subdued hush, almost reverent in its tone. "Novas uncovered the mysteries surrounding the Hidden Sect of the Anti-Mitronians. She discovered that a scarce few disbelievers of Mitron's teachings had eluded his notice. They were not part of the masses which were banished to the Space Arks. Instead, they remained on Gemini, shrouded in secrecy. Some of the lower nobles responsible for preserving Gemini's history were members of the Anti-Mitronians. They encoded the secrets of their sect within the Archives of their families - a practice still carried on to this day by even the nobler clans," T'Poch added, with an insidious smile.

Her beautifully wicked face peered down upon Nimon through the force field, reveling in the unspoken truth she would soon unveil to him. A truth which would shatter even his superior mental control.

"These unsung scribes preserved the real history of Gemini in their writings. They began referring to themselves as the K'Tar. In their teachings they expanded upon the concept of Phoenos. Whereas Mitron saw Phoenos as a peaceful philosophy – an ideal around which he could rally his people to strive for greatness – the K'Tar saw it as a means to harness untold power. Over the seasons, the K'Tar envisioned Dualiity as a means for directing legions of biodgens. With them, they could command – and control - a superior way of life. Through this idea, anything could be accomplished. But they developed more than just their philosophies. They extended their practices into physical skills. By incorporating the specialized crystals designed for biodgens within their own bodies, they would be superior to any other beings. Through conditioning and the introduction of specific trace elements into their system, they were able to achieve what some might consider almost mystical powers. But they could never achieve their ultimate goal - to create a combined 'biodgen-K'Tarian' with which to build their legions."

"Novas studied these Vuu Zon, or Fire Powers, as the Council of Elders would refer to them in their forbidden whispers. As she mastered them one by one, Kronia saw within the young woman the potential for her societal order to become a reality. But Kronia could not support Novas' discoveries openly. The Council would resist. For as you learned in your attempt to persuade the Council that it would be better to use biodgens as tools rather than as religious icons, their favorite defense to ideas they do not support is to ignore them. So, how could Kronia openly support something the Council would choose to ignore?"

T'Poch laughed demonically at the irony of Kronia's situation.

Nimon shuddered at this hideous creature. Simultaneously, he was stunned at the fact that T'Poch knew of his treatise on biodgen control and Dualiity. "How could she know?" he thought.

As if in answer. T'Poch ceased her laughter and looked directly into his eyes, saying, "Nimon, my naive captive. Have you not guessed that one of the Fire Powers about which I speak is that which you yourself possess!? Kronia sensed it during her bond with you at trial's end. Yes, I know of your struggle with her, for I am her agent. She revealed to me what she learned. You have touched Phoenos, ever so briefly, a true wonder to be sure. Having brushed against Dualiity, you move closer to the greatest fear of the Council. They preach about achieving Phoenos, but what they do not say is what it can unleash. They want the glory of the achievement, but wish to suppress the biodgen's true personality. For once the biodgen becomes a free will, a separate entity untethered to the Life

Mentor, the Dual will exhibit the aggression and ferocity which the K'Tar worships, and which the Council fears! The Council knows that a biodgen freed from the suppression of a Geminian mind will become a being wielding untold power. This being is the epitome of the K'Tar! The Phoenos they worship is actually the genesis of a being which represents everything they detest! The Council strictly refuses to acknowledge this fact!"

Taking a deep breath, T'Poch stared into Nimon's very soul, and whispered, "Yet, the secrets within the Archives have been revealed. It was I who breached the sanctum, it was I who rendered your Dual unconscious, and it is I who threaten the Council the most. For I am the Singular Dualiity and Novas is my Life Mentor! Yes, it was my christening so many seasons ago, not that of an anemic, half-breed organic. I was first empowered by Novas on that day, later to be given over to my matron so that I could live free. But that is not the dark secret that Kronia discovered, although a well-kept secret, to be sure. The secret has to do with you, Nimon. What you are, and what you will become."

Reaching into her tunic, T'Poch pulled out an object and held it before Nimon's face. It was a crystal shard – the same one held by Kronia previously during Nimon's trial. She continued, ominously, "You are more like me than you know, my dear Geminian Dual. And..." she continued with a sinister glower, "...you will soon learn we are more alike than you can possibly endure!"

CHAPTER 24

Descartes knew he must continue to goad Steth into revealing the location of Dr. Edison, as well as the fate of Nimon. He could attempt to be subtle, and save himself a few bruises. Or, as was often the case with the renowned life crystal plant manager, he could take the direct approach.

"Steth!" Descartes barked, breaking the Geminian from his rabid tirade. "What does T'Poch plan to do with Nimon? And while you're in such a talkative mood, where is his father, Dr. Edison?"

Steth sneered at Descartes, as would a sadistic animal-keeper while tossing ineffectual scraps to a starving lion. The Geminian realized he was being baited, but his ego prevented him from holding back the information Descartes sought.

"I am in total control of the Earth-man's fate," Steth proffered, "and you can do nothing to alter that fact. Even now I have him detained in the holding area by one of my trusted guards."

Steth sauntered over to the intercom mounted on the Castorian vice-executive's desk.

"A simple word from me..." he taunted, as he feigned to activate the 'Transmit' switch, "...and he will snap his neck like a sun-dried Guavo lizard bone."

Descartes flinched. He thought to himself, "If I act now, would it provoke Steth into killing all of them, or would the Geminian simply unleash his rage on a life crystal plant manager's hapless body?"

As if in response to its master's momentary indecision, a magnificent silver sphere materialized from its timefold and lowered its field of invisibility. An imperceptible sigh radiated through the starlit void as it gracefully released two compact energy spheres along a trajectory to impact the aft defense fields of the Castorian probe ship. Within the hull of the targeted ship, a less poetic scene unfolded.

Rocking violently, the deck of the vice-executive's chamber groaned under the stress of the pulsar concussions. The amber light of the intercom flickered timidly between the aqua-hued fingers of Steth, as they tightly clenched the box for support.

Through the sporadic crackling of the incoming carrier signal, the subdued panic of a youthful Castorian voice could be heard.

"Vice-executive Talor... Solar Corporation life crystal plant... by surprise... stealth device!"

As the static subsided momentarily, along with the rocking of the ship, Talor rushed to the intercom and slapped the 'Transmit' switch through the still clenched hand of Steth.

Punching out his commands, he ordered, "Evasive maneuvers! Divert reserves to defense fields! Now!"

Descartes responded instinctively to his captor's predicament. Vaulting the vice-executive's desk with cat-like ferocity, he planted both heels solidly into the chest of the Castorian. Slamming his target against his Geminian cohort, Descartes smoothly rolled off the desk and shouted, "Brown ... Helicon! Take out the guard!"

Had the Solar executive known what was happening behind him, he would have realized his command was unnecessary. Brown and Helicon had reacted instantly as Descartes pounced upon the Geminian-Castorian duo. With his tail, Helicon lashed out at the guard holding the deactivator to their bindings. The emerald blur of the massive appendage impacted mercilessly across the unsuspecting Castorian's head, immediately snapping his neck. Before Steth could recover from Descartes's attack, Helicon sprayed a jet of bluish fluid from his cavernous jaws into the Geminian's face. The debilitating toxins in the liquid quickly took effect, paralyzing its victim.

Brown recovered the magnetic deactivator from the death-grip of the Castorian guard. Looking up from the lifeless body, he saw his plant manager deliver a final double-fisted blow to the vice-executive's jaw, sending him into the depths of unconsciousness. Pointing the deactivator first at Descartes, then Helicon, and finally himself, he released the energized bands which had tortured their wrists from the very beginning of their captivity.

As Descartes bent over Talor to retrieve the Castorian musket and then tuck it into his belt, he noticed Helicon intuitively doing the same with the guard's weapon.

Curious about the Clionian's fighting prowess, Descartes inquired, "Where did you learn to fight like that, Helicon? You handled yourself well."

Hesitatingly, he replied, "My martial sskillss are remnants of my race's less than peaceful past. It is very rare that we Clionians use them. In fact, we take no pride in acknowledging them - especially to racess with whom we wish to be at peace."

Descartes was shaken by the sincerity in the eyes and voice of the alien before him. "Helicon was actually ashamed of his violent abilities," Descartes thought. He realized what a fool he had been for harboring ill-will against his reptilian ally.

As if a Geminian hypnotic suggestion had materialized the thought in his mind, the reason for Descartes's animosity toward Helicon took form. Vivid memories flooded his mind to reveal the source of his bigotry toward the Clionian.

Descartes had been an operations supervisor in a DNA synthesis station many years ago. Although a simplistic process, it had been the predominant technology before the discovery of life crystal polymerization. The station had been used to manufacture servant drones, a relatively mindless "lifeform" produced for the purpose of manual labor. Tissue donors from across the ten star systems frequented these stations for quick money in exchange for some of their flesh. Crocians, a reptilian race similar to Clionians, were regular customers because of the high price they received for their cells. Their cell regeneration abilities made them ideal candidates as raw material for profitable DNA production runs.

Over the course of Descartes' employment at the station, he had acquired the dislike for the Crocians that a majority of the other employees shared. One ugly, filthy, overbearing Crocian named Garth made a habit of insulting the station technicians at every opportunity. During one drunken visit, he had stumbled against a neutrino cutting station. The accident had caused severe burns in several of the station technicians, including Descartes. As for Garth, the station personnel had managed to save the Crocian with the help of Descartes' knowledge of cellular architechnology. His own burns had been repaired as well, but experience with the reptilian had left invisible scars on his psyche; scars which apparently were only now beginning to heal. The young supervisor had represented his profession admirably by saving Garth's life - knowing that had the situation been reversed, the Crocian would have let Descartes die. Yet Descartes had paid a price for his merciful decision. The Crocian had inflicted much pain on the lives of the station crew. As a result, the desire for compensation from Garth had lingered in Descartes, only to surface as an irrational repugnance toward Helicon.

The plant manager now realized the Crocians and Clionians were similar in outward appearance only. There were no grounds for his animosity toward Helicon.

Looking at Brown, Descartes communicated "Thanks" with his eyes. Turning back toward Helicon, he humbly offered, "Given the chance when we get out of this, I've got some apologizing to do to you."

The Clionian acknowledged the Solar executive with a nod, and replied, "Our team'ss success sso far indicatess you will get your chance."

As if a reminder to tell them their newly acquired freedom was only a small step toward safety, a second barrage of pulsar blasts shook the Castorian vessel.

Snapping back into action, Descartes exclaimed, "Before we do anything, we've got to locate Dr. Edison and get to the safety pod station. The Darwin won't be able to pull its punches for much longer without endangering itself from Castorian retaliation!"

In response, Helicon suggested, "Let me ssee if I can locate the ship'ss blueprints in the vice-executive'ss computer console. That will save uss a great deal of time ssearching for the detention area and pod station."

Adroitly the Clionian applied the lingual-computer skills he had mastered during his research on the Geminian-Castorian link. As he informed Descartes about the locations of various areas of the vessel, the life crystal plant manager formulated a strategy.

"J.B., it will be simpler for you and Helicon to go to the nearby pod station and commandeer it. By borrowing the helmet and gear of our guard here, I'll be less conspicuous as I work my way alone back to Dr. Edison and retrieve him. In the confusion of the Darwin's onslaught, there should be few people in the hallways. My guess is they're being kept pretty busy at their work stations."

Donning the Castorian uniform, Descartes's head rattled inside the massive guard's helmet like a Rovarian backgammon die in its cup. Nevertheless, he was confident that his disguise would prevent a casual observer from questioning him. Brown and Helicon had also prepared themselves for their task at hand. The whisk of the vice-executive's office door as it opened signaled them into action.

*　　*　　*

Descartes had surmised the situation correctly. Nearing the last corridor to the detention area, he encountered only the third Castorian since he had left the vice-executive's office. The previous two had been engineering techs, as best as he could tell, performing much-needed repairs resulting from the Darwin's abuse. This last encounter, however, could prove to be more eventful. The Castorian guard to Dr. Edison's cell standing ten treds down the end of the hallway had to be the result of genetic experimentation. He was built as solid as a duramite rocket booster, and almost as big!

Unable to turn back now without arousing suspicions, Descartes lowered his head and strode arrogantly toward the hulking monster. Recalling the Castorianese he had acquired in order to complete the stealth device acquisition, he prepared a ruse that even the Castorian Chairman would believe.

"Release the prisoner!" Descartes barked. "Vice-executive Talor has found a use for him!"

"You have not been cleared for this area, Little One ..." the giant's voice boomed, "why should I not kill you?"

Descartes responded by pointing a finger in Dr. Edison's direction, at least superficially showing no trepidation from the hulk's reply. "Would you rather be ejected into space instead of him?"

Not giving the walking asteroid before him time to reply, Descartes continued, "Talor plans to use him as ransom for the unconditional surrender of the life crystal plant. If the Solar Corporation fool refuses, he will be catapulted into space. Now I ask again ... would you prefer to take his place?!"

The man-mountain hesitated ... then slowly turned to deactivate the force-field barring the doorway to Dr. Edison's stark quarters. Pivoting sluggishly like an ore barge at one-fifth magneton power, the Castorian was totally unprepared for Descartes's next maneuver. Lowering his head even further, the Darwin's plant manager drove it forward into the small of the behemoth's back. Roaring like a wounded bull elephant, the guard staggered face-first into the still-active force screen. The screen's blue-fire coursed across the surface of the Castorian's skin, momentarily halting his momentum. As it subsided, the massive body crumpled to the floor, unconscious. The only remnant of the field was an acrid, ozone smell, which quickly dissipated into the air-conditioning system of the ship.

Stepping gingerly across the body sprawled before the door, Dr. Edison shook the outstretched hand of his rescuer. Only when he peered into the shadowy faceplate of the helmet did he realize his savior was none other than executive Morgan Descartes!

"Morgan," he exclaimed, "what on Earth is going on?"

"There's really no time to explain at the moment, Dr. Edison. Just follow my lead. And pardon my weapon, but until we make it back to the safety pod station, you'll have to be my prisoner."

"Anything you say, sir. I'm in your hands."

*   *   *

Arriving at the safety pod station a short time later, Descartes and Dr. Edison were surprised at the lack of difficulty with which they completed their journey. As the doors to the chamber parted at their approach, Descartes found his tightened grip on the pulsar musket to be an unnecessary precaution.

Standing with his hands clasped behind him, characteristically rocking from heel to toe, Brown greeted his manager with a smug grin.

"Safety pod station commandeered as ordered, Sir!" the personnel manager piped up, confidently.

"I see that, J.B.. But you make an easy target to anyone trying to correct that situation," Descartes replied.

"Not really, sir," Helicon softly whispered, stepping out from behind the instrument panel to the left of the entrance. Descartes smiled wryly as he saw Helicon lower his own musket.

"My compliments again," Descartes added, nodding his head toward the Castorian technician slumped next to the console, a blue glaze of fluid covering his face.

Dr. Edison moved forward to greet Jefferson Brown with a glowing smile and a warm handshake.

"So good to see you in such good health, Jefferson. It seems I am in your debt," he commented. "And you, Helicon..." he added, turning to the Clionian, "I was under the impression that your skills lent themselves more toward assisting the Geminian Historical Order. I see you are invaluable to my friends in the Solar Corporation as well."

Descartes, surprised at Dr. Edison's familiarity with Helicon, subdued his inquisitiveness for more pressing concerns at hand. "At the risk of sounding pessimistic, I think our success has been a little too easy," he interjected. "Helicon, J.B. ... do the pods check out O.K.?"

"To the besst of our knowledge, sir... although ssspace vessel mechanicss is neither of our expertise," Helicon answered, responding for both himself and Jeff Brown.

As if adding emphasis to Descartes's concerns, the probe ship shuddered again under the impact of the superior power of the Darwin. "No-one onboard this ship should be aware of our escape... at least no-one that's conscious," Descartes thought out loud.

Instinctively, Brown picked up his manager's line of thought and carried it further. "Helicon, what's the duration of Geminian paralysis induced by your venom?"

"Unknown, Jeffersson. To my knowledge, mine was the firsst ssuch exposure," Helicon responded in quiet humility.

Continuing with his speculation, Descartes said, "It's possible that if Steth recovered, he would realize that we would come here to escape. Without transmitters, there's no way to notify the Darwin of our condition. Being forced to use the Castorian pods, we would be easy victims...or would we?"

Descartes remembered that sensor telemetry was required to safely launch an escape vehicle. This prevented a pod from being ejected into asteroid belts, cosmic sheer winds, or other hazardous conditions. He hastily positioned himself behind the alien control panel, glimmerings of an idea materializing in his mind. Mumbling more to himself than to his compatriots, he said, "C'mon, George ... be at your station. Only you can figure out what I'm trying to tell you."

The life crystal plant manager's hands moved tentatively across the unfamiliar controls. Using the short range sensors built into all launch panels, he scanned the Darwin for the precise spot that he knew would accomplish his purpose. Finding it, he began to pulse the output key in a specific, repetitive pattern.

Hundreds of kilotreds away, the Darwin's operations superintendent responded, "Mr. Crescent, we're being scanned by the Castorians... but it's of a very low power level. It's almost as if it were a launch control sensor."

Turning to Saffron One... or was she Two?... acting plant manager and Plant Engineer George Crescent inquired, "Can you I.D. the exact location of the emission?"

"Checking, sir," Saffron Two responded. "According to the updated specifications on that class of ship, the beam is coming from their safety pod station ... but it's too weak and unstable to pinpoint as to what it's trying to scan."

"Amplify the signal, please, and rerun the source location routine," Engineer Crescent prodded.

"Boosted energy source detected, sir," Max Weber interjected, seconds later. "This time it's more powerful ... it's a pulsed launch sensor beam from the same location!" he added with suppressed excitement.

Catching George as he opened his mouth to voice his request, Saffron Two reflexively gave him the information he sought. "Target location pinpointed, sir. Pulsed beam pattern ... repeating... decoding program now activated."

Turning in her console chair to face him, the exotic features of the sensor control technician took on a puzzled look. "Mr. Crescent ... why would the Castorians send a pulsed code launch sensor beam to a conduit linking the plasma stabilizers and the navigational sensor modules? And the pattern is even stranger. It keeps repeating 'pod...pod...pod'."

"Good question, Saffron," George replied, pondering over the possibilities. Thinking back to the conversation he had had a week earlier with his plant manager, a gleam flickered in the engineer's eyes, as a wry grin spread across his star-weathered face.

"You're a sly one ... that you are, my fine manager," George mused. Acting quickly, the Plant Engineer thumbed the communication switch on his control console.

"Engineering department, on my signal activate the stealth device according to the routine I am now downloading. Also, prepare the lander pad to receive safety pods."

Switching to a second channel, George linked to Security. "Gentlemen, just to be on the safe side, send a unit to greet whoever might be coming aboard... stun cutlasses at the ready."

Looking over to Max Weber, "On my signal Mr. Weber, soften the port radial defense field just a might to let in any visitors, and let's see what we get."

"What in Luna's Seas are you doing, Morgan. Since when did you become a launch technician?" Brown asked.

"You don't think I spent all that time in my office just approving vacation requests, do you, J.B.?" came the coy reply.

Before Brown could utter a suitable retort, the whine of a Castorian pulsar musket pierced the room. An anguished cry from Dr. Edison followed, as he crumpled to the floor. Striding in triumphantly, Steth, a bluish slime still oozing down his face, leveled the weapon at Descartes before he could respond with his own.

"Now Earthling, I will have my revenge!"

Descartes could feel the adrenaline surge engulf him as he looked into the mocking face of his aggressor.

Simultaneously, Steth squeezed the key on his weapon.

CHAPTER 25

T'Poch seemed to hover above Nimon as the surging force field surrounding him diffracted the light of her image.

"Yes Nimon. I relish the moment when I shatter your inner control with the truth," T'Poch declared, as she increased the power on the suspensor field.

Nimon's body arched under the oppressive field's energy, helplessly enduring the pain while being forced to listen to her hypnotic words.

Brandishing the crystal shard before his immobile face, she continued. "Do you recognize this? Look closely. Yes, it is the very one that Kronia used in the chamber during your trial. But it is more… much more. You see, it was a simple matter to steal your Ruga'r during the Darwin's visit to deposit you and your Dual on Gemini before your vigil during Royta-Far, the Season of Heritage. It was just as easy to remove this crystal when the plant returned from its archaeological mission in Castorian space. Much information was uncovered during the expedition, as was seen during your trial. However, even more has gone unnoticed. The Clionian was unaware of this relic's hidden power. But soon, you will be!"

Nimon, all but paralyzed, grimaced at the sight of the glistening stone. The mental struggle he endured with Kronia was still fresh in his mind. "What devious purpose did it serve this sinister creature before me," he queried to himself. "She is clearly mad. To proclaim herself the first Singular Dualiity, and a product of my own mother's doing, is insanity!"

The jewel pulsed faintly as Nimon stared into it, or was it his imagination? T'Poch dispelled any doubts. "You still question, me?" she asked. "Do you not sense what is about to occur?" She again increased the current through the field, but this time the energy crackled with blue fire as it was absorbed into Nimon's body. "Ah, good… very good," T'Poch murmured.

"You see, Nimon, this field can not only immobilize your motor neural system, but stimulate the energies within you and the gem I hold, as well!" T'Poch's fingers activated the control keys to the field generator with sadistic pleasure. "I am pleased you are ready to endure more." Waves of white hot pain flooded Nimon's body. Relentlessly, searing heat racked the muscular frame of the technical superintendent; the only salvation being total unconsciousness. Minutes transformed into an eternity, when finally that salvation came.

*   *   *

As Descartes's vision wavered into a truer version of reality, his mental faculties returned. Hovering over him, the broad grin framed in the ebony face of his personnel manager took focus. Past Jefferson Brown's shoulder, Descartes could see Helicon crouched over Dr. Edison. Steth was not within view.

Groggily Descartes muttered the question, "Whut huppened?"

"Sorry about the body-block, boss. If it had been an instant later, you wouldn't be lying here shaking off the peripheral pulsar blast that impacted behind you... you'd just be lying here. Unfortunately, Dr. Edison has been hit pretty badly. We have to get him back to the medtechs on the Darwin."

"Hup me up. I can pilut the pod."

"Under other circumstances, I'd argue with you, but not under these. Helicon's loaded Steth into the baggage compartment. It appears Clionian reflexes win out over a Geminian's when it comes to a shootout. That leaves the four seats for us. But how can we be sure we won't be blown to nanons as soon as we launch?"

"We'll launch an empty pod first," Descartes replied, the slurred speech fading. "That will signal George on the Darwin. Let's hope he understood my message."

In the control room of the Darwin, Mack Weber called out over his shoulder, "Mr.

Crescent, security sensors detect a safety pod launching from the Castorian probe ship."

"Very good, Mack." George Crescent responded, as he tapped the key to his intercom speaker. "Engineering Department, activate the stealth device."

"A second pod has appeared ... no, now there's twelve pods on the screen. Where'd they come from?" exclaimed Mack Weber.

"Activate your filter, Mack, and you'll screen out the false signals. The others are the result of a little modification in the stealth device. I hope that's the gambit our boss was looking for," replied Crescent.

As the dozen pods swarmed across the Castorian screen, the navigator aboard the enemy probe ship swatted at them with his defense pulsars. Satisfaction came as one vaporized under his persistent barrage. He neglected to see another pod arc lazily around the Darwin and disappear into its lander hangar.

Before the thruster whine subsided on the safety pod, Descartes started barking orders to the lander technician, "Get a Med Emergency Team over here, STAT! Security, activate those portable antigrav units and bring them here!"

The care conspicuously passed by Steth, and blanketed the more seriously injured Dr. Edison.

"How serious, mister?" Descartes inquired of the medical supervisor.

"Difficult to tell, sir. Had he been Geminian, he'd be dead. Luckily, the human anatomy differs from that of Castorians and Geminians. Steth instinctively aimed for a kill point on someone from his own species."

Without him needing to say it, the supervisor read on his plant manager's face, "Do all you can for him, son."

Turning to the security men, Descartes said, "Miller, Varochek, take the Geminian to detention. The stun effects should be wearing off shortly, so take precautions."

With a final glance over his shoulder toward the injured father of his technical superintendent, Descartes hurriedly made his way to the nearest omnivator. After a short hop, upon entering the control room, he immediately saw he had left his plant once more in the most competent of hands. Centered in the security vid-comm was the probe ship in a visible state of helplessness. Energy levels ebbing from the futile attempt to destroy the phantom safety pods, the vessel had limped to a safe distance to "lick its wounds".

"Long-range sensors show another probe ship entering this sector, sir," George informed. "I'd wager you it's the other half of the matched set we scuffled with a while back. Any orders, sir?"

"Let's leave them to face the embarrassment of their peers' scorn, George. We've got more pressing concerns waiting for us on Gemini. Ms.

Pomeroy, chart a pathway to the Gemini System. Mack, prepare the crystal polymer tubes for maximum production yield. Next stop, Gemini!"

*   *   *

Nimon climbed upward through the memory strata of pain induced by the suspensor field. As he struggled through the layers of consciousness, he re-experienced it once more. Finally, summoning one last burst of psionic energy, he returned to reality, only to find his tormentor still waiting for him.

"Ahh... I am very pleased, Nimon. Several before you have failed to return to me from those painful depths. Of course, they were unworthy candidates sought out before my discoveries in the Archives, and before I obtained this!" Again she brandished the mysterious gem at the edge of the containment field. "You have confirmed what I suspected. Do you even know the source of the techniques you use? You must, Nimon ... though you still fail to acknowledge the truth. Without knowing it, you have achieved a high level of skill in the Fire Arts of the K'Tar!"

Nimon's conscious mind battled with his subconscious.

"Was it true? Could I be resorting to skills forbidden by my own culture in order to cling to life? I have seen the normal Geminian response to situations which have no solution. Though they loved life, they realized its beauty came from accepting death when it approached," he reflected.

But many times in the past, Nimon refused to choose this alternative. During his first job as a supervisor, linked to Starn he had accompanied a survey party planet side as head of the group. A rockslide had trapped the party past the normal time frame of humans to empower their biodrones. The Terran biodivers had terminated their links, leaving their units entombed. But Nimon and Starn refused to give up. Extending past even their own capabilities, through their efforts a mole hole was tunneled through which they all had squeezed to safety.

"Could T'Poch be right? Had I resorted to techniques which violated the very essence of my homeworld culture? If so, why was it so wrong if it succeeded in preserving life?"

The struggle within his mind continued as T'Poch spoke.

"Using the Fire Arts to subdue the neural shock, you have so far survived the challenge. But here in this chamber, Nimon, away from the disapproving eyes of the Elders - here, on the fringe of the Northern Desert and mountain chain, sequestered between the two climates of Gemini, the harsh, savage desert and the cool peace of civilization - you will become more, much more. Just like you, Nimon, I was suspended between the accepted practices of peace and the harsh savagery of the Fire Arts. But no more!"

"You see, Nimon, I knew everything you would do after my attack on Starn. You would be compelled to try to escape once you learned your Ruga'r had been the instrument of death. You felt you would be the only one who could capture the perpetrator. For the rationale of the authorities would show them that only you could be the true assailant, and they would search no more once they captured you! Again, your savage side subdued your peaceful one, and you sought an alternative that could not exist in the minds of the Geminian authorities. Yet capture was inevitable. Once you were subdued, my plan was simple to complete. My pawn, the Prosecutor, was to make certain of that."

Nimon flinched at the mention of Steth. "His involvement extended beyond persecuting my family?! What could drive him to that depth of hatred for my clan?" His thoughts were transparent to his captor.

"Do I sense surprise in you, Nimon? Had you followed the career of your Geminian nemesis, Steth, you would easily understand his allegiance to me. He was an easy convert to the K'Tar due to his deep-rooted desire for vengeance against your human friends. But he was no match for the accursed Clionian. I sensed from Steth's reports during the proceedings that the desired outcome was being jeopardized. So I chose to accelerate my plan. I used my Castorian followers to seize your father as hostage!"

"You were left with no alternative, Nimon - at least no rational one. I had driven you to a point of no return. By holding your father prisoner, I could accomplish dual goals. First, I could disrupt Novas' efforts to forge a peace between the Castorian Conglomerate and the Solar Corporation. Such a blatant act of terrorism as the kidnapping of a corporate executive's husband from the security of her homeworld would not be tolerated by the Solar Corporation bureaucrats. The link between Castor and the K'Tar would compel them to end the Legotian negotiations." Pausing, she added, "But it is the second goal that will serve to change the course of the stars forever!"

T'Poch laughed wickedly as she boasted of her plan's success.

"Nimon, you poor fool. I know more of what motivates you than you do yourself! Your only choice was to suppress the teachings of peace and choose to follow your savage instincts. You elected the Trial of Survival just as I planned! You followed the path of our savage ancestors to prove yourself right! Once you had started down this path, it was childishly simple to render you helpless. Your training led you to the Brav-Ni cacti to survive. By lacing the plants with serum handed down through the teachings of the K'Tar, I was able to weaken you slowly. I watched your progress through the desert, and when you finally collapsed, I was there."

T'Poch paused, suddenly engulfed in an aura of solemn reflection. Looking at Nimon, yet not looking at him, she continued to speak as if entranced.

"It is now as it was, Nimon. Your eyes show your mounting fear and humiliation at what is occurring here. The irony of this encounter, Nimon, is that even though no-one will know of it for many years, it will have a significant impact on all of Gemini. Yes, secrets long kept will one day be revealed. Novas held secrets. Had it not been for her pathetic duty to her clan, she would not have recorded them in a hidden file in her family's Archives. But she did. My existence, for one. You see, I was unaware of my true origin. Oh, I suspected – that is why I sought to breach the Archives. But not until my suspicions were confirmed did I discover my destiny as the first Singular Dualiity. In that regard, we are much alike. As a pair nears Phoenos, their minds become fragile, much like a set of new born children. Identities become … confused. For me, I was only vaguely aware that I was different. And only now are you becoming aware of your … confusion.

Nimon recoiled from her piercing words, spit at him as if they were venom from a Mobidicus cobra. Tormented, he writhed inwardly, struggling against the field's grip.

"Yes. Nimon. Secrets have been kept from you. Secrets that only Novas, Dr. Edison, and, more recently, Kronia and I know. Do you never wonder why you resist a physical relationship with women, despite their attraction toward you? Do the nightmares you have of the biodrone experiment, when the faith in Phoenos was rejected for the more materialistic ideals, not haunt you? Do you not question how you can exist while your Dual lies comatose in the Institute?"

Nimon's piercing stare into the visage of his captor slowly faltered, crumbling, yielding to the truth she was now revealing.

"That biodrone experiment, when 'you' attempted to empower a biodrone instead of your Dual, did more than induce hallucinations and bouts of manic depressive episodes. It triggered a psychosis that only now, through my use of the Fire Arts and this crystal, plagues you no more." T'Poch built her hypnotic spell to its final conclusion.

"For the truth that you are coming to realize, my dear Nimon, is that, like me, you are biodgen! Starn, lying dormant in his empowering slumber, is the organic!" Pausing only momentarily for the revelation to take its toll, T'Poch forged on, relentlessly peeling away her captive's psyche. The secret is well guarded. No one on the Darwin is aware of your role reversal … they think, as did you, and your Life Mentor, Starn, that he is the bioduotron and their friend Nimon is the organic. A select few at the Institute suspect, for the true purpose of the vigil at the Archive of Families was for them to monitor, and hopefully heal, your psychosis. During her bond with you at trial's end, Kronia discovered the secret, and in turn, informed me. The revelation was beyond my wildest hopes! My plan for an organic transformed into one for which I had not even considered – a scheme designed for biodgens!"

Nimon's initial horror from her rantings melted away, leaving at first a gnawing hunger. As she spoke, her words became nourishment. His starvation craved for each morsel as she fed him the truth that had been hidden for so long. His micro-expressions through the paralysis spoke volumes.

"I perceive within you a growing sense of peace, Nimon. Surprising. For I could barely endure the vile truth behind my creation. When I discovered it, I went berserk. Only my skills in the Fire Arts allowed me to focus this fury and carry out my plan. But my fury was justified, as you will learn. After separating from your mother, my matron raised and mentored me. Novas relied on Kronia to help conceal the secret of my existence, for the rest of the Council, as well as the rest of the ten planetary systems, were not yet ready for Phoenos. Novas was allowed to continue her wholesome career while I was raised by my matron. What Novas did not realize was that my matron was a devout disciple of the K'Tar. You know not of her, but soon, all will recognize the wisdom of P'Teel."

"Do you now see why I hate the followers of Mitron, Nimon? It was they who denied me my true heritage! The followers of the K'Tar were different. They raised me in secrecy, teaching me the Fire Arts which you have just begun to learn! My skills increased through the accumulation of trace elements in the metabolism which followers of Mitron consider forbidden. Ironically, you have gained some of them through your unique genetic makeup. But others are much more difficult to master. For example, under extreme conditions, I can generate enormous thermal energy without damage to myself - but with extreme damage to my target. Perhaps I should show you... perhaps you should be my target! But that would be too simple... and premature. I must first fulfill my promise to you - my promise to tell you the complete truth."

T'Poch paced back and forth at the edge of the suspensor field, a tigress assessing her prey. But instead of the guttural growl of a jungle beast, she continued her soliloquy.

"I mentioned your unique genetic make-up earlier, and the power it provides. I sensed your reaction. But you poor fool, you do not fully understand. As biodgen, we are on the brink of spawning a new race. But you have yet to take the final step, as I did so many seasons before. As

I was handed to my matron, P'Teel, so was a unique gem from the time of Mitron. No, not the one I now hold in my hand, but the one that I absorbed into my soul! It provided the last ingredient that made my ascension to Dualiity possible. The Mitronian crystal was handed down through the generations for one ultimate purpose, my creation. Yet, as unique as it is, it has a mate. This jewel I hold before you is that missing piece. Legend tells of it being carried by Ravar as he and his followers were expelled from Gemini. But it was lost during the journey, as was Ravar. The hopes of the outcasts seemed all but dashed. Though they ultimately made it to their destination, Castor, their numbers were decimated. Radiation sterilized most of the population. Castorians were cursed to be a dying race. Had the Ravarian gem not been lost, their fate could have been reversed using bioduogenetics and Phoenos to propagate their mental essence. As the gods would have it, the Ravarians would have to wait - wait for the missing shard to be discovered by the Clionian on the planetoid that provided refuge to them during their long and arduous journey."

Slowly shaking her head, a rueful expression on her face, T'Poch continued, "How ironic, that the Mitronian gem would be imbedded within a biodgen raised to be a Ravarian … me, and this Ravarian crystal, long lost, is now destined to become part of a Geminian biodgen… you!"

Nimon's mind became flame. Against the laws of physics, his eyes defied the field and turned inward. Minute transformations within his metabolism reached climactic levels. Hybrid cells of living tissue and life crystal technology, sparked by Kronia's bond, activated by T'Poch's witchery, instinctively following the ways of the K'Tar, became the epitome of what happens should a biodgen actually live! Building to a crescendo - the savagery of the construct conscious unleashed - the savagery for Nimon to command! The change went unnoticed by T'Poch as Nimon's hand twitched imperceptibly beneath the blanket of energy. Muscles of tritanium fiber flexed spasmodically against their bonds.

Yet T'Poch's tirade continued.

"This is why I want you! This is why I will have you! You will be mine, Nimon, for the whispers of legend foretell that the crystal halves must be re-united! The Fire Arts must continue. Its followers need a leader - you will help me provide one for them! Your genetics make you a perfect choice - your savagery, barely kept in check, is the way of the K'Tar! We will be the vessels through which the halves become whole. The Ravarian stone, once implanted within you, will spread. Its seed, when combined with those of the Mitronian gem living within me, will provide us with a new, greater leader! This messiah, once raised, trained, and prepared by the K'Tar, will assume control at the culmination of my carefully laid plans for intergalactic war. Through a lengthy process of rebellion and accumulation of power, a legacy of intergalactic rule will be given to the fruit of our incestuous union!"

T'Poch's hands moved over the suspensor field's controls. Quivering with mounting passion, she deactivated the area appropriate for her needs.

Nimon's shame was overwhelming. His mind had all but crumbled under the harsh truth T'Poch had revealed. As T'Poch finished her preparations, feeling returned to Nimon's torso. The deactivated portion of the field allowed the sensation of touch to register somewhere in what was once Nimon's mind. Slowly T'Poch's flesh came into contact with his own. The flames of carnal lust flared within him, as crimson sheets of desire seared the very fiber of his soul. The bestial hunger of the Dual once empowered by his own Life Mentor's mother overwhelmed Nimon's rationality. The reality of her intimate contact was too vile to endure.

T'Poch, now straddling her victim, clutched the Ravarian stone in both hands. Slowly lifting it above her head, she began to sway - rhythmically, savagely - writhing to the cadence of a tribal sound heard only within her mind. As her feral movements neared its climactic end, she brought her hands forcefully downward, plunging the crystal into the chest of her captive!

The last sensation Nimon felt before the fateful blow was the icy-hot tingling in his arms as the field weakened around them. Rationality metamorphosed into bestiality as the savage mindset of ancient Gemini was unleashed. Whether from her trembling hands causing a maladjustment in the field, or due to the ferocity of an ancient Geminian race long-suppressed, it did not matter. Nimon's arms wrenched upward out of the field to grab the bare shoulders of the woman atop him. All traces of control had evaporated within the man-beast. Demons of a primordial time directed the sinewy arms to pull their prey closer. As they wrenched the she-devil through the outer fringe of the energy barrier, the embrace triggered a violent reaction.

The mass imbalance from T'Poch's penetration into the energy flux caused an explosive overload. Nimon's prone body arched spasmodically. T'Poch shuddered uncontrollably. Emotions of a forbidden era flowed together for a brief instant of suspended time. But it was sufficient. The essence of two crystalline shards, long ago separated during a passionate embrace, were unified once more!

The recoil of the imbalanced energy flux shattered the field into arcing bolts of electrical discharges. Bestial-arms, unaffected by the rapidly healing wound left by the crystal, hurled the weakened female from the spent body of the Geminian-human-biodgen. The impact rendered the temptress unconscious, preventing her from observing her victim crawl from the table. Dragging himself through the dark winding passageways, the figure truly resembled a beast of the desert. When he could go no further, he collapsed pitifully within the confines of a stone outcropping.

Separate, yet now forever inseparable, the children of Phoenos slept.

CHAPTER 26

"Entering Geminian Subsidiary System, sir. Exiting time-fold," came Operations Superintendent Weber's methodical report. Conversion efficiency on polymerization tubes 94%. Purity assay at a 7 genix rating. An excellent run."

Descartes allowed himself a small smile as he appreciatively listened to his manager.

"Permission to enter Gemini controlled space granted, sir," Saffron 1 responded to the questioning eye of her plant manager.

"I'm glad to see we're still on speaking terms with Gemini Central, George. How'd you manage leaving the area so abruptly to follow us without flaring them off?"

"It was simple, sir. Once they had their hands on Nimon, they couldn't care less where we went. As soon as you were a bit late on your check-in from the surface, I suspected something was amiss. A quick spectral scan of the area turned up Castorian readings. They launched the whole lot of you up to their probe ship before we could respond. Their stealth device slowed us up, but once we ID'ed their ship's ion trail, we were hot after them. Hope we didn't take too long, sir."

"Your timing was perfect, George. Let's hope our luck holds out so it's just as perfect for Nimon."

Pivoting in his chair to face the technical control station, Descartes inquired, "Mr. Fleming, any progress from the search scan?"

"Sensor modifichhations to detecht only Mr. Edishun's unique metabolism have identified a one-hundred square khlik grid as having the highest probability of chhontaining him, sir. The computer is processing the data to better pinpoint his lochation."

"Very good, Mr. Fleming. Advise me when you have him."

Thumbing the comm-link switch on his console, Descartes reached Personnel. "J.B., we've just about zeroed-in on Nimon. Are you prepared with a medtech to head planet side?"

"We have the lander equipped for ambulance duty, Morgan. Our senior medical supervisor will be staying at the plant to monitor Dr. Edison. The life crystal sutures are taking to his metabolism very well. We've got him under a stasis screen to ward off infection, since any drug we could use would only hinder his body's natural defense system. Other than that, we've just got to wait and see."

"Fine. I'll be joining you personally with a biodrone escort crew, since we don't know what we'll encounter down there. Meet me in the lander hangar when you're ready."

Now directing his attention to his operations superintendent, Descartes continued, "Mr. Weber. Arrange for one Seeker and two Militia biodrones to be loaded into the lander. Check the duty roster to see which empowering techs are up for duty. Also assign medtech Ramirez to accompany us."

"Consider it done, sir," replied Weber, as he activated a switch on his panel.

*   *   *

The appearance of the lander piercing the atmosphere cast an eerie glow against the crystalline-dusted walls of the valley.

Once the surface team disembarked, Jeff Brown gestured toward an opening in a granite outcropping. Moments later, he reported to his plant manager. "Stavros' bioscan of the area registers a Geminoid reading down the corridor beyond that cave's entrance, Morgan. But we've got to get closer before he can tell if it's Nimon."

Stavros was one of the superior grades of Seeker biodrones. Equipped with spectral sensors for radiation ranging from infrared to microwave, he could detect the unique life energy frequencies of any individual to which he was calibrated. Apparently, Nimon was in critical condition, since only a trace of Geminian life energy could be detected over the relatively short distance within the catacombs.

"Formation L then, people. We'll move closer while you keep scanning, Stavros. Keep pulsar muskets at the ready, but holstered. Let's go."

Militia biodrone Cora Xenia took up point as her fellow militia unit lingered several treds behind the group to guard the rear. As they entered the passageway, the faint, acrid odor of overheated circuitry wafted past them.

As the search team moved further into the tunnels, the biodrone Seeker reported, "Organic life energies of an unusual pattern directly ahead at 40.4 treds. I am unable to identify the cause of the irregularity. Haste is suggested."

Now at a steady trot, the group was startled as they rounded an outcropping to see their quarry sitting hidden in a small niche, staring blankly toward them. As the medtech rushed to the near-catatonic figure, Descartes whispered under his breath to his resident sociologist, "J.B., what do you think's wrong with him?"

The gaunt features of the cobalt-skinned Geminian told of the days without food and water. Once neatly groomed hair was now matted and soiled from the mineral waters seeping from the craggy walls. The deep blue of the sun-exposed skin faded briefly to the expected aqua hue on the exposed buttocks, but quickly resumed its darker hue further down his flanks. The most notable feature of the pitiful figure collapsed before the search team were his eyes – his dark, crimson eyes. The glassy stare in a human would immediately indicate catatonic shock, a condition to Brown's knowledge that could not exist in Geminians.

But Nimon was only half-Geminian. Many times in the past, Brown had wished the technical superintendent would reveal more of both his physiology, and the human side of his behavior... until now.

After a thorough scan with his instruments, the medtech Ramirez exclaimed, "We've got to get him to the plant fast, Mr. Descartes. He's experienced a severe trauma. The physical damage appears minimal, but I can't determine the full extent of the psychic trauma without full testing."

Reaching up to activate the throat transmitter clasped to his neck, Descartes established a link to the plant. He urgently ordered, "Have a medical team ready in the lander hangar. Ramirez and Jefferson Brown are bringing up Nimon. Continue empowering the militia and seeker units. We're going to continue searching the area. I'll maintain the normal check-in schedule. Descartes out."

As the lander levitated on a field of energized gravitons, Descartes and his biodrone team moved cautiously through the winding passageway, this time with pulsar muskets drawn. "Anything or anyone that could leave Nimon in that condition is worthy of the precaution," Descartes thought. After forty minutes of searching, they emerged into the chambers from which Nimon had apparently escaped. The human and the three biodiver "others" swept the area with their scrutiny.

The source of the acrid smell was apparent, as the energy field's control panel spasmodically spit its weakened charge from one fused circuit to another. Other than a shoulder bag and loin cloth fashioned out of one of Gemini's indigenous flora, there was no evidence of anyone's presence in the room. The eerie solitude of the chamber began to take effect upon the Darwin quartet, as they looked to each other for solace out of the corners of their eyes.

A staccato of high pitched tones from Descartes's transmitter broke the silence, as Stavros flushed slightly from the start the device's signal had given him.

"This is Descartes," said the plant manager, as he stifled a smile.

"Sir, Saffron 1 here. Jefferson Brown believes Dr. Edison is the key to Nimon's recovery. Though still weak, his wound has healed sufficiently. He felt you would want to know his plans."

"J.B. has good instincts. Prepare the lander to retrieve me."

Turning to Xenia and Stavros, he continued, "Notify the Geminian authorities about this place while continuing your search. Maybe they can shed some light on what's happened here. Keep

Mr. Weber informed about your progress. He motioned the second Militia biodrone to take the point for his return to the lander rendezvous zone. Any questions?"

In unison they replied, "No sir."

"Oh, and Mr. Stavros..." Descartes said with an amiable wink, "...I like that quick reflexes. Keep up the good work!"

*   *   *

As Descartes and his biodrone guard rounded a stony outcropping a few thousand treds away from the two "others", Stavros, the seeker unit, flipped open a small panel on his forearm and aimed it in their direction. "Good," he commented, tossing the comment over his shoulder toward Cora Xenia. "The heat signature of the humanoid registers a clear signal, while the militia unit reading is already showing interference from the minerals in the passage walls. This could be our only opportunity."

"I'm still not sure about this, Stav ..."

Stavros cocked his head slightly toward the militia unit in response to her comment, while still keeping his attention riveted on his scanning grid. The graviton signature of the lander assigned to Descartes had just entered his sensor range. "Time enough for me to convince her," he thought, confidently.

Turning fully toward his comrade, he adopted a softer tone and smiled at her. "Cora, we've been planning this for so long ... waiting for just the right opportunity. This is it," he almost pleaded.

Cora Xenia, one of the most efficient defensive units in the quadrant, hugged herself reflexively, as if to resist a chill that was not there. She looked into his eyes, longingly, for a brief instant. Stavros took a step closer, slowly moving his gaze from her face, down her skin tight fatigues, and back up again. She knew the capabilities of his visual sensors, and couldn't help but flick him a disapproving smile.

"You're such a rogue, Stav." Flirtatiously, she turned her back to him, tossing her shoulder-length auburn lock around her head. Stavros took another step closer, hesitantly, not sure of the signal she was sending. An unspoken moment passed, as each awaited the other to make the next move. Finally, Cora broke the silence.

"Did you remember to bring it?"

Stavros struggled momentarily to understand her question as he fought back the stupefying chemical surges welling up within him. Looking around the cavern awkwardly, he sought for the answer that would mean conquest or failure.

"Well...?" she asked again, peevishly.

The seeker unit took another step closer, coming to within a hand's breadth of her, while he nervously fingered his sensor grid. Looking down at it, he saw the waning signal of the lander as it rose into the atmosphere. Then the answer dawned upon him. Flicking open another panel in his forearm, he produced a micro disc.

"I have it..." he whispered.

Looking over her shoulder, Cora locked her eyes with his and delicately licked her lips. "Let me insert it," she purred.

Stavros shuddered as a wave of expectation coursed through him. Cora placed both hands on the buckle at his waist, still holding his eyes hypnotically. With a savage twist, she parted the protective vest and slid her hands underneath. Taking her time as she explored him, Stavros buried his face into the nape of her neck, drawing in her feral scent. One hand moved to the base of her spine and slowly moved upward with instinctive accuracy. The other brought the disc to her closest hand, frustrated in knowing it would have to interrupt her play, if only briefly. Cora delayed taking it, as she moved him closer and closer to an ecstasy he had only imagined. Then, with experience encoded over the ages, she inserted the disc into the biograft.

"Now we're safe from them," she cooed, as she pulled him down with her onto the cool, cavern floor.

*   *   *

"Crag! What the black hole is wrong with the biod signatures?" technician Hal Xkorp muttered under his breath, using the less accepted epithet for biodrone. "The seeker and militia units have been fading in and out all mission. The lander boost helped some, but now I've got an alarm signature to deal with."

Hal nervously looked over at the "logs" one more time to check their condition. It was a habit he'd have to break if he were to keep his assignment as a biodrone empowerment safety technician. The "BEST" corps was considered a choice assignment on the Darwin. It was their responsibility to monitor the vital signs of the biologicals, or "logs" as they were irreverently called, during their consciousness transmission work shift. Visual checks were pointless, and the first habit of a rookie that needed to be broken, since the biological units were in a catatonic state while they empowered their respective biodrones. The complex monitor system provided all the necessary information to assess the transmitter's condition, and served double duty by tracking the "other" on the surface below. Though the biodrones were fully independent from the BEST technician, it had long been a practice to track specific biodgen emission wavelengths - for what purpose, Hal could not fathom. Since no information ever flowed on those channels, he considered it a mindless procedure that management had imposed long ago that had outgrown its purpose, but had escaped their "all knowing wisdom" to discontinue.

"Got a problem, rookie?" Foreman Lar Heidrick boomed from across the control room. "You'd better say 'No', 'cuz I don't want to have my shift extended havin' to explain to the next foreman why you haven't cleared all your alarm signatures."

Biting the inside of his cheek to keep from snapping back at his Neanderthal supervisor, Hal replied, "This alarm code isn't one they covered in training. And with all the distortion from the caverns, I can't tell if it's authentic or not."

"Call out the ID sequence, and I'll check it on the reference doubloon. And see if you can get it right, huh?" the foreman barked.

Hal called out the code, taking extraordinary pains to speak at a pace that was so slow it bordered on sarcastic insubordination. Moments passed as the foreman paged through dozens of archives, searching for the right reference. Hal glanced at the chrono display with a smirk, knowing that Lar would be late for his daily case of Hofbrau if he didn't find the information soon. A grunt from across the room wasn't as informative as Hal would have liked as he watched the foreman hurriedly punch in a few comm codes. Lar continued to grumble a few more expletives as he shuffled over to his control chair and plopped into it.

Moments later, the door to the outer chamber of the biodrone empowerment center irised open as a hulking form came hustling through. Still struggling to get his remaining arm pushed into the enviro-suit he was wearing, he banged on the glass window to the inner control room and thumbed a command to Lar to come over. Muttering a few insults in Hal's direction, Lar complied. Hal watched innocently as the abrupt jerking movement of the newcomer's head added force to the sharp, but inaudible, instructions he was delivering to Lar. As the foreman's shoulders drooped lower and lower, the verbal abuse suddenly ceased as they both turned to look at Hal.

"Rookie ... c'mere!" Lar commanded. Not giving Hal a chance to completely traverse the room, Lar added with a cock of his head toward the newcomer, "You're with him!" Turning back toward his control chair, the foreman finished his orders, "Get your lousy butt into an enviro-suit while I call the next shift and tell 'em I'm pulling a double." As Lar shuffled off, Hal didn't realize that would be the last order he'd ever have to follow from his "beloved" foreman.

Chapter 27

Hal fidgeted in his enviro-suit as he watched his oversized colleague work through the lander launch preparatory procedure. He hadn't uttered a word since the conversation with Lar in the "log" control room, with only a few brusque hand signals to hurry Hal along or direct him to a certain position well out of the way. As the hanger depressurized and the biocrys skin of the Darwin morphed open, another lander entered the hanger. Hal noted with surprise the plant manager icon on the nose display, indicating that Mr. Descartes was aboard. Hal's curiosity was piqued. The recent activities of the management staff had been communicated to a lesser extent than normal. He had tired of trying to keep up with current corporate events from the weekly downloads. They were only sterilized versions of the facts, and lacked any timely information even if their accuracy wasn't questionable. He preferred to get his news in the various break rooms, listening surreptitiously to bits of conversations while he drank his caffeine cocktails. He'd heard of Technical Superintendent Nimon's troubles, but wasn't clued into the fact that the plant manager had gone planet-side. As he craned his neck to catch a glimpse of the facility manager, he was surprised to hear Descartes' voice snap over the lander comm.

"Eric, what's the status?"

Hal's escort shot him a glance. He then placed a subvocal comm patch on his neck while inserting a companion ear piece receiver. This would allow a private conversation between Descartes and "Eric" ... at least Hal had learned his name ... by transmitting the minute vibrations of his vocal chords without the passing of enough air to produce a sound.

"Mr. Descartes, the "log" control room detected what they thought was an anomalous reading from the surface biodrones shortly after you launched. Unfortunately, the readings were fragmented due to cavern mineral interference. The supervisor took a while in correlating the signal with the appropriate alarm sequence protocol. I can't be sure, but it's possible it's a Level 3."

"Biod-biod?" the plant manager inquired, recalling that levels 2 and 1 were much more severe, and were reserved for more unique situations.

"Yes sir. I assume you'll want the standard precautions?"

Descartes thought for a moment. His safety record was best in class. If an event of this magnitude hit the books, there would be no recovering from it for the rest of the measurement cycle. That meant a lot of bonus lost for a lot of his people.

"Eric, you've proven to be creative in the past. Let's see if we can avoid 'standard procedures', okay?"

Hal saw Eric's face flush a deep crimson, as his jaw clenched rapidly. "Must be some conversation," Hal mused to himself.

"And Eric, just in case ... take the flamers."

Hal decided to take a gamble. "I appreciate the opportunity I got when I moved into the BEST corps," he thought. "Hell, I've even grown used to the mistreatment from Lar ... well, most of the time. But this guy's attitude is just a little over the top. He must think he's a member of Internal Audit, with this voiceless, hyper-secret communications act. Well, I'm entitled to know what I'm getting into on this mission, and he's going to tell me."

Turning his lander chair toward the pilot station, his jaw set determinedly, he made his play, "Listen, Eric, this is all happening kind of fast. I think I ought to know more about this assignment. It doesn't feel like your average landing excursion. These enviro-suits aren't normal issue, especially since the planet's atmosphere is near standard. And guys your age ... umm ... rank, don't normally go planet side. When are you planning on briefing me?"

The supervisor, or manager ... Hal couldn't be sure since he wore no seniority chevron ...

responded with a vicious glare. The same flush of crimson Hal saw during the conversation with Descartes reappeared, and then disappeared as fast as it came. Replacing the look with an approving smirk, Eric fished a data doubloon out of a pouch on his forearm and pitched it toward the young technician. "Congratulations, rookie. No more 'log' tech duties for you."

Not being the reaction Hal had anticipated, he managed to shake off his momentary stupor long enough to catch the memory coin after it bounced off his chest. Fumbling it into the playback socket of his enviro-suit, he switched on the heads-up display option in his helmet.

After a few moments, Eric added, "Helluva way to get promoted, huh?"

Hal's eyes widened bigger than the flip-down ocular display screens inside his head gear. "Jeez ... this is nuts ... we can't do that ... can we?"

"Look closer at the authorization icon ... ever seen one of those?" Eric quizzed.

Hal scrolled the display by focusing on the appropriate pixel on the screen. A logo of a small red sun with a black disk like an eclipse appeared. "Yeah, but ..."

The veteran interrupted. "Listen, rookie. This isn't the first one of these, and it won't be the last."

"I get it now. You've done this before. That's why they sent someone ... ummm ... with your level of experience. And this logo, it's ..."

"Internal Audit Division. And you thought all we did was juggle data doubloons and make your lives miserable." Eric paused and let slip a quirky smile. "Well, some of us still get to do that. But others, like me ... and now, you ... are called on to 'fix' things."

Hal, his mission briefing now complete, and his ocular displays having returned to their niches, stared at the veteran with a puzzled look.

The seasoned IAD specialist kept his attention on his lander control panel, almost a little too deliberately, as he finalized the craft's entry path coordinates. With a sharp jab to the last touch pad key, he whirled his chair to face Hal.

"Listen ... I'm not proud of it, but once you've been on one of these, you know why you have to go, and you pray you won't have to go again!"

"So your god wasn't listening to you last time, huh?" Hal replied, solemnly. After an uncomfortable pause, he quietly inquired, "I've worked in 'log' maintenance for a while, and haven't heard a word of this. So what's it all mean?"

Eric's countenance softened a bit, and he replied, "It means you're a part of this now. You take your promotion, you do your job, and you hope you live to spend your hazard pay."

The lander jolted as it set down on the rocky surface outside the Geminian catacombs. Eric activated a comm link back to the Darwin biodrone control center and barked into his throat microphone. "Switching 'log' transfer control to my field remote." And before Lar could grumble a response, Eric severed the comm link. Just as abruptly, he unclasped the pilot seat harness and made his way over to the safety locker.

"Your file says you're pretty good with a musket, but have you ever handled one of these?" He yanked a wicked looking "defense" sidearm out of its bracket and tossed it over to Hal.

Now all business, the rookie smoothly caught it with one hand, flipped it around his forearm, snapped open the safety and checked the charge. Satisfied, he slapped the butt of the device on his thigh, and twirled it up into a standard ready position. "No, but I'm a quick learner. That's why I can't figure why I've never heard of this."

Eric nodded appreciatively at the rookie's little show. "It's kept pretty quiet, unless you're a 'log' yourself. They won't talk about it for two reasons. Now, get your flamer ready. I'm releasing the hatch. Be ready to cover my butt, and watch yours while you're at it."

Hal placed his hand on the veteran's forearm, preventing him from activating the hatch release. "Two reasons? What two reasons?"

Eric's steely gaze pierced through his own face shield and penetrated Hal's. "One, because they're following orders, like you and me. And two ... because they're planning on breaking them."

"But what orders?" the rookie pressed.

"Why natural orders, of course ... laws of nature ... biods aren't meant to procreate ... surely you've heard of that."

*   *   *

The two IAD members jumped through the lander portal, the younger one landing in a crouched position, flamer at the ready; the senior one, taking point as he darted toward the cavern opening. At the mouth of the catacombs, he activated his shoulder mounted lantern and bathed the darkened corridors with its penetrating beam. Seeing no indications of danger, he motioned his companion forward.

Within the passageways the trace levels of fluorescent minerals, long starved of energy, eagerly absorbed the lantern's beam and doled it back upon the pair as an eerie, green glow. Slowly, deliberately, the two crept forward. Every few treds, Hal jerkily glanced over his shoulder, expecting portions of the rock he just passed to come alive as some monstrous assailant. Eric, always the veteran, stealthily moved around each sharp turn with flamer poised. After what seemed to Hal to be a millennium, they approached a fork in the tunnel.

Eric commanded, "Take the left. I'm on the right. Keep alert. Watch your comm signal monitor. If it drops below 3, alert me. Otherwise, keep quiet until you see something worth talking about."

Following his senior's orders, Hal nodded without a word. Gripping his weapon a shade more tightly, he cautiously kept to the inside wall of the corridor as it twisted its way deeper into the mountain. The temptation to stare at the gauge as it dipped and peaked was overwhelming. He found he had to force himself to count 20 steps before looking at the comm signal. Hypnotically, it competed with his attempts to keep an eye out for the real danger that lay before him.

The fluorescent veins in the walls were becoming less prevalent the further he went. When he glanced back along his path, he could swear the eerie green patterns coalesced into living shapes, warning him to go no further. The ceiling often dipped so low he had to crouch in a Brevorian duck waddle. Rather than crawl, he mimicked the awkward creature so he could keep both hands on his weapon.

As he emerged from one such constriction in his path, he imagined he heard a grunting sound. Adjusting the gain on his helmet headset, he panned the tunnel in all directions to isolate the source. Detecting nothing, he crept forward, beads of perspiration forming on his upper lip and forehead. He fought back the urge to wipe them off, knowing the helmet and protective suit would not yield to such a trivial desire for human comfort. The grunting resumed. Feverishly Hal tapped at his audio controls to locate its origin. The cavern mocked him as it reflected the trace noise back and forth against its rocky surface, blocking any hope of detecting whether the sound was real or the result of an overactive imagination. He knew that if he contacted Eric and he couldn't give him the sound's direction, the veteran's scorn would be relentless. The perspiration was now a chilling sweat that crawled down his back and tensed his muscles into stone.

He pushed himself forward.

The next turn slapped him in the face. The corridor was completely blocked. A sheer rock face cut its way out of the left side of the tunnel. It ended in a jagged, slate edge that angled its way from the base of the opposite wall back up to the center of the tunnel ceiling. Just behind it, another stone face knifed out from the right side of the tunnel, its jagged edge complementing that of its companion. Hal cursed. Turning back would force him to report in to Eric, and he had found nothing worth reporting other than failure and fear. His comm signal maliciously reported a full 7 on its meter.

Stubbornly, Hal directed his shoulder lantern around the stone tomb. Moving closer to the first outcropping, he saw that it was a full tred in front of the one coming from the opposite side. Looking at his wrist controls, he tapped the panel and directed a high frequency sonar burst through the gap between the two rock faces. Staring at the reading for a moment, his scowl slowly transformed into a smile. There was a clear path that "S"ed its way around the two outcroppings. The challenge was whether it was big enough for him to squeeze through. As he prepared to climb across the first slate edge, the grunting sound returned. This time the direction was unmistakable. It was coming from the other side of the barrier!

Hal fought to distinguish himself from the cold granite that surrounded him. Fear crept through his muscles, anchoring him to the rigid stone. Mechanically, he forced his legs up on to the first jagged surface. Talking out loud, he commanded his body to go forward, wedging itself down between the walls. As he twisted his torso into the narrow gap, his shoulder light splashed its beam off the wall into his face, blinding him. Angrily, he slapped the control on his forearm to extinguish it. Purple and orange globes swam in his vision, mixing with the luminescent green tentacles reaching out from the rocks. Pressing onward, an eternity passed as he inched his way deeper into the darkness.

Hal allowed himself a small victory as he reached the end of the first leg of the "S" path. He pulled himself over the second outcropping, only to see his success transform into frustration. The remaining half of the obstacle would force him to crawl. The option of turning back again danced seductively in his mind. Listening intently, the savage grunting sound was gone, leaving a small opening for courage to assert itself. The cold sweat had warmed from the exertion of getting this far.

Hal went on.

Slithering through the reddish powder that resulted from eons of minute grating of the massive slabs, Hal felt like a prehistoric lizard of Geminian lore. Though crawling on his belly, it seemed as if his progress along the second leg was much quicker than that of the first. The eerie green glow a few treds in front of him told him he was nearing an opening. Elated, he hastened his efforts. But his elation quickly faded. What he failed to realize was that the glow also meant something was providing enough light to activate the fluorescent minerals.

And the grunting had returned.

He fought to comprehend it. "Was it coming from an animal in pain? Was it prompted by a savage hunger? Or was it both?" Hal's attempt to replace his fear with rational questions failed. His heart beat rapidly. An adrenalin surge gripped at his throat. Face down, he lay there, shivering uncontrollably.

A hand moved forward. Fingers pulled at a fissure in the tunnel wall. Another hand followed.

Then, simultaneously, they violently clutched the shoulders of the panic-stricken human. With savage tugs, Hal's rigid body was pulled down the rest of the rocky crawl-space. Yanked from the crypt with one quick motion, Hal felt himself hoisted up and slammed against the cavern wall. A blinding light jabbed at his eyes, as he waited for the killing blow.

A gloved hand slapped at his faceplate, jarring his head inside the helmet. Again it came, but the ferocity lessened. Hal unclenched his eyes just enough to see his attacker.

"Rookie! Snap out of it! Get a grip! We've got a job to do!" Releasing his hold on his partner, Eric let Hal slump to the tunnel floor. "What are you doing playing spelunker?"

Hal looked up at the veteran looming over him. A manic giggle slipped out, partially in relief, and partially at his own misplaced fear. Shaking his head slowly, he asked, "Didn't you hear it? Didn't you hear that animal grunting? It was coming from this side of the barrier."

"The only thing I heard was my grunting as I hauled your butt out of that lava tube. And if there was a sound, it could be anything. Look around you. There are minor tube openings all through this section. A noise could be coming from anywhere."

True enough, Hal looked around the tunnel wall and ceiling. There were a dozen openings of all sizes where ancient lava had burned its way through cracks in the rock, leaving tubes as it dripped out and down the craggy surfaces. Pulling himself up, using his weapon as a crutch, he forced himself to regain his composure.

Eric continued, "Our two routes converge further down. I scouted ahead. When I didn't see any sign of you, I backtracked. Now listen, rookie. I need you, and I need you to be sharp. Can you handle it?"

Hal looked back at him, clenching his jaw firmly. "Yeah, I can do this. I just let my imagination run away with me. This is a lot different than sitting in front of a 'log' monitor, you know. But I can do this."

"Well, that's the good news. The bad news is we have another split in the tunnel. And next time somebody grabs you, hit the repulsor disk on your forearm. That'll give 'em a jolt through the surface of your suit they won't forget."

"But what if it's you?"

"I don't think I'm going to have to do that again, do you?" Eric replied, with a slap on Hal's shoulder.

Hal grinned, sheepishly. "I'm sure you won't..." and adding with newfound courage, "... now let's get the job done!"

*   *   *

The manager's stride told of his singularity of purpose as he approached the MedCen. Obediently, the door irised open to allow his entry. Abruptly, hands accustomed to decades of shuffling performance appraisals displayed surprising strength as they firmly grasped the plant manager.

"Morgan, I want you to be aware of Nimon's condition, but you should also know that you can't do anything to help him. We've treated his malnutrition and burns, but it's his psychological condition that's in danger."

"Well what's being done to correct that?" Descartes probed demandingly, his concern showing through to Jefferson Brown.

"That's the problem. Given the damned security clearance needed to treat him, I've had to consult with his family's private physician ..."

"Don't go waving that in my face again ... you know I can't do anything about it. Those orders come directly from the Board!" Descartes barked.

"Like I was saying, you can't do anything about it. But I've conferred with the Geminian expert planet side, and even she's never seen anything like it. But she has recommended a course of action. Her remote psycho- and neuro-scans indicate severe shock. The catatonia can only be broken by providing Nimon with an overriding desire to face reality. Simply put, he needs a reason to return to us. But in order to come back and retain his sanity, he must recall whatever ordeal he experienced and deal with it. The sooner he does this, the greater are the chances for a successful recovery. That's why Dr. Edison's in there with him now."

"Dr. Edison? But J.B., what can he do?"

"The Geminian physician wouldn't say. All I can figure is that Dr. Edison can give Nimon the motive to live in our world, not the one he's created for himself. Dr. Edison claims that the biodgen, Starn, whom Nimon is accused of murdering, is not actually dead. But in order for him to survive ... for them both to survive, Nimon must empower him. It is this 'purpose for living' that must be instilled in Nimon. Dr. Edison has got to convince his son that by ignoring reality, Nimon will be killing Starn, and himself."

"How can he do that? In Nimon's condition, can he communicate with him?" inquired Descartes.

"The expert says 'Yes'. Even in human catatonia, research shows that there can be a fragile link with reality which allows the comprehension of language. It's our only hope."

"So I guess we just wait?" Descartes replied, knowing the answer as he asked. The alternative of waiting had never been Descartes's favorite -under any circumstance. But he had managed to choose it when the situation required. It seemed even more difficult to do so now, with the life of his friend hanging in the balance.

Chapter 28

It had been nearly fifteen minutes since the two had split up for the second time. Hal had forgotten the need to check his comm signal monitor, his newfound courage proving to be an intoxicant that displaced better judgement. It was about five minutes into his tunnel that the signal dropped well below the 3.0 level. His path had been unobstructed, but had snaked its way deeper into the mountain with many bends and turns. Rounding an unusually severe hairpin cutback, things changed. Hal sobered and his courage waned.

The grunting had returned, and with it came an inhuman moaning.

Crouching low and pressing himself against the cavern wall, a glance at his comm gauge drained his courage even further. Refusing to let it disappear completely, Hal urged himself to go on with a self-deprecating curse. Advancing a dozen treds further down the slowly arcing lava tube, Hal sensed a musky odor wafting its way along the dry, sub-Geminian air. A glimmer of light alerted him that the end of his search may be near.

Approaching the opening with musket at the ready, Hal shot a glance around its edge, then flattened back against the wall as his training had taught him. Closing his eyes, he allowed the mental photograph to replay itself in his mind. "A rock-hewn amphitheater ... several openings spaced irregularly around the wall ... was it four or five? ... at its center, a crouched woman ... her back was to him ... was she stripped bare to the waist? ... no-one else in the chamber ... but he could hear the grunting intermixed with a deeper moaning ... damn, he was never good at this during his training ..."

Determined to get it right, Hal inched one eye around the lip of the stone archway. Two decatreds in front of him, the sight came clearly into focus, and it was electrifying.

Exquisitely toned muscles in the female's exposed back flexed rhythmically as her rope of hair swayed back and forth across it. Her Solar Corp.-issued leather tunic had been ripped from her, and lay in a heap across the legs of the seeker biodrone that she straddled. Sensuously, a glimpse of her buttocks became visible above the tunic as she rose and fell. Her arms were hidden from view, as they disappeared around her body to work their magic on her partner. The source of the elusive sounds in the cavern passages was now clear. The forceful, lusty grunts of the militia biod were timed synchronously with the moans of the lover beneath her.

Entranced by the scene before him, Hal failed to notice the scuffing sound he made as he inched forward to get a closer look. Cora Xenia suddenly arched her back, a shudder passing down her, as she stiffly turned her head to look over her left shoulder. Her eyes were pinched shut, as a noiseless scream spread itself across her face. A misplaced sound floated across the room. Hal thought his sensors must have malfunctioned. It was as if wet fabric were being ripped away.

Slowly, Xenia's eyes parted. Gleaming a metallic red, they bore into Hal. Motionless, he stood halfway in the archway, unable to breathe. Seconds passed. Hal knew he had to act, but he couldn't. All he could do was stare into those fiery eyes. Forcing himself with all his will, he traced a path from her eyes to her lips. She was whispering something. Somehow, he managed to move his feet. But rather than flee, he took a step closer. Her lips were wet. Fantasizing, their succulent mango flavor urged him forward. Another step. The lips moved again, but again, the sound was undetectable. Her tongue traced the inside of her mouth. A golden liquid moistened her lips, lips that were so inviting. "Strange..." Hal thought, "that gold liquid ... haunting ... but familiar." Another step, then another. Somewhere in the back of Hal's mind, rational thought struggled to regain control. As her next lover approached, Xenia turned her shoulder further around to him. Hal fought to allow his rational side back into his mind. His gaze moved slowly away from her lips, down her neck, and rested on her shoulder. Her breathing was still heavy from her last conquest. Her heaving allowed Hal the pleasure of watching her breasts rise and fall, their rhythm enticing him ever forward. Both her shoulder and breasts glistened with a gold hue. Hal struggled again to recall where he had seen the fluid. It was mysteriously out of place. Again she whispered. This time, Hal was close enough for his sensors to detect the sound. But the meaning was unclear, his hypnotic stupor keeping rational thought from its duty. Now, only a few treds from her, Hal could do nothing but succumb to her desires. Slowly, Xenia raised her hand from her last lover and brought it around for her next one to see. Clutched within her grasp was a golden nugget, twice the size of her fist. The radiant liquid from the mass drenched her arm, and Hal could see it had coated her bosom as well. Deep within Hal's mind, a caution clarion blared. "I know about this substance!" Hal's subconscious urged.

An intoxicating smile spread across Xenia's face. She raised her hand higher, stretching her prize out to her next prey. She whispered, "You're next."

A flash of horror erased the blissful glaze from Hal's thoughts! "The golden fluid ... it's biod blood!" He had seen it once before in the biodrone recovery room while accompanying a 'log' there after a failed mission. "His heart ... she's killed him ... must escape!" Stumbling backward, Hal fought to regain his senses, and his balance. Xenia laughed wickedly as she pivoted her other arm around to point it at Hal. Still gloved, affixed to it were a variety of devices used by militia units. Hal's eyes widened behind his helmet's faceplate as he scrambled backwards, crabbing his way as fast as he could to escape her. Past her outstretched glove, he saw the head of what was once Stavros loll to one side, mouth agape in a mask of pain and death.

Hal had forgotten he still clutched his musket. All he could think about was escape. Xenia had other plans. Pointing her glove at Hal's weapon hand, a puff and hiss of propellant sent a cable of surgical tungstinium toward its mark. Ensnaring Hal's forearm, a quick jerk by the militia biod tightened the wire, sending a wave of excruciating pain surging through the human. The musket clattered to the stone floor.

Xenia rose from her first victim and pulled the cable again. Hal lurched forward on his knees, trying to relieve the snare's tension before it cut into his flesh, his enviro-suit serving as his last line of protection. The biodrone temptress stood before him, brazenly immodest, bare from the waist up, with only the tattered shreds of her tunic covering her loins. The human didn't notice, the siren's trance now completely broken. Instead, Hal stared in horror at the gaping hole in the seeker unit's chest. Alive only moments earlier, the rookie tried to shake from his mind the thought of what Xenia had done to Stavros.

The image of her squeezing the biodrone's heart rhythmically as she mounted him sickened the human. Convulsing from both that thought and the burning pain in his arm, Hal fought back the urge to vomit. Gurgling a hysterical laugh, Xenia jerked the cable again.

Hal clutched at the wire with his free hand. Grimacing, he looked down at his arm just to prove it was still connected. The disc on his sleeve beckoned. From the mists of his pain, the thought of Eric's last instructions emerged. "The next time someone grabs you, that'll give them a jolt they won't forget." Slapping the disc, Hal allowed himself a vengeful smile.

A blue flash erupted as the charge coursed up the cable and into the harpy. Again Xenia arched her back, but this time not from ecstasy. Hal watched as she jerked and twitched, the current crackling through her synthesized cells. Endless seconds elapsed as she struggled, miraculously staying on her feet. Xenia's grimace failed to elicit sympathy from the human, as he himself gritted his teeth against his own pain. Many more seconds passed. Slowly, the biodrone's grimace transformed. Her convulsions lessened. The crimson slits of her eyes opened wider as a wicked smile spread across her face.

Somehow, she was absorbing the paralyzing power of the repulsor!

"That's impossible!" Hal thought. "No militia biod is equipped to do that!"

Just as mysteriously, a scarlet aura emanated from the militia biod. Pulsing its way along the tether, it neutralized the energy field of the human's suit. As it encompassed him, the suit's micro-compensators failed. Sweat soaked out of every pore in Hal's body as the suit's internal temperature rapidly increased. Unrelenting, Xenia pulled the helpless human closer. As she raised her hand to rip off Hal's protective helmet, its speakers squawked a warning.

"Rookie, down and cover! Now!"

From the mouth of one of the tunnel openings, Eric lowered his flamer and released a charge. A gelatinous capsule impacted on the bare back of the attacker, immediately bursting into a white flame.

"Aaiieee!" screamed the synthetic construct. Futilely, she clawed at the substance. Pulling at anything that wasn't her skin, she jerked off her militia glove and tore away her tunic fragments. Falling to her knees, she hammered at the hard floor with her fists, senselessly beating away an intangible foe.

Hal wasted no time. Feeling the slack in the wire, he peeled it away from his arm and rolled clear of the burning creature. Looking back at her, he uttered a silent curse in her direction.

As if in answer, her screams subsided. Still crouched on her knees and elbows in a semi-fetal position, she raised her head. The hellish eyes glowered at him. In amazement, Hal watched as the white flames condensed around her body, forming almost a second skin of living fire. Placing her palms flat on the stone surface beneath her, she flexed her back up and down, as if readying herself to pounce upon her prey. Unable to move, Hal thankfully heard another charge erupt from Eric's flamer.

The capsule smacked against its target, mercilessly releasing its flaming venom. What was once Xenia jerked at the impact, momentarily shuddering as the fire coursed around her. But instead of succumbing to it, like a phoenix, the flaming creature stood and took a step toward Hal. Not believing the sight before him, Hal sat awestruck, unmoving.

"Rookie ... snap out of it! You said you could do it! Now do it! Grab your musket and aim at its throat! You've only got one chance!"

It seemed as if somebody other than Hal moved his hand behind him and closed it around the musket. It couldn't have been him, because he couldn't take his eyes off of the phenomenon before him. Slowly, the musket was lifted up to his shoulder. A precious heartbeat was taken to level the barrel at just the right angle. The creature took another step. The pulsar musket fired.

The pulse from the musket found its mark. Erupting just below the chin, the head and neck exploded into a fireball. Convulsing uncontrollably, the flaming body of the biodrone staggered with one step, then another, and finally collapsed in a funeral pyre mere treds from the marksman.

Eric rushed to the rookie, who sat crouched, his body shaking fitfully as its adrenalin rush subsided. Looking at his forearm where the cable had bitten into his flesh, he offered some consolation, but only a small dose. "You're going to be okay ... damnedest thing I've ever seen. I've heard tell of stories where Class 3 biod encounters have frightening results, but nothing like that! I'm not surprised at poor Stavros. I've seen it before. But usually the female is found dead as well. Most times a result of her own crazed seizure. But then, the IAD's never been this quick on the scene. I'll have to give this report some thought. Especially since we've still got some things to take care of."

The veteran held out a stringer of a dozen metal wedge-shaped devices, their only defining characteristic being the ominous logo of the IAD. "I want you to place these equidistant around this chamber, doubling them up at the sides of each opening."

Hal was too numb too ask any questions. He just wanted to get away from the unholy scene ... run back to the lander that would take him to the comfort of the Darwin, where he could down some narcotics in the medlab and forget all that had happened. Obediently, he gathered the wedges and trudged off to the far side of the chamber, his arm hanging limply at his side. Eric repeated the process on the opposite side, and waited patiently at one of the openings while his injured colleague finished his duties.

As Hal passed the veteran to exit the cavern, he heard Eric mumble, "One more detail, for what little good it will due on our accident report ..." The comment was followed by the crack of Eric's flamer being fired. Hal turned in awe to see the incendiary charge burst across the sprawled body of Stavros. He flinched, fearful that the unit would somehow rise up, absorbing the flame, and march unrelentingly toward them to seek revenge. But there was no hellish miracle. The biodrone's synthetic biocrystalline form burned as if Cerberus' flaming breath had enveloped it.

Quizzically, Hal looked at Eric.

"I'll explain as we go. Come on."

The duo exited the fiery tomb and jogged back down the tunnel in the direction of the lander. Eric supported the rookie under his arm as Hal's last surge of adrenalin provided barely enough fuel to keep him going.

"What I didn't tell you about our mission is that our job was to salvage these two biods to keep our safety record intact. At best, we could have sacrificed the two rogue units while saving the 'logs' on the ship. That would've kept this at a safety 'incident' level. The infraction between the two could've been covered with what I'm about to do to the chamber."

As they exited the tunnel to the landing area, Eric motioned Hal to move to the side of the tunnel's mouth and press himself against the mountain wall. A strategic tap on the forearm control pad of Eric's envirosuit resulted in a distant "pop", followed by a fiery belch of sulfurous dust and heat from the rocky corridor.

Continuing with his explanation in a matter-of-fact tone, Eric offered, "But I should have disconnected the 'logs' from their link to the biods before they were terminated. The rotten luck was, the mineral deposits in the caves kept that from happening sooner. I was supposed to do it locally. But the militia unit canceled the seeker unit before I could break the link. If I had hesitated long enough to disconnect the militia unit, it would have had you for dessert."

At that moment, Eric's comm unit blared. Looking with downcast anticipation at Hal, he sniped, "That would be Descartes now. I'm sure he's going to gnaw a good chunk off of my backside for losing the 'logs'. I don't have to tell you that a pre-emptive link termination ends up in an agonizing death for the humans on the other side. That's a safety recordable that'll blow our bonus along with everybody else's on the Darwin."

Touching the "Activate" key on the comm link, Eric figured a good defense was a strong offense. "Mr. Descartes, I'd like to offer an explanation ..."

The plant manager didn't give the field operative the chance. "Eric, save it for the official report. Just tell me about the biod units. Are they recoverable?"

Eric hesitated. He knew that regardless of the final outcome, his job was to ensure the units themselves would never be found. "Did Descartes think him a total incompetent?" he asked himself.

He responded with the script he had prepared as if everything had gone according to plan, knowing the conversation was being recorded as protocol required. "Sir, unfortunately, the biod units were lost in a cave-in. The militia unit triggered a chain reaction concussion when we attempted to apprehend her. The geology of the area couldn't take the shock ..."

As if on cue in a holo-play, Descartes responded, "That is unfortunate. Another case of the 'bends', but thank the Cosmos that the biologicals were saved. We'll incur an incident, but your quick action at terminating the link prevented a fatality. Even though the biologicals will have to be transferred out of the empowerment corps while they recover from the loss of their biods, it was still gratifying to be able to see them standing before me a half hour ago."

The veteran looked at his protégé. Both were mystified. "The biologicals were alive?" he thought. "How was that possible? And thirty minutes ago? That was before he and Hal had entered the catacombs!"

Hal returned the puzzled look at Eric and whispered, "If the logs were conscious a full half hour ago, the biods shouldn't have been. What ... or maybe I should ask, 'Who?' did we just flame back there?"

*   *   *

The plant manager severed the link to his IAD operative, content in the knowledge that another level 3 – two Terran biodrones - had been handled. He had never been faced with a level 2, where an organic and biodrone broke the Natural Law. From the stories Eric had told him, he hoped he never would. Level 1 – two Geminian biodgens - wasn't even discussed – even at the Board level. Given Descartes' "officer of the company" position, he would have found out about it, had an incident of that magnitude ever occurred ... even if it had been "adjusted" like the level 3 cases.

But more pressing issues demanded his attention. Hours had turned into millennia, and still no sign of progress had come from Nimon's room.

Suddenly, a deep-throated scream of agony lanced through the sound-deadened walls to shock Descartes and Brown out of their reverie. Both men bolted from their chairs toward the door to the examining room, only to be halted by a tall, lean figure blocking the entranceway. Standing behind the figure was Dr. Edison, struggling to maintain his composure. But nothing could mask the fatigue in his eyes from the emotional ordeal he had endured.

"Nimon! What happened?" both men exclaimed, almost giving in to the urge to throw their arms around him while clapping him soundly on the back.

"All that matters is that I am ... well again," Nimon responded, pausing. His face had resumed a shadowy semblance of control.

Normally, Nimon projected an air of confidence. His quick wit had always been a source of comic relief in stressful situations. But when events required it, he could exude a demeanor of cool business-like control; control of a nature which did not allow for traces of feeling.

But this look was different, at least in Descartes' eyes. It was as if the slightest flicker of an emotion might shatter the resolve of his manager.

"And where do you think you're going, Nimon?" Brown challenged, barring the Geminian from any further progress out of the medical center. The personnel manager had also noticed that Nimon was not himself, regardless of how he stubbornly tried to hide that fact.

"I am needed on the planet surface," came the brief and less than satisfactory response.

"Nimon. You've been through a severe trauma - both physical and emotional. And don't give me that Geminian poppycock about your superior mind and body. I don't care if your blood runs paisley, you're a patient in my department's MedCen, and you're not going anywhere.

Descartes had remained silent throughout the exchange between his managers. Now he decided to take a different tack in the conversation.

"How are you going to explain your disrupted trial of survival to the Council, Nimon? There wasn't any evidence indicating what or who was involved in your being in that chamber. As far as the Council's concerned, we're responsible for turning you back over to their custody. I'd guess they're even a little bit peeved at your being back on the Darwin!"

Before Nimon could reply, Dr. Edison stepped forward.

"I have taken care of that, Morgan. If you recall, it was my testimony that was to be given immediately prior to Nimon's invoking T'Varek Kar. Exerting that right, and given the events that have transpired, I contacted Kronia personally.

Being the husband of a Geminian vice-president and a relative of Kronia through marriage does have certain advantages," he interjected. "Curiously, my briefing to her did not seem to come as a surprise. The mystery around the interference with Nimon's trial has invalidated its necessity, in her mind. She was confident she could convince the Council of Nimon's innocence."

"But Nimon is in no condition to return to the surface!" Brown interrupted, belligerently exercising his personnel manager's prerogative to be omnipotent.

"It is not my condition that is at issue, Jeff. It is Starn's. Probabilities are rapidly dwindling to the point that successful survival from the self-induced coma is unlikely."

"You mean his life is in danger," Brown muttered under his breath.

"I thought I just said that, Jefferson," Nimon replied, ignoring the fact that Brown had not intended his comment to reach his ultra-sensitive ears.

Perking up at Nimon's weak attempt to antagonize him as a sign of the Geminian's recovery, Brown conceded. "Oh ... all right then! You can go! But as plant's sociologist, I demand the right to accompany you to monitor your condition. Solar Corporation's got a lot more invested in you than I would have spent ... and I don't want them docking my pay for dereliction of duty for not protecting your mental health!"

"Jefferson, Corporate has no policy in which a manager's pay is ..."

"He's right, Nimon." interjected Descartes, cutting off his technical superintendent's penchant for correcting his personnel manager. "You do need to be watched. And I think J.B. and I are the best choices to do it."

Nimon's brow furrowed in its characteristic manner when surprised. Looking at his plant manager, he realized that no amount of reasoning would dissuade him once his mind was made up. Besides, time was of the essence.

"Very well, sir. But we must leave immediately if Starn is to survive."

CHAPTER 29

The shimmering transport booth seemed to coalesce into solid matter as it hurtled to a stop near the Institute of Meditative Phenomena. Four figures exited the crystalline dodecagon. Assisting Nimon as they went, the quartet entered the building. The hallways of the Geminian Institute had been vacated as Dr. Edison had requested. Reaching the stasis chamber cradling Starn's motionless form, they peered through the observation glass. Nimon shuddered slightly at the sight of the pale yellow aura of the antigrav field gently pulsing around his Dual.

"Only my sensory system can perceive the beauty of the field's effect," Nimon thought. "Yet how ironic, that I can not only perceive it, but can appreciate it as well," he considered, recalling the dark secret of the nature of his existence. Here he stood - a biocrystalline construct, somehow imbued with both technology and feelings - a construct faced with the challenge to save the being that for so long had given him life.

Turning to his father, he said solemnly, "Your precautions have protected him well. I sense there is still time."

Dr. Edison's only response was a knowing, supportive nod.

Intruding upon the moment, Descartes inquired, "Is there anything we should know or do before you begin, Nimon?"

"Not in this case, sir," Nimon replied. "Nor will any of Jefferson's distasteful psychoanalytical skills be necessary."

It was Brown's turn to furrow his brow. But catching his plant manager's signal to let the remark pass, the personnel manager suppressed his urge to comment. After all, it had been Nimon's childhood exposure to the Institute that caused his distaste for analysts, not Brown's technique.

Nimon entered the outer door to the hygiene lock which sealed out any viral or microbial contaminates. Dr. Edison had insisted on the improved system after Nimon had informed him about Starn's true condition. The Institute had complied. After being bathed in a series of radiation treatments, Nimon continued through the inner door to Starn's chamber.

The sense of Deja vu' was unnerving, but understandable, since he had actually been in this situation just weeks before. "The outcome of this attempt should have a greater likelihood of success," Nimon thought, "since the influence of T'Poch is now improbable. But is it? How will the lingering effect of my recent ordeal with my tormentor alter my psychic prowess? Will the Ravarian crystal shard I still carry within me block my attempts? Are my abilities just another version of the forbidden practices of the K'Tar? Am I truly defying the teachings of Mitron?"

Amidst these subconscious traces of self-doubt, Nimon assumed a Ka'al Ni Kor meditative position. Reflexively, he lightly placed his palms together in front of his chest. Whether prepared or not, he must attempt to save Starn this last time. As his crimson eyes rolled backward and the trance enveloped his mind, Nimon was immediately engulfed in cold darkness. Never before had he experienced such a depravation of sensory stimuli. Space was cold, but there were stars. The galactic boundary was without stars, but the radiation bands were multi-colored and hypnotic. This place was totally devoid of sensation. Even the coldness faded as Nimon's psychic state robbed him of all stimuli, dissipating the phantom numbness to allow more subtle, but vitally important cues to appear.

The life emanation from Starn was undetectable. In his previous attempt, the life-mentor had readily sensed his Dual. But then, T'Poch's abrupt appearance had shattered the link. Undeterred, Nimon came today with the belief the link could be renewed. Until now.

The dank, musty smell of fear crept into Nimon's consciousness. His instinctive response to suppress it faltered momentarily, allowing him to experience his concern for Starn's apparent loss. Suddenly a glimmer of light pulsed faintly below him and faded. Instantly the technical superintendent perceived the connection between the two events. Invoking the matrix Kronia had imprinted in his psyche, Nimon lowered his mental shields briefly to expose the raw savagery lying dormant within.

The light rekindled and flared, guiding Nimon's mind closer. As he approached, Nimon sensed the familiar aura of Starn's life force. "So it is true - it is proven! Somehow, the innate savagery within me, unleashed by the disciples of the K'Tar, holds the key to unlocking the essence of Starn!"

But one question remained.

"Will I be able to endure the violent intensity needed to revive my life-kindred? It is so soon after my ordeal with T'Poch. Should I bring back Starn, if it means using a power forbidden to our people? But what of me? If Starn does not survive, will I continue? To live at the expense of my Life Mentor – would it not be a desecration of the ethos of Phoenos? T'Poch lives, and she does so shamelessly. Am I like her?" Recollection of the sharp pangs from her touch staggered him mentally. His control wavered as he recalled the memory of his mother's concealed truth, and the "truths" of others. "T'Poch was the first Singular Dualiity. Novas had concealed that fact. T'Poch had forced herself upon me. Our bond is forbidden. Do I exist to propagate some untold evil?" Dr. Edison's words revealed an even harsher truth. "The Elders had said peace was the way of Gemini. But savagery had dominated the past. Does it also control my future?"

Nimon's mind reeled. He backed away from the glow of Starn's essence. He could not continue. His conscience berated him, "The lie ... which one would prevail? To save Starn would release me from one – my masquerade as an organic. But to do so means I would propagate another - for it would require a savagery that has been forbidden, yet nurtured by the K'Tar!" Nimon was torn. "How can I prevent myself and Starn from being pawns ... pawns in the struggle between the Council's false ideals and the K'Tar's megalomania?

In fear, Nimon retreated.

The pulsing essence of Starn faded as Nimon recoiled from it. The Terran-Geminian-biodgen bond weakened as mental barriers were reconstructed. The increasing strength of the psychic shields foretold the inevitable, as a precious life force ebbed.

At his weakest, Nimon suddenly sensed another presence ... one of surprising power and energy. He steeled himself for the mental death-struggle he knew would ensue if it were T'Poch. Pausing from his efforts at suppressing Kronia's savage mindset, Nimon directed his attention toward the approaching entity.

"Nimon. Do not retreat from your life-kindred as I did," came the vaguely familiar thought pattern. "The consequences are more far-reaching than you can imagine."

"Novas! How is this possible? How can you be here? Where did you acquire the power?"

"It is not my power. It is yours. I am still with the Legotians in body, and in mind. They have opened my thoughts to yours, but you are the source of this marvel. Your uniqueness has allowed this, with their influence. They have also made it possible for me to experience your memories, if you will allow it. I need to understand why you have turned from your life-kindred. I wish to help. For your actions here are of extreme importance. You ... we ... must not fail in your efforts to revive Starn."

The shock of the Geminian Executive's trans-spatial telepathic probe subsided. Nimon was aware of the Legotians' powers. In the past, they had demonstrated the ability to simultaneously project their holographic images to different points in the galaxy. It had been necessary in order to establish the joint venture between the Earth Exploratory Cartel and the Geminian System. It would not be out of the realm of possibility to connect the thoughts of others over that distance - especially if the participants were as uniquely gifted as Nimon and Novas. "But in all of space and time, why her, and why now?" Nimon anguished.

Cold skepticism replaced his shock. "Of all people in the universe to debate the concept of duty, here is Novas," he groused. "She negated any validity as role model to me when she chose to conceal the existence of T'Poch. How can she speak of duty to another when she could not fulfill her own?"

With that brief thought, Nimon flooded Novas' mind with bitter resentment. Moments passed as the senior executive retreated from the onslaught. Struggling, she called upon all the psychic skills she could muster. Pushing back upon his barrage, Novas finally managed to subdue him enough for him to listen.

"I sense your new-found knowledge, Nimon. That is why I have come. I must make you understand. For the sake of all Gemini!"

Haltingly, Nimon eased his piercing assault. "I have little reason to trust you, after all you have done. But it is irrational to reject knowledge. For now, I will do as you wish. I will leave my mind open to your thoughts ... Mother."

Novas continued, sensing Nimon's bitterness in his reference to her. "In all things, Time is a critical factor. The right thing done at the wrong time will be wrong. Such was the case when Kronia interfered in the Bon-Ka ceremony, inducing me to bestow the Mitronian crystal upon T'Poch. It was right for one of my clan to possess it, for it would be one stone in the foundation to form a new house unifying the clans of Gemini and Castor. But it was too soon. What she wanted was right. I know that now. But when she did it was wrong. Her actions were taken at the wrong time. She interfered in the proper course of Time's flow. And because of that, it has had ripple effects throughout our culture. T'Poch's hatred is but one of those ripples. Yet it is the one that must now be addressed. The irony in Kronia's error is that ultimately you have come to possess the Ravarian shard - as it should be - for you are of the Mitronian clan. But the mate to the life crystal should find its fate not in T'Poch, but one of the Ravarian clan – one yet to be. In a strange way, what Kronia did was right, for your existence has impacted our world more than you can yet know, but Time has yet revealed its ultimate desire."

Nimon failed to grasp what seemed to be the aimless ramblings of a woman possessed. "Had Novas lost her sanity under the influence of the Legotians?" he wondered.

"Nimon, I am not mad. Let me attempt to explain. T'Poch is the first-borne Singular Dualiity, as you have learned. Her ultimate fate was unknown to me until a decade ago. That is when the resurgence of the K'Tar prompted me to investigate their movements. She was at their forefront. I suspected a blood-link with her, based upon my studies, as I am sure she did, yet there was no way to confirm it at the time. Continued probing revealed threads of facts which were gradually woven into the final truth. To reveal that truth - that my own Dual, the first

Singulariity of my essence – was the leader of the K'Tar, would have been without purpose. It would not have altered the course of Time."

Undeterred by the perplexed reaction from Nimon, Novas continued. "Two paths lie before us – one of peace and one of conflict. The Legotians believe I may have the ability to correct events such that a Castorian-Geminian union of the life crystal halves is possible. Although too complex to share with you now, it is the way of peace. Should T'Poch's plan come to fruition, the interstellar worlds as we know them will be thrown into a conflict from which we cannot recover. The way of peace hinges upon you and your success in reviving my son. As is the way of Phoenos, two diverse lives gain strength from one. Once diverged, those two lives can achieve the unimaginable. But the source of Dualiity cannot emerge from a foundation of deceit and succeed. To form a life from deception will doom both to failure. That is what happened with T'Poch. I was misguided by people I trusted. That trust was misplaced when I handed over my biodgen child. Yet you are the product of faithful devotion. From that dedication, you and Starn have brushed against Phoenos – I sense it! That is why you must not turn away from your Life Mentor!"

Novas paused in an effort to contain emotions not often revealed, but only briefly.

"My dear Nimon - my dear son. Yes, though biodgen in origin, you are my blood kindred. You provide balance to my organic child that I was never able to provide to T'Poch. Because of my failure, her devotion toward the Fire Arts are dark and irrepressible. Yet, your existence is destined to reveal the eternal beauty of life. My hope is that with you and Starn, together, the search for Phoenos can move a step closer to completion. For my achievement of Dualiity has fallen far short of reaching the ideal for which Phoenos stands."

Nimon absorbed the meaning, and the emotion, of Novas' thoughts ... emotions that would have been undetectable but for the mind link which they now shared. From those feelings, Nimon realized that she spoke the truth ... at least her truth. But he was unable to share with her the complete truth – the truth of what T'Poch had done. Nimon again fought to suppress the anguish that had overwhelmed him in the hidden chamber on Gemini. Like the secret lair deep within the desert mountains, Nimon closed his mind's tunnels to shield Novas from the thoughts that tore at his very soul.

Novas, in one final attempt, implored him. "I have been with the Legotians. I have glimpsed the future. You are a necessary part of that future. As is Starn. You must save him. Do not let my confused, failed past prevent that. I am unable to express the love for a child as can your father. Yet

I can tell you of my deep ... pride... in your achievements - in what ... in who you are. Do not deny your diversity. Use it. Save your life-kindred ... it is your destiny."

Sensing that he had heard her thoughts, and that he had insulated his own from her, Novas conceded, "I must go now, Nimon. There is still much work left to be done ... by both of us."

As Novas' pattern faded, Nimon's mind probed outward into space after it. "Novas ... Mother ..." it searched. Finally, touching the fabric of the Legotian-Geminian psychic construct, Nimon concluded, "It was real. I had been in contact with Novas. But ... so much was left unsaid."

He had shielded her from the knowledge of T'Poch's attack upon him. He had allowed her the comfort of believing she had reached him completely. So, he would keep his secret from her. "What would it matter?" he thought. "My disgraceful bond with T'Poch is my burden to bear. And her heartfelt confession regarding her failure has revealed to me what I know I must now do."

Hesitantly at first, then with conviction, Nimon pulled back from the trans-spatial link. Steeling himself for what lay ahead, he directed his thoughts to the essence that was his life-kindred.

*   *   *

Days of desert travel had taken its toll on the lone female. Indigo skin screamed its plea for protection against the relentless sun. Half-crazed, no thought had been given to the possibility of using Brav Ni cactus salve. Though clad in black mesh, the journey through dust and wind had torn the fabric and revealed the vulnerable skin underneath. Miraculously, she at last arrived at her destination. Entering the small nomadic encampment, she staggered to a centrally located tent. Throwing back the tarp covering the entrance, the female trudged forward with her final steps. Fighting to hold her chin high, she clung to the last vestige of honor that she could muster.

Lavish tapestries adorned the floor leading up to several richly embroidered lounges. Collapsing into the closest one, the female pulled aside the remaining shreds of protective mesh covering her face. Though weakened, she managed a wicked, crazed smile as she heard the brush of approaching footsteps from an adjoining section of the tent.

The draperies between the compartments parted, allowing the wizened woman to enter. Tentatively, she took a few steps into the living area. Approaching from behind, she noted the odd twitching of the head of the woman she had raised as her own. She looked fondly upon the dark tresses, interspersed with the hereditary silver streaks of those possessing the Fire Arts. But at the same time, she could not suppress a strange sense of uneasiness welling up within her. Softly, she spoke.

"T'Poch, my child, is it done?"

An interminable pause followed. P'Teel inquired again.

"Did you succeed in your quest? Do you have the seed of our future?"

The woman in the lounge mumbled a reply, as she stifled a barely controlled giggle.

Taking a few steps forward, P'Teel pressed, "Are you well? I could not understand you. Did you overcome him? Are our plans fulfilled?"

The response was slightly clearer, the giggle less controlled, "Feeling well ... ah, feeling well. I am feeling well? Our plans, not what we planned. You did not tell me, no, you did not tell me it would be like this."

The unease rose further within P'Teel. Cautiously, she edged around the side of the lounge. Soothingly, she addressed her ward. "T'Poch, you have had a long journey. I see the elements have been unkind to you. Let me care for you."

The giggle rose in its hysteria. "Care for me ... no-one can care for me ... you did not tell me it would feel this way ... you did not care for me." Leaning forward, T'Poch buried her face in her hands as if to smother the fitful laughter. Her hair cascaded forward revealing a blistering line of cobalt skin along the back of her neck.

P'Teel caught her breath. But the reaction was not from what she saw. It was from what she did not see.

"T'Poch!" she challenged, all sentiment draining from her voice. "Where is the necklace? What has happened to the stone?! It no longer hangs from your neck!"

A low growl climbed out from the depths of T'Poch's madness. Head still bowed, she lowered her hands from her face and clenched them into fists. Glaring down at the tapestries, she fought the rage that overwhelmed her. "Necklace ... stone, you care for them? What of me? The pain ... within me ... it is insufferable! I have ... succeeded ... in bonding with Nimon. But, to what end? It was not as planned. The gem - a mind-corridor to bond biodgen and organic? Not so! Did she not tell you? Kronia discovered his true nature... told me... I did as she instructed. But what have ... we done? What have ... you ... done to me?"

P'Teel approached her disciple. Pushing aside her trepidation, she placed her hands on either side of T'Poch's sagging head. Within seconds, the older woman tensed, her body becoming rigid as her mouth gaped open in shock. "Something ... is not right. What has happened?!"

The weathered hands of the aged sorceress pulled her pupil's face up to look at it. The Fire Child's hair tumbled away, revealing eyes of liquid fire. The evil that would be the K'Tar's future looked up at the ancient one, boring into P'Teel's very soul. The guardian of the Fire Arts responded by adjusting her hands ever so slightly, placing fingertips atop the proper nerve points on the face of the succubus. As the psychic link strengthened, the shock waves of maddening fear swept over the aged one. Unwaveringly, innumerable cycles of practicing the Fire Arts empowered her to delve deeper to find the knowledge of what had transpired.

The avatars of the ancient one and her disciple faced each other, surrounded by the dream mists of their mental bond. Scenes swiftly appeared and disappeared just as quickly in eddies of swirling clouds. Were they visions of the future? ... Ghosts from the past? ... Or delusional fantasies shared by followers of the K'Tar? Perhaps all three. T'Poch looked over the shoulder of her mentor, peering into a distant kaleidoscope of images. A young female, sinewy limbs glistening from exertion, dressed in battle garb of an unknown era, raised her weapon, sweeping it forward while fearlessly commanding her followers to charge. The memory cloud billowed toward T'Poch, dispersing, then coalescing into images closer to her. A woman " –Was it her?" - lay on a divan, propped up on her elbows, also coated in sweat, but from a different challenge. Mid-wives scurried around her, fruitlessly attempting to provide comfort as the patient screamed. With the sound as if wet fabric were tearing, the woman collapsed, and a baby's cry pierced the room. The smoky fog surged forward again, sweeping over P'Teel and past T'Poch. It was P'Teel's turn to seek understanding within the vaporous scenes.

P'Teel dismissed the first image, one of her ward relentlessly trudging through the desert. Searching intently, the time-worn sorceress focused on a vision deeper into the mists. Within a craggy chamber, clenched hands came down forcefully, plunging the shard into the chest of the struggling captive. Understanding exploded around P'Teel in a brilliant tapestry of possibilities. Knowingly, she seized one with her piercing gaze, guiding her mind's eye to look into the prismatic scenes hidden within the facets of the jewel. Two figures fought. One she knew to be herself. The other from ages ago. "But was she? The star child I so bitterly hated during the age of Mitron, how could I not have recognized her? They bore the same name – but names are passed down through generations. For the two to be the one, Time's path must be controlled. But how?" The answer was elusive. Narrowing her psychic scrutiny, she relived the combat once more. The young star child had overcome her. Though raw, her Fire Arts were formidable. "Her energy coursing down her arm. I must respond!" The more experienced mistress of the Fire Arts pulled her wrist down and outward sharply, freeing her hand from Novas' grasp. Coiling her arm, she drove it forward with savage force, the glowing palm almost erupting against Novas' chest. But before the concussion lifted the Geminian into the air, the wizened P'Teel, in the midst of the visionary vapors, looked into the eyes of the younger child of the Fire Arts, and saw the future. As the novice hurtled toward the rocky face of the nearby escarpment, this time P'Teel did not smile maliciously. She no longer believed the impact would be fatal. She now knew Novas would survive. She would be a threat to the K'Tar, to her own Dual, T'Poch, and to the unborn creation that would challenge Fate. Such knowledge could be used – utilized to form Desire – molded into Will – forged into Purpose – all for the sake to continue.

And as the desert sands swirled outside the tent beneath the waning shadow of the Silent Giant, a hideous scream pierced the air!

"NOOOOOOO!"

Echoing across the scorched terrain, the fearful cry ceased. Within the confines of the nomadic refuge, the veil of madness lifted, revealing in the visage of the Singular Dualiity the desire, will, and purpose to go on.

CHAPTER 30

The glimmer of Starn's essence was all but extinguished. Nimon knew that to revive him would require extreme concentration. His psionic energy must be focused in a way that would bare his very soul. Nothing could be held in reserve. The link between his two worlds - organic and biodgen - would be the tool that would save Starn ... or kill them both. By lowering his defenses completely, he would be vulnerable to the innermost drives that made him who he was. If they were pure, Starn might live. But if Nimon succumbed to the evil influence of his bond with T'Poch, both he and Starn would die. In the midst of this precarious balance, he would draw upon the subdued energies unleashed by Kronia, and channel them through the Ravarian shard within. Walking the edge of a precipice - on one side the wickedness of the K'Tar, on the other, the mystery of Phoenos – he would reach his Life Mentor.

Together, their destiny would be decided.

The question that now lay before him, "Upon which side will I fall?"

Slowly, Nimon lowered his mental barrier for a final time. Emerging from behind the mask that was Nimon was not the savage construct left him by Kronia. Nor was it the sinister traces of

T'Poch's lust. Instead, Starn's essence was bathed in a radiant energy like none before. It was the love which Nimon's mother could never express for his son. It was the sacrifice the Geminian race had made in their search for Phoenos. It was the bond between organic life and biodgen crystal energy - never before mentioned, but in retrospect, somehow always understood. There were even traces of friendship masked in conflict, as was the connection with Jefferson Brown. Starn's essence did not flare as it did before. Instead, the soft, luminous glow slowly expanded. Its color progressed from the coral hues of Gemini's sands at sunrise to the crimson radiance of the planet's mid-summer day. Its energy engulfed Nimon's consciousness, rapidly escalating in strength from the synergy of life mentor and Dual. Wills merging together, the sons of a new Geminian culture abandoned their unconscious world of future dreams and emerged into the reality of the present.

Descartes and Brown had been anxiously watching their technical superintendent as he bent over the comatose form of Starn. An eternity that had actually been brief moments ended in a sight that would haunt them forever. Nimon stood motionless over his life kindred, one hand placed over his own chest, the other lightly resting upon Starn's. At first, Descartes had to rub his eyes, believing that they were the victims of too many sleepless nights. But peering more closely, he convinced himself that what he saw was true. Nudging Brown, he whispered, "Starn's eyes ... look ... they're moving beneath their lids. Almost like he's dreaming."

Brown replied, "You're the one that's dreaming. Nimon is still standing there. It's not possible for any animation of a biodgen while the living entity is conscious, even rapid eye movement. And as remarkable as it is for Nimon to be able to animate his Dual without telemetry equipment, even he can't do it standing up and conscious."

"Oh no ..." Descartes argued, pointing to Starn, "... then explain that!"

Lying prone upon the medical table, Starn's eyes snapped open. His left hand slowly raised off of the padded surface and gently came to rest on the hand of his life kindred. Instantly, an aura pulsed its eerie glow around them. Starn's head rotated slowly, turning to look up at the figure standing next to him. An expression of puzzlement crept over it as if asking in mute silence, "How is this possible?"

And to the further amazement of the Solarians witnessing the miracle, Nimon spoke.

"Starn, there is precious little time. I cannot fully explain it myself. Much has happened. In violation against the teachings, I have bonded with another. Only very recently have I learned the truth about who ... and what ... I am. I now realize that it is you, not I, who is the living entity. I am the construct. I am the bioduotron. For most of my life ... your life, I have been honored to experience the essence that empowers us both. But it cannot continue this way. My brother, my self, I do not know how, but you are back. It is my gift to you ... your life ... my memories ... that I pass to you. Now I must rest. One day, if Phoenos is with us, we will meet again."

And as suddenly as the essence appeared, it faded. Collapsing to the floor of the medical room, Nimon succumbed to the effects of a biodgen stasis condition. Rising up from the table, Starn gingerly swung his legs down to the floor. Kneeling, he reached for his Dual. Lifting the shoulders of the motionless figure, Starn cradled his life kindred in his arms, and wept.

*   *   *

The control room of the Darwin had resumed its usual ambiance of relaxed efficiency. Tucked next to the omnivator entrance, Saffron Three performed her routine scans of transmission frequencies as expected of a senior control technician during a timefold. Mack Weber was engaged in a standard calibration run of the polymerization catalytic stabilizers while Christi Pomeroy completed a series of navigational plot alternatives through the upcoming Triargent Nebula.

Jefferson Brown had just entered the control room and stopped alongside his plant manager when Descartes inquired, "Estimated time of arrival to the Legotian star system, Ms. Pomeroy?"

"Well, sir... given the ionic activity in the Nebula at this time, we will have to take a slight detour. It should result in our arrival in approximately 16.7 solar days, traveling at cosmic tidal rate theta."

"Very good, Christi, proceed," Descartes responded.

But Brown interjected, "Morgan. What in Gemini's sandstorms are we doing traipsing off to the other end of the galaxy? The crew was scheduled for vacation relief after Helicon's research mission was completed. They're already overdue because of their rescue of us from those Castorian misfits. What's Corporate got in mind for them now ... a data raid on the Therbians?"

"Pull in your claws, J.B. ... We've gotten all recreational provisions in this plant totally revamped during our stay at Gemini. Anyway, the mission's light duty. We've been directed to escort Nimon's mother, Novas, from her negotiations with the Castorians back to Corporate for a full report. The crew can then take extended leave on Earth for their troubles."

"Hmmph! I guess that's a fair deal. Sorry I doubted you," Brown replied. "By the way, speaking of deals, how are the negotiations going?"

"There's been no word since they were started. The Legotians wanted it that way. They don't communicate with us, and we can't communicate with them, until it's over. I can only assume they're approaching an end, since we've been ordered to pick up Novas. But on a different subject, I haven't seen Helicon since we returned to Gemini. What's he been doing? I didn't get a chance to thank him for saving us on that rogue Castorian ship."

"You have been preoccupied, Morgan. It must have been the butt-chewing you got from the Vice-exec of Safety because of Helicon's injuries. You can put your mind at ease. He stayed behind on Gemini. He told me he had suppressed his dislike for humans as long as he possibly could. He preferred the company of the Geminians," Jefferson Brown replied, tongue-in-cheek.

"Yeah, right. Not to mention the fact that he needed to stay on Gemini anyway to complete his work on the artifacts of the Geminian-Castorian ancestors," Descartes added, wryly.

"Minor detail, minor detail," the sociologist retorted, in mock dejection.

"On a more serious note, how is our new staff member?"

"Well, Morgan, he's not exactly 'new'. He has performed on a large number of Darwin task teams and projects over the years."

"Yeah, but that was as a biod, not as a living, breathing person."

Muttering under his breath, Brown sighs, "I just get finished fixing one bias, and another rears its ugly head ..."

"What was that, J.B.?" Descartes pressed.

Immediately covering his criticism with a layer of diplomacy, Brown responded, "I said, you'd better listen to yourself, because your Solarian perspective on bioduogenetics is showing through. You know as well as I that the Geminian-biodgen relationship is a whole different matter than the simplistic one we Solarians use with our biodrones. We haven't even scratched the surface on reproducing the link Nimon ... I mean Starn ... or whichever ... generates with his synthetic life construct."

"Does that mean the medical brains haven't figured out how what happened, happened?" Descartes quizzed.

"That's right. Starn can't even explain it, or isn't willing to."

"So what do we do in the meantime? Nimon was my friend, as well as a member of my staff. Even though I worked with Starn on many assignments, I'm still a little uneasy with the idea of him being the true organic. What are we supposed to do?"

"It's going to take time," Brown counseled. "Even Starn realizes that. He requested that I postpone reactivating him from medical leave for a while."

"What!? Nimon ... I mean Starn ... admitting his own infirmity?"

"I know what you mean. Had it been the stubborn blue-devil asking me, I would have fainted from the shock and would have had to go on leave myself. He never asks me for anything! But we have to realize that Starn has his own personality. So how could I refuse," Brown responded.

Descartes chuckled at Brown's reference to Nimon, and then realized that his friend was no longer among them to defend himself against the rapier barbs of the personnel manager. Solemnly, he inquired, "What's going to happen to Nimon, J.B.? We're going to miss him."

"Well, if there's a silver lining, that could be it. The biodgen construct we knew as Nimon is in good condition ... he's in the typical catatonic state expected of a biodgen ... but all functionality appears to be present. There are no signs of the near-fatal mode that Starn had reached."

"So that means that Starn could reanimate Nimon?" Descartes asked eagerly.

"Not so fast, Morgan. Part of the reason for our trip to Legos is to seek the advice of Novas. Nimon's ... Starn's ... father has cautioned that another link this soon could cost us the 'lives' of both of them. He's anxious for us to arrive so he and Novas can decide what should be done next. The mind's a delicate balance of personalities. Especially Starn-Nimon's. It'll take more than Starn reanimating Nimon to reset that balance. Then there's the matter of the Geminian Council's opinion. They weren't too hot on Nimon's materialistic theories on the application of dual lives in the first place. And after the treatment we got from them when we told them what we saw in Starn's stasis ward, I'm surprised we weren't locked up forever."

"As hard as they try, they're not going to keep this thing quiet, J.B." Descartes interrupted.

"Well, they've convinced me not to talk about it. And I'd advise you to do the same. As far as the outside worlds are concerned, Starn, the true organic, is recovering from a severe psychosis. Part of that recovery is abstinence from empowering his Dual. If we depart from that story line, we risk more trouble than even you can handle. In fact, I believe if not for Dr. Edison's word vouching for us, we were microtreds from the Council taking us into the desert and feeding us to the Vambors to keep this quiet!"

Rolling his eyes at Brown's penchant for exaggeration, Descartes prodded, "I was under the impression that it went even deeper than that, J.B.. From what I could wheedle out of Dr. Edison, it sounded to me like Starn-Nimon is expected to father a new movement in Geminian society ... a movement that all on the Council don't agree with."

"Exactly what I was getting at. In the delicate shape Starn-Nimon are in, I'm not sure we'll ever see Nimon reanimated, much less a part of any socio-cultural revolution!"

Descartes mused, "Well, what I saw in that research center was the closest thing to a religious experience I'll ever know. To see Nimon and Starn, both moving, empowered by one life source, knowing that one of them was synthetic, was nothing short of a miracle! In some sections of the galaxy, it only takes one miracle to start the kind of revolution the Council is afraid of. So, I'd say Starn-Nimon is the best one ... or two ... to do it, if it's going to be done. They've demonstrated breakthrough's throughout their life. You know Nimon ...uh, sorry... Starn, was the first Terran-Geminian hybrid in existence. Plus, building on the technological foundation established by Novas and Dr. Edison, Starn-Nimon organized the utilization of biods throughout the Corporation. You've been there during his performance review by the corporate execs. They whisper that his – er, their – efforts can be traced to the bottom line profits of at least three divisions!"

"I hear what you're saying, Morgan," Brown interrupted, "but after seeing Nimon in the Geminian catacombs, watching him drop like a lead ball in Jupiter's gravity in that stasis ward, and after observing Starn, I'm not so sure. To say he's the next Geminian Gandhi - this I've got to see!" he added, with a theatrical scowl.

"Well, if your skepticism is the only excuse you need to keep an eye on him, then be my guest," the plant manager responded. "Just keep me informed."

*   *   *

A tall, muscular frame cast its silhouette from within one of the observation spheres of the Darwin. The shadow danced eerily against the sphere's inner surface as the myriad lights of the Triargent Nebula choreographed a dazzling display. The sphere bobbed gently in the invigorating propulsion fields as they passed through the hollow core of the Darwin, building in intensity prior to launching the plant into the crest of the time fold. The compartment's transparent walls would provide total protection for its occupant without diminishing the adventure that came from being suspended in infinite time and space during the larger vessels launch.

Starn's body floated in the anti-grav field within the orb, but his mind was elsewhere. He recalled the memories left him by Nimon, and the prior events leading to his first appearance before the Council of Elders after his recovery. Their decision regarding his responsibilities as life-kindred to Nimon left much to be considered. Kronia's words were haunting as he replayed them in his mind.

"Starn. Thee hast returned to us. A rare few knew of your plight. Even fewer know of your return. Those who do are both pleased and concerned as to its meaning. I sense thee are troubled, as well. Reveal thy thoughts to us, that we might better understand."

Kronia's hands unfolded to reveal a glowing crystal. It was not the same one she had used to sense the thoughts of Nimon many days earlier. This stone's synthetic imperfections limited its capability, but it was still a marvel to behold. Starn's fingers went instinctively to the critical points upon the crystal. Instantly, waves of anguish surged from one psyche to another. The elderly woman's head jerked slightly from the impact of the raw savagery. Exercising age-old techniques of suppression, she replaced her pained expression with one of cool, placid control and probed further into Starn's mind. Facing each challenge, Kronia absorbed Starn's fury, countering it with her own.

"We have sensed these same feelings many years before, Starn. They were the thoughts of thy mother. As we counseled Novas, so shall we counsel thee. What has happened is irreversible. The events of the past cannot be changed, so it is futile to attempt such change. Thee must accept this and continue thy path as it has been set. The future of our race is of highest priority. As I counseled thy mother, that future is intertwined with thy fate, and the fate of your

Dual. Starn, thee hast shown us a new way in thy development - and the potential that lies within the Phoenos. The Council shares thy struggle between the desires and fears that accompany your newfound ability, however so brief its expression. But Starn, though thee are of mixed heritage, thy mind doth burn with the flames of Gemini's ancestral savagery. It is important that thee establish a precedence. We must know if the path thee hast chosen can be followed by all Geminians. Can the sensitive life force between you and Nimon exist for others? Can we fulfill the dream of the Phoenos without plunging our culture into the fiery ways of the K'Tar?" A slight upturned twitch of Kronia's mouth, the only sign of her deception, went unnoticed by the entranced Geminian.

Continuing, she implored, "Thy task is clear. It must be determined if thee and Nimon can be sustained. Only then will the Council accept the possibility. That is why the grief thee suffers must be mastered. If thee are successful, thy name will take its place in humble reverence with that of Mitron. Thy destiny, the destiny of Nimon, and the destiny of our race rests with thee. For now, you must go. We will care for Nimon. Thee must follow thy destiny. But I leave thee with this challenge. Give life to the future, son of Novas - new father of the Geminian philosophy of Phoenos."

Ominous though they were, Starn could not totally accept the words of Kronia. She was right in her assessment of his responsibility to Nimon and the Phoenos. Yet he could not discount his other responsibilities. Foremost among them was his involvement ... or more correctly, his Dual's involvement ... in the future of the K'Tar. The influence of T'Poch and her followers on his destiny could not be denied. From the memories shared by Nimon, Starn knew she had committed the basest of evils with Nimon in the secluded caverns of Gemini. But Starn sensed that his own restoration could not have occurred without T'Poch.

"Should I be grateful as Starn, or vengeful as Nimon ... both paths pose hidden dangers," thought Starn. "The responsibility attached to this question could be overwhelming by itself, let alone the questions that still remain to be resolved regarding the actions of my parents, Novas and Dr. Edison." T'Poch's origin as recalled through the haze of Nimon's memories did pose doubts. "What possessed my parents to cause such a thing? How can I be the father of the Phoenos, as Kronia suggests, when my own mother spawned the first Singular Dualiity?" he struggled. "These questions cannot simply be ignored while I busy myself with the salvation of the Geminian race ..." he added, somewhat sarcastically, "... regardless of how persuasive Kronia could be."

Her words came back to him... "The events of the past cannot be changed..."

Starn considered this statement and its infinite possibilities. He recalled the theories leading to the development of the time-folding phenomenon. They had begun in the minds of the Terran fiction writers. From the dream came the essence of the idea. The idea was transformed into substance through the joint efforts of Terran and Geminian astrophysicists and bioduogeneticists. For centuries, Terran scientists had searched for the unifying theory which explained the four basic forces of the universe. Somehow the forces - magnetism, gravity, the weak nuclear force, and the strong nuclear force which bonded atomic particles together - were linked by an all-encompassing principle. The secret of the long elusive principle was hidden within the power of the life essence. A fraction of this power was able to be trapped using the life crystal technology developed by Novas. The crystals could focus the life energy. Once focused, it could be attenuated and amplified to affect the other four better understood forces.

The most notable effect on them was to generate distortion waves. The Terran astrophysicists learned to create vessels capable of producing spatial anomalies that would carry them across the expanse of space. Relativistic theorists confirmed that such travel actually occurred along matter-energy fronts existing in negative time.

Starn knew the theories were still in their infancy. "Could their maturity result in the ability to control the flow of time itself?"

The thought of this power under the control of beings less than gods terrified Starn. He was cognizant of the critical sensitivity of the eddies and currents of time. Probabilities of events could not be fully calculated due to time's ability to fold upon itself. Metaphysicists believed time could link lives centuries apart to cause its future. Parallel courses could exist concurrently, one destined to extend endlessly, the other lasting only long enough to display life's possibilities, then evaporate into oblivion.

But the test was whether time's sensitive balance could be maintained. "Is it within my power to do it ... to right what I believe to be wrong?" The former technical superintendent's mind struggled with the vastness of the problem. Rarely did the Geminian-human utilize the full capacity of his wondrous mental gifts. It was the ability to compartmentalize the brain and to have each portion perform a separate task which made the hybrid's mind so unique. That uniqueness would again reveal itself as all of Starn's faculties were activated. For now, though, the miracle that was Starn's mind indulged itself in the pleasure of witnessing the spectacle about to unfold. Looking out through the chamber's transparent wall, he marveled at the grandeur before him. A vortex formed around the Darwin as the propulsion fields reached their crescendo. The crest of the time-fold engulfed the life crystal plant, hurtling it into a crease within time-space itself, as the vessel winked from its existence in normal space.

*   *   *

A minor lobe of his brain normally dormant began to pulse. He had sensed activity within these neural bundles only a few times in his life, most since he discovered T'Poch's existence. They were now once more sending ominous signals to his subconscious. Recognizing what this renewed neural activity meant, the all but lifeless biodgen steeled himself for the ordeal to come.

None new of – or at least breathed mention about – a Geminian biodgen's psychic condition during dormancy. There were so few of them. Plus, the elite families and the Meditative Institute went to great links to maintain the shroud of secrecy around the almost mystic art of bioduogenetics. To be sure, the Terran process of empowering biodrones was more common, and more studied, but it was also much more simplistic. Nimon's current condition was anything but.

Comatose to the outside world, the subtle activity of the biodgen's brain waves flared. As he expected, the first thoughts of his demonic oppressor were taunting and sinister.

"Dear Nimon ... you have survived, but I sense you are strangely different due to your ordeal. What a pity. None have lived after my previous failed attempts, yet you have. But no matter. You cannot stop me. None can stop me now! Time and space have become insurmountable barriers to those efforts. Know this ... my plan for the K'Tar's new leader is a success! I have suffered loss, but I have survived. And along with my survival comes a new era for Gemini. For I carry its seed!And there is nothing you can do to alter that fact. So, return to your catatonic sleep - abandoned by your life mentor, abandoned by your creators, and most of all, abandoned by me!"

As suddenly as the contact came, it disappeared. Simultaneously, in orbit above the first Singular Dualiity, the Darwin winked out of normal space.

And the eyes of Nimon snapped open!

As her message faded from the turbulent mind of Nimon, it left a deep wound. He rocked his head side to side in fitful regret. The glow of the stasis field surrounding the biodgen strove valiantly to stabilize its patient. But to no avail. The voice in his mind had ceased its taunting, yet he still felt an inexplicable force. The lobe within his brain sensed something powerful ... something ominous. Tentatively, the Solar Corporation manager toggled the switch on an adjacent control pad, discontinuing the stasis field. Pivoting his legs off the side of the table, Nimon straightened to a standing position. Each step was forced, as if he were stepping out on a high wire. The fear of falling choked him. Legs nearly paralyzed with terror carried him toward the doorway as his trembling hand activated the iris. Rigidly, he awaited the presence he felt on the other side.

The door opened ... to nothing.

If he could sweat like a human, the cold rivulets would have streamed down his spine. Instead, the cranial lobe activated stermones which elevated his body temperature. The heat blurred his eyes with a crimson film as he stumbled down the corridor. The sensation intensified as he approached a side passage. A shadow of a figure stretched out across his path, daring him to venture forward. Steeling himself for the challenge ahead, Nimon crouched lower and raised an arm to deliver the first blow.

A dark figure charged around the corner on a collision course.

Startled, Dr. Nicholas Edison looked into the fiery eyes of the Darwin's "inactive" manager, raising a hand to ward off the blow.

It never came.

"Nimon!" Edison shouted, shattering the mind fever that gripped the Geminian biodgen. "How is this possible?!"

The startled manager pulled back a step, lowering his hand to grip his forehead. He inhaled deeply as he tried to regain control of himself.

"You're Life Mentor has entered the spiral wormhole of a timefold! This should not be…"

Struggling to understand his situation himself, Nimon interjected, "Under normal conditions, you are correct, Father … but I sense things will never be normal again. Please allow me a moment."

"I am afraid we don't have a moment, son," replied Edison. "The Elders granted my fellowship at the Institute to further monitor and study your condition under strict limitations, almost Draconian in nature. I suspect forces are in play that, once they learn of your … condition … will terminate my access to you for their own ulterior motives. I saw on the remote sensors that you were in distress, so I came looking for you. Your awakening is of monumental significance, and knowledge of it must be managed with utmost caution. More importantly, you need help, but I fear the Institute is not the place to receive it. "

"I'm not sure I understand," Nimon replied, unsteadily. "So many questions need answers …"

"And you will get them, in due time. But not here – not now. At stake is not only your future, but the future of the known star systems. They are on the verge of becoming embroiled in a conflict of epic proportions, and you are at its epicenter. And, you should know, I'm not going to let you endure this struggle by yourself!"

"Your compassion overwhelms me ..." Nimon murmured, reflexively placing the palm of his hand on Dr. Edison's chest, while he brought his other hand up to rest on his own.

Dr. Edison couldn't miss the wince of pain that flashed across the face of the miracle that stood before him. "What's wrong, Nimon? You appear to be in pain!"

A flash of memory seared Nimon's mind. He saw the stone dangling between the heaving breasts of his captor, as hands ripped at her bodice.

Again, Edison noted the condition of the being before him, and it wasn't a stable one.

"Come, Nimon, you're in terrible shape, both physically and mentally. We must find refuge so I can care for you!"

As quickly as it came, Nimon shook off the effect of the memory flash. Looking up from his own chest, while still gripping his tunic between his fingers, he peered deeply into his father's eyes. "It is true. I need care. You are the sole person that can make that happen, but not here, as you said. The Institute holds too many painful memories … and untold threats."

A grim line formed on the angular face of the Geminian Dual as he and Dr. Edison made their surreptitious departure. The thoughts of what he must do began to form in his mind. Almost gone were any traces of emotional trauma from the harshness of T'Poch's assault. A new resolve flared within him. A resolve that told of the Geminian Dual's ability to overcome. He whispered a promise to himself.

In a quadrant of space far distant from Gemini, the "new" member of the Darwin staff, Starn, walked into the empty corridor, deep in thought. Looking back toward the dazzling nebula display dancing across the steel-glass of one of the plant's portals, the Geminian's lips parted and formed a whisper inaudible to the sharpest of ears.

Simultaneously, two beings, spawned from one mind, murmured, "Nothing is impossible, T'Poch. In time, I will right your wrongs."

And crystal halves, separated by light years of space, in unison pulsed an eerie glow.

EPILOGUE

Ending her trans-spatial link to Nimon, Novas unfolded herself from the Kakan Te position, rising from the floor of the Legotian chamber. The surreal images of the meditative garden, with its tranquil pond, wispy-leaved dwarf trees, and artistically placed stone patterns, faded into the holographic mists.

Emerging from the vapors, a tall, slender figure approached. Gliding across the stone surface, with hands tucked into opposing sleeves of his floor-length robe, the Legotian radiated a sense of calm, his faint golden skin almost glowing with a serene aura. Novas stood - motionless. Though statuesque compared to most Geminian standards, she still came only to shoulder height of the being before her. Subconsciously, she resisted what she felt to be the false sense of security imposed upon her by Chrislar. Even his current form was a facade, as she knew his true nature was that of an energy based lifeform, and not a corporeal being as he now appeared.

Brushing off her skeptical demeanor as if it were nothing but a cool breeze, Chrislar spoke, "You have done well. Your aid to your children has impacted the present as hoped. But your journey along Time's currents has only just begun. Your experience in Mitron's era is incomplete. You ..."

Novas, uncharacteristically emotional, interrupted. "Enough! I am not interested in your continued meddling in the time stream. Look at what it has done to me! I am with child! This defies medical explanation, despite our many advances. As if age were not enough to overcome, I have been ... scarred ... and unable to bear children. Explain this!"

Chrislar, unaffected by her verbal assault, slowly pulled his hands from within his robe's sleeves. Cupping them, with palms facing each other, he slowly rotated them in a spherical motion, clockwise, then counter clockwise. The aura Novas first perceived around the being intensified, flowing down his arms and out Chrislar's fingertips. An energy ball formed – coalescing - pulsing rhythmically, hypnotically. Chrislar continued. "You ... are concerned. We understand. But, our goals are aligned. Your condition demands it. As you say, in the present, you could not - should not - be pregnant. That is why you must return. In Mitron's past - now, your past - you can, and will, bear a child. Look into the portal I hold before you."

Novas yielded. Staring into the undulating orb, scenes flashed by, almost too rapidly to perceive, yet she understood.

Chrislar allowed himself a small smile as he slowly brought his hands together, collapsing the time window. The images within Novas' mind dissipated, like the early morning dreams upon awakening. The more she tried to recall them, the more they eluded her - butterflies dancing in a summer's wind. Chrislar spoke once more.

"We know her as the Time Child," he whispered, glancing down to Novas' midsection. "She has many fates. As do you. The correct one still awaits. You came here, as did the Castorian Executive, to forge a union between your worlds. For that to occur, just as you must, the Executive was required to return to her moment in time. For now, know this. Your lives are inextricably woven together. Within that tapestry lie many outcomes. Immerse yourself in the time pool to discover which outcome will prevail. For the good of the Castorians, the Geminians, yourself, your children … and the Time Child, resume your journey."

Unlike her previous experience, serpentine ribbons did not reach out to her to lift her into the energy globe. Instead, Novas simply turned from the Legotian, lightly treading across the chamber floor toward the quicksilver pool. Unhesitatingly, she waded into the mysterious liquid. Venturing ever further, the fluid no longer lethal, the Geminian Executive shed her corporeal shell, embracing the Fate that awaited her.

About the Author

Lawrence E. Maynard, or Larry to those who know him, enjoyed his formative years during the Silver Age of comics, Saturday morning superhero cartoons, and the interstellar exploits of Gene Roddenberry's Star Trek. His affinity toward science fiction translated into a pursuit of the applied sciences with degrees in Chemistry, Biology, and a Master's in Business Administration. Having completed a career of over three decades in the manufacturing, marketing, and management of building materials, polymers, and coatings, he is able to weave a sense of scientific realism into the fabric of science fiction writing. When not indulging in that creative art, he spends time traveling to visit his family and friends and supports people in pursuit of the American Dream, home ownership. He resides in Knoxville, TN with his wife of 45 years and looks forward to authoring many more science fiction adventures.